# THE RAVEN KEY

## THE FAMIRIAN CHRONICLES BOOK ONE

## HARPER L. CARNES

Print ISBN: 979-8-9862274-2-9

EBook ISBN: 979-8-9862274-3-6

The Raven Key, 2nd ed.



Cover design by James T. Egan of Bookfly Design.

Spanish checked by Juliana Pedraza. She can be found on the site Upwork.

For all those fighting their way through the darkness.

This is a new adult book and not meant for young readers. It contains subject matter that would be expected of the romantic fantasy and horror genres, but also material that may not be, such as depictions of mental illness, past abuse, and non-descriptive discussions of past sexual assault. A list of trigger warnings can be found in the back of the book.

# PROLOGUE

Eliza stood outside her son's room. It was late enough that the world outside was dark and quiet. Late enough that it was safe to assume their neighbors had retired for the night long before now. There was only Eliza awake, standing beneath the harsh glow of the overhead light in the hallway, trying and failing to talk herself out of what must be done.

The turn of the doorknob in her hand seemed loud enough to wake the neighborhood. But no one else in the house stirred with the noise. Not even when the door creaked slowly open.

The light spilled into the room from the hallway and over the bed where Seth slept, his dark brown hair mussed and standing out against the white of the pillowcase he had his cheek pressed into. He looked so innocent in his sleep. So harmless. Like any other six-year-old. But Eliza knew better.

Seth turned onto his back and threw an arm across his face to shield his eyes from the light. Brown eyes. The same as hers.

People often said he looked like her, but she'd always seen more of his father in him. Especially with his freckles and the slight upturn to his nose.

"Mom?"

Eliza held a finger to her lips. Her footsteps were careful as she crossed the room to his bed, avoiding the places in the floor that would have creaked with the weight of her steps.

"Come with me, baby," she urged quietly as she pulled back the blankets that covered him.

Seth slid obediently from his bed with a fisted hand rubbing at his eyes. "What's going on?"

"Shh. Just come with me."

Seth curled his fingers around Eliza's hand when she held it out to him, and she willed it not to tremble.

They moved down the narrow hall with its walls lined with family photos. Familiar faces stared back at them from their picture frames. Their smiles seemed twisted. Their eyes pinpoints of judgment. Eliza looked away.

"Where are we going?" Seth asked, but Eliza didn't answer him.

They passed the kitchen, and Eliza glanced through the arched entryway. The memory of that morning came back to her at the sight of the countertops and the tiled floor.

"I dreamed of this big black bird, Mom." The words echoed in Eliza's head even now. "It had this weird stuff floating off it."

She remembered the dish slipping from her grasp to shatter against the tile floor, but she couldn't recall the sound of the glass breaking, just the noise of her own panicked heart in her ears. The thump of it deafening and quick like a rabbit.

Her husband had put an arm around her shoulders as she'd shouted at Seth to go to his room with tears running down her cheeks. Neither her husband nor son had understood her fury, or her despair.

They reached the small living room with its television set and dark leather couch. Seth's action figures were scattered over a section of the floor, his army men lying like wounded soldiers in the moonlight that she and Seth passed on their way to the back door.

Eliza paused in reaching for the latch. She let out a shaky breath, her mind racing for an excuse not to go any further with this. But there was no other way. She'd been wrong about Seth, and now she had to make things right.

The lock clicked audibly in the stillness of the hour. She opened the sliding glass door, then tugged at Seth's hand, and they slipped out into the darkness.

Eliza hadn't turned the porch light on, and Seth tightened his hold on her hand as she led him down the hill behind the house toward the pond.

Not even the moon could offer some hint of light through the overcast sky, the dew-slick grass that grasped wetly at their bare feet the color of tar to Eliza's maladjusted eyes.

"Mom, let's go back."

Eliza wished they could. Oh, how she wished she could lift Seth into her arms, turn around, and carry him back into the safety of the house. But she couldn't. She had to follow through where she could not before.

They came to an abrupt halt at the water's edge. It was quiet here except for the sounds of insects and the wind sifting through the reeds.

"Mom?" Seth asked in a small voice.

Eliza swallowed. She could feel tears on her cheeks. "We can't let him out."

"Who?"

"No, no, no. We can't—can't let him get out," Eliza whispered, and a tremor ran through her words. She looked at Seth, grief warring with resolution inside her. "You understand, don't you, baby?"

Seth shook his head.

"I'm sorry." Eliza grabbed him by the arm, then spun him around toward the bank as fresh tears slid down her cheeks. "I'm so sorry. I love you."

She let go of his arm and he fell back into the water, already caught off balance from her spinning him. She watched water flood his mouth when he landed hard on his back. He coughed as his head broke the surface, and Eliza knelt to push him back under.

The cold water writhed around Seth wildly as he thrashed and kicked, and she struggled to keep a grip on him, her fingers twisting in his hair to hold him down.

Seth's hand collided with her arm, and he clung to the sleeve of her shirt. She remembered a time when that hand was even smaller. Tiny fingers wrapping around one of her own. She'd protected him back then. Convinced he was different. Certain that he'd been spared.

"I'm sorry," Eliza said once more as that small hand pulled desperately at the wet fabric of her sleeve.

Then, a larger hand closed over her arm and she looked up to see her husband's face. He was breathing hard as if he'd run from the house, but she hadn't heard him. She'd been so focused on Seth. So distracted by her own heartbreak that she hadn't kept an eye out for someone who might stop her.

"No!" Eliza struggled as her husband wrested her back from Seth. "No!"

"Are you out of your mind?" her husband demanded as he snatched Seth up from the water.

He cradled the little boy close, a hand tucking his head against his shoulder as Seth coughed and cried.

"David, you don't understand!" Eliza lunged for her son, but her husband only jerked back and held him more protectively against his chest. "He's dangerous!"

Porch lights were turning on with Eliza's high-pitched wails. First one light flicked to life in the darkness. Then several as the volume rose.

"You don't understand what he is! What's inside him!"

"Listen to yourself!" David urged, his face red and his voice loud enough to counter hers. "This is your son you're talking about!"

People were poking their heads out through doorways or stepping outside to watch.

"It's inside him! He's possessed!" Eliza screeched as she finally got a grip on Seth and tried to yank him from her husband's hold. "Please David! We have to drown him! We have to drown him before it's too late!"

Their neighbor, Yu-jin, who had never been one to stay out of matters that did not concern her, hurried down the lawn toward them as Eliza spoke.

She pulled Eliza from Seth while David stumbled back and Eliza's hands reached out, grasping at air as she fought against her neighbor's hold.

"He's a monster! He has the signs!" Eliza couldn't keep the fear from her voice as David carried Seth away from her, her eyes wide and her hands shaking. "I thought it passed over him! I thought he was different! But I was wrong! I was wrong!"

"There are no signs! There's nothing wrong with him!" David screamed furiously. "He's just a boy!"

Eliza stopped her struggles at last. Her body sagged forward as the sound of a siren split through the night air.

"He's going to kill us all."

# ONE

It was a Saturday, so it didn't surprise Seth when his father plodded into his bedroom wearing a jacket and a woebegone expression.

Every other Saturday, his father would take a trip to visit Seth's mother at the Oak View Psychiatric Hospital. Which meant every other Saturday, Seth would refuse to go with his father to see her.

"I'm heading out in a few," his father said.

Seth didn't even glance away from his history homework. "Okay."

"You're sure you don't want to come?"

"I'm sure."

Seth kept his head bowed as if focused on his assignment, but it was an act by this point. The words in the history book were no longer readable with the tension that coiled inside him. The letters almost seemed to slide off the page as they blurred before his eyes.

"She's your mother—"

Seth tightened his hands into fists to keep them from shaking. "She's a psychopath." He looked up with narrowed eyes and teeth clenched behind a tight-lipped frown.

"She's troubled."

"Troubled?" Seth repeated the word. It tasted bitter in his mouth, the way the water she'd held his head under had. "She tried to *drown me*."

"She didn't know what she was doing, son." His father shook his head. "She wasn't in her right mind."

Seth sat up straighter. "Yeah, well"—he slammed his history book shut—"me showing up wouldn't do her any favors."

Last Seth knew, his mother was still claiming he was some kind of monster. He could remember her calling him as much from the back of a cop car after the police had shown up.

Seth hadn't understood the words the grown-ups used with each other when he was younger. Homicidal. Schizophrenic. Mentally ill. They'd never explained what any of that meant. To him they always just said, "Your mother is sick."

Your mother is sick. A very watered down, kind way of telling a confused and hurting little boy that his mother was having delusions. That she had tried to murder him and would most likely try again if given half a chance.

It wasn't until he grew older that her illness made more sense, and that the terms the adults used became the words Seth used.

The years brought with them the clarity that there was nothing wrong with him. He wasn't possessed. There was no evil spirit. No encroaching apocalypse. Just the ravings of a madwoman.

"Seth, please come with me. She wants to see you."

"No. I don't owe her anything."

His father stared at him in the silence that followed. Seth wondered if his dad could hear him grit his teeth.

When Seth couldn't take the weight of his father's stare any longer, he got up from his bed and made his way across the room to pick up the purple hoodie he'd tossed on the floor earlier.

"Where are you going?" His father's voice was quiet now. Tired.

"Out."

Seth pulled on the hoodie and zipped it as defiantly as one could manage when the zipper got stuck halfway. He tugged stubbornly at it a few times while his father rolled his eyes.

With an annoyed grumble, Seth stalked out of his bedroom door and down the hall to the stairs, which he took with hurried steps. He didn't look back to see if his father followed him, just pulled on the sneakers he'd dumped by the front door yesterday before he headed outside.

There was a chill in the air, and Seth tried once more to zip his hoodie the rest of the way. It was a lost cause, though, and he gave up as he made his way down the porch steps.

He'd planned to go for a drive, but the breeze felt good on his skin, so he kept walking. A few yellow and orange leaves crunched beneath his shoes as he headed down the sidewalk.

It was only the second day of September, and yet some people along Seth's street had already begun to decorate their houses for Halloween. Here and there were fake cobwebs stretched over hedges or clinging to the sides of houses.

As Seth continued to walk, he spotted a few vinyl ghosts stuck to a window two houses down, and a cardboard witch tacked to a doorway across the street from him.

It occurred to Seth then that his eighteenth birthday wasn't too far off. On October 27th, he'd be considered an adult. The thought itself felt strange, because he'd never felt like a child. Not after what his mother had done.

They'd moved to Twin Oaks shortly after the trial. His father had wanted to be closer to the psychiatric hospital where his wife was confined. As towns went, it wasn't the worst. Their house was smaller now, but newer, and Portland was only a short drive away.

A bird landed in Seth's path, and he stopped to look at it. At first, he thought it was a crow, but its size alone made him realize it was actually a raven.

It regarded Seth with a tilt of its head and a ruffle of feathers, seemingly unafraid of him. Seth's eyes tracked it as it moved closer.

Seth's phone rang, startling raven and boy alike. He watched the bird take flight with a long low *kra* of a call as he pulled his cellphone from his pocket to answer with a customary, if slightly unnerved, "Hello."

"Hey, Seth," his friend Evelyn said in a cheery voice. "I heard about this house party over in Portland from one of my college friends. I was thinking we could go tonight if you're not busy."

"I'm not sure I'm in the mood for a party," Seth admitted.

The idea of driving out to Portland to hang out in a house filled with drunken college students held little appeal. Especially when Evelyn would probably get bored with Seth's lack of enthusiasm and leave him to entertain himself.

"Oh, come on, Seth," Evelyn said, and added in an almost conspiratorial tone, "You can get drunk. Maybe even meet someone."

"Now you're just being a bad influence," Seth huffed, but a hint of a smile pulled at the corners of his mouth. Evelyn's enthusiasm was contagious.

"Say you'll go."

Seth smiled, feeling a touch lighter. "Okay, I'll go."

"Oh, good!" Evelyn squealed. "Because I'm almost at your place."

A huff of laughter escaped Seth, and he shook his head. "Right. You'll want to park along the curb. My dad is heading out soon."

"Okay. I'll see you in a bit."

Seth pocketed his phone after the call ended and turned to look back at his house. A blue Foursquare with white trim and a gray roof. So different from the bungalow they used to live in. There was more space between the houses in this neighborhood, too. "Room to breathe," his father had said when they'd first moved in years ago.

Seth was still waiting to breathe. Still waiting for the pressure around his chest to loosen. It never seemed to go away.

When he reached the driveway, he loitered out on the concrete next to his own car, a 2001 Subaru Outback that his father liked to call a rattletrap. But it was entirely Seth's, given he'd saved up his earnings from the local coffee shop to buy it.

Evelyn's car caught Seth's attention immediately when it came down the street—a bright red BMW that her father had bought her.

The car eased up to the curb and a moment later Evelyn emerged with a smile that twisted into a frown of disapproval.

"You're not actually going dressed like that, are you? I mean, no offense, but it's not exactly the best choice for a party."

Seth looked down at himself. At the ratty old hoodie and the edge of the black T-shirt that stuck out from underneath it. He could see her point. Even if he would deny it until his dying day.

Evelyn looked more done up in an understated but pretty blue dress and her long red hair in a half-crown braid.

"It's my favorite hoodie," he said.

"Maybe so, but I think you should go change."

Normally, Seth would ignore her comments and insist they leave. This time, he didn't argue. It was one of those Saturdays, and he already felt drained.

The front door opened as Seth turned back toward the house. It was his father, car keys in hand, with the Pikachu key chain Seth had made in third grade dangling from them.

They watched him get in his old truck. The sound of the engine started a moment later, and he gave them both a perfunctory wave before he backed out of the driveway.

A part of Seth wished he had gone with his father. Like he always wished every other Saturday when his dad would drive out to the psychiatric hospital. But Seth's anger and fear had always been stronger than his longing.

"Come on." Seth tilted his head in the direction of the house as the sound of the car engine faded into the distance. "Help me figure out what to wear."

Evelyn followed Seth as he led the way inside the house, then up the stairs to his bedroom.

"You get into another fight with your dad?"

"I'd rather not talk about it," Seth said as he pushed the door to his bedroom open.

Evelyn pressed her lips together as if she wanted to say more, but had decided against it. She headed over to Seth's closet instead and opened the slatted white doors while Seth sat on his bed after taking his hoodie off to wait for her choices.

"Well, this is horrifying," Evelyn stated as she took stock of Seth's closet. "I'm pretty sure you own more plaid than I do, and I'm a lesbian."

"I've never even seen you wear plaid."

Evelyn didn't respond to Seth's comment as she rifled through his clothes. Instead she said, "How are you gay? I thought gay men were supposed to have a fashion sense."

"There was probably a mix-up with the mail when they were sending out the certificates." Seth nodded. "Somewhere a well-dressed man is living a lie."

Seth smirked when Evelyn paused long enough to roll her eyes at him before she returned to her task. She pulled a black long-sleeve shirt off a hanger then discarded it with a sigh when she found a thumb-sized hole in the sleeve.

After what felt like eons, Evelyn finally turned toward Seth with a red sweater in her hands, her eyes focused on the garment and her mouth set in a grimmer line than the sweater probably deserved.

"Look," Seth said at last, "if you have something to say, just say it."

"I think you should visit your mom." It was said tentatively, as if Evelyn expected Seth to yell at her, or throw her out of the house. For a moment, the thought did cross his mind.

"You haven't seen her in years," Evelyn continued hurriedly, "and it could actually be good for you. Maybe it would help—"

"How in the world would seeing the woman that tried to murder me help?"

Evelyn flinched when Seth snapped at her, but continued anyway. "She's still your mom. You try to act like you don't care about her, but I can tell you do."

Seth wanted to hold on to his anger. The heat of it simmering beneath his skin was always preferable to the cold numb of depression. But he was tired, and Evelyn looked so panicked he thought she may actually cry if he raised his voice again.

He took a deep breath to calm his nerves, then stood to take the sweater Evelyn clung to like a shield. It had been a Christmas present from his father last year, but he'd only worn it twice since then. He wasn't sure why, since the fabric was comfortable against his skin when he changed into it.

"Let's get going," Seth said, refusing to address the subject he could still sense on Evelyn's mind any further. "I need a drink."

He ignored the way Evelyn stared after him as he left the room. After a moment, she followed him with the same silence his father so often had with him these days.

# Two

Over an hour later, Seth was leaning against a wall drinking cheap beer from a red Solo cup. He'd lost track of Evelyn a while ago after she had gone to flirt with a girl that had smiled at her from across the room.

With a sigh, Seth pushed off from the wall. His cup was empty, so he headed to the kitchen where the keg was being kept.

It was loud, and despite the decent size of the house, crowded. People moved about in all directions as Seth tried to pick the path of least resistance, some of them dancing, others talking animatedly to one another.

Someone shoved past Seth and he stumbled forward into a firm body in front of him. A loud crunch of plastic accompanied the collision as the red Solo cup crumpled between them.

A hand touched Seth's shoulder, but whether it was to steady him or leverage for some space between them, he wasn't sure. He took a step back anyway and looked up at the man he'd knocked into. Then he kept staring while heat rose in his cheeks.

The man he'd collided with was gorgeous, and older, if the strong frame and heavily stubbled jawline were anything to go by.

Seth stood there awkwardly as he took in the short black hair and straight-toothed smile. A flustered apology tumbled from his mouth the next second. He was caught off guard more by the beautiful green eyes that gazed back at him than the collision.

"It's fine," the man said in return. "Don't worry about it."

Seth ducked his head as he mumbled another apology all the same, then stepped to the side to continue on his way to the kitchen, his embarrassment a familiar heat that spread all the way to the tops of his ears.

"Hey."

Seth turned back with the single word, both confused and intrigued that the guy had spoken to him at all. He actually glanced around to be sure he wasn't making an even bigger fool of himself if tall, dark, and handsome hadn't actually been talking to him.

"How old are you?" the man asked, and the *thump-thump-thump* of the bass from the song that blasted over the sound system meant Seth had to move in closer to catch what he said.

"Twenty-one," Seth lied, with a glance at the crumpled Solo cup still in his hand.

"You don't look older than nineteen."

"I get that a lot." Seth patted his own cheek. "Just baby-faced, I guess."

"What's your name?"

"Seth," Seth replied, while he moved in closer still.

"I'm—"

"Gabriel!" A young woman with long blond hair threw her arms around the man's neck from behind before he could finish speaking. She smiled, overly familiar in the way she tucked her chin against his shoulder as he looked at her. "Everyone's waiting for you."

Seth looked away, feeling even stupider than he had before for assuming this guy—Gabriel—would have any interest in someone like him.

Seth wasn't anything like Gabriel at all. He was fair-skinned, pale almost, with tousled brown hair and a frame that was more slim than toned.

Gabriel, on the other hand, was broad-shouldered, his body lean and fit in a way that was obvious with the tight shirt he wore. His skin was darker than Seth's own—an olive brown that was even more noticeable when compared to the light complexion of the woman that hung off him.

He was out of Seth's league and, by all appearances, taken.

"Oh, hey, Haley," Gabriel was saying. "I got sidetracked."

"Well, it's time to meet up with everyone." She pulled away, only to snag his hand in hers so she could lead him through the throng of bodies.

"Nice meeting you!" Gabriel called over his shoulder to Seth with a raised hand and an almost apologetic quirk to his mouth.

"Yeah, you too!" Seth called back as Gabriel disappeared into the crowd.

Seth stared after him for several minutes before he weaved his own way through the press of bodies to the entryway of the house. He wanted nothing more than to go home now, but he didn't want to ruin Evelyn's good time.

He decided he'd go for a walk rather than ask her to take him home. He'd come back in an hour or so when it was late and she'd be ready to leave.

With a last glance around, Seth dropped his plastic cup into an overflowing trash can on his way outside. He took a deep breath once he was on the front stoop. The air in the house had been stale and warm, with the number of people packed inside. Outside it was colder and carried the crisp, earthy smell of fall that Seth now breathed in deeply.

The lawn sloped down toward the sidewalk and Seth picked his way down the small hill with careful steps to the concrete. He hunched in on himself the farther he got from the light that spilled over the grass from the house. He hated the dark. Even before his mother had led him from their home on the night she'd tried to kill him, Seth had feared what might hide in it. But he kept walking once he reached the sidewalk all the same, his eyes on the ground.

Seth didn't look up again until he found himself under the glare of a streetlamp. He slid his hands in his pockets as the wind picked up and a few dead leaves skittered over the concrete with a dry rasp.

His gaze tracked after them, the wind whisking them toward a park across the street, and Seth stepped off the curb to head in that direction.

There were a few areas like this in Portland—spaces of nature that had managed to not be consumed by city expansion and growing residential areas. Collectively, they were referred to as pocket parks. This one, according to its green and yellow sign, was actually called Piccolo Park.

A playground sat toward the center with a wooden jungle gym and a swing set. The wind made the swings sway and the chains creak as he drew closer.

The sound reminded him of being small and going to the park near their old house with his mom. He could barely remember what she sounded like outside his dreams. But he thought she'd seemed happy when she pushed him on the swing, or watched him as he went down the slide. Back then, she had loved him. He wished he knew what had changed.

Seth sat down on a swing, his hands wrapped around the chains to keep himself steady. The swing was too close to the ground for the length of his legs to swing, so he sat there silently and scraped his foot through the dirt and wood chips.

"Everything alright?"

The voice belonged to Evelyn, so Seth didn't bother to look up to see who had spoken. He kept his gaze on the ground and let his hands slide down a few links in the chains before he tightened his grip again.

"I saw you leave the party."

Evelyn sat on the swing next to him when he still didn't respond. He could sense her eyes on him and he finally looked over at her.

She was holding on to the chains the way he was, but hunched forward to look at him. Her swing swayed back and forth with the way she'd tucked her legs up so the blue flats she wore barely scuffed the ground.

At five-foot-ten, he was taller than Evelyn. A few inches more and he'd have been as tall as that Gabriel guy.

Seth still couldn't get him out of his head. Especially how beautiful his eyes were.

"That guy you were talking to looked pretty cute."

"He also looked pretty straight with that woman hanging off him," Seth replied.

"Yeah, well, there's no accounting for taste, I guess." Evelyn winked at him. "I mean, come on. We both know you're the better catch."

Seth huffed a laugh that came out more derisive than humorous. "Maybe if I was a few months older, or a few years. The age of consent for Oregon is eighteen."

They fell back into silence. The only sound for a time was the creak of the chains in Evelyn's hands as her swing swayed and the scrape of Seth's shoe through the dirt.

"You're thinking about him again, aren't you?" she asked.

"Who?"

"Who do you think? Adam."

Seth shrugged, not willing to admit the memory of the boy was always somewhere in the back of his mind. As were the events of the day Seth went to school after their breakup to find everyone knew about what had happened to him when he was a child. What his mother had done.

The sound of wings drew Seth's attention to the air, where a barely visible black shape circled lower. A few seconds later, a raven landed on the side of the slide across from the swing set. Its talons clicked against the metal as it stared at Seth. Expectant. Waiting.

"Seth?" Evelyn asked as Seth stood slowly. "Hey, earth to Seth."

The bird tilted its head but didn't retreat. Even when Seth crossed the wood chips to the slide, it didn't startle or spread its wings to fly away.

"Wait," Evelyn protested. She rose from her swing to hurry over to him when Seth reached out a hand. "Don't touch it! What if it has rabies?"

"Birds can't get rabies."

"It could still have something!" Evelyn shouted as she snatched Seth's hand back.

The raven rasped a call as it spread its wings and craned its neck with an angry ruffle of feathers. It took flight a moment later, its talons narrowly missing Evelyn's face as it flew past.

"Crazy-ass bird!" Evelyn shouted after it, whirling around to watch it go.

"I saw one earlier today too," Seth said as he watched the bird disappear into the night. "Do you think it's the same one?"

"I doubt a bird followed you all the way to Portland." Evelyn shivered and wrapped her arms around herself. She hadn't worn a jacket and her sleeves only reached her elbows. "Let's go. This place is giving me the creeps."

The party was still going on when they reached the car that Evelyn had parked along the curb. The music from inside could be heard even out here.

"You sure you want to leave?" Seth asked. "I mean, we drove all the way out here."

Evelyn looked back to the house with its white trimmed windows and gray siding. "Yeah. It's getting late and I don't need my parents on my case."

"Right." With a sigh, Seth got into the car.

The drive home was mostly quiet, except for that soft rock music Evelyn liked to play.

The light in the living room window was on when they finally pulled into the driveway, so Seth could count on his father still being up.

"Say hi to your dad for me," Evelyn said as Seth exited the car.

"I will."

Seth closed the door of the car and Evelyn gave a wave, which he returned before she drove away. Once she had gone, Seth turned toward the house with a deep breath. He headed up the driveway, shoving his hands in the pockets of his jeans as he went.

The hall was dark when he got inside. He could have turned on the entryway light, but the glow that spilled into the hallway from the living room gave enough for him to see by so he didn't have to stumble about in the dark.

His father sat on the couch in the living room, his head in one hand and a glass of scotch in the other. He was only in his forties, but he looked older. Stress had lightened his hair from the dark blond it used to be and set worry lines in his face.

"Hey Dad," Seth offered lamely as he stood in the doorway.

His father sighed and dropped the hand against his face to his lap. "Where've you been all night?"

"With Evelyn," Seth replied. "At a party. She says hi."

His father sighed again before he took a drink. He didn't seem angry. Just defeated. Somehow, that was worse.

"You remember that trip we took up to Lake Tahoe?" he asked.

"Not really."

But Seth did remember. Those days were some of the last happy ones he'd had with his mother. They'd rented a cottage on the water for the weekend. Nothing extravagant or out of the ordinary when he looked back on it now. But when he'd been a child, it had felt like an adventure.

"Your mom taught you to skip stones out on the beach."

Seth glanced away. He blinked hard with the heat behind his eyes and swallowed around the lump that had formed in his throat.

He remembered that day on the beach with his parents. It had been their last day at the cottage and they'd all gone for a walk as a family.

The lake had been so still it had almost looked like glass until his mother had picked up a stone from the sand and sent it skipping across the surface five times before it sank. It had seemed like magic when Seth had first seen it, and he'd begged her to teach him.

"I miss days like that," his father said. He finished his drink and set the empty glass down on the table. "I miss when we were a proper family."

His father reached for the half-empty bottle of scotch to lift it from the table. He had tipped it to refill his glass by the time Seth reached for him to still his hand.

Seth set the bottle back on the wooden coffee table with a solid clunk and his father huffed a sound that could have been a chuckle, but it sounded sad.

His father stretched out on the couch the next minute with his head on the armrest. He didn't look to have any intent to rise soon. In fact, he was already dozing off.

Seth pulled the blanket that was folded haphazardly over the top of the couch down. He shook it out to its full length before he lay it over his father and turned off the lights on his way out of the room. It cast him into darkness for a few moments while he got his phone out and turned the flashlight function on.

He found his way back down the hall then up the stairs by the small beam of light. Once he was in his room with the door closed, he toed off his shoes and climbed into bed without bothering to change.

Seth took a deep breath, then let it out slowly as he lay on his back and stared at the ceiling. He felt tears in his eyes, and he blinked them back, only to end up wiping away the stubborn ones that slipped down his cheeks.

It was easier in the light of day to convince himself that his mother had set all this in motion. That he and his dad lived the life they did now because of her choices. But, on nights like this, Seth couldn't help but think the problem was him. That he'd somehow destroyed their family.

# THREE

Seth blinked his eyes open to the sound of a rhythmic *tap-tap-tap-tap* against his window. He couldn't remember when he'd fallen asleep, but apparently, he had.

He lay still in his bed, watching as the shadows of tree branches swayed along his ceiling. Their dark shapes were stretched and misshapen from the light of the moon.

It was quiet now, but he still held his breath as he listened. Waited. Until finally it came again. A repetitive *tap-tap-tap-tap-tap* against the glass.

Seth forced himself to sit up and swing his legs over the side of the bed so he could get a better view of his bedroom window. A black shape sat outside the glass. Barely distinguishable from the darkness of the surrounding night, and revealing itself only in the way it moved to peck at the glass of his window once more. *Tap. Tap. Tap. Tap.* It was becoming increasingly insistent, more urgent as it went on. *Tap. Tap. TAP. TAP. TAP.*

Another raven.

Seth wasn't particularly keen to open the window to his unsolicited feathered visitor, but the tapping only grew louder and he worried it might wake his father. With a calming breath, he rose from his bed and crossed the short distance to his window.

The large black bird turned its head to the side, almost expectant in the way its dark eye regarded him. When he didn't open the window immediately, it went back to pecking at the glass until Seth undid the latch, then pushed the window up from the bottom.

The raven hopped onto the windowsill, then down onto the desk beneath it to peer up at him with a *kra* and a ruffle of feathers along its body. Its talons dug into the wood and its beak was sharp and curved like a Bowie knife, but Seth reached out to it all the same.

He let his fingers curve over the raven's back as he brushed his hand down its glossy black feathers.

The raven almost seemed to purr under Seth's touch—a low croaking rumble of a noise that sounded nothing like a cat, but seemed to express approval all the same.

Something dark rose from its feathers to twist around Seth's hand before he could jerk it back. It sank into his wrist to move up along his arm beneath his skin, and he grabbed at the place that undulated with its presence. A vain attempt to stop its progress.

Seth saw it again as it rose through his skin and slipped out from between his fingers. It curled like smoke, yet rippled with the same fluidity as the surrounding water. He could see points of brightness and swirls of color in it. They blinked in and out of sight with the way it twisted around itself.

The floorboards creaked behind Seth, and the raven let out a shrill cry of alarm as it looked beyond him.

"We can't let him get out, Seth."

Seth didn't have to turn around to know who the voice belonged to. He'd heard that voice in his nightmares for years.

"You're not real."

A damp palm settled over the back of his neck. His mother's icy fingers gripped tight as her nails dug angry crescents into his skin.

"You're not real. This is a dream," Seth repeated stubbornly, even as he flinched with her touch. "It has to be a dream."

The raven shrieked, and Seth pressed his hands to his ears to block out the sound. To block out his mother's repeated whispers of, "No, no, no, we can't let him out." He tried to pull away, but he couldn't move. He was anchored in place by his mother's hand on his neck.

Something cold and wet sloshed over his feet. It drew a shiver of fear from him, and he dropped his gaze to the floor to find water inching up around his ankles.

"You understand, don't you, baby?"

The water rose quickly. In no time, it was higher than his bed. Almost as high as his waist. It lapped at the top of his desk, soaking his notebooks and carrying his pencils away.

Seth stared at the rippling darkness that rose from him. Panic heavy in his gut with the proof of the thing inside him that his mother feared.

The raven stepped back. Its wings flapped as it continued its rattling cries of rage and the water continued to rise, forcing it to retreat to the windowsill.

"I'm sorry," his mother whispered.

Seth went under with a splash, his mother fighting to hold him down when he struggled. He twisted around and kicked out, but she only adjusted her hold around his throat, her hands choking him as she sank under the water with him.

The familiarity of his bedroom faded out around him until there was nothing but the water as far as he could see, and he sank down with his mother further and further into the cold and the dark.

Seth woke with a heaving gasp as he hit the floor, his legs tangled in the sheets and the rest of him half-hanging off the bed.

His dad opened the bedroom door as Seth kicked himself free of the bedding and dropped his legs to the floor.

"Are you okay?" His dad asked when he saw Seth sprawled on the ground. "I heard the thud."

"I'm fine. I just fell out of bed."

"Another nightmare?"

Seth nodded as he sat up.

"I think you should go back to that therapist."

"Dad, I'm fine, really. It was only a bad dream."

His father stared him down. "I'm making you a therapy appointment."

Seth shook his head.

It wouldn't do any good. It never had. The only thing therapy had done was make him feel even more broken and talked over. But every few months, his dad would make him go, hoping, maybe even praying, that this time things would be different. That this time, Seth would get the help he needed.

"I'm not going."

"Oh, you'll go," his father insisted. "Even if I have to drag you there myself."

"You sure you'd be sober enough for that?"

Seth regretted the words as soon as they left his mouth. His father's face fell and his eyes took on that somber look they did so often now. Seth knew he should apologize. He even wanted to. But the words stuck in his throat.

I'm sorry. I'm sorry for all of this, Seth thought, but what he said was, "I have to get ready for work."

His father didn't comment as Seth got to his feet then moved past him into the hall to make his way to the bathroom.

Despite the nightmare, Seth had somehow overslept. Which meant his shower was rushed, his clothes wrinkled, and his stomach empty when he made it out the front door and down the porch steps to his car.

The drive to work at least wasn't too long. Though the early morning traffic was the tedious stop and go kind, leaving Seth just enough time to make it inside and clock in if he didn't dawdle.

Seth parked in his usual spot near the side of the building and headed inside, the cap he'd grabbed from the passenger seat where he'd tossed it after his last shift clutched in his hand.

The Happy Beans Café was part of a brown-bricked section of shops along Main Street with a rainbow awning over the door and a sign in the window that proclaimed the café's slogan: Better Gay Than Grumpy.

A couple of yellow metal tables and chairs sat outside the shop front, and with the fall weather being fair—even sunny—today, it wasn't surprising that a few patrons had taken advantage of the option to sit outside while they sipped their drinks. Some of them glanced Seth's way before returning to their coffee or conversation as he opened one of the double doors to go inside.

Aaliyah was already behind the counter for her shift, tying the yellow apron with the smiley face on it around her waist, while Kevin clocked out at the register. It was always somewhat amusing to see the goth girl dressed in dark clothes with even darker skin donning the hideously bright apron.

"You look terrible," Aaliyah drawled without preamble. She pulled her ponytail through the back of her cap—which was also a hideous shade of management-mandated yellow—as her gaze swept over Seth. "Did you sleep at all last night?"

"Enough to be standing," Seth replied flatly. He clocked in once Kevin had left and took his apron from a hook by the locker where the staff stored their bags and, during colder months, their coats and boots.

"You need to go to bed earlier," Aaliyah said.

"Sleep and I aren't on good terms with each other."

Aaliyah clucked her tongue at him and tapped the rim of the cap the café forced him to wear so it covered his eyes.

As Seth righted the cap, the bell over the door chimed. He looked over with the sound only to see tall, dark, and handsome from the party last night walk in.

"Oh, shit," Seth blurted, and ducked behind the counter when Gabriel looked in his direction.

"What are you doing?" Aaliyah asked in a voice that dripped with judgment. She looked down at where he sat on the floor with his legs sticking out in front of him and his back against the glass door of the display case where they kept the muffins.

"Hiding."

"Why?"

That was a perfectly valid question. One Seth didn't have an answer for himself. He'd lied about his age to the man, yes. But nothing about working in a coffee shop was revealing of that.

Fortunately, Aaliyah stopped questioning him once Gabriel reached the counter. She chose instead to lean forward with her elbows on the glass to make eyes at him while she twirled a piece of black hair tipped with red around her finger.

Seth was more used to seeing her flirt with girls that came into the café, maybe because it was a safer bet that the girls who came in would have some interest. But he had seen her come on to the occasional guy as well.

"Hi, can I get a latte?"

Aaliyah stopped twirling her hair and reached for the travel mug Gabriel had set on the counter before he'd even finished speaking.

"You don't usually come in on Sundays," Aaliyah commented, "or get lattes. You always order plain, black coffee."

"I told a friend I'd try it."

"Are you out here to see that friend then?"

Seth tilted his head until he could see Gabriel at the counter talking to Aaliyah. She worked more shifts than Seth, so she knew more of the customers that came in regularly than he did.

"I was visiting with some friends yesterday," Gabriel replied, "and then I stopped by my parents' house for the night."

"You weren't visiting anyone special?" Aaliyah cast him that look again. The come-hither one that Seth had seen her use to reel in and land a date before.

"Still single," was the only response Aaliyah received, followed by a polite smile.

If Aaliyah was disappointed by his seeming lack of interest in her, she hid it well. Though she did avoid direct eye contact with Gabriel as she finished cashing him out at the register. When that was done, she headed to the fridge to get the milk. Her slip-resistant shoes squeaked softly as she walked away from them both.

"Seth, right?" Gabriel asked from just above him.

"Uh huh," Seth mumbled in return as he pressed his face into his hands, the heat in his cheeks burning against his palms. It had just occurred to him he was sitting behind glass, which every person in the shop could see through.

"You okay down there?"

"Yeah." Seth tipped his head back to look up at Gabriel, who was peering over the counter at him, his brow knit in worry.

Seth used one of the shelves they stored bags of coffee beans on to leverage himself up from the floor and said, "Yeah, I'm fine. I just lost something."

"What'd you lose?" Gabriel asked as Seth straightened up.

Seth sighed. "Only my dignity."

Gabriel pressed his lips together as if he were trying for a neutral expression, but the corners of his mouth kept twitching upward like he was trying not to laugh. "Did you find it?"

"Not yet. It's hard to find when I'm distracted by a pair of gorgeous green eyes."

Aaliyah made a choked off snort of a sound from where she was steaming the milk and waiting on the espresso shot. But Seth ignored her, because Gabriel smiled and dipped his chin with a laugh.

"You'll have to tell me if it turns up," Gabriel said.

"I promise you'll be the first to know," Seth said as Aaliyah placed Gabriel's order on the counter.

A moment went by in which Gabriel considered Seth before he appeared to come to a decision. "Can I borrow your pen?"

"My pen?" Seth mumbled, even as he took it from the pocket of his apron and held it out.

Gabriel took the pen and picked up one of the napkins from the holder on the counter. "I just realized you'd have a hard time telling me when you found your dignity without my number."

It was Seth's turn to smile as Gabriel slid the napkin across the counter to him. He hadn't expected Gabriel to respond to his poor attempt at a come on, let alone give him his number. But there it was in his hand. All ten digits scrawled neatly across the brown paper in black ink, with the name Gabriel Caballero Ortiz just above them.

"I will definitely call to let you know."

"I look forward to it, *Seth*..." Gabriel prompted.

"Cunningham."

Gabriel nodded as he sent one last smile Seth's way before he picked up his travel mug and turned to leave.

"What just happened?" Aaliyah asked slowly, stunned. Her eyes flicked between Seth and Gabriel's retreating back.

Seth couldn't blame her. He had considered pinching himself to be sure he wasn't dreaming, though the lack of horrific imagery suggested he was very much awake.

"What are you doing now?" Aaliyah asked when Seth pulled his phone out of the pocket of his apron.

"Calling him," Seth replied, already punching in the number on his phone.

"He hasn't even left yet." Aaliyah observed.

"I can see that. Thank you."

"You're supposed to wait like a day or two before calling so you don't look like a desperate loser."

Seth pressed his cellphone to his ear as he glanced at Aaliyah. "But I am a desperate loser."

He watched as Gabriel pulled his own cellphone from the back pocket of his jeans and answered on the third ring.

"Hey," Seth said, trying for nonchalant and probably failing miserably, but Gabriel had turned to look back at him all the same. "Since I've already made a fool of myself and things couldn't possibly get any more embarrassing by asking you this now... Do you, maybe, want to go out with me tonight? Unless you're busy tonight. In which case we could go out tomorrow night, maybe?"

Gabriel smiled slowly, and Seth felt a blush heat his cheeks.

"What?" Seth asked.

"You're cute when you ramble."

Uh-oh. Cute wasn't usually a good sign. Cute for a guy was brotherly and let's-just-be-friends territory and—

"I am actually busy tonight. But if you'd be up for it, some friends and I are going out on a sailboat tomorrow. We could do a kind of double date."

"I'd be good with that," Seth agreed, even though the idea of going out on the open water made his gut go cold.

"Great. I could pick you up if you want?"

That was a terrible idea. If Gabriel knew where he lived, then he could show up unexpectedly. God help them both if Seth's father was home.

"Or you could meet me at my apartment?" Gabriel said, seeming to sense Seth's hesitation.

"Yeah, that would work. What time should I get there?"

"Maybe around one?" Gabriel suggested. "We want to get to the marina before three and it's over an hour's drive."

Seth cringed internally. To get there by one, he'd have to leave school early. He wasn't eighteen yet, so he couldn't sign himself out. Which meant he'd have to ditch about an hour before school ended. It seemed a small price to pay to see Gabriel, though.

"One will work."

They stood staring at each other happily until Gabriel seemed to realize he was having a phone conversation with someone he was standing only five feet away from. Not only that, but people had begun to look over at them with curious stares.

"I'm going to hang up now," Gabriel said, but he was still smiling, albeit more self-consciously.

Seth lowered his own phone and slipped it into the front pocket of his apron after Gabriel hung up.

"I'll see you tomorrow," Gabriel said.

"Yeah, I'll see you then," Seth replied.

Seth couldn't help his smile as he watched Gabriel leave. He hadn't gone on an actual, proper date in months. Not since he'd broken up with Adam.

He was happy. Excited even. He could barely remember the last time he'd been excited like this.

# FOUR

Seth's heart hammered in his chest as he drove down the road from school. He'd never skipped out of class a day in his life, but there was a certain thrill to breaking the rules—the same way there had been excitement in sneaking through the hallways of his school when he should have been in class already.

His hands had shaken when he'd pushed open the door that led out to the parking lot. His heart raced as he'd darted to his car.

That excitement had gone now, and Seth took a deep breath to ease his anxiety as he changed lanes to take an exit that was coming up. The knot in his chest was tighter than ever before, but he was used to its presence in the same way one became used to an unwelcome but old friend.

The traffic was light, with people being at work or school, and the GPS was a reassuring guide to a destination he hadn't been before. Gabriel had texted him the address early that morning.

The apartment Gabriel lived in came into view about twenty-five minutes later: a white-bricked building about three stories high and set near a small grove of Douglas firs.

Gabriel was already outside when Seth pulled into the small parking lot. He was loading a blue cooler with a red flannel blanket folded on top of it into a gray Jeep Wrangler when Seth parked a few spaces over and got out of the car.

"You made it," Gabriel said with a grin, abandoning the still-open trunk to meet Seth halfway and give him a tight hug.

Gabriel smelled almost like mint, but woodsier, and with a hint of something similar to citrus. It smelled good, the scent sharp and bright but not overpowering.

"I'm glad you're here," Gabriel said as he pulled away. He was still smiling. Beautiful and warm in a way that made Seth smile in return.

"You ready?" Gabriel asked.

"I think so."

"You look nervous."

"I am nervous," Seth admitted. "The truth is, I'm not that great with water."

"What do you mean?"

There was an uncomfortable amount of silence before Seth answered. "I almost drowned when I was a kid, and I never learned to swim after that."

Seth didn't want to tell Gabriel the details. He didn't want Gabriel thinking of him as the damaged guy that was almost killed by his mother. He wanted Gabriel to think he was normal for as long as he could.

"So, you're scared of going out on the water?"

"Yeah."

Gabriel considered Seth for a time before he said, "Look, if we get there and it's really too much for you, we can go do something else."

"You sure?"

"Yeah."

Seth smiled. "Okay."

"Great. We should get going."

The drive out to the marina passed by more quickly than Seth had expected. Probably because he had Gabriel to talk to. When the tall masts of boats came into view, he fell silent and stared out at the blue of the water as they drew nearer. He hadn't seen the ocean since he was a little kid.

There were a few other people milling around on the docks where the boats were moored and as they parked Seth spotted a familiar head of blond hair out by one of the larger sailboats—the woman Seth had seen with Gabriel at that party. Her name was Haley, if Seth remembered correctly.

A man with darker hair than Haley's stood near her, and as Seth watched, he caught Haley by the waist to spin her around while she laughed.

Her boyfriend, probably. It felt ridiculous now that Seth had once thought she and Gabriel were a couple. The man holding her close seemed a much better fit for her.

Gabriel got out of the Jeep when Haley and the man she was with started kissing.

"Cool it, will you?" Gabriel teased. "There are children present."

For a horrifying second, Seth thought Gabriel meant him. Then he saw the little boy and girl with their parents further down the dock. As he watched the mother bent to help the little boy with the zipper on his coat. She reminded Seth of his own mother in a way, with her long brown hair and deep brown eyes.

There was a sudden ache in Seth's chest at the sight, the empty kind that threatened to swallow him down into a bottomless pit of loss, of grief, over what he no longer had and would never know.

"Hey, are you okay?" Gabriel asked. He came around the Jeep and touched a hand to Seth's elbow.

"Yeah." Seth nodded, but he was looking toward the water now, at the ocean of blue. And he was remembering the stillness of the pond behind his house before his mother had shoved him beneath the cold water—the spasm in the back of his throat and the fire in his chest when the water had rushed in to fill his lungs.

"You sure?"

Seth looked away from the water too quickly. His gut twisted nervously, and he slipped a hand into Gabriel's. "I'll be fine."

It was a lie. Gabriel had to know it was a lie. Seth's hand was shaking.

"We can go do something else," Gabriel reminded him.

"No. I want to meet your friends."

Gabriel squeezed Seth's hand gently. "You don't have to go on the boat to meet my friends."

"I don't want to ruin everyone's fun."

"You won't. It's fine. Really." Gabriel leaned in closer. "Besides, it gives me an excuse to be alone with you for a bit."

Seth felt his cheeks warm with Gabriel's words and they strode down the walkway that led to the dock. Haley and the man she was with came forward to meet them halfway, but Seth couldn't quite bring himself to step out onto the weathered wood that stretched out over the water.

"So, this is Seth?" Haley smiled over at Gabriel when she had reached them.

"This is him."

Haley turned her focus back to Seth, and her gaze swept over him. "You were at that party a few nights ago, weren't you?" Haley asked, and Seth nodded. "I thought you looked familiar. I'm Haley."

Seth held out a hand toward her. "It's nice to meet y—"

Haley had moved in. Her arms going around him in an unexpected gesture of affection.

"Oh, okay," Seth mumbled as he patted her on the back awkwardly.

Haley pulled back and clasped Seth's hands in her own. She seemed about to say something, but a spark arced between their fingers that made them both draw their hands back sharply.

"Are you okay?" her boyfriend asked as he took Haley's hand in his.

"It was just a little static shock. I'm fine," Haley said as she curled her fingers over his. She smiled at Seth. "This is my boyfriend, Josh."

"It's okay," Josh said. "We don't have to hug."

"So, you two ready to head out?" Haley asked.

"Actually, Seth and I thought we might go for a walk instead," Gabriel replied. "You should go though, and we'll meet you back here in about an hour?"

"You sure?"

"Yeah." Gabriel nodded. "I wanted to spend some time alone with Seth."

"Oh, gotcha." Josh gave Gabriel a wink and a pat on the arm.

Gabriel smiled back even as he rolled his eyes.

"We'll see you two in a little while," Josh said as he walked back down the dock.

Haley gave a wave as she hurried after him.

"See you!" Gabriel replied, while Seth waved.

Gabriel and Seth walked down the beach side by side. The warmth of Gabriel's hand as it slipped into his was a comfort in the chill of the afternoon.

"I probably should have warned you Haley's a hugger," Gabriel said, finally breaking the silence.

"It's fine."

Seth smiled and breathed in the ocean's smell. His eyes fell closed as a breeze ruffled his hair, and he looked over at Gabriel when he gave his hand a squeeze.

"When was the last time you saw the ocean?"

"I think I might have been five? And it was actually in California," Seth replied. "It's not really the ocean I remember, though."

"What do you remember?"

Seth glanced toward the water. He remembered the hotel they'd stayed at with its king-sized beds and white sheets. The abundance of palm trees that seemed to line every sidewalk when they went outside for a walk. The heat of the sun overhead and the smell of sunscreen.

He remembered going to eat at a Japanese restaurant, and how his mom let him try sushi for the first time. He remembered how his dad had smiled at the face he made when he first bit into the raw salmon, and the way his mother had laughed brightly.

The most he remembered about the beach was building a sandcastle with his mother. How he'd shaped the wet grains of sand into something resembling a tower. His mother beside him with a plastic shovel that was too small for her, digging up sand to build a moat. Her long brown hair wet from swimming with him earlier, the damp strands sticking to the tanned skin of her shoulders and neck.

Seth looked back over at Gabriel. "Sushi and sandcastles mostly. It's weird the things you remember sometimes."

They continued on down the beach, their steps just out of reach of the waves that lapped at the sand.

"So," Seth began, "I think you mentioned to Aaliyah you were visiting your family? Do they live in Twin Oaks?"

"My family's place is a few minutes out from there," Gabriel replied. "It used to be a farm. It actually still has the barn and everything."

"Do you mean that one farm with the hex sign on the barn? The one that looks like an eight-pointed star?"

"That's the one."

Seth blinked at him. When he was younger, Seth and some of the neighborhood kids used to sneak out at night and ride their bikes to the woods that bordered that farm.

Strange noises could be heard coming from the barn at night. Rattles and howls that had been enough to tease the imagination of children into believing in witches and monsters.

Sometimes they'd dared each other to see how close they could get to the barn before getting spooked and scurrying back to the safety of the woods.

"It's actually an animal rehabilitation center," Gabriel continued. "My parents inherited the place from my mom's father. It's part of the reason we moved to America, and why I'm studying to be a vet."

"Is it okay if I ask where you're from originally?"

"Yeah. It's fine," Gabriel said with a shrug. "I lived in Bogotá until I was ten."

"Where's that?"

"It's a city in Colombia."

Seth thought for a moment. "That's in Latin America, right?"

Gabriel nodded.

"I probably should have guessed that from your last name. So do you speak Spanish too, then?"

"Pienso que eres lindo," Gabriel said without missing a beat as he smiled at Seth, "y realmente me gustaría besarte."

Seth considered the words, but he couldn't remember most of what he'd learned last year in his Spanish class. He hadn't gotten any better since then without any lessons he was required to study for.

"That—actually sounded really sexy, but I didn't understand most of it."

Gabriel ducked his head with a laugh, the sound of it bright and amused. Seth really liked his laugh.

"It means," Gabriel said, pausing with one of those smiles that made Seth feel weak, "I think you're handsome, and I'd really like to kiss you."

"Yeah?" Now Seth paused and turned toward Gabriel.

"Yeah."

Seth brought a hand up to cup Gabriel's cheek, feeling the brush of thick stubble beneath his palm. Then he leaned in to press his lips to Gabriel's in a soft kiss. A first kiss. The kind of kiss that asked a question in its shortness and uncertainty.

The answer was there in the moment Gabriel closed the space between their mouths again to kiss Seth back—to pull him in closer and kiss him more firmly.

Seth shivered with a gust of wind. It was colder by the water, the chill biting through the long-sleeve shirt Seth wore, and he regretted forgetting his jacket in his locker in his rush to leave school.

Gabriel pulled back from the kiss to look at him. "You cold? Or am I just that good?"

"I'm a little cold," Seth admitted with a smile. "I'll be fine though."

Gabriel had already shrugged out of his jacket before Seth could finish speaking, and Seth stared at him when the jacket was placed over his shoulders.

Seth had never had a guy give him his jacket before. It was so old school. The kind of thing he'd only seen in eighties rom-coms where the guy always got the girl in the end.

The jacket was big on Seth, but it was warm where it draped over his shoulders, so he slipped his arms through the sleeves then drew it closed around himself to ward off the cold.

"Thanks," Seth said, still surprised. He wasn't used to being looked after like this. "Won't you be cold though?"

Gabriel shrugged, seemingly undisturbed by the chill in the air. "I'll be alright. Besides, I have a sweater. You don't."

Seth made a sound of agreement, then bent to pick up a stone. He turned it between his fingers a few times. It was gray and smooth and just flat enough to suit his purpose.

He hooked his finger along the edge the way his mother had taught him, then tossed it out toward the water. It skipped three times before it plunked beneath the surface.

"I never could get the hang of that," Gabriel said.

"My mom taught me how," Seth said, and a quiet sense of surprise ached in his chest. He rarely, if ever, talked openly about his mother. "She's not really in the picture anymore."

Gabriel was silent beside him, and Seth started looking for a second stone to toss, his shoe toeing the sand.

"May I ask why she's not around?" Gabriel asked at last.

Seth didn't answer Gabriel right away, choosing instead to stare out at the water. The breeze that came in off the ocean carried the smell of salt with it. It smelled the way tears tasted. The pond his mother had taken him down to hadn't been like this. It hadn't been wavy or the color of sapphires. It had been still and dark as ink.

"I'd prefer you didn't," Seth said honestly. He turned to look up into Gabriel's eyes. "Those aren't happy memories."

"Okay."

Gabriel's arms went around Seth's waist to pull him close. The gesture felt almost like an apology and Seth smiled at Gabriel's touch.

"Thank you."

"For what?"

"For not pushing."

"My parents taught me to respect the people I date. Whether it's a girl or a guy."

"So they know? Your family?"

Gabriel nodded. "They know. They actually figured it out when I was pretty young."

"How?"

"I crashed into a parked car."

Seth blinked up at Gabriel with a tilt of his head. "Yeah, I'm going to need some more information to understand that one."

Gabriel glanced upward. His brow furrowed with thought. "I was fifteen, maybe sixteen years old, and my dad was trying to teach me how to drive, right?" He looked at Seth, who gave him a nod to prompt him to continue. "So, we're in this parking lot driving in circles, and this really, *really* insanely hot guy jogs by and I start watching him instead of where I'm going. So, the next thing I know I've crashed into one of the only parked cars in the lot."

"Oh, shit."

"Yeah, it was bad. But anyway, my dad looked over at me and went, 'Son, you might be gay.' Which, not exactly, because I'm actually bisexual."

"Was he okay with it, though?"

"He was okay with me being attracted to guys. Just not so much what I did to the car."

"Right."

"What about your dad?" Gabriel asked. "Does he know?"

"Oh, he *definitely* knows. He, uh, actually walked in on me and my first boyfriend, in the middle of things, because he was bringing in the laundry. Which ended up all over the floor because he put the basket over his head."

"That might actually beat my car-wreck experience."

"Yeah, he didn't talk to me for a week afterward. Wouldn't even look at me." Seth let his fingers play over the back of Gabriel's hands. "Then one day I came home from school to find a box of condoms on my desk with a note saying I'd be doing the laundry from then on."

"But it's been okay since then?"

"Yeah. I mean, we don't talk about it much, but he doesn't give me a hard time about it either."

Seth spotted another flattish stone and pulled away to retrieve it. He repeated the motion from earlier, sending it skipping across the water.

"Can you teach me how to skip stones?" Gabriel asked. "I've never been able to do it right."

Seth grinned playfully. "I will in exchange for another kiss…"

Gabriel smiled at that and leaned in to kiss Seth again, the press of his mouth making Seth shiver as he kissed him back. The kiss deepened as Seth let his hands slide up along Gabriel's back.

Gabriel pulled back from the kiss first and leaned his forehead against Seth's. His breaths were coming quicker now, and Seth couldn't help but feel smug.

"You're going to want to find a rock that's pretty flat," Seth said.

"What?"

"To throw," Seth explained as he stepped away from Gabriel with a teasing grin to look for an appropriate stone. He finally found a mottled gray one that was relatively flat and held it out to Gabriel, who took it from him, his fingers brushing across Seth's as he did. "If you throw that," Seth told him, "I can see what you need to do differently."

Gabriel held the stone awkwardly. His toss was more heavy-handed than Seth's had been—more of a chuck than a sidearm—and his stone immediately plopped beneath the surface of the water.

"Here." Seth stepped over to Gabriel after he picked up another stone. "You're not holding it right."

Seth positioned Gabriel's fingers on the stone, getting him to hold it with his thumb and middle finger, then firmly hook his index finger along the edge.

"You're going to throw it more like this," Seth said as he showed the correct movement with his own arm.

Gabriel tossed his stone toward the water the way Seth had shown him. This time it skipped once before it sank.

"Better." Seth smiled.

They skipped stones for a while longer, until the wind picked up and the water became too choppy for it. At that point Seth strode to Gabriel's side and took his hand in his to lead him back to the Jeep.

Gabriel let go of Seth's hand to head over to the trunk while Seth leaned against the side of the vehicle with his own hands in his pockets. He smiled when the trunk closed with a *thunk* and he spotted the flannel blanket Gabriel had tucked under an arm.

Gabriel made his way back to the front of the vehicle and Seth followed him, watching as Gabriel climbed up onto the hood of the Jeep.

"Come on up," Gabriel said with a tilt of his head.

Seth climbed up onto the Jeep. Gabriel was probably expecting him to sit beside him, but instead he situated himself between Gabriel's legs and leaned his head back against his shoulder.

Gabriel smiled in response.

"You totally planned this," Seth said as Gabriel wrapped the blanket around them both.

"I figured at some point we'd get some time to ourselves," Gabriel admitted, tucking his chin against Seth's shoulder.

"You're a hopeless romantic, aren't you?"

"Maybe." Gabriel chuckled as he cupped Seth's hands between his own. His skin was warm despite the cold, and his hands rubbed gently over Seth's to chase the chill away. "Or maybe I've just seen one too many romance movies because I have sisters."

"You have sisters?"

"Yeah." Gabriel nodded. "Diana is fourteen and Naomi is twenty-five."

"And how old are you?"

"I'm twenty-two."

It was younger than Seth had thought. He'd guessed twenty-three, maybe twenty-five at most.

"So, I know your sister's names. What about your parent's?"

"Daniela and Carlos," Gabriel replied. "What about yours?

"My dad is named David."

"And your mom?" Gabriel asked hesitantly when Seth went quiet.

"Eliza." The sound of his voice was almost lost to the wind as it picked up again, but Gabriel didn't ask him to repeat himself.

Seth snuggled in closer to Gabriel as he watched the sailboats out on the water. There were only a few boats out today, the weather perhaps cold enough to convince the less adventurous to stay on shore. One of those boats belonged to Haley and Josh, and Seth thought it might be the one with the yellow on its sail that seemed to be working its way closer to the dock slowly.

"That's them, right?" Seth asked, pointing out the boat.

"Yep. That's them."

They watched together as the sailboat Haley and Josh were on pulled back up to the dock a while later, and they disentangled to walk back to the marina to greet them.

# FIVE

There were dark clouds overhead by the time Seth and Gabriel said their goodbyes to Josh and Haley, the group parting ways in the parking lot to head to their respective cars. A few drops of rain now dotted the pavement.

Seth was happy despite the turn the weather looked to be taking. The rest of the visit had gone well. They'd all sat at a wooden picnic table and talked over the lunch Gabriel had brought in the cooler. Seth had decided he liked Gabriel's friends. They were kind, and funny in a way that drew a laugh from Seth more than once.

Thunder rumbled in the distance, and Seth tipped his head back to ponder the sky overhead once more, his steps coming to a halt so he could watch the clouds approaching from over the water. The ocean looked dark and reddish with the sun setting on the overcast horizon.

"Seth?"

Seth made a sound of acknowledgment as he cast his gaze in Gabriel's direction. He had his keys in his hand, and was almost to the Jeep, while Seth had fallen behind.

Gabriel gave him a smile. "You coming?"

"Yeah," Seth replied with a grin as he jogged forward.

"Better hurry and get in before it starts pouring."

"Thank you," Seth said when he reached the Jeep, and Gabriel looked at him from the other side of the car. "For being understanding about the whole water thing."

Gabriel smiled at Seth. "You're welcome."

Seth ducked his head as he got in. He buckled his seat belt and glanced over at Gabriel with the sound of the car keys turning in the ignition.

The radio hummed to life a moment after the engine, the sounds of a rock band playing over the speakers as Gabriel backed the Jeep out from its parking space then drove from the lot.

Seth's phone vibrated in the pocket of his coat. He'd put it on silent last night before bed and had forgotten to switch the sound back on.

He pulled it from his pocket now. The message from Evelyn in his notifications didn't surprise him, but the missed call alert did. Seth stared down at his phone with a growing ache in his chest, at the name of an ex-boyfriend he never thought he'd hear from again. Isaac Easton. The first boy he'd ever loved.

It'd been months since they'd last spoken. Months since Seth had allowed himself to think of the tall boy with the wavy dark-blond hair and blue eyes that had made his breath catch when he'd first looked into them.

But he still remembered. He still remembered that day in class before they'd broken up. How Isaac had run a hand through his hair—a gesture Seth recognized as a nervous tic. Only this time, it was different. This time Isaac had stiffened when he brought his hand back down.

"Isaac?" Seth had whispered as he'd leaned forward in his seat. "Hey, are you okay?"

Isaac bolted up like he'd been slapped. He hurried from the room and Seth ran after him.

The teacher called out to them, but Seth ignored their words. His entire world narrowed down to the person he cared for most.

He found Isaac in the bathroom with his head bowed over the sink and his hands planted flat on either side of the basin, his face pale and sweat beading along his forehead, and a twist to his mouth like he was about to be sick.

"Isaac, what's wrong?"

Isaac shook his head, his hands balling into tight fists against the counter.

"Seriously, Isaac, talk to me. You've been avoiding me all day."

It was true. Anytime their eyes had met, Isaac had turned abruptly to hurry in the opposite direction. It wasn't until they had language arts together that Isaac let Seth get anywhere near him.

Isaac raised his gaze to meet Seth's. There was an almost bone-weary sadness in his eyes that made Seth reach for him and Isaac let himself be drawn into the hug, his body hunched forward to make up for the height difference, and his hands clutching the back of Seth's shirt.

Isaac took a ragged breath, like he couldn't get enough air, and Seth felt the dampness of tears against the skin of his neck.

"Hey," Seth soothed when Isaac made a choked sound. "It's okay. I'm here. I've got you."

Isaac jerked back when Seth brought a hand up to run through his hair, his own hand shooting up to touch the strands like they were made of glass. The rise and fall of his chest inconsistent and unsteady. His cheeks damp and face flushed.

"I don't think we should see each other anymore."

"What?" Seth's heart sank in his chest like a ship being dragged down by its anchor. "Why?"

Isaac squeezed his eyes shut as if Seth's question physically hurt.

"Did—did I do something wrong?" Seth asked, and he could feel heat behind his eyes, the dampness of tears welling up and threatening to spill over.

Why was this happening? He must have done something for Isaac to be saying this. His Isaac, who had always been so understanding with his issues. Who had never hesitated to soothe Seth's fears or his pain when things became too much.

Maybe that had been the problem. He'd been too much. Too vulnerable. Too noisy. Too needy.

Seth took a step forward but didn't feel the ground beneath his feet. Couldn't feel anything other than the numbness in his limbs and the slowed patter of his heart in his chest. "How can I fix this?"

"You can't."

"Isaac—"

"Please don't make this harder than it is," Isaac said, then abruptly headed past Seth for the restroom door.

"Isaac, wait. Please. Tell me how I can fix this!" Seth pleaded, tears sliding down his cheeks as he watched Isaac's retreat. "Isaac?" But he was talking to himself, the door in front of him already swinging closed. "I don't understand," Seth had choked out through the hot rush of tears. "What did I do?"

Seth still didn't understand it now. Any of it. Not why Isaac had gone from loving him one day to wanting nothing to do with him the next. Not why they'd parted ways. And certainly not why he would contact him now after all this time.

A few drops of rain hit the windshield of Gabriel's car. The sound drew Seth's focus in time to see an animal dart out from the trees. It stopped in the middle of the road ahead of them, and for a second, yellow eyes met Seth's own.

The next instant, Gabriel's palm smacked against Seth's chest to hold him back as he slammed on the brakes. Too late.

There was a sharp snap as flesh and bone met metal.

The cellphone flew from Seth's hand with the abrupt stop, going who-even-knew-where, and his body jerked against Gabriel's hand.

Gabriel said something Seth didn't catch. His attention was focused on the streak of red across the road and the black mess of fur beyond it. He could feel the ratcheting thump of his heart against Gabriel's palm with each breath he took.

"Seth?"

The rain had become steadier, and Seth squinted through the water that ran like small rivers down the windshield. The animal on the road lay still and wet in the downpour.

"Seth?"

"W-what?" Seth asked, and finally turned to look at Gabriel.

"Are you okay?"

"Yeah. Yeah, I'm okay."

Seth climbed out of the vehicle into the rain before he could think better of it. One of his hands gripped the door as he stared at the bloodied lump of dark fur lying a short distance away—a wolf, or what was left of it.

"Seth, wait."

Against Gabriel's advice, Seth walked toward the animal. His steps were slow, cautious, because despite the blood smeared over the asphalt a part of him half expected the wolf to leap to its feet with teeth bared and fur bristling.

It didn't move though. Not even when Seth crouched beside it.

This close he could see the blood on its gray-flecked fur. Its body was wirier than Seth imagined wolves were supposed to appear, but it was obviously old. Old and now dead in the middle of the road.

Sadness swelled in Seth's chest as he once again took in the sight of the blood and the stillness of the animal before him. The dark-furred body gave rise to a sense of familiarity he didn't understand. He'd never seen this wolf before. Yet he couldn't shake the feeling this wasn't the first time he'd seen it.

The fur along its belly stirred and at first Seth thought it was only the wind, but then he realized it was breathing. Shallow, but there.

"I think it's still alive," Seth said when he heard Gabriel come up behind him.

The wolf's paw twitched and its eyes squinted open. The sudden movement drew Gabriel closer, and Seth moved aside so he could crouch down to have a better look.

Gabriel ran a hand along the wolf's back, possibly to check for breaks to its spine, or maybe to comfort it. Seth had no idea which was more likely.

The wolf let out a long, low whimper when Gabriel's touch moved down along its side. His fingers pressed carefully into its flank. Definitely checking for wounds now.

Another pained whimper and Gabriel made a soothing sound as he found what he'd apparently been looking for. A bloody gash arced along the wolf's flank when he parted the fur there.

The wolf's paw twitched again, and it shifted its head against the road. "You can help him, right?"

Gabriel frowned in a way that made Seth's heart sink and shook his head. "Not here I can't. But if I get him to my family's rehabilitation center quickly he may have a chance."

Seth held his gaze, and after a moment Gabriel nodded back toward the Jeep.

"Go spread the blanket out over the trunk so he has something more comfortable to lie on," Gabriel instructed.

Seth rose from where he'd knelt. It was pouring now and large droplets of water pelted him as he ran back to the car.

The back door offered some coverage once he was beneath it, the rain drumming an angry percussion against the metal and glass above him.

Seth unfolded the flannel blanket, doing his best to keep it dry as he spread it out over the bottom of the trunk—not that it would matter with the wolf already soaked in rainwater and its own blood.

He backed away as Gabriel stepped up beside him, the wolf held carefully in his arms. It occurred to Seth how easy it would have been for the animal to turn its head and bite him. It didn't seem to have the will, though. Aside from a few pained whimpers it stayed docile in Gabriel's arms.

Seth shivered as rainwater ran down his neck into the collar of his already drenched shirt. But he didn't complain about the cold, or the sodden state of his clothes as he watched Gabriel situate the wolf on the blanket.

Once the trunk was closed again, they both rounded the vehicle to their respective sides, sliding into the dry air of the Jeep to slam their doors shut against the rain.

Gabriel had his phone against his ear when Seth looked over at him, his other hand on the steering wheel to guide the Jeep forward while rain pounded against the windshield and a whimper rose from the back.

# SIX

The place Gabriel turned into had changed little since Seth had last seen it, back when he was a kid. Though this time around, he was better able to recognize it for what it really was. Not a farm, as the large red barn had made him believe, but a rehabilitation center for wildlife.

Instead of wooden fences to corral in horses or cattle, there were chain-link fences that held wilder animals. From that alone, Seth knew it was safe to assume the barn housed wild animals as well, rather than horses or a tractor.

A woman ran through the rain to meet them as Gabriel parked the Jeep. She was shorter than Gabriel, but not by much. Her dark hair was tied back in a ponytail that dripped water, and her skin was the same shade as his. But her eyes were a dark brown when she looked in Seth's direction.

"Who's this?" she asked. Not bothering to hide her curiosity.

"Naomi, this is Seth."

Naomi didn't look like she quite believed him. "This is Seth?"

"Yeah," Gabriel replied simply, already headed toward the trunk.

But Naomi didn't follow. Her gaze swept over Seth as he trailed after Gabriel, the look in her eyes too suspicious for his liking.

"Veintiuno mi cola," Naomi said to Gabriel in a voice that sounded almost accusatory. "Se ve como un peladito."

"Dijo que tiene veintiuno."

"Te confías mucho. Obviamente te está diciendo mentiras."

Gabriel rolled his eyes as he opened the trunk of the Jeep. "No me molestes y más bien ven a ayudarme."

Naomi huffed as she came around the Jeep with a shake of her head. "No me vengas llorar cuando la policía aparezca en tu puerta."

Seth stared between them. He barely understood a word of what was said, yet he was certain it was about him.

The wolf whimpered at the three of them, its head lifting enough to stare at them with fear in its eyes and more blood on its fur than there had been before.

"Poor thing," Naomi said as she pulled a pair of gloves from the back pocket of her jeans and put them on.

"Can you save him?" Seth asked.

"I can try." Naomi slapped a second pair of gloves against Gabriel's chest. "Help me get him up."

Gabriel made an annoyed sound as he pulled the gloves on. "You have a terrible bedside manner."

"You're not my patient."

Between Gabriel and Naomi, they managed to get the wolf inside the small clinic that was connected to the farmhouse and onto a metal table.

Seth came inside after them to stand uncertainly off to the side, shivering as rainwater dripped down his face from his hair and Naomi took medical supplies out of a cabinet.

"Diana!" Naomi yelled, after a glance in Seth's direction. "Diana! Oye! Get in here!"

There was a sound from behind Seth and he turned in time to see a young girl with light-brown skin and a long braid open a door that appeared to lead into the house.

"What?"

"Take Gabriel's date and get him some dry clothes."

Diana's eyes flicked over Seth and she smiled brightly when she looked at Gabriel. "Okay, I approve. He's cute."

Gabriel gave her a smile in return. "At least *someone* thinks I have good taste in men."

Diana giggled and Naomi rolled her eyes at Seth's grin as she stepped back to the metal table they'd laid the wolf on. Gabriel came up beside her to help.

Seth didn't see any of what happened next as Diana led him into the farmhouse, then around a corner and up a flight of stairs. She let go of his hand to hurry ahead of him, and Seth had to quicken his steps to keep up.

Seth's gaze trailed over the collection of family photos on the walls as he followed Diana down the hall at the top of the landing, his eyes picking out the familiar image of brown skin and green eyes from group shots of family and friends. Birthday parties, holidays, outings. Seth paused to look at a high school graduation photo: Gabriel in a cap and gown in front of what was unmistakably Seth's school.

A crucifix hung on the wall as well. Which either meant that Gabriel was Catholic, or that he had at least been raised in a Catholic household.

"Hey," Diana said, and Seth turned to find her leaning out of a room at the end of the hall. "You coming?"

Seth gave a nod and headed into the room after her.

The bedroom he found himself in was relatively small. The light of sunset filtered in through the large window, illuminating a few pictures that hung on the dark-blue walls—mostly more family photos, but there was one of Haley and Josh as well. It must have been Gabriel's room from when he'd still been living at home.

Diana headed for a closet on the left while Seth gazed around.

A chest of drawers stood against the wall closest to the door and the headboard of a bed against the one opposite, books stacked on top of the dark brown wood and in shelves built into the sides.

"Here. These should fit," Diana said. The words drew Seth's attention to her and the clothes she held. "At least I think they should."

"I'm sure they'll work fine," Seth replied as he took the jeans and black sweater.

"Right. The bathroom is across the hall." Her eyes swept over him. "Feel free to use one of the towels in there. Lord knows you need it."

She disappeared out the door after that, leaving Seth to wander on his own to the bathroom, a generous word for what was little more than a glorified closet with a toilet and shower. The counter with the inlaid sink was narrow and looked barely big enough for the number of people it would have had to accommodate while Gabriel was still living at home.

The linen closet was easy enough to find though, and Seth took out a towel before he stripped out of his wet clothes, which he set on the bathroom counter rather than let splat to the floor in a puddle.

By the time Seth had dried and changed he could hear voices from downstairs. One of them was Gabriel's, so he headed back down with his wet clothes to ask if he could use the dryer.

Gabriel was talking with Diana when Seth reached the bottom floor, his eyes tired and his clothes soaked.

"Hey," Seth said, and Gabriel looked at him as he went on. "How's the wolf?"

"Stable from what we can tell. He's out in the barn now."

Seth gave a sigh of relief, then glanced from his handful of clothes to Gabriel. "Is it okay if I use your dryer?"

"Yeah. Diana can show you where it is. I need to go"—Gabriel gestured at himself—"get cleaned up."

"Follow me," Diana said after Gabriel excused himself and headed upstairs.

She half skipped her way to the laundry room as Seth followed.

"So how did you and Gabriel meet?" Diana asked after he had tossed his clothes in the dryer and she'd pressed a few buttons to get it running.

"He came into the coffee shop I work at." Seth thought for a moment. "Well, actually, we technically met the night before that at a party, but I didn't ask him out until the coffee shop."

Diana smiled. "So, it's kind of like fate wanted you together."

Naomi called Diana to the kitchen to help make dinner before Seth could respond, and he wandered a short distance behind her as she headed back that way.

They found Naomi at the stove, cooking chicken with vegetables in a skillet. She didn't waste any time in directing Diana to cut some avocados.

A boy around Seth's age stood near Naomi, his clothes spotted with rainwater and his hair damp. He was stirring something that Seth suspected was rice.

"This is Marcus," Naomi said when she caught Seth watching him. "He's our cousin. The storm is so bad he decided to stop here to wait it out. His house is farther up the road."

"I'm Seth," Seth said, then added when he realized that probably explained nothing, "Gabriel's date."

Marcus gave him a nod and turned back to what he was doing.

Seth felt like he'd fallen into a different world. This whole place was somehow more vibrant, more alive than Seth's house ever felt, and it had nothing to do with the brightly painted rooms he'd wandered past or the way the light seemed to fill each one—though it certainly didn't hurt, as Seth's house was mostly white walls and drawn curtains.

It was more the sense of family. Of constant movement from one room to the next. The way they'd brush by each other in their rush to get something. They were comfortable in each other's spaces.

Seth didn't have a lot of that. He and his father only had small moments here and there together. Sometimes Seth felt more like he had a roommate he had to clean up after and feed than a father.

Which reminded Seth that he hadn't texted him with his whereabouts yet. He looked back toward the front door with the rain and wind on the other side. He'd forgotten his cellphone in the Jeep.

"Seth." Naomi gestured him over and he made his way to her. "You think you can handle making a salad?"

Seth felt insulted. "I know how to cook. I've been making all the meals at home since I was a kid."

"Well, at least I know Gabriel won't starve if the two of you ever get married," Naomi replied.

Seth blinked at her, stunned.

"Jesus, Naomi," Diana hissed to her sister. "Will you cool it? They only just started dating."

Naomi waved a dismissive hand toward Diana. "If he's serious about him, it won't matter."

"I'm standing right here."

"It won't turn into anything serious if you scare him off," Diana said. "I give it a week."

Seth gestured widely with his arms. "Still standing here."

"Ignore her," Diana sighed as she moved away from the counter to the fridge.

She returned a moment later to the counter closest to Seth, where she placed a head of lettuce, a cucumber, and a few carrots. A cutting board was pulled down from a cabinet overhead, and a knife from a drawer, followed by a vegetable peeler, were placed on the counter beside it.

Seth took up the space Diana vacated and started peeling a carrot without further prompting. A comfortable quiet settled over the kitchen as they focused on their separate tasks.

Gabriel appeared shortly before dinner and helped by setting the table while the rest of them brought the food over—plates of chicken with vegetables, rice, what looked like some kind of avocado dressing, and the salad Seth had made.

Seth was seated next to Gabriel and across from Marcus.

The conversation at the table flowed easily while they ate until Naomi said, "Maybe after dinner Gabriel can play us something on the piano."

The entire energy of the room shifted.

Gabriel stiffened and Diana looked down at her plate with a nervousness that made the corners of her mouth tighten. So different from the perpetual smile Seth had grown used to in the few hours he'd known her.

"You play the piano?" Seth asked with a glance at Gabriel.

"Oh, he's been playing piano almost as long as he could speak," Naomi said, and Seth turned back to her when she spoke. "It was basically like a third language for him by the time we moved to America."

"He quit though." Diana's fork scraped against her plate as she made piles out of her rice. "Like ten years ago."

"He tried to quit before that, but Mom and Dad made him keep going." Naomi cocked her head. "Almost a year after that, he threw a fit and refused to go anymore. When Mom took him anyway, he ran three blocks before she caught up to him."

"Can we talk about something else?" Gabriel asked sharply.

"I'm just saying I don't get it. You're not the type to up and quit. You wanted to go to Berklee and everything. Then a few weeks into us getting you lessons again, you say you don't want to play anymore."

"And you've been reminding me of the fact for the past ten years," Gabriel grit out. "So can we please, please, stop talking about it?"

Naomi sat back in her chair with a frown and a raised brow. "Yeah, well, Mom and Dad spent a lot of money on that piano we have. It was over three thousand dollars, and you won't even touch it."

Seth looked from Naomi to Gabriel, who had gone ashen and quiet, his gaze unfocused and his breaths uneven.

Seth knew panic when he saw it and he reached for Gabriel's hand beneath the table to intertwine their fingers, while Naomi kept saying things that were making Gabriel's hand shake in Seth's. Kept pressing for an answer that Gabriel obviously didn't want to give.

"You need to stop putting him on the spot like this," Diana said in such a quiet voice Seth almost missed the fact that she'd spoken.

"I will when he gives me an answer."

Diana's brow furrowed. "He gave you an answer. Years ago. It was too much pressure for him to handle."

Naomi shook her head in disbelief. "But—"

"I'm actually getting fed up with you doing this too, Naomi," Marcus interrupted. "It's upsetting for everyone."

Naomi pushed her chair back from the table and stood. "For the record"—she leaned forward with her palms flat on the table—"I'm not buying what you're selling, Gabriel. There's more to the story than what you've told us." With that, she left the kitchen. Though her voice reached them a moment later when she called Diana and Marcus to help her feed the animals.

"So, Naomi is..." Seth trailed off as he searched for the right word once he and Gabriel were alone.

Gabriel looked over from where he was still seated at the table. "Kind of a dick?"

"I mean, I wasn't going to put it like that but—*yeah*."

Gabriel laughed like a weight had fallen off his shoulders. "Yeah, well, she's always been more of the tough love type, and sensitivity isn't really in her vocabulary. Also, my mom inheriting this place was only part of why we moved. The other half of it is that my parents could tell how serious I was about Berklee." Gabriel shook his head. "So, Naomi got uprooted from everything she'd known because of what I wanted, and then I didn't live up to my end of things."

"It sounds like you're saying she resents you."

"I think on some level she does."

Seth let the topic of conversation settle into silence. It was a heavy discussion to be having so soon into their relationship. He hoped it didn't cause his next question to be taken as a means of escape even as he rose from his chair. "I think I left my phone in your car. I should get it."

"I can text Naomi to get it on her way back in," Gabriel said as he pulled his own phone out of the back pocket of his jeans. "There's no reason for you to get all wet again."

"Thanks."

"Are you okay?" Gabriel asked as he sent the text off. "Did Naomi stress you out?"

Seth shrugged a shoulder and Gabriel slipped his phone into his back pocket, then rounded the table to close the space between them.

"I bet I can cheer you up."

"Yeah?" Seth said, and already the hint of a smile ghosted across his lips.

Gabriel's hands slid down his sides, long fingers splayed against his hips when they came to a rest. "Yeah." Gabriel nodded, a confidence in his smirk that made Seth's stomach give a warm flutter.

It was a novelty. He hadn't had butterflies over someone since Isaac.

When Gabriel leaned in the next moment and kissed Seth, that flutter of warmth spread up from his stomach to his chest. His heart skipped like the rainwater off the windowsill, and he pressed in closer.

Seth's hands stroked up Gabriel's back when he kissed him a second time. The cotton of his shirt rode up and he dug his fingers into the fabric to feel the warmth of skin beneath it as the kiss deepened. Gabriel's tongue slid against his own, and if Gabriel kept kissing him like that, Seth's mood wasn't the only thing that was going to be up.

When Gabriel pulled back, the smile he wore made Seth want to kiss him again, and he knew he was beaming just as brightly.

"That's better," Gabriel said.

There was the sound of a door opening, then Naomi's voice calling to them.

She was taking her raincoat off when they got there, her clothes damp and her hair just as wet. A few strands that had escaped her ponytail were stuck to her cheeks.

"Thanks," Seth said when she handed him his cellphone. "I needed to call a cab."

"You're kidding, right?" Naomi asked, while Seth's fingers hovered over the screen. "It's terrible out. We have two guest rooms. You should just stay the night. Marcus is."

Marcus glanced over at Naomi like he wished she'd leave him out of it.

Seth blinked at the offer. "I, um…"

Naomi crossed her arms and cocked her head at him. "You have somewhere you need to be?"

Only home, so his dad didn't worry. Only school the next morning, so he didn't get in more trouble than he was already. But Naomi was looking at him like she expected as much.

"No," Seth said with a shake of his head. "Nowhere important."

"Then stay the night. It's not safe to be driving anywhere right now."

"Mom and dad would not approve," Diana warned, holding her sopping raincoat at arm's length. "They won't even let me go to a sleepover. They'd definitely never let me have a boy stay over."

"Well, they're not here because their flight was canceled, and if they were, I think they'd understand with the way the weather is. Also, you're fourteen and Gabriel is an adult. There's a difference."

Diana looked unconvinced. Her eyes narrowed and lips pursed.

Naomi turned her attention back to Seth. "You're better off safe than sorry."

"Okay," Seth agreed, and when Naomi turned her back, he sent a quick text to his father, lying to him about staying the night at Micah's so he wouldn't worry.

# SEVEN

It was still raining. Seth could hear it against the window where it ran in rivulets down the glass. But it was the sound of thunder that had woken him.

According to the clock on the nightstand, it had only been around four hours since Gabriel had shown Seth where the guest room on the second floor was and kissed him goodnight. Seth went to bed with a smile on his lips for once, instead of a lump in his throat.

A flash of lightning lit up the room, and Seth rolled over onto his back with the rumble of thunder that followed. The rain rattled the windowpanes, and eventually he sat up. There was no way he could get back to sleep while the storm hammered against the house like this.

Seth threw the covers aside and swung his legs over the edge of the bed, as restless as the wind through the tree outside the window.

He rose to his feet, deciding he'd get a glass of water. The floorboards creaked beneath his steps as he walked—a reminder of how old this house was. He opened the door of the room, then leaned into the hall with a glance around the corners. He was half checking for people and half trying to get his bearings in the dark house that he barely knew.

The boards were cool against the soles of his feet as he made his way downstairs and headed for the kitchen when he reached the bottom.

He stopped before he passed the living room when he glimpsed Gabriel in front of the piano. He was reaching a hand out toward the keys, his fingers almost brushing them before they curled in against his palm.

Seth shifted his weight to take a step back, and the floor creaked where he stood with bare feet and borrowed pajamas. The sound seemed to draw Gabriel from his thoughts, and he turned to look at Seth.

"Sorry," Seth said, feeling like he'd broken something and was about to step on the shards. "I was going to get a glass of water and—"

"It's fine."

It didn't feel fine. It felt like he was intruding.

"Were you going to play?" Seth realized after he asked that it was a stupid question for the middle of the night with everyone else in the house asleep.

"No." Gabriel glanced back at the piano. "No. I was just... thinking."

There was a nagging urge to ask what Gabriel had been thinking about, but the sadness in his voice and the tension in his shoulders stopped Seth from asking. He knew when to leave things well enough alone.

Seth looked around for something to change the subject to. His gaze fell on a pile of photo albums that sat on the wooden coffee table in front of the couch and he pointed to them.

"So, if I looked through those, would I find any embarrassing baby photos?"

The tension in Gabriel's shoulders eased and he smiled as he said, "Maybe a few. Actually, I think those are the ones from when we lived in Bogotá."

"Oh," Seth mouthed as he picked up one of the albums, his curiosity piqued.

Gabriel joined him on the couch. Seth leaned back into him, and Gabriel looked over his shoulder at the album he opened.

There was a house in one of the photos that drew Seth's eyes. It was a two-story, with white concrete walls and an orangish clay-tile roof. A boy sat in the driveway with a pile of chalk next to him and a smile on his face as he looked up at the camera from where he was drawing a yellow sun.

"That's our old house."

Seth pointed to the little boy. "Is that you?"

"Yeah."

"You were *so cute*."

Gabriel gave a small laugh. "Am I not cute now?"

"You grew up handsome." Seth smiled and rested his head on Gabriel's shoulder as he turned to the next page in the album.

The next two pages had photos of a crowded beach, a few people half-buried in the sand—one of which Seth suspected was Naomi. A few of the other photos were of kites in the air, all with bright colors and intricate designs that stood out sharply against the blue of the sky.

"I think that was at Festival de Verano," Gabriel said, then explained when Seth stared at him, "It means Summer Festival. They have concerts and events to celebrate Bogotá's birthday."

There were photos of a little boy Seth recognized as Gabriel over the next few pages. He looked about eight in these and was seated at a piano, much like the one in the living room with them now. He was clearly in his element and so happy, his eyes alight and a wide smile on his face.

Seth swore he could feel Gabriel's heartbeat quicken where his shoulder pressed up against his chest. His body seemed to tense as he stared down at the photograph of himself.

Seth wanted to ask what had happened. Why Gabriel had actually chosen to quit playing the piano when he'd obviously loved it so much.

He turned the pages without a word until they'd passed that section of the album. Gabriel relaxed against Seth again.

Seth realized with a glance upward that the rain had stopped. The haze of dawn was now breaking through the cloud cover to light the window in the dull glow of early morning.

"I should feed the animals," Gabriel said with a glance from the clock to Seth. "Did you want to come?"

"Yeah, sure."

"Okay, meet me in the kitchen in a few minutes. I need to get changed."

They parted ways. Seth gathered his clothes from the dryer to dress in the downstairs bathroom before he met up with Gabriel in the kitchen again. He found him by the counter with two bottles of formula in his hands.

They headed outside and toward the barn. The ground was muddy with the rain from earlier, and the grass was glistening with droplets.

Even from this distance, Seth could see two fawns in one of the pens up ahead. Their heads turned toward the sound of their footsteps and their bodies tensed as if ready to run. The fawns regarded them warily and Seth hung back, slower to approach than Gabriel, worried about how they'd respond if he got too close.

Gabriel entered the pen. The fawns cautiously moved toward him, their steps tentative and ears twitching in Seth's direction.

"It's alright. They won't bite you," Gabriel reassured him, seeing the way he hesitated inside the gate.

"I don't want to scare them," Seth whispered.

"They're pretty fearless when there's a bottle involved." Gabriel smiled. "It's every other time outside of that they seem to spook. Here"—Gabriel held out the second bottle to him—"just don't let them pull it out of your hands because they'll run off with it."

Seth took the bottle from Gabriel, and, copying his crouch, held it out toward the other fawn. It regarded him with large, dark eyes and sniffed in his direction, stretching its neck out toward the bottle. Eventually, its mouth closed hesitantly over the nipple.

Seth wasn't entirely sure what he was thinking when he reached out to touch it. An urge he couldn't control pushed his hand forward until his fingertips brushed the soft fur along the fawn's neck.

Sparks jumped from beneath his touch and the fawn bleated a terrified cry. Both of the fawns clumsily fled to the other end of the enclosure to huddle there, their wide eyes on Seth.

Shaken, Seth took a step back as an apology fell from his lips. He'd never seen an animal look so frightened.

"They just spooked, Seth. They'll be fine," Gabriel said as he straightened up. "It happens."

Seth didn't argue. Just curled his fingers in against his palm. The pad of each one still thrummed with energy.

"I think I gave it a static shock. Like with Haley at the docks."

Gabriel glanced from the fawn to Seth. "Do I need to get you a pair of rubber gloves?" he teased.

Seth rolled his eyes.

"Maybe a lightning rod?"

"Ha ha, very funny," Seth retorted, but he couldn't help the chuckle that followed.

"The fawn will be fine, Seth. Come on."

Gabriel took Seth to the barn where there were several wooden pens that at one time must have been horse stalls and a few smaller cages that held things like squirrels, birds, and rabbits.

It was much louder in here than it had been in the pens outside with their individual shelters—a noise that only grew when Seth stepped inside. The animals backed into the corners of their cages or sought shelter in provided hideaways. All except for the wolf, which Seth spotted in one of the converted horse stalls.

A refrigerator was tucked in a corner toward the far wall, and Gabriel headed over to it. He set the bottles from earlier on top of the fridge, then extracted a few Tupperware containers from inside. Some looked to be filled with different chunks of meat, others a mix of vegetables.

The wolf raised its head at Gabriel's approach, its tail swishing to greet him.

"Hey, Silver," Gabriel said as he filled a metal bowl that had been set out by the pen with the chunks of meat, then slid it through the space at the bottom of the door.

"Silver?"

"Diana insists on giving all the animals names," Gabriel explained.

The wolf rose up off the ground slowly with a soft whimper. It now had a bandage on one of its front legs that it favored and another on its side where its fur had clearly been shaved.

"Is he alright?"

"So far," Gabriel replied. "He's very old, though. So that could change."

Seth leaned cautiously against the top of the pen to get a better look at the wolf while it ate. When the overhead lights glanced off the gray in its fur just right, it did shine a little like silver, and Seth could see why Diana had given it such a name.

"It's a miracle he survived at all," Gabriel said from where he was feeding an ornery-looking raccoon.

They finished feeding the rest of the animals, Gabriel taking some extra time with a rabbit that was missing its eyes. Seth thought it was sweet the way he talked to it in a soft voice to coax it out from where it had pressed itself into the corner of the cage with distress. He finally earned its trust enough for it to hop forward and take a carrot from his hand, and Gabriel set the rest of the vegetables close by so it could find them more easily.

The sound of a car coming up the gravel drive drew them to the barn door. A gray station wagon stopped outside, and Haley and Josh stepped from the car a moment later.

"You guys are here early," Gabriel said.

"Haley wanted to see the wolf," Josh explained, with Haley already heading past Gabriel into the barn. "It's all she's been able to talk about after you called last night."

Gabriel seemed to watch Haley almost expectantly, as if waiting for her to determine something about the wolf that now met her eyes. Its gaze held hers for a few moments before she looked away and nodded to him.

Gabriel's brow rose, his eyes going wide. And Seth got the sense he was missing something important.

They all headed for the barn entrance a few minutes later. All except Gabriel, and Seth turned back to find he still stood before Silver's stall, his hands clutching at the wooden gate and his eyes locked with the wolf's yellow ones.

"Yes." Gabriel's whisper was so soft Seth almost missed it.

Silver let out a whimper and collapsed with a heavy thud, while Gabriel slumped over onto the ground in almost the same instant, his limbs jerking in a fit.

"Shit!" Seth shouted. "Gabriel!"

It was hard not to give in to the panic that washed over him, but Seth managed to push his building hysteria back as he dropped to the damp dirt of the barn floor.

Seth used to have a friend that was epileptic and knew enough from experience to turn Gabriel on his side, which Haley helped him do with some effort.

He counted every second it went on. Hoping with each one that it would stop. Waiting out first one minute, then two. At five he should call an ambulance, but he had already reached for his phone when his count hit three.

He had the first digit of 911 keyed into his phone when Gabriel finally stopped moving. It should have been a relief, but it left Seth unnerved to see him so still and quiet. Especially when he didn't respond right away to Seth speaking his name.

"Hey," Seth said when Gabriel blinked his eyes open at last, his gaze unfocused. "Hey Gabriel. Are you okay?"

Gabriel stared up at him and Seth squinted at the burst of yellow around his pupils that spiked out into the green of his eyes. It was like looking at the rays of the sun from between blades of grass. It was beautiful. It also wasn't supposed to be there.

Gabriel blinked a few times. The fog cleared from his gaze after a moment more, and he moved to get up. Seth helped him ease into a sitting position, where he sat with his hands over his face for a few minutes before he let them drop.

"Are you okay?" Seth asked again.

"I'll be fine."

"Are you sure?"

Gabriel nodded, but Seth remained unconvinced, his hands not moving from his shoulders.

"Josh, why don't you help Seth get Gabriel back to the house," Haley suggested. "I'm sure he's exhausted."

Seth narrowed his eyes at her. "Shouldn't we call an ambulance?"

"It wasn't long enough for that."

"But if it's the first time he's had one—"

"It's not," Haley almost snapped, and Seth fell silent. "He's had them before. Just get him inside. He needs to rest."

Seth and Josh helped Gabriel stand, and between the two of them, they got him to the couch in the living room. Haley trailed in after them a short time later, and Seth assumed she'd looked in on Silver. Her downcast eyes and deep frown told Seth all he needed to know. Silver was gone.

# EIGHT

Seth had been shooed from the house by Naomi, who had been insistent that Gabriel rest. He'd gone when the taxi arrived rather than argue with her.

The subsequent drive to get his car took longer than Seth had expected. Not so long that school had ended, but after he received an angry text from his father, he thought it best to head home rather than try to sneak into class.

It was late afternoon by the time he made it to his house. His father was seated on the steps when he pulled into the driveway, clearly waiting for him.

With a deep breath, Seth got out of his car. He was dressed in clothes Gabriel had lent him after he'd gotten mud on his own from the barn, and he was very much aware of that fact as his father's eyes swept over him, no doubt taking in the jeans and T-shirt that didn't fit quite right.

"Do I want to know why you're dressed like that?"

Seth didn't say anything, just stood quiet and sheepish in the drive.

"Come inside when you're ready. We need to talk."

Seth watched his father rise from the porch step, the book he'd been reading before Seth arrived in his hand.

It took Seth a few minutes to talk himself into going inside. He'd expected to find his father waiting for him in the living room, but when he heard the opening of a cabinet in the kitchen, he headed in there rather than further down the hall.

Seth found his father taking out two mugs. A tin of hot cocoa was already out on the countertop and Seth sat himself on one of the stools at the small kitchen island.

"So, the school called me at work Monday," his father said as he scooped powdered chocolate into each of the mugs, all the while not looking in Seth's direction.

Seth could tell from the tension in his father's voice though that he was upset, and they both fell into silence while Seth's father filled each mug with milk, then set them in the microwave to heat.

"You want to tell me where you went?" his father prodded. He turned to look at Seth now. "And why you had to leave school?"

"Not especially."

"How about who you were really with? Because I checked with Micah's parents and they said they hadn't even seen you."

Seth said nothing. He didn't know what to say. He couldn't tell his dad about Gabriel. He would never understand, and Seth couldn't risk Gabriel being arrested. So, he only stared down at the countertop.

The microwave beeped a shrill interruption in the heavy silence. His father sighed, took the mugs from the microwave, stirred the contents, and then slid a mug of hot cocoa across the countertop in Seth's direction.

Seth clasped the mug between his hands but didn't raise it to his lips.

Hot cocoa was something his father used to make when Seth was having a hard time of things as a little kid. His mother had been around back then, and she used to drop a handful of those little rainbow marshmallows in Seth's cup with a wink as if it were a secret, even though his dad would be standing right across from them.

Since she'd been gone, there had been no marshmallows. His father probably didn't have the heart to do what his wife once did, and Seth didn't feel right doing it himself.

"Look," his father sighed. "You're almost eighteen, so I get that you're starting to feel like you can make these decisions for yourself, but I'm still your father and I would prefer it if you didn't skip class."

"I know. I just..." Seth trailed off.

He just what? Wanted to go out with his college boyfriend and meet his college friends and pretend to be a college kid?

His father stared at him expectantly, waiting for some further explanation.

"I'm sorry," Seth mumbled. "I don't know what I was thinking."

Except that he wanted to see Gabriel. Talk to Gabriel. Kiss Gabriel.

"We're supposed to go in for a meeting with your principal tomorrow before classes start."

Seth deflated with a heavy breath and rubbed his hands over his face.

His father set his own mug of undrunk hot cocoa down on the counter. "I feel like there's something you're keeping from me. Something more than the school stuff."

Seth didn't look up, just sat silent and anxious while his father scrutinized him.

After a moment of silence, his father asked, "Is it something bad?"

Seth shook his head quickly. "No."

"There's nothing going on I need to be concerned about? You're not in any kind of trouble?" his father continued, and Seth kept shaking his head. "I don't need to worry you're going to end up hurt, or worse?"

"No. No, it's nothing like that."

"But it is something," his father concluded.

Seth glanced away, feeling caught out and not sure what to do or how to respond.

His father laid a hand on his shoulder, and Seth's hands gripped more tightly around the dulling warmth of his mug. "You know you can trust me with anything, right?"

"I know."

Seth's father sighed. He seemed worried, maybe even annoyed, but resigned. Probably because he realized Seth wouldn't give him anything more than what he already had. "I'm here when you're ready to talk about whatever is going on." He gave Seth's shoulder a squeeze and when Seth looked up at him, he said, "I love you."

"I love you too, dad."

"And it's because I love you that I'm setting up a therapist appointment for you."

"Dad—"

"I found this one therapist, and she has more experience than the last one you saw," his father continued, a glimmer of hope in his words. "So maybe this time will be different."

Seth shook his head. He doubted it would help at all, but he also didn't want to take the hope from his father's eyes by saying so.

He finally took a drink of his hot chocolate. The now lukewarm but still sweet liquid reminded him of happier times and he almost stopped drinking it as the memories made it settle uncomfortably in his stomach.

He made himself finish the rest of the drink quickly and gave his dad a hug. Then he went upstairs to crawl into bed, that lump of nervous anxiety lodged in his throat once more.

# NINE

The principal was a pale, wiry man with glasses that perched on a sharp nose and a bald spot atop his head that probably blinded birds when he walked outside on sunny days.

He had rattled on about the importance of attendance for a good twenty minutes while Seth sat and nodded agreeably, knowing better than to argue unless he wanted things to turn out worse for him.

The principal flipped through a paper-filled folder that was undoubtedly Seth's school record.

"You don't have many extracurricular activities," the principal commented. "I think it might be best to get you enrolled in something. Keep you out of trouble."

"I play soccer," Seth said with a sheepish frown.

The principal waved a dismissive hand. "Unless you plan to get into college on an athletic scholarship, I think we should focus on an extracurricular that's more academic. Besides, you missed your last practice."

"What about Spanish?" Seth ventured.

"Spanish?" both his father and the principal said at the same time. His father seemed dubious with the sidelong look he slid Seth's way, while the principal looked intrigued.

"I know it's too late to sign up for the actual Spanish class, but I could do it as an independent study."

More looks were exchanged, this time between the principal and his father.

"I mean, knowing a second language would look good on a college application or even a resume, right?" Seth reasoned. "And I'm pretty sure I know someone who'd be willing to tutor me."

They talked for a while longer on the subject. The principal finally agreed after some convincing, while Seth's father didn't seem as easily persuaded, and was still staring at Seth after they'd left the principal's office.

"I thought you hated Spanish."

"I don't hate it. I just didn't see the point of it before," Seth explained. "You know. Like math."

His father closed his eyes with a pained sound. "Do I want to know what your midterms are going to look like?"

A grin pulled at Seth's mouth. "I'm kidding."

"Hilarious."

"I thought so."

Seth's father patted his shoulder. "I'll see you at home."

"Yeah. See you then, Dad." He flashed his father a quick smile before they went their separate ways.

The school hallways bustled with bodies, students hurrying about on their way to their lockers or clumped together in small groups as they talked with their friends.

Seth was among the ones headed to his locker, intent on putting away some of his books that he wouldn't need until later in the day. It was as he finished up that he spotted Evelyn a short distance away.

She headed over to Mary, who was only a couple of lockers down from Seth, which made it easy to listen in on the conversation.

"Hey, can we talk?" It was asked meekly, as if Evelyn expected to be dismissed, or even yelled at.

Mary didn't answer. Not at first, anyway. Her eyes were directed stubbornly toward the open door of her locker.

"Mary—"

"I have nothing else to say to you."

"Mary, please—"

"I already told you. You can like girls just as long as you know it's sinful."

The "and change who you are" went unspoken, yet was loud enough to catch the attention of several other students in the hall who glanced over toward the two of them. Some looked sympathetic, but most of them seemed curious.

"So, I'm good as long as I believe I'm bad?" Evelyn replied. Her cheeks pinked as her conciliatory tone turned to one of anger. "Why do you have such a need to control me?"

Mary's hand tightened on the book in her locker as she finally pulled it out. "I'm not sure how you think you're not being manipulative," she huffed haughtily as she closed her locker door with a hard *clack*. "I've been nothing but respectful."

Evelyn bristled visibly at the flippant dismissal of her emotions, her shoulders rising as if buoyed by a wave of anger. "You haven't been respectful. You've been civil. There's a difference. And being civil is a far cry from being kind."

"You're just trying to make me feel bad, and I don't have to be friends with someone who makes me feel bad."

Tears glistened in Evelyn's eyes. She was clearly hurt and frustrated by the situation.

Then the bell rang for class and students hurried by them at a clipped pace so as not to be late.

Seth couldn't help but step in. "Why do you always twist things into something they're not?" he asked, ignoring the ring of the bell that echoed through the halls.

"I'm not twisting anything," Mary retorted, her already narrow eyes thinning even further.

"That's all you ever do," Seth said as he closed the distance between them. "I mean, you made a slam book about Evelyn, then played the victim the entire time while you and your friends picked her apart for not being Christian and liking girls."

"That's not true," Mary said with a shake of her head that made her black hair brush against her shoulders, "and it wasn't a slam book."

Seth rolled his eyes. "Yes, it was. But you'll never take any real responsibility, because you always have to be the one in control, and heaven help anyone who doesn't bow down to your personal beliefs and moral standards."

"Now you're just being as manipulative as she is," Mary replied. Her mouth thinned and her brow lifted as she tilted her chin up.

"Do you ever stop and listen to the things you say? Or think about the people you hurt?"

"I'm not hurting anyone. Like I said, I've been respectful." Mary shook her head, almost as if she were shaking off Seth's words.

He glanced at Evelyn—watched as she wiped tears from her cheeks—before he looked back at Mary. "All you ever do is hurt people."

Mary gave Seth a shove and Seth caught her hand when she moved to do it again. His fingers were a stark white against the golden brown of her skin, and a tingle like electricity ran from beneath his fingertips—just like it had with Haley at the marina, and the fawn at the rehabilitation center.

"Let go!" Mary hissed as she tried to jerk free.

Seth gave into his anger, that same kind of urge he'd felt yesterday with the fawn making him tighten his grip. "Say you're sorry."

"Go fuck yourself!" Mary snapped and managed to yank her arm away with some difficulty, the momentum it took to free herself causing her to stumble back. "You have no right to treat me like this!"

"You're one to talk. With all your telling people what to think and who to be."

"You're just trying to make me the bad guy when you two are the problem!"

With those last words, and a toss of her hair, Mary headed off down the hall without so much as a glance back.

"You're better off without her." Seth followed Evelyn when she headed toward her own locker. "She treats you horribly. Her and her friends."

Seth still remembered last year in art class when three of Mary's friends had sat themselves at his and Evelyn's table, their gazes determined and their mouths set in tight lines, looking like they were on some kind of mission.

They'd tried to convince Evelyn that "God's unconditional love" was the love she should be pursuing. That her attraction to women wasn't even real, and that she was just in love with female friendship.

The art teacher had sat only a few feet away, painting one of her pet project bird houses, and clearly listening in, while doing absolutely nothing to stop the situation.

They shouldn't have even known Evelyn was gay, since Seth and Mary were the only ones who were supposed to have known. Which meant one of them had outed Evelyn, and it hadn't been Seth.

"We've been friends for years. She wasn't always like this," Evelyn said in a voice that sounded strained, as if she might cry. "I feel like if I could only say or do the right thing, it'd stop."

"There isn't any right thing to do or say," Seth reasoned. "People like that just want control, and they'll never be satisfied. They'll take and take until you're not even yourself anymore."

"I don't know why I feel like the bad guy when she's the one acting like this."

"Because she's good at manipulating you," Seth said. "She's good at manipulating and controlling everyone. She always has been."

"I just want my friend back." A few tears strayed down Evelyn's cheeks when she spoke this time. "I want the person I used to know, the person who cared about me, back."

"That person probably doesn't even exist anymore."

"She does to me."

Seth slung an arm around Evelyn's shoulders and led her toward their first class of the day, which was math.

Micah was already there when they arrived, and Seth took his seat at the desk next to him while Evelyn slouched into the desk in front of them.

Micah, per usual, had his nose buried in some work of fiction, which left Seth sitting with his gaze on him pointedly for several minutes after he'd cleared his throat loudly and still received no response. He was about to try again when Mrs. Fields walked to the blackboard, the click of her heels against the linoleum floor drawing his attention to her.

She was, by Seth's best guess, somewhere in her forties. Her sharp cheekbones and high forehead were all the more accentuated by the way she wore her black hair pulled back in a tightly braided bun. Her skin was dark like her daughter Aaliyah's, and Seth was reminded of his coworker anytime he looked at her.

When Seth looked away from her to Micah, he was still reading, but with the paperback hidden behind his math book.

Seth rolled his eyes and tapped Micah on the shoulder with a whispered, "Hey, dude. Come on. I'm way more interesting than a book."

"That's debatable," Micah replied without looking up.

"Seriously?"

Micah finally looked at Seth and pushed his glasses up his nose. The round frames made his brown eyes look larger. Almost owlish. "Fine. What's so important that you have to interrupt me just when Gandalf is facing off against the Balrog?"

Seth squinted at him. "Lord of the Rings? You're reading— You know there's a movie now, right?"

Micah shook his head at Seth as if he were pitiful.

"Okay, whatever," Seth continued. "Never mind the book. I'm sure J.R.R. Tolkien's three-hundred-page description of a tree is riveting." He waved a dismissive hand. "I need to ask you a favor."

Micah shook his head and the movement made his dark curls sway. "The last time I did you a favor, I ended up grounded for a week."

"Look, I swear this is different from helping me get alcohol. I just need you to tell my dad that your cousin Edmundo is giving me Spanish lessons if he asks."

Micah stared at Seth with narrowed eyes, causing his glasses to slip back down his nose. "Why?"

"I can't tell you why."

Micah rolled his eyes. "Then no."

"Dude, come on."

"No." Micah turned back to his book. "Knowing you, it's probably something illegal."

"I really am learning Spanish, okay."

Micah side-eyed him.

"It's just, not with your cousin." Seth paused. "How about this? If you help me, I'll get you whatever book you want from Barnes and Noble."

Micah tilted his head, considering the offer. "Okay. Fine. I accept your bribe."

Seth clasped his hands together in front of him. "Thank you."

Now Seth just needed to get Gabriel on board. He slunk lower in his seat as he took his phone from his back pocket and sent him a text.

"I'm going to regret agreeing to this, aren't I?" Micah guessed.

"Probably," Seth mumbled in response, distracted.

"Seth." Mrs. Fields' voice startled him so badly he nearly dropped his cellphone.

"Give me your phone."

Seth felt panic tighten in his gut. He needed his phone. What if Gabriel texted back? Oh god, what if Gabriel called and Mrs. Fields answered?

Mrs. Fields pressed her lips together in agitation and made to reach for Seth's phone, but a loud *thwack* against the window startled them both.

It came again and again, and Seth felt his heart beat faster when he realized it was a raven. Just like the one from his dream.

Seth sat and stared silently as the raven beat itself repeatedly against the window like it had gone mad, a growing smear of blood marring the glass.

His classmates were panicking. The room was awash with the sound of horrified shrieks and gasps as the raven finally went still against the glass, half-stuck to the window by bits of its own brain matter.

Seth didn't look at his classmates. He did his best not to glance toward his teacher. He just stared at the broken bird where it slumped against the glass, its neck and wings bent at odd angles. It dropped off the sill a moment later. Its descent drew a few less timid students to gather around the window with morbid curiosity.

Seth stayed in his seat as they chattered loudly, their faces pressed as close to the glass as they could get. Some of the horror that had overtaken the room seemed to have dissipated with the bird's fall.

"Alright! Class! Everyone!" Mrs. Fields raised her voice to be heard over the noise. "Back to your seats!"

Only a few students listened to her. The rest stayed huddled close to the window, talking loudly over one another. Mrs. Fields practically had to step into their clustered group to herd them back to their seats.

Seth tucked his cellphone back in his pocket with the hope Mrs. Fields would forget she'd asked for it in the commotion. She didn't.

"Your phone, Seth," she insisted with a hand outstretched, when she'd restored order from chaos. "Now."

Seth took it back out of his pocket, then handed it over to her with a frown.

"You can have it back after class." Mrs. Fields walked back to her desk, where she placed Seth's phone in the top right-hand drawer before she returned to the lesson she'd been teaching.

Seth tried to focus on the equations on the board and then on his algebra assignment. But he had other thoughts that vied for his attention—Evelyn, Gabriel, and the raven that now lay bloody and broken on the ground beneath the window.

To make matters worse, every time he looked up from his equations, Mrs. Fields seemed to be studying him. Maybe it was his imagination, a kind of paranoia from getting in trouble at the start of class. But he was sure she was keeping a closer eye on him than usual.

Class finally let out with the ring of the bell, but Seth hung back while the rest of his classmates packed up their books and worksheets. After most of them had cleared out, he picked up his own backpack and, slinging it over a shoulder, made his way up to where Mrs. Fields sat at her desk.

"You said I could have my phone back after class," Seth said when he stood in front of the desk.

He shifted from foot to foot awkwardly while Mrs. Fields regarded him before she finally reached for her desk drawer to retrieve Seth's phone. She held it out to him, but when he went to take it from her, she kept a firm grip on it.

"Tell me, Seth," she said in a quiet voice that sounded more calculated than curious. "Have you seen anything like that happen before?"

"I don't know what you mean."

"Any other birds or other animals behaving strangely?"

Seth thought of the other ravens he'd seen. He thought of the way they had watched him and didn't immediately take wing when he stepped toward them.

He shook his head. "No."

Mrs. Fields made a contemplative sound, like she didn't quite believe him, but she let go of Seth's phone all the same.

"I don't want to see your phone out in class again."

He gave a nod and left the classroom as he checked for a message from Gabriel. A smile spread across his face at the response he found, which quickly became a frown when he saw the text from his father telling him he'd made the therapy appointment. At least it would be a few weeks before he had to go judging by the message.

Seth tried to put it out of his mind for the time being.

# TEN

Seth and Gabriel fell into a routine of spending a few hours studying Spanish and stealing kisses between nouns and adjectives before going out somewhere. So far, it had been the happiest three weeks of Seth's life.

The Spanish lessons had been meant as an excuse to spend time with Gabriel without his father thinking twice over where he'd gone for the day. But Seth had grown to enjoy them, had come to appreciate what Gabriel's mother tongue meant to him, and in turn, the ways he could connect with Gabriel through it.

They'd decided to go out for dinner this time. It was busy at the steakhouse they'd chosen. But from what Seth overheard the hostess saying, the wait wasn't terrible. Only around fifteen minutes.

Seth patted down his pockets, realizing that he didn't feel his wallet on him. "Shoot."

"What's wrong?" Gabriel asked.

"I think I left my wallet back in the Jeep."

"I can pay."

Seth shook his head. "No. You paid last time. Why don't you put your name in while I run and get it?"

"Okay," Gabriel agreed and handed Seth the car keys.

Seth's wallet was exactly where he'd thought it would be on the passenger side seat when he reached the Jeep. He stuck it in his back pocket after retrieving it and locked the car up before he headed back toward the restaurant.

He had almost made it there when he caught sight of a familiar face, one that he'd spent a considerable amount of time dodging in the hallways of his high school: Adam. The boy he'd dated after Isaac and before Gabriel.

He was the opposite of Isaac with his brown eyes and dark brown hair. The length of it just passing his chin while Isaac's had been shorter and wavy instead of straight.

The few times he had run into him, he'd been with Evelyn or Micah, who had acted like a shield. It had become a habit to stick close to them when traversing the space between classes. He was alone now though, and that simple fact had him turning back in the direction he'd come.

"You running away from me, Seth?"

Seth's steps faltered. A chill ran up the back of his neck when a hand clamped down on his shoulder.

He gave a panicked jerk at the touch, pivoting on his heel as he stumbled back, far enough that he was out of reach, but not so far that he didn't catch the smirk on Adam's face. The turn of his lips was almost as crooked as his nose.

Adam huffed a laugh. It almost sounded like he was disgusted with Seth, and a hot spark of anger shot through the cold shock of fear that had anchored Seth's feet to the concrete, the heat of it reaching his cheeks and making him grit his teeth.

"You're not worried about Isaac hearing about this? Because I'm sure he'd love to take another swing at you." Seth wished he could snatch the words back the moment they'd left his mouth. He knew all too well it was the wrong thing to say, that it was a memory that knocked at Adam's wounded pride.

"You think you can threaten me?" Adam demanded as he slammed Seth up against the nearest building hard enough to knock the breath from his lungs. Seth flinched as the cold brick dug roughly into his back.

Adam drew back a fist and Seth squeezed his eyes shut.

A flapping sound brushed past Seth, followed swiftly by a bewildered cry of pain. The grip Adam had on him fell away.

There were cuts on Adam's cheek when Seth opened his eyes again: three thin stripes of red that slowly swelled over with small droplets.

Seth raised his eyes at the sound of a familiar kra and his gaze landed on a raven atop one of the streetlamps. A speck of blood dripped from its talons to run down the yellow bulb as it ruffled its feathers in warning.

After a moment another landed beside it, then another, their talons tapping against metal as they settled. It had brought friends.

Adam's gaze flicked from the ravens to Seth. The look in his eyes suggested he thought Seth was somehow responsible for them being there. "You really are a freak, aren't you?"

Seth flinched at the remark, and he glanced from Adam to the ravens as his heart beat a frantic rhythm in his chest. "It's just a couple of birds—"

"Birds that seem to follow you around," Adam said. "Even when we were dating, I'd see them around you. Just always... there. Watching."

"So what? You think they're protecting me?"

Adam cast his gaze back up to the ravens. As if that were answer enough.

Seth shook his head, but even as he did, he tried to recall his time with Adam. Tried to remember if the large black birds had been around even back then, and he thought maybe Adam was right. That they had been. Though never as close as they were now.

A shadow from above on the sidewalk. A gronking cry from overhead or a tree. Maybe. But nothing like this. Nothing like the bird that had left scratches across Adam's cheek or beaten itself against the window of Seth's math class. It was as if they were becoming bolder. More aggressive in their task of watching over him—if such a thing could be believed in the first place.

"I think we should test it," Adam suggested. The look in his eyes made Seth try to step around him.

"I'm gonna pass. Thanks."

Adam shoved him back against the wall. Hard enough to make Seth wince. The ravens flexed their wings and called out a warning.

"I wasn't asking."

Seth's heart beat in his throat as he watched Adam raise his arm again—only for him to be jerked back abruptly. The motion sent him stumbling a few feet away, and Seth let out a relieved breath when Gabriel situated himself between them.

Adam stared wide eyed at Gabriel. Absolutely seething. "What the fuck is your problem man?"

"I'm pretty sure that's supposed to be my line," Gabriel retorted. "Especially after what I just saw."

"Maybe you should learn to stay out of shit that doesn't involve you."

"Put your hands on him again and I'll show you involved."

From where he stood with his back pressed to the building, Seth couldn't see Gabriel's expression—but it coupled with the threat was apparently enough to make Adam take several steps back. His gaze flicked to Seth briefly before he seemed to think better of going up against the guy in front of him and took off at a quick pace.

Even after Adam had gone, Seth's mind raced. Adam's accusations over the ravens played on a loop in his head.

It was stupid. Seth knew it was stupid. They were just birds—a common species of bird at that.

They weren't following him. They weren't guarding him. He was being ridiculous. Adam was being ridiculous. It was all nothing but some bizarre coincidence.

Gabriel had turned his attention to Seth. His gaze swept over him and he closed the space between them to rest a hand on Seth's shoulder.

"Are you okay?"

Seth nodded, shrugging further into his jacket. He felt weirdly exposed. Like he'd let slip a horrible secret. "Yeah. I'm fine."

"Are you going to tell me what that was about?"

"That was Adam," Seth replied sheepishly. "An ex of mine."

Gabriel looked in the direction he'd last seen Adam go. There was no sign of him now, though. Just a few people along the sidewalk ignoring their existence to avoid the situation.

"He seemed like a real charmer," Gabriel said sarcastically as he turned back to Seth.

Seth stared down at the concrete and fiddled with the cuffs of his coat when Gabriel's attention didn't shift from him. He felt like he was being scrutinized—or pitied.

"Was he always like that?"

"Not always. He could be really sweet sometimes."

"And the times he wasn't?"

Seth wrung his hands together as he thought back to it.

It had seemed like such a small thing at the start. A small shove here. A punch to the shoulder there. If he said anything, he was always given a laugh, and a grin, followed by, "I'm just playing around. Don't be so serious. Smile." And Seth had. The corners of his mouth had lifted obediently each time.

After all, it was only a joke. Adam didn't really mean to hurt him. It wasn't like that. If his skin darkened in places afterward, it was only because Seth bruised easily.

When the argument happened, when the first slap came, he'd still somehow been shocked by it.

It had happened twice more by the time Seth got up the nerve to say anything to anyone. But by then Adam had already told people about Seth's mother, what she had done, where she was now. Before long, the entire school had known—so Seth had stayed quiet—because the last thing he'd wanted was to give anyone another reason to see him as broken.

"Pretty much what you just saw."

"He hit you?"

Seth glanced away, trying to hide the flush of shame in his cheeks. "I should have done a better job of protecting myself."

"Why is it your job to protect yourself rather than his job to be the kind of person you don't need protection from?"

"That's... a good point."

Gabriel squeezed Seth's shoulder gently. "You're really okay?"

Seth met his eyes. "Are you?"

"No. I regret letting him go so easily."

"If it makes you feel any better, my first boyfriend—Isaac—figured out what he did and got a few good hits in."

Seth could still remember the sharp crack of plastic overlying the even sharper crunch of bone when Isaac had smacked Adam in the face with his lunch tray. The force of it was enough to break Adam's nose and send him careening to the floor. It had taken two teachers to pull Isaac off him once he'd had him under his fists. And Isaac had screamed like a maniac as he was dragged away that he'd kill Adam if he ever touched Seth again.

"Did he put his weight behind his punches?" Gabriel asked.

Seth nodded. He couldn't help the smile that pulled at the corners of his mouth.

"Good."

"I hate to be a drag, but do you think maybe we could do the restaurant another night and just go back to your place?" Seth asked quietly. "I don't feel up for being out after all that."

"Yeah. That's fine, and understandable."

"Thank you."

They started walking back to the car side by side. A shadow glided across Seth's path, a dark shape against the wash of orange across the concrete from the setting sun.

Seth stopped short at the sight of it. His shoes scuffed against the sidewalk as he took a step back. With a wary breath, he lifted his gaze to the sky to see a single raven circling directly above him.

"Seth," Gabriel called, and Seth looked at the hand that was held out to him. "Come on."

Seth took Gabriel's hand in his and he let himself be drawn forward. An arm went around his shoulders when he was at Gabriel's side again. The simple contact was enough to ease his anxiety.

"Movie night?" Gabriel suggested when they reached the Jeep and parted to open their respective doors.

Seth nodded. "Sounds perfect."

It was a short drive to Gabriel's building and an even shorter walk up to his apartment. The last of Seth's unease fell away once they were behind closed doors and in familiar territory.

He'd always liked Gabriel's home. It was all soft lighting, plush furnishings, and warm colors. A cozy space adorned with family photos and a sense of safety that Seth was grateful for every time he stepped through the doorway.

One of Seth's favorite things had become curling up with Gabriel on the large couch. Sometimes with one of the fleece blankets draped around them like a cocoon, and other times with just Gabriel's arms around Seth, holding him close against him like he never wanted to let him go.

He looked forward to some of that now. He could use the comfort.

Seth got sodas from the fridge while Gabriel made popcorn. The both of them were more at ease now and conversation flowed between them about what to watch.

It was domestic in a way that had Seth smiling, and he wondered—if they somehow got past the issue of his age when it came out—if living with Gabriel would be anything like this. Comfortable. Easy.

They finally settled on a Sci-Fi film. Which Gabriel had seen already but was apparently intent on having Seth watch to introduce him to one of his favorite actors.

"Should I be jealous?" Seth joked as they settled on the couch together and Gabriel turned on the movie.

Gabriel smiled and slipped his arm around Seth. "He's definitely competition, but you'd be hard to give up."

Seth smiled and let his head rest on Gabriel's shoulder while the film played. He was only half watching the screen, more focused on Gabriel's arm around him, the softness of the sweater against his cheek, and the warmth of skin just beneath the thin layer of fabric. It was grounding. After everything, it made Seth feel safe.

# ELEVEN

A few boys from the soccer team were kicking a ball between them, even though practice had ended. Their girlfriends were huddled together on the stands a few rows off from Seth.

It was getting colder out, and more than one of the girls complained about the chill in the air. But Seth's body was still warmed by the exertion from the game and the cold hadn't settled into him yet.

Seth had missed his last few practices, and he'd forgotten how good it could feel to play out on the field with his teammates. The way soccer could keep his mind off the things he would rather not think about. Like how he'd run into Adam several days ago and had to confess to Gabriel what had happened with him.

He looked up from tying his shoe at the sound of footsteps on the bleachers coming toward him to find himself penned in by Evelyn and Micah.

"So," Evelyn began as she sat down to the left of Seth and Micah took up the space to his right, "are you going to tell us what's been up with you lately?"

"What do you mean?" Seth asked.

"We mean the fact you barely spend any time with us anymore," Micah supplied.

Seth side-eyed the two of them. "Why does this feel like an intervention?"

"It's not an intervention," Evelyn said. "We just haven't seen you outside of school in forever."

"You're seeing me now."

Evelyn sighed. "We're worried about you."

"You don't need to be," he said, shaking his head. "I'm fine."

"You know what we mean, dude," Micah insisted, "Ever since you started your so-called Spanish lessons, you've been AWOL."

"Because I've actually been learning Spanish."

Evelyn tilted her head and frowned, like she thought Seth was lying, and he looked over at Micah in time to see him roll his eyes.

"Okay. This is ridiculous," Seth said, holding up a finger in annoyance. "I am telling the truth."

A half-truth—yes. But still the truth.

Micah shifted forward. "Dude, just tell us what's actually going on."

Seth shook his head. "Nothing is going on."

"Then why am I lying for you?" Micah pressed.

Seth huffed a sigh and looked away.

"Are you seeing someone?" Evelyn asked. "We're not having a repeat of what happened with Adam, are we?"

"I'm just learning Spanish."

Evelyn rested a hand on Seth's shoulder, and he jerked away from the touch. "Seth—"

"What? What? What do you want to hear, *hm*? Do you need me to say it in Spanish so you believe me? Dije que estoy bien," Seth snapped, waving a hand for emphasis as he spoke. He picked up his bag and slung the strap over a shoulder as he stood. "Ahora deja de molestarme."

Micah narrowed his eyes. "I'm pretty sure that just proves you're dating whoever is teaching you Spanish."

"Oh, he's definitely dating whoever it is. He'd need some kind of incentive to get to this point."

Seth looked skyward with a roll of his eyes at Evelyn's comment. His gaze settled back on them with an aggravated sigh as Micah nodded his agreement.

"Like if he gets a word right, then he gets a kiss?"

"Definitely a kiss." Evelyn confirmed.

"I'm leaving."

"I'll tell," Micah said, and Seth stopped short. "If you don't explain what's going on, I'll tell your dad and the principal that it's not my cousin that's tutoring you."

"You wouldn't."

Micah crossed his arms over his chest and lifted his chin. A challenge clear in his eyes even from behind his glasses. "Try me."

Seth stared daggers at him and Micah stared right back.

"Should I go to the office now?" Micah asked, starting to stand.

"Okay. Alright." Seth relented. He dropped his bag to the ground. "Maybe I am seeing someone."

Evelyn grinned. "I knew it."

"Do we know him?"

"Oh, no. He uh... He goes to a different school than us."

"So, what is he like?" Evelyn asked.

"He's really handsome, has a great sense of humor, and he's smart—like, super smart." Seth smiled to himself. "And I really like him."

"And he's the one teaching you Spanish." Micah concluded.

"Yes." Seth nodded and retrieved his bag. "He's the one teaching me Spanish."

"You already sound like you're getting the hang of it." Evelyn pointed out.

Seth shrugged. "I picked up more than I realized from my Spanish classes—so I'm farther along than I thought I'd be."

"So why the secrecy?" Micah asked.

"You know how awkward my dad can get with this stuff. I just don't want to deal with more crap than I already am."

Evelyn nodded at that.

"I actually have a lesson today I need to get to."

"Really? You can't hang out with us for a while?" Evelyn asked.

"I really can't. But I will call you guys to do something when I get a chance. I'll see you later."

The two of them reluctantly said their goodbyes to Seth, and he waved in return before he headed to his car to drive to the apartment building.

He was grateful the traffic was heavier than usual. It gave him time to talk himself out of his anxiety.

Evelyn and Micah knew he was dating Gabriel now—but they didn't actually know who Gabriel was—or his age. They just knew he was Seth's boyfriend.

He remembered Evelyn had seen Gabriel and him talk at that party weeks ago. He was certain she'd never heard his name though, and as long as she didn't see him in person, she wouldn't make the connection. At least, that's what Seth hoped.

Gabriel was waiting for Seth outside when he arrived. He was sitting on a step that led to the door. A book on his knee. His body hunched and head down to stare at the open page, enthralled.

It wasn't an uncommon sight. Gabriel often came outside to read while he waited for Seth to arrive.

"Hey," Seth greeted as he got out of the car and approached. "What are you reading today?"

Gabriel closed the book and turned it so Seth could see the cover. It showed two young men on a hill in front of a lake with pine trees.

"The Alpha's Son." Seth smiled. "I didn't know you liked werewolves."

Gabriel flashed Seth a grin in return. "I love stories about werewolves."

"They're one of my favorites too. Maybe I should read it after you."

"I'd be open to letting you borrow it."

Gabriel stood and Seth followed him up the rest of the stairs, then into the building. He stole a kiss once they were inside. Gabriel pressed close to him. A smile on his lips when they parted, and Gabriel's free hand took hold of Seth's, leading him the rest of the way to his apartment.

They settled in beside each other on the couch once they were inside, Seth with the notebook he'd copied his Spanish questions into, and Gabriel with his biology textbook and worksheets. Occasionally, Seth would get stuck on a translation and Gabriel would help him along, giving him just enough guidance that he could figure it out on his own still.

Gabriel made a bored sound several hours into their homework session and tipped Seth's head up with a hand beneath his chin. The kiss he gave Seth made his heart flutter and warmth bloom in the pit of his stomach. He loved when Gabriel kissed him like this. Soft and slow, like they had all the time in the world.

Seth licked his lips when Gabriel pulled back. "We'll never get anything done if you do that."

"You want me to stop?"

Seth shook his head, a smile overtaking his face. "Never."

Gabriel kissed him again. Just as slow and sweet, but deeper. His tongue slipped between Seth's lips unhurriedly and one of his hands cupped the back of Seth's head, his fingers brushing gently over his scalp.

Gabriel let himself be pushed down on the couch when the kiss ended. His breath hitched when Seth dragged his lips down along the shell of his ear before sucking at the lobe. Gabriel's hands slid beneath Seth's shirt, and his fingers dug into Seth's skin as his lips found him again.

Seth let his mouth trail lower, over Gabriel's jaw, then down his throat. His name was murmured softly as Gabriel shifted his hips up, a strong leg hooking over Seth's thigh to pull him in closer.

Not too long ago, Seth would have read into Gabriel's responses and moved a hand down to touch him more intimately, but Gabriel didn't feel comfortable doing anything below the belt without a clear and informed yes being given. And Seth didn't want another explanation about how arousal wasn't consent.

Gabriel stared up at Seth with shaky breaths, his hands tightening in the back of Seth's shirt when he ducked his head for another kiss. The yellow in Gabriel's eyes shined brighter—not only that—but it looked like it was spreading. The yellow fanning out more and more to overtake the green.

"Why do they do that?"

"What?"

"Your eyes," Seth clarified. "Why do they turn yellow like that?"

"They don't."

"They do."

Gabriel averted his gaze. "They've always had some yellow in them. It's just a central heterochromia."

"No," Seth insisted. "It wasn't there until after you had that seizure."

Gabriel stared up at him. More than a little apprehensive.

"You can trust me with this. It's happened before and I never said anything to anyone," Seth whispered. "Are you like the guys in that book somehow? Is that why you like werewolves so much?"

Gabriel disentangled himself from Seth and rose quickly from the couch. His shoulders tensed and his eyes looked anywhere but at Seth as he crossed the room.

Seth got up to follow him. He rested a hand on Gabriel's arm when he reached him—only to have him pull away. His heart constricted at being cast aside so easily. His anger warring with his worry as he watched Gabriel pointedly ignore him.

"Why won't you just tell me what's going on with you?" Seth demanded. "I know you're something more than human. I'm not stupid."

Silence was Gabriel's only reply. He still wouldn't look at Seth. He just stood there with his back to him. Uncomfortably quiet and breathing too fast.

"Do you think I'd put you in danger if I knew the truth? That I'd run off and tell people?"

No response.

"I wouldn't do that!" Seth shouted. His anger winning out over his panic enough to make him raise his voice. "I'd protect your secret! I'd protect you! I'm basically doing it already!"

A phone rang, and Gabriel moved away from Seth. Clearly intent on answering it.

"Seriously? Gabriel, I'm trying to talk to you," Seth snapped. Irritated. "You can call whoever it is back."

A glare was sent Seth's way as Gabriel picked his cellphone up from the coffee table. He was still staring at Seth when he pressed it to his ear.

Seth got the sense it was one of Gabriel's sisters on the other end of the line, probably Naomi with the way Gabriel's brow furrowed. His face always got a pinched look when he talked to her.

Seth didn't stick around to find out if he was right. He gathered up his things while Gabriel spoke on the phone and slammed the apartment door shut on his way out when he couldn't put words to the hurt he felt.

He hurried down the stairs then out the front door into the chill of the evening. The cold cooling his heated cheeks as he made his way to his car.

Seth slammed the front door open when he got home and he tossed his bag angrily to the floor. He was furious with Gabriel—but also with himself for saying anything at all. He should have known better than to ask.

He was beginning to think he wasn't built for a relationship. Maybe that was why Isaac had dropped him like he meant nothing, and Adam hated him so much.

His dad wasn't home. As evidenced by the fact he didn't come to find out why Seth was so upset when he kicked the door closed, but there was mud on the floor when Seth clicked on the lights. A line of footprints that led down the hall and into the living room. A reminder of his father's presence in his absence.

Seth sighed and shook his head before he went to retrieve the cleaning supplies from the laundry room.

His dad was probably at the bar in town. It was where he usually went at this time of night. A fact Seth had once hated, but in more recent years had used to his advantage to stay out later or clean the house without interruption.

Not that his dad really noticed either of those things. He was too drunk most of the times he came home to check that Seth was in bed or wonder where the mess he'd left behind had gone.

In hindsight Seth felt a weird fondness for those times his father showed concern for where he had been all night—because they weren't the standard response.

Seth started his chores for the evening by mopping the hallway of the footprints. Mud was ground into the carpet when he inspected the living room, and he spent almost an hour scrubbing at the mess. He tidied the kitchen afterwards, cleared trash from the counters, and rinsed plates before placing them in the dishwasher. He moved on to laundry next. Which was the one he actually hated, and the only chore he'd convinced his dad to do for a time until he'd walked in on Seth that night he was with Isaac.

The mind-numbing monotony of the whole routine gave Seth time to clear his head and feel an ache in his limbs. One that had more to do with scrubbing surfaces and lugging about baskets of clothes to be thrown in the wash or placed in their respective drawer than his anxiety.

He remembered the first time he'd done this he'd been eight and tired of living with the mess. After that it became an expectation. One that grew over time to include things like shopping and cooking. Things that most kids probably didn't deal with all on their own until they were older.

By the time Seth finished cleaning it was past ten o'clock, and still his dad had not returned. He probably wouldn't for several more hours.

Seth considered going to the café. Maybe getting a cup of tea and calling Evelyn or Micah to see what they were up to. It would be better than being home alone.

His phone rang before he could decide. He pulled it from his back pocket to find Gabriel's name on the screen.

He thought about ignoring him—the way Gabriel had ignored his questions—but ended up taking the call. Not liking the way anxiety moved through him when he tried to hold off on answering.

"Hi," Gabriel said quietly and when Seth said nothing in return, he added, "I'm really sorry."

"Are you?" Seth questioned as he wandered down the hall and into the kitchen. "Because that's easy enough to say."

"Seth I—"

"I asked a simple question, and you treated me like crap for it."

"I'm not sure I'd say anything to do with this is simple."

"You know that's an admission in itself, right?" Seth said as he dropped into a chair at the kitchen island.

"I know." Gabriel paused, and Seth stayed quiet, waiting for him to speak again. "Would you let me make it up to you?"

Seth hesitated. He really shouldn't allow his lie to go any further, and here he had the perfect excuse to end things. It would be so easy to blame it on the fight. On Gabriel keeping secrets. It would be better for the both of them. Especially Gabriel. For so many reasons.

A no rested on the tip of Seth's tongue. His grip was too tight on his phone and Gabriel's worried silence was like a scream against his ear. He tried to force the words he needed to say out, but they wouldn't come. He stayed silent as his heart beat out the seconds against the confines of his ribs and his thoughts raced with all the reasons to put an end to what they had. To say goodbye.

"Please, Seth."

"I need some time to think about things."

"I am really sorry."

Gabriel sounded so sincere. So sad. And Seth hated himself for putting that pain inside him.

"I know. I'll call you in a few days, okay?"

"Okay," Gabriel replied quietly.

"Okay... Bye."

"Bye."

Seth ended the call with a heavy heart. He set his phone down, then leaned forward. His elbows on the counter and his head in his hands. The sound of Gabriel's defeated voice ringing in his ears.

He hated himself at that moment. He was demanding honesty when he couldn't give it in return.

His father came home a few hours later. Just as drunk as expected and tracking mud over the floor Seth had spent considerable time cleaning.

"Stop. Stop," Seth said, moving to intercept him before he could make it to the living room. "We're going to aim for sleeping in an actual bed tonight."

His dad looked down at the hands on his arms, and then at Seth.

"Sit," Seth instructed as he indicated the stairs, and his father sat down on them without a word of argument so Seth could crouch to untie the laces of his boots and tug them off.

It was dirty work given his dad wore them to construction sites, and Seth dusted his hands off on his jeans as he stood. The boots having been dropped near the wall.

"Okay." Seth gestured up the steps to get him moving again. "Let's go."

Even with his hand on the railing to steady himself, his father still needed Seth to catch him when he tripped.

Seth almost lost his footing with him as he worked to keep him upright. One day his dad was going to make them both topple down the stairs.

They made it into the bedroom at the end of the landing. His father shrugged off the coat he hadn't taken off downstairs as he walked ahead of Seth.

He couldn't quite keep the annoyance from his voice as he asked, "Do you think you can get ready for bed on your own this time or—"

His dad collapsed on the mattress with a grunt, still fully clothed.

"Well, I suppose that works too."

He took the time to cover his father with the bedspread before he turned back to the door. He had just clicked off the light when he heard him mumble, "Don't forget you have that therapy appointment in a few days."

Seth laughed. It shouldn't have been humorous, only it was to him given the state his father was in.

Of all the times to play at being a parent. Seth thought bitterly.

"I'll remember."

Seth closed the door behind him. The house was suffocatingly quiet now. All he had was the sound of his breathing, and the rampant repetition of his thoughts as he made his way back downstairs to clean the floor again.

# TWELVE

It had been three days since Seth had last talked to Gabriel. Three days where all he'd wanted to do was call Gabriel and fix things between them. He hadn't given in, though. A part of him was too anxious to make the call.

Instead, Seth begrudgingly sat in the passenger seat of his father's car after school. He didn't want to be there, but his father had been insistent he keep the therapy appointment.

"One appointment," his father had said. "Just one, and if you don't like her, you don't have to go again."

That alone made it seem easier to just get it over with than argue.

"Do you want me to drop you off at your boyfriend's place after the appointment?"

Seth shifted uneasily. "I don't have a boyfriend, dad."

He didn't need this right now. He didn't need to have this conversation with his father ever. Especially not when he was having issues with his boyfriend.

"Seth, come on. I'm not stupid," his father insisted. "All these nights you've been gone. Coming home in clothes that aren't your own. The sudden interest in Spanish. Not to mention all the times I've caught you talking in Spanish over the phone with that dopey smile on your face."

Seth looked over at his father. "I don't have a dopey smile, and I don't have a boyfriend."

His father glanced at him with a tilt of his head and a not-buying-it frown. "I know you have a boyfriend. What I don't know is why you think you have to hide it from me."

"I'm not hiding anything. I'm not dating anyone."

"Is it because he's Mexican? Did you think I wouldn't be okay with that?"

"Oh my god, Dad, seriously. I do not have a Mexican boyfriend." That at least was true. Gabriel was Colombian.

"Okay. Well, if you want to go spend time with your non-existent not-Mexican boyfriend, you have my permission."

Seth rolled his eyes but said nothing. He just looked back out the window.

The office building was tucked off a winding drive that they passed once before they realized where it was. His dad circling around in the parking lot of a fast-food restaurant to head back to it.

Seth stared up at the oak trees spread out around it once they were parked and he was out of the car. Their branches cast shadows across the sidewalk that led up to the door.

Seth trudged along the concrete after his father. He kicked at a rock in his path and watched it tumble off into the grass and then lifting his head. His hand caught the door before it could close on him after his dad opened it, then he stepped inside.

The waiting room contained a few wooden chairs with well-worn cushions. A receptionist was straight ahead. Seth's father told the woman behind the desk they were there to see Debra Thompson.

Seth took a seat in one of the chairs, his elbows resting on the glossy wood of the armrests. And his father joined him a few minutes later, crossing his legs as he picked up a magazine from a pile on a small square table between the chairs. His eyes didn't meet Seth's as he flipped the magazine open to the middle.

Seth looked down at the floor. The carpet had seen better days—the brown faded to a dirty beige in places from all the people that had sat where he sat now. Depressed. Lost. Looking for some form of release from the pain in their lives. He wondered if any of them had found what they needed to heal. Twelve different therapists since the day his mother had tried to kill him and he never had.

He wasn't sure how long he waited there with his eyes trained on the floor before a voice spoke his name, the sound of it breaking him out of his circling thoughts.

When Seth raised his head, he found a woman who looked to be a few years younger than his mother only a short distance from him. There she was. Therapist number thirteen. With a patient smile on her face that faltered when Seth met her eyes.

But the surprised tilt of her lips was gone the next second as she gestured for him to follow her, which Seth did with the air of a man being summoned for his execution.

Seth's father dropped the magazine he'd been reading on his chair, standing as if to follow them, but she stopped him with a few words on needing time to speak with Seth alone. She preferred her first session to be with her patient before she got the parents involved.

She led Seth down a hallway into a small room absolutely covered in plants. He passed by a potted fern on his way to the couch, across from an armchair where he assumed Debra would sit.

Sure enough, Debra soon settled herself in the chair. Her skirt creased as she bent forward slightly, picking up a notebook that had been sitting on the coffee table between them—one of those black and white ones Seth sometimes saw at the dollar store in town.

"So, your father told me a bit about why you're here already."

Seth looked away from her, deciding to focus on a hanging plant. The way the vines cascaded from it reminded him of teardrops.

"Your father mentioned you've been having nightmares about your mom." She paused as if to give Seth time to respond, her pen poised over her pad of paper, waiting to jot down something in regard to his reply. "Do you want to tell me about that?"

Seth said nothing.

He'd answered this question before for other therapists. One of them had suggested his dreams typically started with a false-awakening because the night his mother had tried to kill him, he'd been asleep when she'd come for him. But knowing that didn't help him sleep through the night. It changed nothing.

"Seth?"

Seth slid his gaze in her direction without moving his head, brow raised and lips pressed tightly together. He didn't see the point in answering her. She would draw her own conclusions regardless of anything he said. She probably already had, as most therapists did before he ever opened his mouth.

Debra set her pen down on her notebook and considered Seth with a tilt of her head. "I can't help you if you won't talk with me."

"What makes you think you can help me at all?"

"Someone has to at least try."

Seth met her eyes again. Darker than his own. Her hair was lighter than his though. A honey-blond that brought out the pink in her cheeks, and the length of the strands was short enough to be considered a pixie cut.

"Pretty sure I'm a lost cause," he said.

"No person is ever a lost cause."

"That's not what the last therapist I saw for more than a session said."

"They said that?"

Seth nodded. Annoyed to relive the memory.

It was right before he'd been dropped by them for not writing down any goals he had for the next five years as a homework assignment.

It wasn't even that he'd refused to do it. It was that he didn't know how to think through all the horror and pain to something positive he could accomplish.

If the therapist had just taken some time to talk with him—helped him brainstorm possibilities for the future—he might have been able to come up with something.

He found it cruel. How could they think he'd be able to imagine so easily where he'd be in five years when he was so deeply depressed he didn't know if he'd make it the next five days?

He hadn't seen a therapist beyond a single session since then. What was the point if the person meant to help you was only going to hurt and reject you like everyone else?

"Well, let's hope they were wrong."

Seth frowned and crossed his arms over his chest. He didn't find Debra's response kind either.

Debra gave him a small smile, one that almost seemed more curious than sympathetic. "Your mother's name was Eliza, wasn't it?"

"Still is."

Some emotion Seth couldn't quite catch flickered across her face like a long-forgotten memory had risen to the surface before being shoved back down. It was an expression Seth had seen one too many times on his own face in the mirror.

Debra cleared her throat before she asked, "Do you think about what she did a lot?"

Seth sent a perturbed look to the succulent on the coffee table in front of him, wondering if he was just imagining Debra's unease. "It's not like I want to. I wish it would all go away. It just won't."

"Have you ever talked about her with anyone?"

"A few times."

Debra picked up her pen again and jotted something down. "Who was the last person you told what happened?"

"I—" Seth stopped and slouched further into the couch. "I told an ex of mine. Though we were dating at the time so I guess they weren't an ex."

"And how did that go?"

"Horribly?" Seth rolled his eyes. "When we broke up, they told everyone what my mom did."

Debra frowned, acting sympathetic toward his pain. "Have you had trouble going to people for help since then?"

Seth gave a reluctant nod, and Debra made another note as she relaxed further back into her chair.

"Are you dating anyone now?"

Seth glanced away, hesitating. "Yeah. Kind of..."

"Kind of?"

"We had a fight."

"What about?"

Seth shifted uneasily. "Honesty."

"So, they did something that made you question whether you could trust them?"

"No. Not exactly." Seth thought about it for a moment. "He seems like a good guy. He's just—private."

If Debra was surprised he was dating a man, she didn't show it. Just made a note in her journal and continued on with the discussion. "You want him to open up more?"

"Yeah..."

"Have you told him what happened?"

Seth shook his head. "No."

"Have you considered that for him to open up, you might need to do so first?" Debra asked gently, her pen pausing over the page she was on.

"I'm scared of what he'll think of me."

Debra tilted her head and said, "That doesn't sound like you trust him."

"I don't trust anyone with that anymore though." Seth lowered his gaze to the floor. "That's not his fault."

"How long have you been dating?"

"Over a month now," Seth replied. "But it feels like longer since we see each other so often."

"Why so often?"

"He's been helping me with some school stuff." Seth looked down as he fidgeted with a loose thread at the hem of his shirt. "It's been nice, but I've probably messed it all up."

"Because of the fight?"

Seth nodded.

"People fight Seth. It's a normal part of relationships," Debra reminded. "It doesn't necessarily signal an ending."

"Maybe it's better if he leaves me though."

"Why do you say that?"

There were so many reasons. Least of all the fight. That was insignificant compared to the secret Seth was hiding from Gabriel. But Debra was expecting an answer, likely one less complicated than the truth.

"It's just so much baggage to deal with," Seth replied, still not looking at her. "It'd be less for him to put up with."

"What if he doesn't want to go? What if he wants to stay with you?"

"He won't. People don't want someone like me." He thought of Isaac. He thought of Adam. "They always leave when they find out what happened."

"If someone leaves you because you're honest about how you're hurting, then there's something wrong with them. Not you."

Seth wished he could believe that. Wished it was something that rang true, but everything in his being screamed that he was the problem. He was the reason people left and never looked back. There was something wrong with him. Something broken that could never be fixed. Something wretched that could never truly be loved.

"I know it won't last," he said. "It never does."

"Did it last with your parents? Even after everything?"

"My dad always seems to be on her side. Like she just made a mistake or something."

"He still loves her."

"Yeah," Seth agreed, then glanced away again. "I probably shouldn't be mad about that."

"You feel betrayed by him?"

"I guess, but I also feel like I tore them apart."

"You were six when she tried to kill you, right? How could a six-year-old be to blame for that?"

Seth only shrugged. Logically he understood her point. Emotionally it had always felt different. Like he must have caused it all somehow.

"Did your other therapists ever do any containment exercises with you?"

Seth looked back at her. "I'm not even sure what that is."

"It's where you imagine a container of some sort. It can be a box, a vault, a room, just so long as it has a lid or a door that you can open or close as you please."

"And I'm supposed to, what? Put all my bad feelings inside it?"

"Basically. Until you can handle processing them."

"You know I'm not six years old anymore, right?" Seth scoffed. "I don't play make believe. Imagining a box isn't going to help anything."

"I can only make suggestions. It's up to you whether you want to try them." Debra checked her watch. "I'm afraid we're almost out of time."

Seth blinked at that. He hadn't realized he'd been talking for that long.

"If you want to set up another appointment, you can speak with Rachel at the front desk."

"I'll think about it." Seth paused, raised his eyes to meet Debra's gaze. "Do you have to tell my dad I'm seeing someone?"

"No." She gave a small smile. "It can stay between us."

"Thank you."

Seth didn't book a second appointment at the reception desk. He simply told his father the same thing he'd told Debra, that he'd think about it.

# THIRTEEN

Seth was getting out of his dad's car to go up to their house when his cellphone rang.

He hesitated when he saw it was Gabriel. Not sure if he was ready to talk to him yet, but he did miss, and he didn't want to ignore him. He really didn't.

Seth answered the phone—but fell silent when he heard pained noises—a series of whimpering groans that made panic stir in his chest and slither down into his gut.

"Gabriel? What's wrong?"

"There were hunters... I was shot."

Seth's stomach rolled and his hand tightened on his cellphone. Afraid he'd drop it.

"Please tell me you called an ambulance before me."

"They wouldn't know how to help me. It's not a normal bullet. It had witchbane in it," Gabriel replied weakly. "I called Haley... but she's in Portland. I'll be dead before she reaches me."

Seth didn't even know what witchbane was, but he assumed if hunters were using it then they hadn't been out looking to shoot squirrels or even deer. No. They'd been looking to kill whatever Gabriel was.

"Where are you?"

"Seth, what's going on—"

Seth held up a hand to silence his father and moved farther from him to hear Gabriel's response.

"I'm in—in the woods outside of Twin Oaks."

"That's not enough to go off. Where are you exactly?"

"About a mile out of town... you'll see the remnants of a white fence. There's a path into the woods next to it." Gabriel panted. "Follow it... until you see a large boulder. I'm near there."

"Out of town toward Portland, or toward the farmhouse?"

"The farmhouse."

"Okay. Okay." Seth nodded, already forming an idea of Gabriel's location in his head. "What do you need me to do?"

"This will sound insane, but... I need you to bring me water, lavender, and silver."

The request made Seth pause. Gabriel was right. What he was asking for didn't make any sense—but then, neither did the yellow in his eyes.

"Where the hell am I supposed to get lavender?" Seth demanded, already jogging into the house to look. "I don't just have that lying around."

"I don't know... but I'll die if you don't get—"

"Gabriel?" There was no response. "Gabriel, you there?"

Nothing—and Seth looked down at his phone to find the call had been lost.

"Shit," Seth muttered, and he ran to search through the house while he swore under his breath in a panic. "Shit. Shit. Shit."

His dad watched with utter confusion as Seth sprinted from room to room, ransacking drawers and tearing through the closets until he found the wooden box of silverware that had once belonged to his paternal grandparents tucked in one. He remembered his father telling him years ago that the utensils were made of silver, and he opened the lid to snatch up a spoon from its velvet lined resting place.

Seth stood frozen for a moment as he pondered over where he could find lavender. Some cleaning products they had were scented with it, but he doubted they would work. Same with the lavender candle in the living room, and the old bottle of his mother's perfume. The one his dad kept tucked away in a drawer and thought Seth knew nothing about.

No. He needed the actual plant.

If it were warm out, he'd go to the neighbor's house. They grew it out front in their garden and Seth could often smell it on summer nights when he left his window open. But it had been particularly cold the last few weeks and any lavender that had flowered in the warmer months would be gone now.

He had to think. Where could he find it? What did he have on hand that would have lavender in it?

"Tea!" Seth exclaimed so loudly his father jumped as he ducked past him and into the kitchen to rifle through the cupboards. Wooden doors banged and items scattered as he moved from one to the next. "Tea... Tea... Where's that fucking lavender tea you always get?"

"But you hate lavender tea."

"That's not an answer!"

His father blinked in surprise when Seth looked at him with panic.

"Oh god." He stared at his father in horror. "Don't tell me you drank it all."

"I think it's behind the coffee."

Seth hurried back to the open cupboard with the coffee in it. The red container of Folgers toppling from its shelf to spill across the kitchen when he shoved it aside to reach the metal canister behind it.

"Jesus, Seth," his father complained, staring at the mess on the counter and tiles.

"I'll clean it up," Seth said hurriedly. "Just not right now."

"Seth, what is going on?" His father demanded as Seth shoved the spoon and purple container of tea into his coat pockets.

Seth didn't respond. Too busy getting out a thermos and then filling it with water from the tap.

"Where the hell are you going?" His dad wondered as Seth headed to the front door while he screwed the cap on to the thermos.

"Uh... I'll explain later."

When he had a believable excuse. When Gabriel was safe, and Seth's heart didn't feel like it was about to rupture through his chest with how hard it was beating.

"Explain it now."

"There isn't time."

Seth dodged his father's grab for his arm and sprinted out the front door. He got inside his car and locked it. By the time his father was there, he was already leaving the driveway.

He almost missed the fence along the side of the road as he sped along, and had to reverse back to it. He caught sight of the path as soon as he was out of the car. A stretch of dirt in an otherwise overgrown area of forest.

The boulder took longer to happen upon than he had expected. He had hoped it would be nearer the road, but it was deep among the trees.

He found Gabriel on the other side of the great white stone.

A path was scraped through the dirt like he'd dragged himself to where he lay crumpled now. Blood coated the leaves around him and had soaked through the fabric of his shirt along his stomach.

That was when Seth saw the claws. It stopped him in his tracks and had him staring wide-eyed—stunned silent—until Gabriel's lips drew back in a grimace and Seth caught sight of fangs.

Seth did make a noise then. A startled gasp that lived and died in the back of his throat.

He had suspected Gabriel wasn't an ordinary human. Had even entertained the idea he was some kind of werewolf, but to see it—not just the yellow in his eyes—but the claws and fangs on full display, was unnerving.

Gabriel shifted, his leg drew up and his fingers flexed against his wound before his limbs jerked in a fit. It was enough to make Seth skid those last few feet to drop to his knees beside him.

"I got it." Seth's voice came out high and thready. "I got the stuff you needed."

Gabriel didn't speak after the seizure had passed. He just lay there dazed and Seth blinked back tears as he rested a hand gently on Gabriel's shoulder. Not knowing how to help him.

"Tell me what to do."

Gabriel didn't respond. His eyes unfocused and flickering yellow, like a lightbulb with a loose connection.

"Hey. Come on." Seth patted Gabriel's cheek until he focused on him. "Tell me what to do."

"Put... lavender and silver in the water... You need... you need to..."

Gabriel's body went stiff, legs and arms locked tight as his eyes rolled back. A fresh series of convulsions wracking his frame. It had Seth scrambling to get the items he'd brought out of his pocket.

He uncapped the thermos and hastily poured some water into the lid then added the lavender. He stirred it with the silver spoon, then realized as he stared into it expectantly—waiting for something to happen—that it would only react when it was against the wound.

Seth peeled Gabriel's shirt up. The fabric was tacky with blood and it made Seth's stomach turn.

He nearly lost his nerve to panic when he saw the wound. The hole itself looked black, almost rotten, with a pattern of dark veining that erupted from it and seemed to bleed yellow into the surrounding skin.

With Gabriel not being in a state to tell him how to proceed, Seth guessed at what to do next. He scooped out palmfuls of wet lavender and moved closer to Gabriel to press the wet bits of herb against the wound while Gabriel jerked under his touch.

The lavender warmed under his palms and Seth drew back his hands, watching as it almost seemed to soften into a paste that seeped into the wound.

Gabriel settled against the ground. His body going loose-limbed and still other than for the occasional aftershock. Like he'd just survived an earthquake inside himself.

A purplish steam rose as the darker sections along the torn flesh peeled away, then flaked off. Allowing the edges of bloody skin to knit itself back together.

Seth nearly collapsed with the surge of relief that ran through him. He'd thought for a moment he'd been too late. That he'd lose Gabriel shaking and whimpering in the dirt—and the near miss had rage swelling inside Seth. An overwhelming urge to find whoever had done this and rip into them made his teeth clench so hard his jaw hurt.

When the last traces of discoloration had faded from Gabriel's skin, Seth carefully shifted him so that his head rested in his lap while he looked him over.

Other than the wound that had been in his stomach, Gabriel didn't appear to have any other injuries. But he still looked sick, and Seth didn't know if that was something to be worried about or if the cure took time.

A twig snapped somewhere in the distance. The sound was enough to make Seth hold his breath and hunch over Gabriel protectively. As if shielding him with his body would make any kind of difference against somebody bent on killing him.

The steps drew closer. It sounded like a single person from the noise of the footfalls. Maybe it wasn't hunters. It could be a hiker, or his dad following after him, or—a figure stepped into view from around the side of the boulder they were huddled behind—Seth took in the sight of long blond hair, and a flash of yellow in otherwise gray eyes.

Haley.

That's right. Gabriel had said he'd called her.

Haley let her gaze sweep over Seth, then the lavender tea container and the silver spoon that still rested in the thermos's lid.

"He told you," Haley said. Somehow, it sounded like an accusation. Like some line had been crossed.

"He was *dying*."

Haley fell silent at that, and Seth let his knuckles stroke over the side of Gabriel's face, trying to soothe him while he sweated and shivered. He could feel Haley's eyes on him still, but he kept his focus on Gabriel.

He watched the too shallow rise and fall of his chest as he breathed. Noticed the pallor of his skin. He looked near death—and Seth tried not to imagine what he would have found if he'd arrived any later than he did.

"The first time with witchbane is always the worst," Haley said, this time in a softer tone. "It's a real shock to the system, and he has no tolerance built up to the poison—or the cure."

"But he'll be okay, right?" Seth asked as he brushed dirt and bits of leaves out of Gabriel's hair.

"He'll make a full recovery."

Seth let out a shaky but relieved breath. With how Gabriel looked, he'd started to worry there would be lasting damage.

"But he needs to be with the pack, and you can't go with him. You're going to have to let me handle that alone."

Seth raised his gaze to her. "You want me to leave him?"

"You're not pack Seth. You're not family. You're not his mate. You can't be here. They'll kill you."

"I'm his boyfriend," Seth protested. "That has to count for something."

"It counts to him, and to me. But it won't to them," Haley replied. "The safety of the pack is more important."

Seth looked down at Gabriel when he shifted against him. One of his hands found Seth's to hold as he cracked his eyelids open slowly. He squinted up at him. His eyes were still too bright, but not as dazed and glassy as they once were.

"I need to take him, Seth."

Seth nodded and rolled his lips together to hold back the sound that wanted to escape him. The horror of what he had seen was still fresh in his mind.

He let Haley take Gabriel from him and watched her get him up. The fact she could keep him standing on her own with how much he was leaning into her spoke volumes of the strength she possessed.

"Wait." Seth picked up Gabriel's cellphone from among the leaves and rose to his feet. From the way the screen stayed dark under his fingers, it was safe to assume the battery had died. Which explained why the call from earlier had cut out. "He'll uh... he'll need that."

Haley accepted the phone with a nod. "I'll give you an update on how he is when I can. It might be a while."

"Right. Okay."

A part of Seth wanted to follow them as they left, but he understood that would only put all of them in danger. At least he knew now why Gabriel hadn't wanted to tell him anything about what he was. He'd been trying to protect him.

Seth gathered up the supplies scattered over the forest floor, and headed to where his own car was parked. He sat in the driver's seat for a time once he was inside the vehicle, just staring down at the blood on his hands and trying to process everything.

He felt sick as he shrugged off his hoodie and used it, along with some water from the thermos, to scrub Gabriel's blood off his skin.

If his father saw it, there would be questions. Ones that would be much harder to deal with than why he had rushed from the house in a panic.

The hoodie ended up tucked beneath the passenger seat. Hidden away from prying eyes.

Seth tried to gather his thoughts enough to think of a convincing lie he could tell his father. One that was believable for why he'd torn the rooms apart before taking off in his car. Even as he turned ideas over in his head, he knew nothing he could come up with would be believed.

# FOURTEEN

The coffee grounds were still all over the counter and floor when Seth got home. It didn't surprise him that his father hadn't cleaned it up. Though the broom and dustpan were already in the kitchen, as if waiting for him.

It was as he was getting things tidied up that his dad made an appearance. His gaze swept over Seth like he was looking for anything out of place, and Seth hoped he hadn't missed a spot of blood somewhere on him.

"You going to tell me what all that was about?"

"I can't," Seth replied lamely. "It's... personal, and I wouldn't want to violate my friend's privacy."

His father huffed and turned away. "Right. Well, the day you feel like telling me what happened, I'll be here."

His father left the kitchen, angry, and Seth stared after him. The broom handle clutched too tight in his hands.

The evening crept up on Seth unexpectedly as he first finished cleaning and then cooked dinner.

Cooking was the last thing he'd felt up to doing, but he didn't want his dad more upset with him than he already was.

He ended up making a simple dinner of lemon pepper chicken with a side of green beans. Though he didn't eat more than a few bites himself.

His dad ate without a word. Still upset. Though his obvious aggravation eroded gradually into something more resembling concern as he watched Seth shuffle his food about his plate with a fork.

"I wish you would just tell me what's going on."

"Nothing is going on."

"Did something happen with your boyfriend?"

Yes, he almost died. Seth thought.

"No. I already told you I don't have a boyfriend," he said.

"Okay," his father groused. "If that's the way you want to play it..."

Seth slammed his fork down on the counter. His chair scraped against the floor as he stood from the kitchen island in a huff.

"Seth—"

He ignored his father and stomped his way out of the kitchen. The stairs creaked under his steps as he hurried up them.

Seth paused in opening his bedroom door and looked towards his father's room. He'd only just remembered there was a silver locket in his mom's old jewelry box. One that was large enough that he could put some lavender in it. His dad kept it in the same drawer as the bottle of perfume.

He crossed the landing to the door and pushed it open quietly. The light on the bedside table was still on, casting a soft glow that didn't reach the far corners.

The room was still relatively neat from the last time Seth had cleaned it. Only a few stray articles of clothing tossed carelessly to the floor disturbed the otherwise tidy space.

It was more sparsely decorated than Seth's own room, with only a few family photos on a dresser: pictures of the three of them from their vacation at the ocean, ones of his parents from their wedding with his mother in a light-blue dress rather than white, and ones of Seth from when he was so young that his hair hadn't darkened from blond to brown yet.

It hurt to look at them. To see how the three of them had been happy once.

Seth stepped up to the dresser with the pictures on it and knelt to open the bottom drawer where his father kept his mother's belongings. He paused for a moment, looking over the items and remembering her in a way that was almost foreign to him now.

It was why he rarely opened this drawer. The things inside reminded him too much of who his mother used to be.

He found the jewelry box under a floral print scarf. The box was simple and white, with a few sliding drawers and a soft melody that played when the lid was lifted.

Seth couldn't remember the name of the song now. Though his mother had told him years ago.

He tried one drawer on the box. Then the other. The second one he opened held the locket and he pulled it out to examine it.

The light in the room glinted off the circular compartment at the end of a longer than average chain. One side had a crescent moon. The other the sun.

Small engravings adorned the rounded edge and Seth traced them with his thumb. The markings almost looked runic, but if they held some meaning it was in a language he didn't understand.

He undid the latch when his thumb brushed up against it. A small sachet falling free when he opened the locket up.

Seth plucked it from where it had fallen. The smell of lavender invading his nostrils as he brought it up to his face to look at. He'd smelled it earlier, but had thought the scent was from his mother's perfume.

Footsteps sounded by the door and Seth looked up to see his father step into the room. His gaze traveled first to Seth, and then the locket.

"Sorry," Seth apologized. "I was just um..."

"Going through your mother's things?"

"Yeah..." Seth sat back on his heels. Too tired to think of an excuse.

"You can have it if you want," his father said after a long moment of silence where he just stared at Seth. His gaze sympathetic.

"Really?"

"You don't have anything of hers to hold onto. So, yeah. If you want it, keep it."

Seth stood from the floor then crossed the room. His hand curled around the locket and the chain dangling from between his fingers. "Thank you."

His father nodded as he let Seth step passed him to leave the room.

"Seth," his father said, and Seth turned back with the sound of his name. "I know you're the kind of guy that really doesn't like to talk about his problems... but holding everything in will only hurt you more in the end."

"I'm fine."

"No, you're not"—his father shook his head—"and I know some of that is my fault."

Seth glanced away with the admission.

"I just hope whoever you're with—"

"Dad, I'm not—" Seth broke off when his father raised a finger to indicate he be quiet.

"—is someone you feel safe enough to open up to, and loves you enough to not quit on you."

Seth scuffed his shoe against the carpet. "I should get ready for bed."

His father didn't say anything else as Seth turned away and slipped the chain around his neck. The locket a reassuring weight against his chest as he went about his bedtime routine.

It was after nine by the time he was settled in bed. The blankets pulled up to his chin. He tried to focus on the warmth around him and the rhythm of his own breaths. Anything to distract himself from the mess of his thoughts.

Haley hadn't called him yet. She hadn't texted either. His phone was wretchedly silent beside him on the bed.

Seth's thoughts raced. What if the pack smelled Seth on Gabriel? What if something had gone wrong? What if the lavender hadn't been enough? What even was witchbane?

He ended up googling witchbane on his phone. Apparently, it was a type of low-growing evergreen shrub that was more commonly known as rue.

Google offered a plethora of witchbane photos, and Seth scrolled through them for a few minutes. The unassuming clusters of yellow flowers made him think of Gabriel's wound though and he set his phone down on the bed after exiting out of the webpage.

His fingers toyed with the silver chain of the locket still around his neck as he stared up at the ceiling and tried to force away the worries that ran in a loop inside his head.

He heard a flap of wings outside. A raven settling in the tree near his window to stand guard—if Adam was to be believed—and its presence was strangely calming. But Seth really didn't want to think about his ex—or his theories.

He didn't want to think about Gabriel either though. At least not in the way he was.

The memory of him lying on the forest floor, blood caked over his stomach, and seizing—dying. He didn't want to remember him like that.

But the image was seared into his brain. Details he hadn't even processed at the time made the horror that played behind his eyelids all the more vivid.

The way the lavender had sizzled with small bubbles along the edge of the wound. How Gabriel's claws had raked tracks through the dirt, rustling leaves and snapping the occasional twig. The specks of blood on his lips where he'd nicked himself with his own fangs.

Seth felt tears on his cheeks and he took a deep breath then let it out slowly.

He needed Haley to text him. Call him. Something. Anything to calm his heart and his head.

An update didn't come until the next day. The ding of his cellphone waking Seth from a restless doze he didn't remember falling into, and he snatched up his phone to check his messages.

The text simply said: *He's doing better.*

They were the most calming three words Seth had ever read, and he sagged into the mattress with relief.

The fact whoever had done this was still out there occurred to him and he sent a response asking: *Will he be safe? Are they going to find who did it?*

Haley replied: *The pack is working on it.*

With a deep breath, Seth sent off one last message, asking Haley to tell him when Gabriel headed home and seeing if she could give him Diana's number.

# FIFTEEN

The plastic grocery bag made a crinkling sound as Seth set it on the counter. He'd gotten a text from Haley a short time after school let out that Gabriel was back at his apartment. Followed some time later by a second text from Diana with the recipe he'd wanted.

The ingredients for the soup had been relatively easy to find at the grocery store. Except the yuca, a brown, almost tube-like root that had taken him forever to locate in the produce section of the store simply for the fact he'd never seen one before.

He stared at it now. The recipe didn't instruct him how to prepare it exactly, but he assumed he was supposed to peel it like a potato.

"What are you making?" Seth's father asked, stepping into the kitchen a few minutes after Seth had gotten things started and the smell of chicken was in the air.

"Sancocho de gallina."

"And that's what in English?"

"It's basically a chicken soup."

Seth's father looked at the pot on the stove where Seth was bringing the corn on the cob, chicken, bouillon, aliños, and plantains to a boil.

"I was planning to take some with me when I see Edmundo today." Seth looked away from his father when he said the name, not wanting him to catch something in his expression that would give away that he was telling half-truths.

"You're bringing your Spanish tutor soup?"

"I figured I'd do something nice for him. You know, since he's teaching me for free and all."

His father smiled faintly, almost knowingly.

"What?"

"Nothing. Call me when it's ready."

By the time the soup was finished cooking, it was almost noon and Seth hurriedly set a bowl on the kitchen island along with a small plate of rice and sliced avocado.

He called to his father that dinner was ready as he ladled soup into a Tupperware container, being careful not to slosh it over the counter in his hurry.

His father entered the room just as Seth snapped the lid on the Tupperware and put the container in a paper bag. A second container with rice joined it, along with two avocados and a few limes since Diana had mentioned Gabriel liked lime in his.

"All set to go?" his dad asked.

"Yeah. Don't wait up. I'll probably be back late."

His father nodded as he sat down at the table. "Drive safe."

"Thanks," Seth said as he took hold of the handle of the paper bag.

He headed out then, and after an uneventful drive, arrived at Gabriel's apartment just in time to slip inside after a woman carrying her groceries.

Gabriel answered the door when he knocked, and a surprised smile graced his features.

"Hi," Seth said quietly. "Haley said you were back at home."

"I wasn't sure I'd see you again," Gabriel admitted. "I thought maybe everything that happened would have scared you off."

Seth shook his head. "I'm just glad you're okay." He hesitated, glancing about to be certain they were alone before asking, "Did the pack find the guy who did it?"

"Not yet."

"Not—" Seth rested a hand on Gabriel's arm. "Is it safe for you to be home? What if they—"

"You don't have to worry about that. We have a kind of truce with the hunters. We don't kill anyone, and they don't kill us."

"Then it was like... a rogue hunter?"

"You could put it that way."

"So it was just because they happened across you and realized what you were?"

Gabriel nodded. "Just in the wrong place at the wrong time."

"You're sure they won't come after you?"

"I don't think they'd want to expose themselves. There are some pretty nasty consequences for breaking the truce. Besides, I don't think they actually know my name or where I live."

"I hope you're right."

Gabriel stepped to the side to let Seth inside the apartment. The paper bag Seth held bumped up against Gabriel's hip as he moved past him, pulling his focus away from Seth momentarily.

"What's that?"

"Oh." Seth glanced down at the bag himself. "I made sancocho de gallina."

Gabriel raised his gaze from the bag to Seth's face. "You made me my favorite soup?"

"Yeah. I got the recipe from Diana."

Seth headed into the kitchen, where he set the contents of the bag out on the table.

"You want to get the bowls and spoons while I cut these?" Gabriel asked, picking up the avocados.

"Sure."

Seth had spent enough time at Gabriel's apartment that he knew his way around the kitchen well enough. He could locate the bowls and silverware with ease while Gabriel cut the avocados at the counter.

Once they were seated Gabriel explained that he typically dipped the rice instead of dumping it in the bowl as he took a spoonful and did so. Seth followed his example. Both of them were quiet for a time as they ate.

"You should try it with lime," Gabriel recommended, having added some to his own bowl.

"I detest lime."

"You might be surprised."

Seth picked up one of the lime slices after a moment of contemplation and squeezed a small amount into his soup before he took another—more reluctant—bite.

There was an exception to his rule apparently, as he found the lime juice actually brought the flavors of the soup together nicely.

"Okay. I admit it, that's pretty good."

Gabriel grinned in response and went back to eating.

Even with that smile and the conversation, Seth couldn't help but feel things weren't quite right. The energy between them had an awkward, almost stilted quality that Seth didn't know how to fix.

They were both pointedly ignoring the weight and pain of what had happened. It lived and breathed in the silence between their conversations. An uneasiness that was loaded with unspoken tension.

"There's somewhere I'd like to take you tonight, if you're not busy. It's a bit of a long drive though," Gabriel said as they were finishing up. An almost anxious tone to his words.

Seth looked up from his nearly empty bowl. "Where?"

"Is it okay if it's a surprise?"

"I guess so."

They took care of their dishes and stowed the rest of the soup in the refrigerator before they headed out to the Jeep.

Seth wondered where Gabriel was taking him as he got settled in the passenger seat. He couldn't imagine it was anyplace crowded or noisy with what still sat between them. He got the sense Gabriel would want to talk things over. Though Seth doubted he'd do it during the actual car ride. He wasn't the type to cage Seth into a conversation that way.

Gabriel hadn't been kidding about the drive being long. They were over two hours outside of Portland before they turned onto a private drive surrounded by evergreens. The Jeep rocked along the dirt road and the carefully casual discussion they were having broke off as Gabriel stopped the car.

Seth got out of the Jeep along with Gabriel. He took in the space as he did so. It didn't seem overly special. Just an area of cleared land circled by pines with more dirt than grass from the cold weather.

"What is this place?"

"My inheritance from my grandparents."

"Oh. Okay." Seth glanced around. Still not understanding the purpose behind their road trip. "Why did we come here?"

Gabriel moved to lean back against the front of the Jeep and nodded toward the sky. "Look up."

When Seth lifted his gaze, he gasped audibly. He'd never seen the stars so clearly. Not with the lights from the towns and cities he frequented. "Oh... *Wow*."

"I come here sometimes when things start to feel like too much."

"I can see why." Seth smiled as he moved to stand beside Gabriel. His eyes were still fixed on the sky. "It's beautiful. I've never seen the stars like this before."

Seth slipped his hand into Gabriel's and Gabriel gave it a gentle squeeze. He Probably needed that connection just as much as Seth did. An unspoken promise that the bond between them was still there. That it had survived the hurt and fear of the past few days.

Silence settled between them for a time. Companionable and quiet in a way that felt calmer than before.

They stood staring at the points of light overhead. The sky was clear enough that Seth could just see the milky way. But he couldn't help eventually turning his eyes on Gabriel. He was more beautiful than the stars to Seth—and just as much of a mystery to him.

"That day in the barn," Seth began, and Gabriel met his gaze. "That seizure you had. It wasn't something that had happened before, was it?"

Gabriel stayed quiet, and at first Seth thought he wouldn't get an answer. That Gabriel would pull away in a repeat of that day in his apartment, because of pack rules Seth had only begun to understand. But then Gabriel took a deep breath as if to steel himself, let it out slowly, and said, "No."

Relief flooded Seth, and he closed his eyes briefly with the rush of it. "What happened that day?"

After what felt like another eternity of silence, Gabriel said, "The wolf we hit... he wasn't an ordinary wolf."

"Then what was he?"

"A familiar."

Seth blinked at him, surprised by the answer. "Like a witch's familiar?"

"Yes. Exactly like that. The family line he was bound to died off," Gabriel explained. "When that happens, a familiar loses its powers. It becomes corporeal and will eventually die a mortal death, unless it finds another witch to serve, or someone to act as a host for it."

"So you're possessed by a familiar?"

"More like fused. Our spirits are joined together now."

"Wow. That's... completely different from what I thought you were."

"Oh?" Gabriel leaned closer. "What did you think I was?"

"You're really going to make me say it?" Seth asked and Gabriel grinned. The yellow in his eyes grew brighter and Seth pulled in a breath, fixated on the way Gabriel looked at him.

"Yes."

"I thought you were a werewolf."

Gabriel chuckled. "I had a feeling that was it from what you said about that book I'd been reading."

"So, what is this kind of thing called, then?"

"The word for what I am is famirian. Werewolves are probably some kind of misunderstanding that came out of wolf famirians, but they're not real."

Seth thought for a moment, turning things over in his head. "If only the pack can know about any of this, then how did you know about Haley? I mean... you knew, right?"

"The pack isn't just wolf famirians. It's also the families of those of us who joined with a familiar," Gabriel explained. "My family has been pack ever since my great grandfather married into it."

"So, you suspected Silver was a familiar, and that's why Haley came over? To confirm it?"

"His name is actually Kit—but yes." Gabriel nodded. "Familiars can sense suitable hosts, and given my family's history, it seemed strange that a wolf of all things would just show up like that."

"Yeah. I can see how that would seem like too much of a coincidence." Seth thought for a moment, trying to decide what to ask next. "Were your great grandparents mates? Haley mentioned something about mates."

"No, uh... mates differ from family, or even a married couple," Gabriel said. "It's a bond that links two people together for life. You're never truly alone after it takes place, since you always have a sense of your partner, mentally and emotionally. It goes beyond normal intimacy."

"How does it happen?"

"Through a bite." Gabriel lifted a hand and dragged his thumb over Seth's neck, near where it met his shoulder. "Right here."

"I'm guessing that's where the story around werewolf bites came from?"

"Probably. Few choose to do it these days, though." Gabriel let his gaze sweep over Seth. "This doesn't freak you out? Not even a little?"

"It did at first, and I know it probably still should, but I also know you'd never hurt me."

"You're right. I never would." Gabriel looked guilty the next moment. "Not intentionally anyway."

Seth shook his head. "I shouldn't have pushed so hard for answers. I should have let you tell me in your own time." He held Gabriel's gaze with his own. "I'm sorry."

"I'm sorry too." Gabriel paused, looking Seth over as if to get a read on him. "Are we okay?"

"Yeah." Seth gave Gabriel's hand another squeeze. "Yeah. We're okay."

Gabriel sighed with relief and smiled. "Good."

"So, what was the phone call about?"

"What?"

"The phone call that day in the apartment? I'm guessing from Naomi?"

Gabriel's brow rose and his eyes widened with surprise. "How did you know it was her?"

"You get this look like someone shoved a lemon wedge in your mouth when you talk to her."

Gabriel laughed. "I do?"

"Yeah." Seth nodded, amused. "You do. Pretty consistently."

"I didn't realize."

"So, what was it about?"

"Um... something broke into the pen the fawns were in. Naomi found one of them half-eaten, and the other was missing."

"Oh geez..."

"That's actually why I was out in the woods that day," Gabriel explained. "Someone called about a fawn that wasn't acting right."

"Not acting right how?"

Gabriel shook his head. "I don't know. I didn't find it before..."

Seth pulled Gabriel into a hug when he trailed off. His hands fisted in the back of Gabriel's jacket as strong arms slid around him in return.

A suffocating and fierce anger bubbled up inside Seth as he remembered the way Gabriel had suffered, and he tightened his hold.

"I want to hurt them for what they did to you."

"Don't say stuff like that."

"It's true, though."

"I know. That's what scares me," Gabriel said as he moved back a step to look at Seth. "I can hear your heartbeat. I can smell your anger. I know you're not lying."

Seth pulled back and stared at him. He probably shouldn't have been surprised Gabriel had such abilities. So did wolves after all.

"I just keep seeing you in pain, and thinking of what would have happened if I'd been any later." Seth shook his head. "Or if I hadn't found what you needed... or answered the phone. God, what if I hadn't answered the phone?"

"But you did."

"I don't even know how that stuff you told me to bring worked."

"Silver with water purifies the wound and lavender binds the spirit," Gabriel explained.

"Honestly, I still don't get it."

"I'm okay. That's what matters."

Seth glanced away with how his eyes burned with unshed tears, and he brought a hand up to rest over the locket hidden beneath his shirt. He could tell from Gabriel's sympathetic gaze that he knew Seth had lavender with him.

"Seth..." Gabriel tipped Seth's head up with a hand beneath his chin. "I'm okay. Really."

Seth surged forward and their lips met in a bruising kiss.

Gabriel let Seth take what he needed and gave it just as strongly. His hands slid down Seth's back and came to rest about his waist. The weight of his palms a steady reassurance.

He kissed Gabriel again and again, pressing in as close to the heat of Gabriel's body as he could.

Kissing was better than crying. So much better. The warmth of Gabriel's lips offered comfort—and a clarity he hadn't expected.

Seth was in love with him.

He'd had a sense of it before. It had seemed too soon to call it love, though. But that's what it was.

Gabriel's tongue coaxed Seth into opening his mouth for him, and he shivered with the brush of Gabriel's tongue against his own when he gave in. He'd missed this. Being the focus of Gabriel's desires.

Seth pulled back when the kiss broke, only allowed as far as the circle of the arms around him. Gabriel not ready to let him go yet.

A kiss was pressed to Seth's forehead in the next instant. Arms tightened around him as he let himself be drawn close again and Gabriel's head inclined so his face was against Seth's neck.

It occurred to Seth after a moment that Gabriel was breathing in his scent. He realized Gabriel had done that before—many times. He'd just been far more subtle about it in the past.

Seth imagined the part of Gabriel that was a wolf found some comfort in it.

They stepped away from each other after a few more minutes. Their movement's reluctant but necessary if Gabriel wanted to get the blanket he had from of the back of the Jeep.

They curled up on it together once it was spread over the ground. Seth on his side with his head pillowed on Gabriel's chest and an arm draped over him, while Gabriel held him close. Their eyes on the stars again.

It was nice to just lie there together, gazing up at the heavens. Both of them safe and happy in each other's embrace.

"Are you planning to do anything with it?" Seth asked eventually into the otherwise quiet night.

"Hm?"

"The land."

"Oh..." Gabriel thought for a moment. "I was thinking I might build a cabin here one day. After I graduate, probably."

"You mean like a vacation home for when you need to get out of the city and just be you?"

Gabriel smiled. "You mean be a wolf."

Seth grinned in return. "I do mean be a wolf."

"Yeah," Gabriel admitted. "I mean, there's land around here to run too, and sometimes the wolf in me needs that freedom."

"Sometimes I feel like I need that, too. The freedom from everything back home, I mean."

Gabriel's gaze flicked over his face with worry, and Seth wondered if it was his scent or the beat of his heart that gave him away.

"Is everything okay at home?"

Seth shrugged his shoulder, making the hand Gabriel had there shift with the movement. "I'm just juggling a lot."

"Is there anything I can do to help?"

"Not unless you want to do meal preps for me."

"I can do that."

"What?" Seth blinked at him. "Really?"

"Yeah. I mean... probably nothing fancy, but I can do some simple dishes like lasagna or stuffed arepas."

"Are you serious?" Seth asked. "Because that would actually be amazing."

"Yeah. I can do it."

"Thank you," Seth said. "Really."

"You're welcome."

They fell back into a comfortable silence. The stars less of a focus now than each other.

Gabriel's hand came up off Seth's shoulder to trace over his neck. Right over that spot where he would need to bite him to form the bond.

Seth closed his eyes with the touch and stretched his neck to open himself up to it more. A pleased rumble came from Gabriel with the gesture, and Seth felt it where his head still rested on his chest.

He knew what Gabriel was thinking. It felt good to be wanted that way. Even if he wasn't ready to take that step. He doubted Gabriel actually was, either. It was just a fantasy of connection that played between them.

"We should probably head back soon," Gabriel said reluctantly.

Seth nodded his agreement, but didn't get up. A few more minutes wouldn't hurt anything.

# SIXTEEN

By the time they were back at Gabriel's apartment it was almost ten, but Seth followed Gabriel up the stairs to the second floor, wanting to at least see Gabriel to his door and kiss him good night before he left.

Gabriel paused with the key in the lock to look back at Seth. "Do you want to come in?"

"I have work tomorrow."

"You could head out from here," Gabriel said as he finished unlocking the door and opened it. "In the morning."

Neither of them moved to go inside the apartment. They stood there while the implications of Gabriel's words settled between them.

"I bought an extra toothbrush, back before everything happened," Gabriel blurted out, unprompted, and Seth smiled knowingly.

"So, you've been planning on asking me to spend the night?"

Gabriel nodded. He was more bashful now as Seth moved closer.

Seth put his arms around his neck and leaned into him. "You're blushing."

"Am I?"

"Mm-hmm."

"I just... I don't want you to go."

Seth kissed him. A brush of lips just to tease him, let him get a taste of what could be.

"If I'm honest, I don't want to leave," Seth confessed with a smile as he pulled back from the kiss.

"Yeah?"

"Yeah," Seth nodded. "I'll stay. I just need to grab some things from my car really quick."

"Okay. Do you want me to go with you?"

"Nah, it will only take me a minute."

"Here." Gabriel handed Seth his keys. "You'll need those to get back in the building."

Seth turned back the way they'd come. He waved the keys at Gabriel and said, "I'll be right back," before he went down the stairs.

It was almost dark outside. The last signs of the sun were vanishing below the horizon, the oranges and pinks it left behind in the sky gradually being swallowed by the darkness.

Seth headed out into the parking lot. He unlocked his car and slid into the front seat to reach his backpack. He grabbed his phone charger from the front pouch of his backpack then opened the glove compartment, a few papers falling free as he moved things around until he found the box of condoms he kept buried in the back behind his registration.

He took three in case one ripped when he was getting it open or if they wanted to have sex more than once. He stuck them in the back pocket of his jeans, left the car, and headed back to the door of the apartment building, sending a quick text to his father that he was spending the night at Micah's house. He felt a bit guilty about the lie but it was short-lived.

It took him a moment to figure out which key to use for the door, but once he was inside he took the stairs back up to the second floor at a clipped pace. He didn't bother to knock, since Gabriel was expecting him back, just opened the door and headed inside.

Gabriel wasn't in the living room, or the kitchen, where Seth left his phone to charge since the battery was almost dead.

He found Gabriel in the bedroom, lying on his back on the bed with his textbook held in front of him.

"Hola," Seth said with a smile as he stepped into the bedroom.

Gabriel looked at Seth from over the textbook he had been reading. "You've missed your Spanish lessons that badly?"

"I missed my tutor more." Seth grinned as he made his way over to the bed. "How do you say 'You look handsome' in Spanish?"

Gabriel chuckled and dipped his head. When he looked back up to answer, it was with a smile on his lips. "Te ves lindo."

Seth leaned forward with one knee on the bed so he could kiss Gabriel. He kept the kiss chaste. Sometimes shorter, softer kisses were better than the longer ones.

"Te ves lindo," Seth said when he pulled back from the kiss.

"Te adoro," Gabriel said as he cupped a hand to Seth's face and stroked his thumb over his cheek.

"'I adore you'?"

Gabriel nodded in reply, and Seth smiled, his cheeks warming with the affection.

When Gabriel pulled his hand back Seth settled himself more fully on the bed and asked, "Were you doing homework?"

"Just reading ahead," Gabriel answered. After glancing at the textbook again, he set it on the bedside table.

Seth curled in close to him, his head resting on his shoulder. "How do you say 'You make me happy' in Spanish?"

Gabriel looked at Seth with a soft smile. "Me haces feliz."

"Me haces feliz." Seth repeated the words warmly as Gabriel slid an arm around him. "How do you say, 'I love you'?"

Gabriel stared at Seth. His gaze softened and his lips parted in an awed smile. "Te amo."

"Te amo."

Gabriel pressed a kiss to the top of Seth's head then rested his cheek against his hair. "Yo también te amo."

Seth smiled at the response, knowing that it probably meant I love you too. "I like the way that sounds. Te amo."

He let his fingers trail over Gabriel's jaw, felt the prickle of stubble against his fingertips and let his eyes map out Gabriel's face while he tried to figure out how to ask for what he wanted.

"How do you say, 'I want to make love to you'?"

"And I thought I was the old-fashioned one," Gabriel teased, but there was warmth in his smile and interest in the way his gaze slid over Seth.

"Sometimes I like old-fashioned. After all, I like you just fine," Seth pointed out, and Gabriel smiled.

"You'd say, 'Te quiero hacer el amor.'"

Seth tilted his head back so he could look into Gabriel's eyes. "Te quiero hacer el amor." He was quiet as Gabriel's fingers ran through his hair. "Would you want to?"

Gabriel leaned in closer. "Sí, mi amor. Te quiero a ti dentro de mí," he whispered against Seth's ear with a suggestiveness to his tone that made Seth shiver.

"I understood 'Yes, my love' and that you want something, but not what you want."

"You want to know what it means?" Gabriel asked as his lips brushed against Seth's ear.

"Yeah," Seth breathed, tilting his head with the drag of Gabriel's lips lower along his neck. A tingle of heat shivered across his skin and made him smile. "Yeah, I definitely want to know when you say it in that voice."

"It means I want you inside me."

Seth pulled back enough to look at Gabriel. He looked interested, yes, but there was a kind of nervous tension to the way his eyes flicked over Seth before he looked away again.

"I mean, if it's not your thing—" Gabriel started.

"Oh no, it is definitely my thing," Seth interjected. "I am totally into topping. I am really into that. Into... being in you. I brought condoms."

Gabriel ducked his head and pressed his lips together as a smile toyed with the corners of his mouth.

"Why are you laughing?" Seth asked, going for mock-offended and failing when he couldn't fight back his own grin.

"I'm not."

"Yes, you are."

"It's just..." Gabriel shook his head with a fond smile. "You're still cute when you ramble."

"Oh, I'm cute?" Seth pushed a hand against Gabriel's chest to lay him out flat on the bed and Gabriel went down with a smile. "I'm cute now?"

Seth straddled him then cupped a hand to Gabriel's cheek, pressing his thumb in against his jaw to tilt his head back, making Gabriel stretch his neck out for him so he could kiss along the length of it.

When Seth nipped at his neck beneath his jawline, Gabriel's breath caught and his hips pushed up into Seth.

"Is that cute?" Seth whispered.

"Muy tierno," Gabriel replied with a teasing smile, but his breath came out heavy.

"That's cute in Spanish, isn't it?"

"Very cute." Gabriel nodded.

"I was going for sexy, so guess I'll have to try a little harder, hm?"

Seth leaned back in to kiss from Gabriel's mouth to his jaw, the stubble there rough against his lips. The sweater Gabriel wore hindered his progress when he kissed down his neck again and wanted to move lower. So he slid his hands down Gabriel's sides, his fingers gripping at the hem of the garment when he reached it to pull it up. The process was helped along when Gabriel sat up partially and raised his arms so Seth could get the sweater off him.

Seth let his gaze roam over Gabriel's naked torso as he lay back down against the rumpled bedding. There was an assuredness in the way he looked up at Seth and shifted under his stare.

Seth knew the lines and angles of Gabriel's hips and stomach from the times his shirt rose when he'd reached for something on a higher shelf of a cabinet or stretched his hands over his head when he was sore. But he'd been left mostly to his own imaginings when it came to the full scope of what it would be like to have Gabriel laid out shirtless on the bed beneath him—his skin a warm tawny in the lamplight and a dark trail of hair disappearing beneath the waistband of his jeans.

The quirk of Gabriel's mouth was like an invitation. One that Seth accepted happily, leaning in to kiss him. And Gabriel's lips parted beneath his. Eager. Wanting. His arms tightening around Seth to pull him in closer. Seth licked his tongue into his mouth for a taste of him and Gabriel responded eagerly.

"You're gorgeous," Seth said when he pulled back from the kiss.

Gabriel smiled. His hands slid down to grip Seth's shirt and Seth didn't protest when Gabriel peeled the article of clothing up and off, though he did chuckle when Gabriel tossed the shirt across the room as if it had personally offended him. His chuckle quickly shifted into a sharp inhale when Gabriel pressed a line of kisses down his neck, his mouth warm and the light burn of his stubble sending a hot tingle across Seth's skin.

"I want to taste you," Gabriel murmured against Seth's throat while his hands slid down Seth's body, and his fingers undid the button, and then the zipper, on Seth's jeans when he nodded his consent.

Seth let Gabriel press him down against the bed. His pants and boxers weren't even fully off before Gabriel licked up along the head of his dick with the flat of his tongue, circling his lips around it to suck.

The sudden onslaught of sensation made Seth gasp. Gabriel's mouth was all suction and wet heat when he bobbed down further, the feel of it making Seth clutch at his own hair and spread his legs wider.

Gabriel took advantage of the movement, running his hands up Seth's thighs to grip at his hips. His fingers dug into Seth's skin as he held him down and Seth panted as his body pushed up against that hold, wanting more of what Gabriel was giving him.

Gabriel's eyes fluttered closed and he moaned like he was savoring him. Like Seth was the best thing he'd ever tasted. Like he'd decided his new life's purpose was to drive Seth mad with his mouth.

Seth trembled. The muscles in his stomach tensed with each slow bobbing suck of Gabriel's mouth.

"God, you're good at this."

Gabriel rolled his tongue along the underside of his cock and Seth moved his hands from his own hair into Gabriel's, his fingers flexing with the slide of Gabriel's mouth.

"Really, really good." Seth breathed. "You should stop, though. Unless you want me to come."

Gabriel released Seth from his mouth and a grin overtook his face when Seth moved to push him down against the bed again, effectively reversing their positions. Seth pressed a kiss to Gabriel's mouth that he couldn't help but smile into.

When Seth pulled back from the kiss, he moved off the bed just long enough to get his jeans and boxers off the rest of the way, being sure to get the condoms from the back pocket of his pants before he abandoned them to the floor. The locket he wore followed more hesitantly.

Gabriel's dick was a hard line in the denim of his jeans when Seth moved back onto the bed, and he dropped the condoms to the mattress so his fingers could trace over him, Gabriel canting his hips up into the touch.

"Your turn." Seth let his mouth move down Gabriel's chest, then stomach, his teeth grazing against muscle, his tongue tasting skin.

Gabriel bit at his lip when Seth popped the button on his jeans open, then slid the zipper down with a soft rasp, and Gabriel arched so Seth could get the rest of his clothes off him. Seth wanted to make Gabriel arch his back for a different reason.

The clothes ended up on the floor and then Seth ducked his head down to let Gabriel have what he wanted.

He closed his eyes briefly, reveling in the warm, musky taste—the wet skin smell that grew as he kept sucking.

A muffled groan caught in his throat when he opened his eyes to Gabriel watching him, his hips pushing up for more, just this side of too much. Seth's name fell from Gabriel's mouth and his back arched with a moan on his lips when Seth let his mouth slide over him faster.

Gabriel beckoned him back up with a few words, a smile on his lips as he pulled Seth down into his arms to kiss him. Seth moved his hips for the velvet glide of friction, Gabriel hard against him, and his fingers trembled against Gabriel's skin as they moved together. Gabriel held Seth more tightly to him as he kissed him harder.

"Lube?" Seth asked breathlessly when the kiss broke.

"Second drawer of the bedside table."

Seth leaned across the bed and fumbled for the handle of the drawer, then hurriedly pulled it open to sort through it until he found what he needed.

Gabriel had already turned over for Seth with the click of the bottle cap, his body shifting against the sheets to get comfortable while Seth spread lube over his fingers.

"Ready?" Seth asked.

Gabriel nodded, his head turned to the side against a pillow that he dug his fingers into when Seth slowly pressed a slicked finger inside him.

It was the first time Seth wasn't someone's first time. He figured the same rules applied though. Go slow. Use plenty of lube. Be mindful of his partner's reactions.

Gabriel was noticeably more experienced with this kind of thing than Seth's previous partners had been though. He knew how to relax into it and didn't need Seth to stop repeatedly to give him time to adjust. He took the first finger easily, his breath hitching with excitement as it sank inside him. The second had him shaking as he rocked back into it, a needy groan escaping him when Seth bent his fingers just right.

"Seth. *God.*"

Seth pressed in with his fingers again to see how Gabriel tensed and trembled. He did it again just to hear the noises he made, the way he said Seth's name like a prayer.

He pressed kisses up along Gabriel's spine as he continued to move his fingers inside him, and he smiled against Gabriel's skin at the way he could feel him shake beneath his mouth.

Seth eventually pulled away. But not far. Just enough to retrieve the condom and do what needed to be done. Then he lined himself up, and Gabriel's hands flexed against the pillow as he eased his way inside.

"Te amo," Seth whispered against Gabriel's ear as he dragged his hands down along his sides. Gabriel shivered under his touch, his body rocking back into the push in.

Seth pressed a kiss to Gabriel's neck, and pulled back slow, then pressed forward just as carefully. He had to close his eyes and concentrate on not coming at the sounds Gabriel made and the way his body gripped him tight. Pleasure sparked through them both on every slow drag back and shove forward, his eyes open to watch Gabriel move to meet his thrusts.

He kept up the gentle rhythm until he felt he had control of himself, until Gabriel begged him to go harder.

Gabriel pressed his face into the pillow beneath his head and took everything Seth gave him. His breaths came out harsh and punctuated with soft moans as they shared his body.

"You're gonna make me come," Gabriel whined low and desperate.

The words made heat unfurl low in Seth's belly and a groan escaped him. His hips snapped forward harder, while Gabriel said a mess of things, his voice rising. So close to coming apart for Seth, because of Seth.

A long, drawn-out groan fell from Gabriel's lips when he came over the sheets and Seth's hands slid over Gabriel's. Their fingers intertwined as Seth moved into him, chasing his own orgasm.

Gabriel urged him on in a voice that trembled, his hands squeezing Seth's when Seth tensed and shook with his own release.

Seth rested his forehead against Gabriel's back as he worked to catch his breath afterward. "God, I love you," he panted, "and you should get used to me saying that because I'm going to be saying it a lot from here on out. Like, a lot a lot. You're probably going to get sick of hearing it."

"I don't think I could ever get sick of hearing that. In any language."

"Good, because I really do love you."

"I really love you too."

Seth was still inside Gabriel, and he shifted his hips slightly, a smile pulling at his mouth with the hot little sound Gabriel made in response.

"Can we do it again?" Seth asked.

Gabriel looked back at Seth from over his shoulder. "Get me a coffee and I'll consider it."

"It's almost eleven o'clock. How do you sleep with all the coffee you drink? You'll be up all night."

Gabriel smirked, his brow rising. "Do you not want me to be *up* all night?"

Seth couldn't help the laughter that bubbled up out of him. He was still laughing when he got up from the bed to dispose of the condom in the nearby wastebasket.

Gabriel turned over onto his back as he did. "You remember which cupboard the coffee is in, right?"

"Bold of you to assume I'm agreeing to this bargain," Seth said with a teasing grin.

Gabriel lifted his hands above his head, smirking with his arms crossed at the wrists as he stretched his body in a slow, languorous motion that made Seth catch his breath.

"Oh god," Seth breathed as he let his eyes roam over Gabriel's body. "Yeah. Yeah, I'm gonna go get you that coffee." He headed toward the bedroom door. "You have excellent negotiating skills, you know that?"

"I just know what's on offer," Gabriel called after him when Seth was almost to the kitchen, "and that you want it."

Seth chuckled to himself as he fixed Gabriel his coffee. He didn't get a cup for himself and handed Gabriel the mug in exchange for a kiss when he climbed back onto the bed.

A few minutes after Gabriel had finished off his drink and set the mug down on the bedside table, he leaned in to kiss Seth's neck. Seth tilted his head slightly for a better angle as coffee-warmed lips brushed against his skin, a smile spreading across his face with the attention.

"Can I top this time?" Gabriel asked in a whisper against his ear.

Seth stiffened and Gabriel pulled back, seeming to notice the change in the way Seth held himself.

"Look, I've actually never bottomed before, and honestly, I'm not sure I'm ready for that yet. Maybe one day, but not now." Seth rubbed at the back of his neck, a lump of dread in his gut when he remembered how badly Adam had reacted when Seth had turned this very thing down. "Please don't be mad at me."

"I'm not mad." Gabriel shook his head and then shrugged with his next words. "Maybe a little disappointed, but it's not a deal breaker for me or anything like that."

"You swear? You're not just saying that?"

"I'm not mad. I promise."

Seth took a deep breath and glanced away, the tension draining out of him.

Gabriel touched a hand to his shoulder. "Are you okay?"

"Yeah. I just feel like I ruined the mood."

Gabriel shook his head. "You didn't ruin anything." He pressed a kiss to Seth's mouth that Seth responded to tentatively then readily when Gabriel pulled him in closer.

He tasted like the coffee he'd just drunk. Subtle notes of caramel-like sweetness with a nutty undercurrent lingered on Seth's tongue when Gabriel pulled back enough to speak.

"I still want to. Do you?"

Seth nodded before his mouth claimed Gabriel's once more.

Gabriel's hands urged Seth to follow him as he lay back against the bed, and Seth obeyed the grip on his skin so he was settled between Gabriel's thighs.

"Hazme el amor otra vez," Gabriel murmured against Seth's lips between one kiss and the next.

Some of the words were familiar, and Seth guessed it meant, "Make love to me again," a request Seth had no issues fulfilling.

He snagged a fresh condom and the bottle of lube from where it lay on the bed. It wasn't long after that he sank back inside Gabriel. Gabriel lay on his back this time, which Seth loved because he could kiss him, and watch the way pleasure played across his face—the way his breath caught and his eyes seemed to glow.

"Look at me," Seth said when Gabriel closed his eyes to no doubt hide the effect Seth was having on him, and Gabriel did. His gaze found Seth's again, and Seth cupped a hand to Gabriel's cheek as he watched the flicker of color.

It fascinated Seth, the way the yellow in them pulsed with every thrust Seth made into him. How it grew steadier and brighter, the closer Gabriel got to coming.

Seth moved inside Gabriel more slowly this time around, wanting to make it last, to be close with him for as long as he could, wrapped up in each other's embrace. And he could feel Gabriel's fingers flex and dig into his skin with every thrust.

When Gabriel did come, it was with Seth's name on his lips and Seth's mouth at his throat. His eyes were a deep yellow when Seth pulled back just enough to look into them.

Gabriel was still shaking when Seth found his own release, his lips brushing Gabriel's in a kiss that was interrupted by groans and panted breaths, Gabriel holding him close as pleasure shuddered through him.

When it was over, and after they'd cleaned up, they lay in bed together. Gabriel's head was on Seth's chest, while Seth ran fingers through his hair and down his neck.

Seth had missed having these quiet moments with someone, the ones where he could just lay in silence with his eyes closed until the world didn't even seem to exist outside of the two of them. The touch of skin and the gentle sound of breath lulled him into sleep when he let it.

# SEVENTEEN

Seth woke alone. The bedroom was quiet and dark. Not even the street-lights, which should have come on by this hour, cast a glow of light through the windows for him to see by. He blinked his eyes, waiting for them to adjust to the surrounding darkness.

"Gabriel?" Seth called out. Only silence answered him.

Seth slipped from the bed then crossed the room to the open bedroom door to peer out through it. The living room just as dark and empty as the bedroom had been.

"Gabriel?" Seth tried again.

Footsteps came from behind him. But they sounded too light to belong to Gabriel.

Seth inhaled and exhaled shakily. He knew it was her without turning around.

He ran for the front door before he even heard his mother's voice speak his name, but the knob refused to turn. He slammed his hands against the hard oak of the door as if he could somehow break through it.

"Why can't you understand, baby?" his mother asked from behind him, and Seth balled his hands into fists against the door.

He stopped trying to run. There was no point. She always caught him in these dreams.

"Go away!" Seth bowed his head forward and closed his eyes as his mother's arms slipped around him, her hands cold against his skin. "Just go away! Please, please, please go away!"

"We can't let him out."

"I don't know what you mean!" Seth screamed as water rose around his ankles, rushing in from beneath the door. "Who's he? Who?"

"He's inside you," his mother replied, in a voice that sounded as if it were meant to be soothing. She stroked a damp hand through Seth's hair, her nails scratching over his scalp like talons.

The water was up to Seth's knees now.

"I don't understand," Seth choked. "Why did you do it? Why did you try to drown me?"

The surging water hid the sound of his tears. It sloshed around his waist now, but he didn't try to pull away anymore. Not when it rose up to his chest. Not when it inched past his shoulders.

"Just tell me why," Seth pleaded hopelessly. "Why did you want me to die?"

His mother dropped her hand from his hair to tighten her arms around him as darkness began to seep from beneath Seth's skin and she repeated that same phrase once more. "We can't let him out."

When the water reached Seth's mouth and rose to cover his nose, he tried again to pull away as he choked, but the arms wrapped around him only tightened. He was drowning, like the dream before this, and the dream before that, and the time he was a child. He would always be drowning.

"Seth."

He struggled at the sound of his name against his ear. Why? Why did she want to kill him? Why did she despise him so much?

"Why?" The word came screaming out of him. A ragged, wrecked cry that left his throat raw and his chest aching.

"Seth!"

He jerked against the arms that restrained him, convinced the hands on him were his mother's until his mind recognized that the voice that called his name was far too masculine to belong to her.

"Seth, it's me. It's just me. It's okay."

Seth stilled with a choked-off cry. His eyes blinked against the tears and sweat that blurred his vision until bits of recognition started to filter in through the fog in his mind.

Gabriel's voice against his ear with whispered words meant to calm him. One hand pressed to Seth's head and the other gentle against Seth's bare shoulder. The softness of the blanket wrapped around him. All things that made reality feel more solid, and forced the last of the dream to slip away.

Seth couldn't bring himself to look at Gabriel. He was too afraid of what he'd see reflected back at him in those all-too-expressive green eyes.

"I'm fine. I'm fine," Seth insisted as he wiped at his face.

He pulled away from Gabriel and from the concerned touch that followed after him. He didn't much feel like being touched by anyone right then, and he pulled the blanket around himself like a shield.

"You didn't sound fine when you were screaming two seconds ago."

"It was only a nightmare. I get them sometimes. It's just, something I have to live with."

Gabriel shook his head. "That was not a nightmare. That was a night terror."

"There's a difference?"

"Yes. You can't move or scream during a nightmare because, unlike night terrors, they happen during REM sleep, when your brain releases chemicals to prevent movement. Also, you don't have difficulty waking from them like you just did."

"Okay. Well, I have both then... probably."

"Very few adults have night terrors. When they do, it can be a sign of stress or even trauma."

"You know I've always loved how smart you are—until now."

Gabriel was quiet for only a moment, but the silence between them felt like an eternity. "You know you can talk to me, right? About anything."

"I've heard that before from other people," Seth said quietly. "They've never really meant it."

"You don't think you can trust me?"

"I think I don't want to lose you, and everyone has a limit."

"I promise I'm not going anywhere."

Seth pressed a hand over his eyes as he took a shaky breath, on the verge of tears once more. "You can't say stuff like that."

"Why?"

"Because I'm going to want to believe it."

"You can believe it," Gabriel assured, resting a hand on Seth's shoulder, "and you can tell me what happened."

Seth could feel the warmth of Gabriel's palm even through the fabric of the blanket, and a part of him wanted to turn with the touch—let the man draw him in close until he felt safe again, until he felt steady. But he didn't move. He stayed right where he was, hunched in on himself with his hand over his face to hide his tears.

Even if he could trust Gabriel's words, Seth knew it wasn't fair. He didn't have a right to put this on Gabriel. He'd seen how his pain had worn down everyone else around him. He couldn't do that again. Not to Gabriel.

He'd learned it was kinder to deal with it on his own, so he didn't drown the people he loved with him.

"I'm sorry," Seth said, pushing himself up from the bed. "I shouldn't have stayed."

"Seth, wait," Gabriel said as Seth retrieved his pants and pulled them on. "You don't have to leave."

Seth started picking up the rest of his clothes from the floor. "If I stay, you'll just keep asking what happened to me."

"Because I care about you."

Seth took a deep breath and closed his eyes. "I wouldn't even know where to start trying to explain things. I don't talk about it anymore. At least, not outside of therapy."

He could feel the heat rise in his cheeks at the admission he'd seen a therapist before, shame twisting in his gut with a sickening familiarity. It didn't help that Gabriel said nothing in response, and Seth turned the shirt he held right side out rather than look to see Gabriel's reaction.

"I mean—everyone knows what happened. I'm just not the one that told them." He shook his head. "I made the mistake of telling this guy I was dating that my mom was put in a psychiatric hospital and why. So of course, after we broke up, he told everyone about it."

"Hey." Gabriel touched a hand to Seth's arm before he could put his shirt on.

Seth looked down at Gabriel's hand. His fingers were loose where they rested against his skin, and Seth could have easily pulled away. He could have easily gotten up and walked out the door. He didn't. He met Gabriel's eyes at last and waited for him to speak.

"Did your mom try to drown you?" Gabriel asked as gently as one could ask such a thing, and when Seth just stared at him wide-eyed and open-mouthed, he added, "You just said your mom was committed. Plus, when you were asleep you said some things about being drowned, and you did tell me awhile back you almost drowned as a kid."

Seth didn't say anything. He could feel the heat of fresh tears prick at the corners of his eyes and he blinked them back as he looked away.

"Hey, Seth, it's okay," Gabriel said in a soft voice, the same soft voice Seth had heard him use when he'd coaxed the rabbit out of hiding at the farm all those weeks ago.

Seth hated him for it. Hated that he was being handled like a frightened animal. He hated himself more though, for being so weak that he hadn't even been able to push a single-syllabled yes from between his lips.

Gabriel moved forward and when Seth didn't push him away, he gathered him close like he thought he could force all the broken pieces that made Seth up back together if he held him tightly enough.

Love was nice, and love could be a comfort. But Seth had learned over the years that love couldn't fix him. It wouldn't stop the nightmares. It wouldn't cure his depression, or his PTSD, and people thinking it could was typically what brought about the beginning of the end.

"What happened to me is always going to be there, and it's never going away," Seth warned.

"I can handle it."

"Can you?" Seth pulled back enough to look Gabriel in the eyes. "Because most people can't."

"I can try," Gabriel said, and that at least sounded like a more honest answer. "If you'll let me."

"Okay," Seth said at last. "Just, not tonight. I don't want to talk about it anymore tonight."

Gabriel nodded. "We'll talk when you're ready."

"Thank you."

"Will you come back to bed?"

"You sure you want me to?" Seth asked. "I could have another nightmare, or night terror, apparently."

"I'm sure."

Seth nodded and took his pants back off before he settled into bed with Gabriel, a short distance from him this time because he still felt like he couldn't breathe and he needed some space.

It was dark and quiet in the room but not in the way it had been in his dream. There was a muted glow from behind the blinds where the streetlights shone from down below and he could hear Gabriel breathing softly beside him. The sound was a reassurance that he wasn't alone, that he wasn't in danger.

"It still doesn't make sense to me," Seth confessed quietly when he couldn't calm the thoughts that raced through his head. "I mean, I know that she thought there was something wrong with me but—I don't understand it."

It was easier to speak the truth into the darkness when he couldn't see Gabriel's face or the pity that would certainly be in his eyes.

If Gabriel was surprised that Seth had decided to open up to him after all, he didn't comment.

"I was six years old..." Seth trailed off as the memory of that night came to him. He could almost feel his mother's fingers tangled in his hair, almost taste the scum of pond water on his tongue. He squeezed his eyes shut and sucked in a harsh breath. "I was six years old, and my mom tried to drown me."

It didn't sound real even as he said it. How could that ever be real? What mother would do that to her own child?

"There was a pond out back of our house and my mom took me down there one night and—" Seth broke off. He swallowed, and tried to force the rest of the words out, but his voice kept breaking.

Gabriel let a hand skim gently up and down Seth's arm. He was still silent, but there. Somehow that was comfort enough.

The room was quiet. There weren't even traffic sounds outside the window at this hour. It made Seth's voice seem louder than it probably was when he finally managed to speak again.

"She said she was sorry. She said she loved me. Which is insane. How can you love someone but want to kill them?" Seth closed his eyes against the tears that wanted to spill down his cheeks. "It was so cold, and I couldn't breathe. I couldn't—"

Gabriel's arms encircled him, pulling Seth in close so his back pressed into the warmth of Gabriel's bare chest. He hadn't realized how badly he was shaking until he felt how still Gabriel was against him.

Seth opened his eyes to find Gabriel's hand to take in his own. He intertwined their fingers and Gabriel squeezed his hand gently as he whispered soothing things into Seth's hair—some kind of muffled nonsense that Seth didn't entirely understand with half the words getting lost against his head, but it eased Seth's anxiety to know Gabriel cared.

Finally, after what felt like forever, Gabriel asked, "Where did they send her?"

"She's at Oak View."

Seth turned over so he could see Gabriel and try to gauge what was going through his head by the expression on his face. He just looked concerned, and sad.

Seth swallowed against the lump in his throat. "I haven't seen her since the trial."

"Do you want to see her?"

"I don't know. A part of me does but... I'm mad at her." Seth's face felt hot and he squeezed his eyes shut to stave off his tears. "I'm so mad at her."

Gabriel stayed silent, giving Seth the space he needed to articulate his emotions, though he did rub a hand over Seth's back.

"But I miss her," Seth admitted. "I miss her every day."

"I think you should go see her," Gabriel said, and Seth started to pull away only to have Gabriel catch at his shoulder. "I just think you have a lot of unanswered questions, and you need some closure in order to heal."

"I don't know if it's a good idea." Seth shook his head. "She still thinks there's something evil inside me. I'd only upset her."

"Are you still seeing a therapist?"

"No. Medication helps some, but therapy never worked for me, and everyone keeps acting like I'm just not trying hard enough with it," Seth admitted reluctantly. "But I tried that route for three years, really tried, and went through multiple therapists. With the way everyone talks about it, sometimes I feel like a freak or a failure because it didn't help."

Gabriel brushed Seth's bangs back from his face. "Therapy can be a good place to start, but everyone is different, and everyone heals in different ways. You're not failing just because one thing you tried didn't work for you."

"You're the only one that seems to think that." Seth sighed. "It doesn't help either that everyone feels like I should forgive my mom, and not just the therapists. My dad. My friends. They all think that's what will help me."

"You don't have to forgive her. People are always talking about needing to forgive, but forgiveness by its nature means letting people off the hook. You don't need to do that," Gabriel said softly. "I don't think people understand that it's not forgiveness they're actually talking about when they say things about letting go, and moving on. They're talking about unburdening. Which is different from forgiving. You don't let people off the hook when you unburden, you just move on from what's not yours to carry."

"I never thought about it that way."

They didn't speak for a while after that and Seth lay in Gabriel's arms while gentle hands rubbed circles over his back. The touch helped Seth relax, his shoulders sagging as his anxiety left him. Though he couldn't quite bring himself to close his eyes yet. He was still all too aware that sleep meant dreams, and dreams could so easily become nightmares.

"I love you," Gabriel whispered.

"Yo también te amo," Seth answered quietly.

# Eighteen

The next morning Seth woke to the sound of Gabriel's gentle breathing. One of his arms was still wrapped loosely around Seth's waist. It made Seth wish he didn't have to get up for work, that he could instead continue to lay there sheltered in Gabriel's space. But he knew it wouldn't be fair to call in on such short notice and leave Aaliyah to handle things on her own while they tried to find someone to cover for him.

Seth shifted out from beneath the arm Gabriel had draped over him then climbed from the bed to pad across the room to the jeans and long-sleeve shirt Gabriel had left out last night before they'd gone to bed. They were old clothes, worn soft with use. The shirt was a bit loose on him and the jeans a little long in the legs, but they were comfortable against his skin.

He wondered if these were more clothes Gabriel had outgrown years ago and meant to donate, like the ones at the farmhouse that Diana had handed over to Seth to wear.

It was still early. He wouldn't need to leave just yet, so he ambled his way into the kitchen to make coffee.

He checked the fridge once the coffee was brewing and found creamer on the bottom shelf. The sight of it made him smile, because he knew for a fact that Gabriel couldn't stand creamer. Especially the white chocolate raspberry kind that Seth favored.

Seth added some to his cup when it was ready, then drank it while he leaned back against the counter, his thoughts circling over the previous night.

He felt somewhat self-conscious about his nightmare and tried to reassure himself by thinking over Gabriel's reactions. The way he'd drawn
Seth in, instead of putting up walls or sending him on his way.

A smaller person would have been repulsed by Seth's brokenness.
Would have done everything in their power to discard him along with
the baggage he carried. Not Gabriel though. Gabriel loved him. He really,
and truly, loved him.

Seth smiled to himself as he poured a cup of coffee for Gabriel. No
cream. No sugar. Just plain, strong coffee.

He was still asleep when Seth walked into the bedroom. Though he
did stir, blinking his eyes open when Seth set the mug on the bedside
table.

"Morning."

"Mornin'," Gabriel mumbled in return, still groggy. His hair was
sticking up in odd places in a way that Seth found adorable.

"I'm not sure how you can stand to drink coffee black," Seth commented with a glance at the mug he'd set down.

Gabriel shrugged and looked to the mug on the bedside table. "I've
been drinking coffee since I was little."

"Kids drink coffee over in Colombia?"

Gabriel gave a nod. "Yeah. My parents would give us coffee with milk
after dinner as a treat. Did after we moved here too. I think I was about
thirteen when I switched over to plain coffee though. It's how my dad
always drank it, so I guess I picked it up from him."

"Wow. I wasn't allowed to drink coffee until I was sixteen. My dad always said it would stunt my growth." Seth let his eyes drift over Gabriel's
tall frame and the lean muscles of his torso above where the blankets had
slipped down to gather at his waist. "Clearly I was lied to."

Gabriel chuckled and Seth grinned along with him. He sat down
on the edge of the bed, a hand reaching out to comb fingers through
Gabriel's hair.

"Thank you," Seth said, and his smile turned softer. "For being there
for me last night."

Gabriel pushed himself up enough to press a kiss to Seth's forehead. It was reassuring in its tenderness, and Seth let out a slow breath, his eyes falling closed with the press of Gabriel's lips.

"You should go," Gabriel said reluctantly when he pulled back. "You don't want to be late."

Seth stood. Though not before he gave Gabriel a hug goodbye and a quick kiss.

"I'll call you," Seth promised. Then he gathered up his things and headed out of the apartment to drive to work.

Aaliyah was in the middle of preparing what Seth guessed was a cappuccino when he stepped inside the café and he gave her a smile as he retrieved his apron from the hook it hung upon.

"You seem happy," Aaliyah commented as Seth stepped behind the front counter, tying his apron as he went up to the register to clock-in. "Like, actually happy. Not that forced, customer-service happy."

The timer over the coffee pot went off, signaling it was time to dump the now cold pot and make a fresh one they kept on hand for customers who wanted a regular coffee.

"I actually am happy," Seth said as he dumped the old coffee down the sink.

He could feel Aaliyah watching him as he set the pot back, and then picked up the bag of coffee beans from the shelf beneath the counter.

"Oh. So, any reason?" she asked conspiratorially. "Gabriel, maybe?"

Seth smiled. "Maybe."

"So, the sex is good, huh?"

Seth nearly dropped the bag he had been pouring into the grinder. His cheeks were hot when he turned to look at Aaliyah, who gave him a good-natured laugh and a teasing wink.

The bell over the door chimed and Seth looked over at the sound, relieved to have a distraction. At least until he realized it was Evelyn coming into the café, with downcast eyes and a frown firmly on her face.

"Hey, Eevee." Seth greeted her with a sympathetic smile.

"Hi." Evelyn sighed, and tucked a stray hair from her braid back behind her ear.

"Everything alright?" Seth asked.

Evelyn gave a downward wave of a hand. "Fine. I'm just tired."

Seth frowned. He'd heard the phrase from Evelyn more than once at school. He knew she was still hurting over Mary, but he didn't know what to do to help her.

She placed a plain black travel mug on the counter, and Aaliyah approached to take it.

"You want your usual cappuccino?" Aaliyah asked. Her eyes flicked over Evelyn's bedraggled appearance and the sadness that shadowed her eyes. "It's on the house."

Evelyn managed a small smile. "You're so sweet. Yes, please. And thank you."

Seth let Aaliyah make the coffee, his focus on Evelyn who talked quietly with him for a time. Not about Mary. She was probably trying not to think of her for all the good it did.

When Aaliyah came back with the coffee, Evelyn gave her a small smile and a shy "Thank you" before she retreated to one of the empty tables near the window. Aaliyah watched her go.

More customers came in. Most presented travel mugs to be filled, but a few requested a to-go cup. The majority hurried on their way once their drink was paid for and passed to them. A few though picked an empty table and enjoyed their coffee in the ambiance of the café.

Aaliyah had turned the radio on and Indie music piped out into the small space. The sound of it was interrupted occasionally by a laugh or bit of conversation Seth caught from one of the tables nearer him.

Seth didn't think much of it when he heard the bell over the door chime once again about an hour and a half later. But when he looked up, he saw that Mary had stormed into the coffee shop.

"What did you do?" she demanded, and Seth flinched back as she shoved her hand in his face.

Seth's eyes widened. The fingers of her left hand had begun to turn a deep red, as if she'd dipped them in ink and let it run down her skin.

"What is this?"

He stared at her from between the fingers of her hand. "How the hell would I know?"

"Don't play dumb! It started right after you grabbed me!"

Seth sucked in a breath. He'd forgotten, but he had, hadn't he? In the hall that day at school when Mary and Evelyn had gotten into that argument. He'd grabbed at Mary when she'd shoved him for getting in the middle of things.

"Mary, stop it."

Seth's eyes slid to Evelyn, who had abandoned her coffee at the table she'd been sitting at to join them. Her gaze was angry, but there was a spark of worry there too when her eyes took in Mary's skin.

"He did this!" Mary snapped.

"How could he have? You're being ridiculous."

Mary whirled around to face her. "Am I? Haven't you noticed that anytime something bizarre happens it's when he's—"

A heavy *thunk* sounded through the coffee shop and Mary's words dissolved into a startled yelp.

Several people jumped up from their seats screaming, their eyes trained on a raven as it slid down the window.

It left blood smeared across the glass as it descended. Blood that Seth would no doubt be charged with wiping up.

"What the hell—"

There was another *thunk* accompanied by a sharper sound as a crack ran up along the glass and Evelyn broke off from whatever she had been about to say.

"Are those ravens?" Mary asked. "Like the one at school?"

Another bird hit the glass and floundered to the ground, stunned but not dead like the last two.

"What the hell is wrong with these birds?" Mary demanded when three more smacked into the glass.

They came faster now. One after the other. The window creaked with each black, feathered body that slammed into it. And the crack elongated with sharp white lines that branched out across the glass.

"It's like they've gone crazy," Evelyn said so softly that Seth almost missed the words.

Everyone who had been seated near the glass was on their feet now. A bit farther into the coffee shop, people were still seated but had a tense grip on their chairs, as if ready to bolt if they needed to.

"They're going to get in," Aaliyah said, just before the glass shattered.

Ravens flooded the coffee shop.

Some flew at the customers, who ducked and tried to shield their faces. Most of them though headed for Mary, with talons outstretched toward her face.

The black croaking mob descended upon her, and she was forced down to the floor by the sheer number of them.

Seth caught glimpses of her between black wings as she flailed. The dark tangled strands of her hair grasped tight in a talon. A red gash along a golden-brown arm. The white of her teeth as she screamed.

Aaliyah grabbed Evelyn and pulled her away from Mary when she tried to get to her. A few of the ravens followed. Drawn by Evelyn's attempts to help.

Seth rushed forward and tugged Evelyn into his arms when she broke free of Aaliyah's hold on her. His head ducked down over hers and his eyes squeezed shut with the flash of talons in front of him.

The pain he expected didn't come though. No scratch of talons. No peck of a beak.

When Seth dared to open his eyes, he found the ravens circled him closely but didn't so much as brush him with their wings. They veered off from him with intent any time they came within reach.

Seth kept a tight hold on Evelyn, who wailed and thrashed against him, still desperate to reach Mary. But as long as he kept her close—the ravens let her be.

Everyone else in the coffee shop wasn't so lucky. The ravens going after quite a few of the customers and leaving them bloody from pecks or deep scratches.

Aaliyah grabbed the fire extinguisher from the wall behind the counter. She turned it on before the birds could react and attack her as well.

The white spray it emitted drove the ravens away from Mary. They shrieked angrily as they found other places to settle, bobbing their heads and flapping their wings.

"Get out!" Aaliyah yelled, moving in closer with the extinguisher as she directed the hose to blow the birds back. "Go! Get out!"

The ravens flew out of reach of the extinguisher, their feathers ruffled and their flight haphazard. Customers ducked as the birds made their way back out into the daylight through the broken window.

"Mary!" Evelyn shouted. Seth let her go, let her run to the girl who had been nothing but cruel to her yet somehow still mattered.

Seth closed his eyes as his ears rang with Evelyn's horrified screams.

When he opened his eyes again, it was to find Aaliyah staring at him, her breaths shaky and her hair stuck to her cheeks with sweat.

"They didn't come after you," she said, and her eyes pinned Seth to where he stood. "Why didn't they come after you?"

# Nineteen

Seth drove Evelyn to the hospital in her car, following the ambulance Mary was in as it sped down the streets, the lights atop it flashing.

The girl inside was a mess. The ravens had left her with bloody pock-marked hands and a popped eyeball that oozed fluid down scratched cheeks. The one she had left was filled with tears when Seth moved to stand beside Evelyn, who had been kneeling on the ground next to her. Not caring that her dress became splotched red by the blood on the floor.

Mary's shirt and leggings fared far worse, the ravens having scratched and tugged bits of fabric free to get at the flesh beneath.

Seth looked over at Evelyn. Her hair was free of the braid she'd had it pulled back in when she'd come to the café and was now a tousled mess from running her fingers back through it. Her make-up was smudged and her cheeks stained with tears. She was so far from the girl he was used to seeing.

"I'm sure she'll be fine," Seth offered, trying to sound encouraging, but even to his own ears the words came out sounding hollow.

Evelyn pushed her fingers through her hair again and shook her head in a way that was more resignation than disagreement.

"She lost an eye, Seth," she said at last, "and that rash on her hand... what could do something like that?"

Seth didn't reply. A sense of dread lodged in his throat and Mary's words still rang in his ears. Could it really have been his fault?

Seth pulled into the parking garage at the hospital. He let Evelyn lead the way to the elevators once they left the car and then up to the lobby to find the nurse's station.

"Hi," Evelyn said, and the nurse on duty looked up from her computer. "My friend Mary Chapman was brought in a little while ago. I was wondering if you could tell us where they would have taken her?"

The nurse typed at her computer while Evelyn waited with hands clasped on the counter, and Seth fidgeted with the string on his hoodie.

"The doctors are with her now. If you have a seat, I'll let you know when there's more information."

Evelyn stepped back from the nurse's station. She found a chair not far into the waiting area, and sat herself down resolutely to wait while Seth followed her.

"Hey," Seth said, shoving his hands in his pockets as Evelyn looked up at him. "Do you want anything? Water? Coffee, maybe?"

"If you could get me a coffee, that'd be great. I never finished the one at the café."

"Do you want anything in it? Cream, or sugar?" Seth felt somewhat ridiculous, but he couldn't help falling back on what he knew. He knew how to prepare coffee. He had been doing it for the past two years now.

Evelyn seemed so tired as she said, "Both. Please."

Seth nodded and excused himself to find where they kept the vending machines. He eventually found them tucked in an alcove around the corner and down a hallway.

It was just as he finished putting the sugar in the steaming cup that he saw her. Isaac's mother.

She seemed exhausted, with dark circles under her eyes and clothes wrinkled like she'd slept in them. Her blond hair was pinned back from her face, one of the bobby pins precariously close to falling out.

Seth took a step toward her, worried not just about her, but why she would be at the hospital.

She spotted him a second later. A deep frown furrowed her brow.

"You've got a lot of nerve showing up after all this time," she practically shouted as she stalked toward him.

The fury in her eyes was enough to make Seth stumble back. "What are you talking about?"

"Don't act like you don't know!" she screeched. "He's been dying of cancer all this time and you couldn't even show up for him!"

Seth didn't even feel the coffee cup slip from his hand. Barely heard the dull thud of it when it hit the floor or felt the hot liquid that sloshed over his shoes and pant legs.

"What the holy hell are you yelling at him for?" Evelyn demanded, stomping across the tiled floor to put herself between Seth and Isaac's mother. "Can't you see he has no idea what you're talking about?"

Seth could see when clarity seemed to settle over Isaac's mother. Her brow smoothed, and her mouth loosened to part in surprise.

"He never told you." she realized.

Seth focused on the floor. He felt numb, almost dizzy. "He never said a word."

"Oh, Seth, honey, I'm so sorry. I thought you knew."

Seth raised his head to look at her. "He's going to be okay, right? The treatment's working?"

She shook her head, and the world seemed to tilt beneath Seth's feet. "He's not in treatment anymore."

"What?"

"He refused to continue treatment a while ago."

"Well, make him do it then! You're his mom! You don't just let him stop!"

"I can't make him do anything. He's eighteen."

"I'll talk to him then. I'll—"

"It's too late," Isaac's mother said tersely. Her hands went to Seth's shoulders to steady him when he staggered forward. "It's spread from his lungs to his brain. He's too far gone."

"He's dying?"

Isaac's mother nodded, and Seth swallowed against the bile that rose in his throat. His hands shook at his sides as he remembered the missed call he'd found from Isaac on his phone just before the wolf had stepped out onto the road. A call he'd never returned.

Seth looked at Evelyn, and she gave a nod of understanding.

"Do what you need to, Seth. I'll be fine."

"Can I see him?" Seth asked as he turned back to Isaac's mother.

"Of course, sweetheart." She pressed a gentle hand to Seth's back to steer him forward then down one of the hallways. "You should know, he gets confused. Sometimes he can't remember why he's here, or he thinks he's living at a different point in time." She was quiet for a moment before she added, "He's been asking for you."

Seth was still trying to wrap his brain around the fact that Isaac had cancer. But then they were in front of Isaac's room. Isaac's eyes brightened when he saw him, a relieved smile spreading over his face.

"Hey," Isaac said. His voice was hoarse, thin, like he was winded after running a mile. "I missed you."

Seth sucked in a breath that felt like ice water filling his lungs, like being held under when all he wanted to do was kick his way to the surface. But life kept pulling him down.

Isaac's eyes were as blue as he remembered, but the rest of him was so far gone from the boy he'd known. He was even thinner now than when Seth had seen him last, his cheeks gaunt and eyes sunken.

A tube for an IV was taped to his hand and wires of differing colors were attached to his chest and the monitor next to the bed. Another tube was looped over his ears with a pronged part inserted into his nostrils and while Seth couldn't see an air tank, he knew that's what it had to be for, because Isaac could no longer breathe properly on his own.

Seth walked through the open door into the room and took the hand Isaac held out to him. It felt so fragile, he was afraid to tighten his grip.

"Are you mad at me?" Isaac asked as he looked up at him.

Seth wasn't sure what he was referring to. The breakup? The fight with Adam? Keeping his diagnosis a secret?

"I know I shouldn't have pushed you to go to church with me."

Oh god. He was talking about their first fight, the one that had ended with Seth not speaking to him for two days.

"I just don't want to lose you, ever."

Seth felt a few tears slide down his cheeks and he glanced away to wipe a hand over his face. He wanted to be mad. For the lies. For the secrecy. Being mad was far preferable to the hollowed out void Seth was feeling inside him now.

"Seth..." Isaac gazed up at him imploringly when Seth looked back at him. His hand was shaking in Seth's own, and there wasn't any way for

Seth to know whether it was a nervous reaction, or from the cancer that had weakened Isaac's body.

God. Cancer.

Seth felt like he should have known, that he should have pushed Isaac to tell him why he had given up on them so suddenly instead of sinking into self-pity.

"You are, aren't you?"

Seth hesitated with a thought for Gabriel and what they meant to each other. How much he loved that man now. How he should be loyal to that love.

But Isaac stared up at him with worry and Seth moved to stretch out on the hospital bed next to him, being careful with his movements and the way he put an arm around him so as not to disturb the tubes and wires that seemed to be everywhere.

"No. I'm not mad at you."

Isaac smiled softly as his head came to rest on Seth's shoulder like it belonged there. Like they'd never broken up. And Seth held back his tears as he let his fingers pet over Isaac's hair, which was now buzzed short, and Seth assumed he'd done it himself once he really started losing it to the chemotherapy.

Isaac's body settled gradually. His eyes fell closed and his chest rose so faintly that Seth looked at the heart monitor to reassure himself that he was still alive.

"He gets tired easily these days," Isaac's mother whispered as she moved from the doorway to the side of the bed. She reached out a hand to adjust the tube tucked back behind Isaac's ear with practiced ease. It was routine. It was her life now.

Seth eased out from beneath Isaac carefully so as not to wake him. "I should let him rest."

"You'll come back, won't you?" Isaac's mother asked quickly when Seth stepped toward the door. "I just— I can't bear to keep breaking his heart when he asks after you."

Seth knew she was asking him to lie to Isaac. To pretend they'd never broken up. To help make his passing easier. Just that little less painful and less lonely.

Seth nodded. "I'll be back tomorrow if not today." His gaze went instinctively to Isaac once more. To the paleness of his skin and the labored rasp of his breaths. "Did they say how long..." Seth's throat closed up around the rest of the words.

Asking Isaac's mother how long her son had left to live felt cruel. Isaac dying of cancer at eighteen felt infinitely crueler, and Seth couldn't understand how either of them could worship a god who would be responsible for such things.

"A few weeks. Maybe more, God willing."

God willing. Seth's mother had likened him to a god. A destroyer of worlds. A being of infinite power. Yet here he was, as helpless in the face of this as he'd been in every other instance of pain and death that had snaked its way into his life.

By the time Seth made it back to Evelyn, Mary's parents had arrived, or who Seth assumed to be Mary's parents, given how distressed they sounded while they spoke with Evelyn.

He'd never met them before, and while he'd known Mary was adopted, it hadn't really registered until now when he saw that the man and woman were fair-skinned when compared to their Korean daughter.

Evelyn sent Seth a sympathetic glance as she continued to answer the Chapmans' questions. Not having the space to do more than that for the time being. Though Seth suspected she'd check-in with him when she could.

# TWENTY

They made it back to Evelyn's place around dinner time. The both of them entering her house with subdued expressions.

"You think that's why Isaac broke up with you? The cancer?" Evelyn asked, continuing the conversation they'd had in the car about his condition.

"Yeah. I do."

Before Evelyn could continue, there was a *tap, tap, tap* from around the corner, and for a terrifying moment Seth thought it was another raven, until a voice with the speed of molasses sliding down the side of a jar croaked, "Is that the Cunningham boy I hear?"

Evelyn's grandmother, a rickety old woman with gray hair that was restrained in a messy bun, appeared around the corner. Her cane of twisted oak tapped against the floor as she walked.

She squinted at Seth as if she couldn't quite make him out. Her blue eyes were so much like Evelyn's that it was unnerving to see them set in a face that life had mapped with wrinkles.

"Ah," she breathed, and her eyes crinkled at the corners even more when she smiled, "it is you. I thought I recognized that voice."

"Nana, you should be resting," Evelyn said in a worried tone.

Evelyn's grandmother waved off Evelyn's worry with little more than a glance in her direction.

"I have strength enough to say hello to your friend." Evelyn's grandmother turned her gaze back to Seth. "I knew some Cunninghams back in my day. They were rabbit-hearted as their name suggested, but"—her eyes swept over Seth from head to toe—"somehow the spirits gave you wings."

Seth smiled at her, indulgent in the way people were with the elderly when time had caused their minds to slip. She always said the same thing to him every visit.

Evelyn's grandmother looked between the two of them. "Has something happened?" Then without waiting for a response and giving a look at Evelyn, "Those girls didn't give you trouble again, did they? I've told you already, my dear, to not heed the words of such folk. Their kind are of small minds and even smaller hearts. You do no good ruining your calm over them."

"I know Nana," Evelyn said as she guided her grandmother back toward her room, "and I think it's time for you to head back to bed. You need your rest."

"Careful now. Don't step on Timmons," Evelyn's grandmother said with a look to the empty air near Evelyn's feet. "He'll be yours one day."

Seth still had no idea who Timmons was supposed to be, or why he would supposedly belong to Evelyn someday. He'd assumed for years that Evelyn's grandmother was talking about an animal, probably a beloved pet that had passed on years ago. Like a cat. He could picture her owning a cat.

Their voices drifted down the hallway as Evelyn helped her grandmother back to her room.

"Strange," Evelyn's grandmother said. "So strange that friend of yours. How does he have wings?"

"Nana, you know Seth doesn't have wings. He's just a normal guy."

"Ah, child, you just can't see them yet. But your time will come. Your eyes will open."

A door opened and closed in the direction of the entryway and a moment later, Evelyn's mother appeared in the living room. She glanced up at Seth while stowing her keys in her purse. Her brown hair, which was cut into a tidy bob, brushed against the scarf she wore about her neck, the dark green of it offset by the gray of her eyes.

"Oh, hello Seth. Are you staying for dinner?"

"I actually have to head home to make dinner for my dad. I just wanted to make sure Evelyn got home alright."

"I see," Evelyn's mother said as she continued toward the stairs. "Well, you're always welcome any time."

"Thank you. I'm going to go say goodbye before I head out."

Seth found Evelyn pulling a quilt up over her grandmother when he entered the room.

The quilt was a vivid blue with a cloud of darkness spiraling toward the center, where a green, red-throated bird seemed to swallow it.

Seth wondered if there was a story behind the embroidery, if the intricate design held some greater meaning than simple aesthetic.

"You know she made it herself." Evelyn looked over at him when she spoke again. "She made all the quilts in here."

Evelyn's grandmother smoothed out the quilt over her lap with fingers that shook. "I had much steadier hands back then."

Seth smiled. "It's a beautiful quilt."

"Thank you, dear. It's one of the last I made."

Seth tilted his head as he examined the bird in the center of the quilt once more. "Is it a hummingbird?"

"Yes." Evelyn's grandmother smiled. "I always liked the story my mother used to tell me about the hummingbird spirit. A tiny little thing that manages to stave off the darkness. I always saw it as a reminder that even in those moments when we feel small, we can overcome our darkest times if we choose to hope."

Seth's gaze was drawn toward the bottom edge of the quilt when the fabric rippled as if something had run out from beneath it.

"Settle down now, Timmons. You'll spook the boy."

Seth blinked. First at the edge of the quilt, where it still swayed, then at Evelyn's grandmother, who was giving him a knowing smile.

When he raised his eyes to Evelyn, she had her head tilted, and her eyes narrowed with concentration.

"Did you hear that?" she asked in a whisper, and her gaze flitted to Seth.

"I didn't hear anything."

Evelyn blinked. "I thought I heard a voice."

Seth contemplated telling her what he'd seen. That the quilt had moved. But then he noticed the window across the room was open a crack and a breeze was ruffling another quilt that lay over the back of a rocking chair.

"The window is open." Seth gestured toward it. "You probably just heard someone from outside."

When he stepped out into the hall with Evelyn, who closed the door of the room behind her, she said, "It wasn't from outside."

"Eevee—"

"I know you're going to think I've lost my mind," Evelyn said, turning to him. "But I've been hearing things. I heard something at the coffee shop too. A voice."

"What did it say?"

"'Run,'" Evelyn replied. "It just kept saying 'run.'"

Seth's cellphone rang, and he reached into the back pocket of his jeans for it. He gave Evelyn an apologetic look before answering.

"Are you okay?"

Seth faltered when he heard how strained Gabriel's voice sounded. His reply got caught in his throat, because no, he wasn't okay. Not after the day he'd had.

"Just tell me you're not hurt."

"I'm not hurt," Seth forced out.

"Thank god." Gabriel breathed a sigh of relief that Seth could hear even over the phone. "The café is all over the news."

Seth blinked. "Oh."

"And you hadn't called, so I thought—"

"I'm okay. Really. I'm sorry I made you worry. I was with my friend Evelyn at the hospital," Seth explained. "One of her friends got hurt, and then I found out someone I used to date has cancer and that he's dying. It's been a day."

"Yeah. It sounds like it."

"I'd like to visit him at the hospital. My ex, Isaac. He sometimes forgets we broke up but, I mean, nothing's going to happen between us and—"

"You don't need my permission. I trust you, okay?"

Seth fell silent. He'd fallen into old habits for a second, had forgotten how different Gabriel was from Adam.

It was Gabriel who broke the tension at last by asking, "What if there was a cure? For Isaac, I mean."

"There's not. It's cancer."

"But what if there was?" Gabriel pressed.

"Why are you asking me this?"

"I know this woman. She's had some luck with terminal patients."

"She's a doctor?"

"More of a spiritual healer," Gabriel replied, with a hesitancy to his words that made Seth nervous.

"So, like what? Some new age healer?"

"Of a sort."

"You want me to ask Isaac's incredibly religious parents if a new age spiritual healer can treat their son?" Seth scoffed. "Even if I did believe in that kind of thing, which I don't, his parents would never go for it."

"You'd be surprised what desperate people will do."

Seth fell silent. There was an ache in his chest when he thought of the alternative. Isaac dead. Isaac gone forever.

"You really think she can help him?" he asked, still hesitant.

"She's rather unorthodox, but yeah, she can help."

"Okay," Seth agreed. "I'll ask his parents. Can you go ahead and call her today, please? Just in case they say yes."

"I'll see what I can do. I should warn you, there are risks involved. It could kill him."

"He'll die anyway if we do nothing." Seth took a few more steps away from Evelyn before he added, "Thank you for trying to help. I love you."

"I love you too."

"I probably won't be coming by tonight though." Seth glanced back in Evelyn's direction to find her watching him intently. "Evelyn needs me right now."

"That's understandable. I have some stuff to check over to make sure I'm on track with my courses anyway."

"Right. I forgot you're almost done with your prerequisites. It was Oregon State University you were going to transfer to, right?"

"Yeah. That's the plan."

Seth had wondered about what would happen with their relationship when Gabriel changed schools. They hadn't really talked about it outside of Gabriel mentioning he'd be moving after he finished his current courses.

"It's going to suck not having you so close."

"That's only if I get in."

Seth smiled. "Oh, you will. They'd be stupid not to take you. So yeah, I'm going to hate the distance."

"We'll figure it out."

"Yeah. I know. Have a good rest of your night."

They said their goodbyes and Seth ended the call. Evelyn was staring at him with a frown when he turned to look at her.

"Your boyfriend is in college?" Evelyn narrowed her eyes. "And definitely not a freshman from the sound of it."

"He's a senior." Seth admitted.

"Why wouldn't you tell me? We tell each other everything." Evelyn shook her head. "I even just told you about the voices I've been hearing."

"I wanted to tell you—"

"That is such a cop out," Evelyn retorted. "If you wanted to tell me, you would have."

"I couldn't tell *anyone*. He's twenty-two."

Evelyn stared Seth down, and some of his guilt must have shown through because she asked, "Does he know you're seventeen?"

"No," Seth admitted. "I haven't gotten up the nerve to tell him yet."

"So, you've been lying to everyone then."

"I didn't lie to you."

"Well, you didn't tell the truth either." Evelyn shook her head. "And lying about your age, do you even understand how crazy that is? How much trouble you could get this guy in?"

"Right. You're hearing voices, but I'm the crazy one."

Hurt flashed across Evelyn's face. Her eyes narrowed and her mouth thinned as she clenched her teeth.

"Get out," Evelyn snapped, turning abruptly to stalk across the living room toward the stairs. "I don't need your help."

"Eevee—"

"Just go! I don't want to hear it!"

"Eevee, I'm sorry."

She whirled on him before she reached the staircase. "I said *leave!*"

Seth staggered back as a tremor ran through the wooden floor beneath his feet. A picture fell from the wall and Seth winced at the shatter of glass when it hit the floor. In the same instant, the TV toppled from its stand with a heavy smack.

Seth's back hit the wall, his eyes still trained on Evelyn, who stood as still as before.

The rumble from beneath their feet stopped as abruptly as it had started. It had maybe only lasted a minute or two, but it was enough to make Seth forget his anger.

Evelyn hadn't moved. Her body was rigid, tensed in a way that reminded Seth of the fawns on Gabriel's farm when he'd stepped into the pen with them.

Slowly, they both lowered their gazes to stare at a long crack that now ran through the space between them, the edges jagged with splintered wood. The foundation beneath it crumbled into the split-open dirt below.

Evelyn was the first to stumble back from it, but only because Seth already had his back to the wall. He skirted the crack in the floor to reach her, where she had now collapsed onto the bottom step of the staircase. Her eyes were still fixed on the floor.

"Are you okay?" he asked as he crouched in front of her. When she didn't respond, he shook her, trying to get her to focus. "Eevee?"

She raised wet eyes to him and he pushed a few strands of stray hair back from her face, reading the shock in her wide eyes.

"I did that," Evelyn said at last.

"Eevee, stop it." Seth gave her shoulder a comforting squeeze. "It was an earthquake. That's all."

Evelyn rose unsteadily to her feet, the movement dislodging Seth's hands.

"Why can't you just believe me?" Her hand shook as it went to the railing of the staircase to steady her stance. "This is too much to be a coincidence."

Seth stared around at the devastation. At the glass along the floor and the cracked TV. At the wooden coffee table that was now crooked and farther from the couch than before.

"The ravens, Mary's hand, and now this," Evelyn insisted, and Seth turned his gaze back to her as she spoke. "Something is happening, Seth. Whether you want to believe it or not."

"It was an earthquake."

Evelyn shook her head and let her eyes fall closed briefly. She looked frustrated, drained, but most of all, upset.

"Go home, Seth. I need to check in on Nana."

"I could help."

"You've helped enough."

"Eevee—"

"I'll call you later."

It was a dismissal, one that was followed by her passing him to head back to her grandmother's room. Seth watched her go before turning with slumped shoulders to head out the front door.

# TWENTY-ONE

The call from Evelyn never came. She never texted either. Seth didn't even see her at school the next week and a half, and when he tried to reach out himself, worried, there was no reply.

He'd done his best to distract himself with other things and people. He went to every soccer practice, kept up with his homework between his visits with Isaac, and always went to his tutoring sessions with Gabriel—typically cleaning the house beforehand.

When Seth arrived at the apartment building after his chores that evening, Gabriel was already waiting for him, the door propped open with his shoulder.

He heard the click of the door as it closed behind them and the sound of Gabriel trailing after him. He was quiet in a way that made Seth well aware that he knew something was wrong.

Seth turned once they were inside Gabriel's apartment and rested his forehead against Gabriel's chest. When Gabriel wrapped his arms around him, his eyes closed and he breathed in deeply, picking up the smell of citrus with woodsy undercurrents he'd grown used to.

"Is everything alright?"

"I'm just stressed." Seth sighed before he lifted his head and said, "Honestly, I'd rather not talk about it." He looped his arms around Gabriel's neck and smiled at him. "I'd prefer you distract me instead."

"Are you trying to get out of your Spanish lesson?" Gabriel teased.

"Teach me in the bedroom."

Gabriel was the one to kiss Seth this time and Seth relaxed into it. He let his hands slide into Gabriel's hair to tug gently at the strands, making Gabriel groan against his mouth.

"I'm not sure that was even a word," Seth teased, pulling back just enough to speak.

"You know there are other things I could teach you in there that are a lot more fun than Spanish."

"There might be a particular lesson I'm interested in." Seth grinned. "But you have to get me naked before I tell you what it is."

Gabriel urged Seth backward as they continued to kiss and Seth's hands gripped the hem of Gabriel's shirt to slide it up. The two of them parted just long enough to get it off, their shoes and socks following suit before they were kissing again.

"You wear too many layers," Gabriel complained when they had to part once more to get Seth's flannel and then T-shirt off.

"It's cold out," Seth said, his voice muffled from where he was lost beneath his shirt until Gabriel got it the rest of the way off him. "Not all of us can be a living furnace."

"Is that your way of telling me I'm hot?"

"Maybe." Seth grinned and pulled Gabriel in by his belt loop so he could pop the button on his jeans and get the zipper down. "Though I can probably think of more inventive ways."

Gabriel caught his breath when Seth sank to the floor. He could imagine what he looked like on his knees, gazing up at Gabriel with hooded eyes and kiss-bitten lips.

Seth dragged Gabriel's pants and boxers down so they pooled around his ankles. Gabriel stepped out of them when Seth prompted him.

He wet his lips with the tip of his tongue and cupped his hands to Gabriel's rear to pull him in closer.

The noise Gabriel made when Seth took him into his mouth had him moving a hand down to squeeze himself through the denim of his own jeans. He'd always loved the sounds Gabriel made during sex, from the heavy gasps to the desperate moans he could bring out of him.

The bedroom was the one place Seth had ever heard Gabriel raise his voice. He was so much quieter than Seth most of the time. So much more reserved in both manner and speech that it had become a point of pride for Seth to get him to be loud.

He knew how to do it by this point too—familiar with what Gabriel liked and how to read his reactions, how to make him groan openly, sounding so needy while Seth sucked him that Seth couldn't help but moan in return.

Seth's fingers dug into the flesh of Gabriel's rear as he took him in deeper, and he loved how Gabriel shuddered in response. How his fingers slid into Seth's hair and tightened. The way his hips bucked when Seth found a sensitive spot with his tongue.

Seth pulled off when Gabriel pressed a hand to his cheek and said his name. They kissed when he stood, Gabriel licking into his mouth and burying a hand in the back of his hair.

"I want you to top," Seth said when there was a pause between one kiss and the next.

Gabriel pulled back enough to look at him. "What?"

"I want you to top," Seth repeated.

Gabriel shook his head. "You don't have to do that, Seth. I don't mind— "

"I want to." Seth took a step back as he unfastened the fly of his own jeans, making quick work of getting the rest of his clothes off before he stepped back into Gabriel's space.

Gabriel watched him silently.

"I know I said no when you asked before, but I think I'm ready now."

Something in the way Gabriel looked at him shifted. His gaze seemed to grow softer as he leaned in to kiss Seth again, letting their lips meet gently as his hands came up to cup Seth's face.

Seth let himself go pliant as Gabriel walked him slowly back to the bed while they kissed.

When Adam had tried that, he'd been more insistent, more forceful. His hands left bruises on both of Seth's arms before he'd managed to shove him away, bluish-purple marks that Isaac had noticed in gym class the next day when Seth hadn't been quick enough to change in the locker room.

He'd been scared when Adam had pushed for this, but it felt different with Gabriel. It felt safe.

Gabriel guided him down with the next kiss and Seth sank onto the bed. His breath shuddered out against Gabriel's lips as he spread his legs wider to make room for him, and Gabriel was pressed right up against him, warm and hard, and it was like Heaven. He reached a hand down to guide them against each other while he rocked his hips forward and back. Seth sighed out as he moved into it.

"Tell me what you want," Gabriel said.

"I want your mouth on me."

Gabriel kissed Seth in response. His hands cupping his face again, a tender gesture that Seth had begun to crave.

"Not exactly what I meant."

"I know. Say what you want in Spanish," Gabriel said when he pulled back enough to speak, "and I'll do it."

"Quiero tu boca en mi."

"Good. But can you be more specific?"

Seth laughed. "This is what I get for asking you to teach me in the bedroom."

"Mm-hmm." Gabriel nodded, grinning. "This is what you get."

"Quiero que me... something."

"It's chupes." Gabriel chuckled and pressed a brief kiss on Seth's mouth before he added, "But I'll still suck your cock, even though you couldn't remember the right word."

Gabriel's mouth trailed from Seth's lips to his jaw, then down along his throat to his chest where he paused briefly to lick a wet stripe over one of Seth's nipples. The shock of pleasure made Seth's breath catch sharply.

A shiver ran through him at the promise of what was to come as Gabriel moved lower again, his lips tracing paths between freckles, and Seth's skin warmed with his breath.

Soft lips finally circled the head of his cock, and a moan fell from Seth's mouth with the warm slide of Gabriel's tongue. Gabriel's hands held him down at his hips while he sucked him, because Seth was never good at staying still during this. His body always wanted to push up into that wet heat.

Sometimes Gabriel had let him—when he wanted Seth to come with just his mouth, and they didn't have the time to drag it out. He'd let Seth set the pace.

This wasn't one of those times though. Gabriel went slow and teased Seth with his tongue until he trembled beneath his hands.

Seth made a soft noise of complaint when Gabriel pulled off of him, and Gabriel chuckled, low and throaty. His head ducked down once more to press a kiss to Seth's hip.

"Muéstrame lo que es sentirte dentro de mí," Seth said, wanting to be shown what it would feel like to have Gabriel inside him.

Gabriel breathed in slowly and Seth saw the yellow in his eyes brighten as he leaned forward to cup a hand to Seth's cheek. "You're sure you want to do this?"

Seth nodded in response. He was sure. Completely. "Completamente."

Gabriel moved away, and Seth blinked after him, wondering if he'd gotten the wording wrong.

"Did I not say that right?"

Gabriel glanced back at him. "You said it right."

"Then where are you going?"

"To get the lube out of the bedside table."

"Oh, right. Yeah," Seth said as Gabriel opened the drawer and rooted around inside. "Lube is good. It's a good idea. A great idea really. Don't want to be doing this without it."

Gabriel grinned as he settled himself back on the bed, lube and a condom in hand. "You're doing that cute rambling thing."

"I think we should start calling it sexy rambling," Seth suggested as Gabriel set the condom aside, "so my ego feels less threatened."

Gabriel laughed warmly. "Your ego will survive. Trust me."

"I do trust you."

Gabriel paused with the weight of Seth's words. There was a smile on his lips when he leaned in a moment later to kiss him, sweet and slow in a way that had Seth carding his fingers in Gabriel's hair.

"Hand me that pillow," Gabriel instructed when he pulled back from the kiss and he gestured to the one next to Seth's head.

Seth snagged it without question and handed it to Gabriel. His hips rose up off the bed the next moment without prompting so Gabriel could get the pillow under him before he settled back down.

There was a click as the bottle of lube was opened, and Seth tensed reflexively when he felt the touch of slick fingers a few moments later. They didn't press in right away, though. They just touched him. Gabriel's fingertips massaged circles against his rim in a way that made Seth catch his breath and shift impatiently into the sensations after a few minutes.

"You get off on teasing me, don't you?"

"You've learned trust," Gabriel said. "Should we work on patience next?"

"It's definitely a weak point of mine at times." Seth chuckled.

Gabriel smiled softly. "I've noticed."

Seth wet his lips with the tip of his tongue and closed his eyes as he relaxed into the touch. That was when Gabriel finally pushed a finger inside him, and Seth took it in past the first knuckle before he tensed.

"Oh. Okay." Seth winced slightly, opening his eyes the next second. "Maybe you're not just a tease."

Gabriel paused, his gaze sliding over Seth's face. "Does it hurt?"

"It's not bad. I just need a minute. Sorry."

"It's okay. You don't need to apologize," Gabriel murmured into the skin of Seth's thigh. A soft kiss followed his words. "We'll go as slow as you need."

"Okay."

Gabriel pressed more kisses into his skin, the soft brush of lips and the rougher graze of stubble soothing in its familiarity. Gabriel had touched him like that over a dozen times before.

A flush heated Seth's cheeks when he nodded and felt Gabriel's finger push in deeper. It crooked carefully after a moment of gentle searching, and Seth arched with a gasp.

Seth's hands fisted in the bedding and his fingers flexed as Gabriel stroked up against that spot inside him over and over. The pleasure made Seth shake and move instinctively into the thrusts.

The finger withdrew eventually, and Seth felt weirdly empty. He wanted it back inside him. He almost asked for it, but then there was a second finger pushing in alongside the first. Both of them slicker than before, Gabriel being liberal with the lube, and Seth bit his lip to hold back a moan as they sank slowly inside him.

Gabriel talked him through it. Made sure Seth was okay as he worked to open him up as gently as he could. Made sure it wasn't too much or too fast. His fingers paused now and then when Seth needed him to wait.

When Seth was ready, Gabriel drew back to pick up the condom he'd dropped on the bed earlier, his fingers tearing the packet open and then putting the rubber on while Seth watched and waited. His hands reached for Gabriel when he shifted closer after picking up the bottle he'd set aside earlier.

More lube, on Gabriel this time, and then he was lining himself up to press against him. Inside him. Soft words fell from Gabriel's lips when Seth gasped.

It hurt just enough to make Seth question his choices. His body tensed up, legs hugging Gabriel's sides, and Gabriel went still.

"Do you want to stop?" Gabriel asked.

"No. No, I just need you to wait again. Can you— here just— just touch me," Seth said as he guided one of Gabriel's hands to his cock. A tremor ran through him when long fingers wrapped around him and stroked with a firm grip. "Yeah, I like that. That feels good."

A beat of silence passed between them where Gabriel watched Seth beneath him, gauging his reactions. He leaned in a minute later to brush a kiss over Seth's mouth, a soft press of lips that repeated gently, and Seth focused on the warmth of Gabriel's mouth against his and the caress of his hand over his cock.

His own hands slid into Gabriel's hair to pull him down into a firmer kiss. His fingers tightened in the soft strands to tug the way Seth knew he liked.

It helped, the distraction, and Seth opened his mouth beneath Gabriel's as he relaxed into the press of his lips. The stroke of his hand.

"Okay," Seth murmured against Gabriel's mouth when he felt ready. "Keep going."

A gasp escaped him as Gabriel eased in deeper—deep enough that Seth went tight all over. The same hot jolt of pleasure ran through him that he'd gotten from Gabriel's fingers. Only this felt more intense, more significant with the way Gabriel looked at him. His gaze was soft and his touch gentle as he let his knuckles brush over Seth's cheek.

"Are you okay?"

"Yeah." Seth smiled up at him and pressed a hand to Gabriel's hip to urge him to move. "Just go easy on me."

Gabriel nodded. His hips rocked back then forward carefully and repeatedly when Seth relaxed beneath him again. He had one hand on Seth's cheek and the other on his hip to guide him.

Seth's eyelids fluttered with the slow drag of Gabriel inside him, and a moan left him with a tremor of pleasure that had his legs shaking. It hurt a little still, but that got better gradually. The hint of pain faded the longer it went on.

"Still okay?" Gabriel asked softly.

"Yeah. Yeah, I'm okay."

The yellow in Gabriel's eyes brightened as he leaned in to kiss Seth's throat, and Seth tipped his head back in offering. His hair stuck to his forehead with sweat and his skin flushed with need.

A noise somewhere between a groan and a growl that was going to haunt Seth's fantasies rumbled across his skin, and a hard suck at the pulse point of Seth's throat the next second made him gasp then moan.

Gabriel pulled back to look at him, his thumb dragging over the mark he'd undoubtedly left on Seth's neck. His gaze focused on Seth's face as he drew pleasure from him with every thrust.

"God, you look so good like this, mi amor. You're doing so well."

Seth shivered with the praise, warmth pooling low in his belly with the words. Gabriel calling him that was going to be his undoing.

Mi amor. My love. It meant Gabriel loved him, and he knew it was true. He could feel it in Gabriel's touch, in the gentle roll of his hips that moved Seth toward a growing heat.

The pleasure inside Seth built in a way that made him shake and drag his hands up along Gabriel's back to grip at his shoulders. His fingers dug in as he shifted to meet the next thrust, and the next, again, and again. His eyes fell closed as he lost himself to the sensations.

If he'd known it could be like this, he would have done it sooner. He wouldn't have refused when Gabriel had asked for this days ago. He would have asked for it himself to begin with.

"Faster," Seth panted.

Gabriel moved into him quicker with the softly spoken word. Not enough for Seth to be overwhelmed, but enough that he could feel the difference. The steady drag inside him made his toes curl against the bed and he couldn't help the words or desperate, needy noises that escaped him.

Gabriel kissed him. Maybe to stop his breathless rambling, or maybe just because he wanted to. Either way Seth welcomed it, his lips parting beneath Gabriel's to let him in.

The kiss broke when Seth tipped his head back at the touch of Gabriel's hand over his cock. His fingers were tight as they slid over Seth, making him moan with the spike in pleasure.

Seth dug his fingers harder into Gabriel's skin as Gabriel's thrusts and the quick slide of his hand pushed Seth to a point of no return. His breaths became harsh and shallow, and he trembled as he rode the cresting wave of pleasure.

"That's it, mi amor."

Seth's body went wonderfully tight with the next push in, and he gave a panting cry as the pleasure overtook him. His hands tugged Gabriel in closer, deeper.

Gabriel let himself be drawn in with a stuttered breath, his body knotting tight as he held Seth, deeper in him now than he'd ever been before, and Seth clung to him as they shook, and groaned, and finished together. Gabriel's eyes a deep yellow when Seth gazed up into them.

Seth let his head drop to Gabriel's shoulder and he breathed hard against his skin when it was over, while Gabriel combed his fingers through Seth's hair, his blunt nails dragging over his scalp in a way that made him shiver.

"Oh, wow." Seth sucked in a breath then let it out shakily, a hint of a laugh in his voice. "Is there anything you're not good at?"

"Knitting."

Gabriel smiled fondly when Seth laughed, and he let his thumb stroke over Seth's cheek.

They lay tangled together for a while longer as their breaths settled, but eventually Gabriel slipped out of him and cleaned the come off Seth's stomach with the corner of a sheet before he rose to dispose of the condom. Seth pulled the pillow out from under himself and resituated while he was gone.

A thumb slid over the mark on Seth's neck when Gabriel returned. He felt a gentle ache that let him know it was there when Gabriel applied just enough pressure to make Seth's eyelashes flutter.

"I may have gotten a little carried away there," Gabriel said as he stretched out on the bed next to Seth.

"It's okay." A smile slipped across Seth's face. "I like it."

Fingers petted through Seth's hair again, and Gabriel kissed him sweetly, easing them back into the intimacy of before.

Seth watched as the glow in Gabriel's eyes calmed slowly. The green was becoming more prominent again bit by bit. Soon the yellow wouldn't stand out so harshly.

Most people never even noticed it, and if they did, it usually resulted in a compliment rather than suspicion of the supernatural. But then, none of those people had ever seen Gabriel like this, with his skin flushed and his hair a mess, his body tired and contented against rumpled sheets with Seth tucked in close against him. The yellow in his eyes too bright still to be dismissed as anything ordinary.

It made Seth smile. Gabriel had trusted him with his secret. He'd let him in rather than risk losing him, and now for Seth, Gabriel's eyes were just another thing that was beautiful about him in that moment.

Gabriel's forehead came to rest against his, and they lay like that for a time. Seth was in no hurry to move, and Gabriel showed no need to rush him.

Seth closed his eyes, basking in the press of fingers along his skin, and the warmth of the body next to him. The comfort of it all lulled him into a light doze.

The mattress shifted some time later, and Seth blinked slowly from where he now lay on his stomach as Gabriel traced patterns over the skin of his back with the tip of a finger.

"What are you doing?"

"Mapping the constellations on your skin."

It took Seth a moment to realize Gabriel meant his freckles, and that he was drawing lines with his finger between the more prominent ones.

"I hate my freckles," Seth mumbled into his pillow.

"I think they're beautiful."

"You think every part of me is beautiful though," Seth said with a lazy smile.

"Because every part of you is."

Seth smiled wider. It probably should have come across as sappy, but Gabriel had a way of making those kinds of things sound sweet.

"Do they have names?"

"Hm?" Gabriel's finger paused on Seth's skin.

"The constellations you're mapping," Seth clarified. "Do they have names?"

"Yes." Gabriel pressed a kiss to Seth's shoulder, then traced a pattern of lines over it. "This one here would be Cervus."

"What does that mean?"

"It's Latin, for deer."

"You know Latin too?"

"A little," Gabriel replied. "Mostly plant and animal names from my classes."

"I'm dating a genius."

Gabriel huffed a laugh, then pressed a kiss between Seth's shoulder blades. "If you say so."

"Will you tell me the other names?" Seth asked, still not ready to move yet.

"Yes, mi amor."

Seth smiled softly. "I like it when you call me that."

"Good. I like making you happy," Gabriel said as he dragged his fingertips lower to trace another pattern, sharp angles and lines that made up shapes Seth didn't recognize. "This one is Lupus the wolf and..." He drew a half circle with a finger just above it. "It's howling at Luna, the moon."

Gabriel walked his fingers up Seth's spine then slid them back down about an inch or so to draw a line left then right. "Gladium, the sword."

Seth closed his eyes when Gabriel slid his fingertips over his lower back with a lighter touch. It was a sensitive area for him and Gabriel knew that.

"What's that one called?" Seth asked when Gabriel drew what felt like a series of triangles.

"Colibrí. It means hummingbird," Gabriel said, and Seth smiled when he kissed his shoulder. "That one's actually Spanish. I can't remember the word for it in Latin."

"My friend's grandmother actually mentioned a story about a hummingbird. Something about how it symbolized hope."

"That reminds me of The Hummingbird and the Cave of Misfortunes," Gabriel said, then—when Seth looked at him expectantly— he continued, "It's a myth. A really old, and not very well-known one."

"What's it about?"

"It's a bit like the story of Pandora's box," Gabriel replied. "Only, the hummingbird doesn't stay locked up the way hope does. It comes out to stop the darkness and ills of the world."

"Why do you think it's different?"

Gabriel shrugged. "Maybe the person that created the myth realized waiting and hoping wasn't enough. That hope is just the thing that keeps you going while you move forward."

Seth shifted against the pillow, his thoughts drifting over Gabriel's words. He liked the moral of this story better than the one about Pandora's box.

"Can you spend the night?" Gabriel asked.

"I have to be somewhere by five," Seth replied, remembering he had a soccer game. "But I can come back after."

"Now that you mention it. I actually have to be somewhere too." Gabriel slid his fingers through Seth's hair. "We could meet back here at seven?"

Seth smiled. "Yeah. I'd be good with that."

Gabriel pressed a kiss to the back of Seth's neck, and Seth wished he never had to leave. That they could stay here, like this, always.

Eventually though, Seth forced himself to move from the bed to dress and head home to get ready for his game. His dad was expecting him back soon since they'd planned to drive together.

# TWENTY-TWO

The floodlights shone down on the soccer field as Seth took his position on the grass for kickoff. They were playing against Beaverton High School tonight. Their orange and black uniforms clashed sharply with the blue and white that Seth's team wore.

"Seth?"

Seth raised his eyes to the player from the other team that stood in front of him, and he froze. They both did. Dark brown eyes stared back at him in shock.

"Marcus?"

They'd only met the one time. But Seth still remembered Gabriel's cousin from that evening at the farmhouse.

Marcus didn't say anything in return. His eyes moved to the bleachers on the opposite side of the field.

Seth swore he felt his heart skip several beats as he followed Marcus's gaze and then it stopped dead in his chest.

Gabriel.

Gabriel saw him too, his body stiff and his eyes wide.

No. No, no, no. This had to be some kind of horrible dream.

This couldn't be real. It couldn't be.

It couldn't really be Gabriel in those bleachers. Not his Gabriel, moving quickly as he made his way down from the metal stands, his steps carrying him across the grass and toward the parking lot.

Seth took off at a run across the field after him. He nearly ran into a member of the other team as he swerved around the players, trying to reach Gabriel before he could get in his car to drive away.

"Cunningham!" Coach Pembroke yelled after him as he ran off the field, his cleats clacking against the concrete. "Where the hell do you think you're going?"

Seth ignored the anger of his coach and the confused shouts of his teammates. Gabriel was what was important.

They reached the car at nearly the same time, and Seth opened the passenger-side door to slide in after Gabriel before he could drive away.

Seth panted for breath as the door clicked closed behind him, a stitch in his side from how he'd run to catch up.

Gabriel took several deep breaths of his own. Though Seth had the sense they were meant to calm Gabriel's nerves rather than anything to do with him being winded.

"So how old are you really?" Gabriel asked finally.

"Seventeen," Seth croaked.

Gabriel stared at him in shock—the kind of shock that hardened into anger just beneath the surface, making Seth feel like he'd only seen the tip of the iceberg. That the rage Gabriel held back was the kind that could sink ships.

"Get out," Gabriel said in a voice that was unsettlingly quiet. His knuckles shook against the steering wheel.

Seth wanted to take his hands in his own to calm him, but that was probably the last thing he should do.

"Gabriel—"

"Go!" Gabriel shouted. "Get out!"

Seth didn't move. For a moment, he couldn't even breathe. He felt dizzy. His eyes burned with wet heat and the sick twist of his stomach.

"I'm sorry." Seth licked his lips before he continued. "I'm sorry I lied to you. I just—I really liked you and—"

"You're *seventeen*." The look Gabriel gave Seth was enough to make him flinch back. "Do you have any idea how much trouble I could be in if someone were to find out about us?"

Seth bit his lip and glanced away.

Gabriel's eyes went wide. "Oh, god... Who knows?"

"My friends and my dad know I'm dating someone—but they don't know how old you are. Well, except for..."

"Except for who?" Gabriel demanded when Seth trailed off.

"Evelyn."

"Oh, *fuck*."

"She won't tell anyone." Seth reached out a tentative hand to rest on Gabriel's arm when he dropped his head against the steering wheel. "Please, I love you."

Gabriel bristled and pulled away from Seth's touch. "You're a *child*!"

"I'm old enough to know how I feel!"

Gabriel shook his head. "I'm not having this conversation with you."

"Why?" Seth demanded.

"Because you're *seventeen*!" Gabriel snapped, an almost hysterical edge to his words.

"You keep saying that..." Seth threw his hands up. "As if one year—not even a year, by the way, just less than two weeks now from eighteen—is supposed to make any difference."

Gabriel looked away from Seth. His lips pressed together tightly and a muscle in his jaw twitched.

"Give me one good reason why we can't be together," Seth insisted. "One good reason that has nothing to do with my age."

"Because you lied to me."

Tears spilled down Seth's cheeks and Gabriel looked like he was close to crying himself. It made Seth want to reach for him again. He wanted to hold him in his arms, and tell him all the reasons they could get through this. All the reasons why Seth's age shouldn't matter. He didn't dare.

"G-get out," Gabriel said again. This time his voice shook. This time it cracked. "*Please*."

Seth listened this time. His hand fumbled at the door handle as tears blurred his vision but he finally swung the door open and stepped out of the car. He had barely managed to close it behind him before Gabriel drove off, leaving Seth standing alone in the parking lot.

He stared after him, his face hot with tears and the pain in his chest. He wrapped his arms around himself and sobbed.

The idea of going back to the field, where he was sure Gabriel's cousin would still be and maybe even the rest of his family, made Seth feel sick to his stomach. His dad had driven him here though, so if he wanted to leave, he'd need to find his dad to give him a ride home.

Seth didn't have to look far, because when he turned back in the direction of the field, he found his father stood a short distance away with his hands in his coat pockets. His expression was a strange mix of upset and understanding, his gaze soft but his mouth a thin line.

"Dad..."

His father didn't say anything. He just walked over to Seth, took his hands out of his pockets, and pulled him into a tight hug. It only made Seth cry harder.

"Come on, son," his father said gently. "Let's go home."

They didn't talk on their way to the truck or on the drive to the house. In fact, they didn't speak at all until Seth had kicked off his shoes with what little energy he could manage and let himself fall face-first onto his bed.

He could hear his dad in the doorway, probably leaning against the doorframe as he usually did.

"He's older than you." Were the first words out of his father's mouth since the parking lot.

Seth sat up slowly. He felt heavy, hollowed out, like someone had bored out a hole inside him and filled it in with lead.

He hadn't stopped crying since Gabriel had left him. Even now his nose ran and a few tears slid down his cheeks.

"He thought I was twenty-one." Seth's voice sounded as weak as he felt. He wished Gabriel was there to hold him, and the ache that thought carved out in his chest just made the tears come more steadily.

"So, you lied to him."

Seth nodded. His throat tight and his eyes sore.

"And now that he knows the truth, he doesn't want to go out with you anymore."

The words slammed into Seth like a physical blow. They hurt because they were true. Gabriel would probably never even speak to him again.

"What's his name? His actual name."

"Gabriel," Seth answered quietly.

Seth's father sighed heavily and strode over to the bed to sit down next to him. He put an arm around Seth's shoulders and Seth let himself lean into his father.

"How old is he?" his father asked after a long moment of silence.

"Twenty-two." Seth sniffled.

"Which is way older than you."

"He's only four years older."

"More like a few months shy of five years older, and that's still a big difference when one of you is seventeen," his father pointed out.

Seth hung his head. He wished he was older. He wished Gabriel was younger. He wished he lived in one of the states where Gabriel didn't run the risk of arrest just for being with him.

"I'm almost eighteen."

"But you're not eighteen yet, and you're in two completely different stages of life. You haven't even started college yet, and he's probably close to graduating from it, right?"

"He's actually transferring after he gets his prerequisites done. He wants to be a vet, so it's longer than most schooling."

"That doesn't change anything. And what were you planning to tell him when it was time for you to go to college?" His father furrowed his brow, clearly confused. "You didn't think the truth would come out then?"

"I was hoping it wouldn't matter by then."

Seth's father shook his head and gave Seth's shoulder a pat, like he was sympathetic but also exasperated.

"I love him."

"I know. But sometimes love isn't enough. Sometimes honesty matters more."

Seth ached inside. It felt like something vital had broken. He took a shaky breath and pulled away from his father to lay back down on his bed, his hands gripping at his pillow as if it could somehow anchor him.

His father's hand was on his back a moment later, a small spot of warmth in the cold numbness Seth had fallen into.

"You want anything to eat?" his father asked, and Seth turned his face away to hide in his pillow—the thought of food made his stomach turn. "We could order pizza."

"I'm not hungry," Seth mumbled. He didn't look back at his father to answer, and curled in on himself more tightly.

Seth wanted to stop existing. Everything felt meaningless now. Everything felt like a lie. Gabriel had promised he wouldn't leave him. He had promised.

He pressed his face harder into his pillow, trying to hide the fact he was crying full out again, but he was certain his father knew anyway. The pillow could only do so much to muffle his sobs, and it did nothing to stop the way his body shook.

Gabriel had promised to always be there, and he'd left him. His thoughts always came back to that fact.

"We could watch some TV," his father suggested. "It's better than being up here all alone crying."

Seth wanted to be alone, though. He wanted to lay still in his bed and cry until he wasn't able to breathe anymore.

"Just go away," Seth choked.

"Alright." His father patted him on the back before he stood to leave the room. "I'll be downstairs if you need me."

Seth heard his father's footsteps leave the room and then head down the staircase. After a short time, the sound of the television could be heard from the living room, lively and cheerful and all the things Seth wasn't in that moment.

He longed for this to be a dream. One of his nightmares that he'd wake from in Gabriel's arms, upset and unsteady, but also safe and loved.

# TWENTY-THREE

It was late when Seth snuck out of the house the next night. He'd heard about a bonfire out in the woods from some of his teammates before the game had started yesterday. It seemed as good a distraction as he could hope to find in town.

He could see the soft glow of fire from between the trunks of trees as he drew near the outskirts of Twin Oaks. A large group of people around his age milled about in the open space of a clearing when he followed a dirt path off the road and into the woods.

A portable speaker that had been hooked up to an iPhone blasted music from where it sat on a tree stump near an open cooler full of beer.

Seth swiped two cans and wandered away from the more crowded area near the bonfire to drink them. He wasn't looking for companionship or to dance like some of the other people there. He just wanted to numb himself to the memories in his head and the answering twinge in his chest.

It worked. For a while anyway. Though Seth had to go back for two more beers to silence his more stubborn thoughts.

Halfway through his last one, someone approached him from behind. Seth didn't turn around though, hoping that his disinterest would dissuade them from conversation. He just wanted to be left alone.

"What do you think you're doing?"

The voice was all too familiar, and Seth turned slowly to find the source of all his heartbreak staring him down.

Seth blinked at Gabriel, surprised to see him at a high school party. He looked pretty in the flicker of the flames from the bonfire. An almost otherworldly shine to his eyes when the light hit them just right.

"I'm getting drunk. What are you doing?"

"Your dad texted me from your phone," Gabriel replied, and Seth had never seen him look so unamused. "He asked if we were back together because he couldn't find you anywhere."

"Oh..." Seth narrowed his eyes in thought. "How did *you* find me?"

"Do you really think I don't know your scent?"

"So you... what? Drove around town with your head out the window smelling for me?"

Gabriel looked half embarrassed and half ticked off.

"You did," Seth concluded. "You sniffed me out."

"Yes. Okay. I got worried."

"If you're not careful, I might think you still care about me."

"This is not the time or the place for this," Gabriel said pointedly with a nod to indicate the people around them. He took a step in the road's direction. "Now come on. Let's go."

"No. I'm not ready to go yet." Seth turned away and gave the beer can a shake. "I want to finish this."

"Not read—" Gabriel broke off, flustered. "You shouldn't be drinking at all."

"If you have a problem with it, you're free to go. It's not like you want me around, anyway."

"Why are you being like this?"

Seth tossed his beer to the ground in a fit of anger. "Because I'm pissed at you!"

Gabriel gestured toward himself, his hands pointed at his chest. "I'm the one who was lied to, but you're mad at me?"

"You weren't exactly honest, either. All your talk about being able to trust you, and you just drop me like I'm nothing." Seth threw a hand out. "And there are still things you haven't told me about the pack. Oh, and not to mention, you never told me why you won't play the piano anymore. Even though Naomi is clearly right and something happened."

Gabriel looked away with that last one, shame in the way his eyes narrowed and the downward curve of his mouth.

"See"—Seth waved a hand in Gabriel's direction—"right there. You just shut down."

Seth's heart jolted in his chest at the way Gabriel looked in the next instant. It reminded Seth of a time he'd come over unannounced and caught Gabriel in a rare dark mood.

Gabriel hadn't cried, or yelled, or even talked much that night. He'd just been sad, in a quiet, despondent way Seth hadn't seen until then and that Gabriel wouldn't explain.

Seth shook his head. "You know, you act sometimes like you have this enormous weight on your shoulders, but for all your talk about being there for me, you never once let me be there for you."

Gabriel met Seth's eyes, and sadness colored his tone when he said, "Yeah, well, it doesn't matter now because it's not your place to know anymore."

"Because you left me."

"I did what was best for you."

"Who are you to decide what's best for me?" Seth shouted. "You left me standing alone in a parking lot when you had promised you'd always be there. Only hours after we—"

"I know."

"I trusted you."

"I know."

Silence fell between them, and somehow it was more deafening than the music that filled the air.

It started to rain. The bare branches overhead offered little cover, and Seth frowned with the cold that ran down his skin in droplets.

"Just let me take you home," Gabriel insisted. "Your dad is really worried about you."

Seth gave a reluctant nod. "Fine. But only because it's raining."

He let Gabriel take him by the hand to help him forward through the throng of people headed for their own cars. Given how badly Seth was stumbling as he walked, it was probably for the best.

The rain picked up, and heavy drops plopped against Seth's head. His hair stuck to his scalp with the dampness, a lump of dread in his throat with the tug of Gabriel's hand to lead him out to the road.

He was reminded of his mother's hand in his. The way she had pulled him out the door when he was young. Out into the dark and down to the pond to kill him.

Rainwater ran into his mouth as he was pulled forward, and it made reality as slippery as the grass beneath his shoes.

"Seth—" Gabriel started, but didn't finish whatever he meant to say as Seth slipped from his grip and fell to his knees.

Seth squeezed his eyes shut and pressed his forehead to the wet grass along the side of the road. He dug the fingers of both hands into the earth, trying to ground himself with tactile sensation. Remind himself the water that made his hair and clothes cling to him wasn't in a pond. That the hand that had been pulling him along in the dark hadn't been his mother's.

He wasn't sure how long he huddled there on the ground with his fingers in the dirt and tears on his face as memories played behind his eyelids. His stomach twisted with the terror in his body and he spewed up the beer he'd drunk.

Voices filtered in and out around him. Too many people. Too much noise.

Seth coughed around the sour taste in his mouth. His fingers flexed against the grass as he blinked his eyes open, only to close them again with a groan.

Gabriel bracketed Seth from behind when he managed at last to stumble to his feet, an arm around his middle and a hand on his chest to keep him upright.

The crowd parted for them as Gabriel helped him the rest of the way to the Jeep, then into the passenger seat where he buckled Seth in like a concerned parent before he closed the door. Seth watched him round the vehicle while he tried to sort through the mess of his thoughts.

"Are you okay?" Gabriel asked when he slid into the seat next to Seth.

"My mom was holding my hand when she took me down to the pond. I wanted to go back, but she just kept pulling me forward."

Gabriel stared at him. Horrified. "Me holding your hand did that?"

"It was more a combination of things..."

"What—"

"Can you just take me home?" Seth interrupted quietly. "I don't feel well."

Gabriel had Seth give him his address for the GPS, then started the car.

The Jeep rolled along the road faster than was probably legal, Gabriel following the directions the voice from his cellphone gave him. It was the only sound in the car. Neither of them had spoken a word since they'd left and the silence was getting to Seth. It was so much different from how they used to be.

"I hate this." Seth glanced in Gabriel's direction. "Not having you in my life hurts."

"You know I'm not doing this to hurt you," Gabriel said quietly.

Seth rested his head against the cool glass of the window. Tears slid down his cheeks and Gabriel was quiet next to him.

"Why can't you just be with me?"

"Because you're a seventeen-year-old boy and I'm a twenty-two-year-old man."

"I'll be eighteen soon—"

"That doesn't change what you did."

"—and we've already slept together. So why are you acting like my age still matters?"

"Because it should," Gabriel said. "I'm just trying to do the right thing here, Seth."

Seth shook his head against the glass. His heart hurt like it had crumpled in on itself. "Why does loving me have to be the wrong thing?"

Gabriel gave a weary sigh and Seth looked over at him. Really looked.

He was a mess, his eyes red-rimmed with dark shadows under them that looked as sore as Seth's felt. As if he'd been up for the past two days crying like Seth had.

It made Seth's chest ache to know it was his fault, and he swallowed against a fresh wave of nausea, the taste of something bitter in the back of his throat.

Seth's house came into view and a moment later Gabriel had idled the Jeep up alongside the curb.

"What am I supposed to do without you?"

"Go back to being a teenager."

Fresh tears stung Seth's eyes. "As if I ever got to know what a childhood was like in the fucking first place."

Seth shook his head but swung the door of the Jeep open all the same. It wasn't like he had much of a choice.

The porch light flicked on. The door of Seth's house opened, and his father came out of the house to stare at the Jeep.

Seth got out unsteadily. He slammed the door on Gabriel's next words, then weaved his way across the lawn toward the front door of his house.

He fell halfway there and heard the opening of a car door from behind him. Gabriel was at his side a moment later to help him stand.

"Don't," Seth protested, and gave Gabriel a shove back that made them both stumble. "Just go. Okay. You don't want me, so just *leave*."

Gabriel stared at him, his eyes downcast and brow furrowed. There was a silent kind of hurt in the way he shoved his hands in his pockets before he turned away and back toward the Jeep.

"Was that Gabriel?" Seth's father asked when he tripped his way into the house.

"Yeah."

"I thought you two broke up."

"We did. We are," Seth snapped, scared and angry and taking it out on the wrong person. "He was just making sure I got home safe."

Seth started up the stairs, his hands on the railing to steady himself, while his father stared at him in shock. He looked like he didn't know who Seth was or what to do with him.

"Are you drunk?"

"Yep," Seth replied.

His father made a flustered sound before he waved a finger upward. "Go to your room."

The attempt at parenting made Seth double over the banister in a fit of laughter. "That's the best you can do? Go to your room?"

"Now!"

"Okay." Seth laughed as he headed up the stairs. "Okay. I'm going. Look, I'm going. I was already going. Wow, parenting figure of the year here."

"And straight home from school for a month. You're grounded."

"Yeah. Wonder how long that'll last."

"You want to make it two?"

"You know kids learn by example," Seth shot back from the top of the steps. "Maybe if you didn't want me drinking, you should have been a better role model."

"Two months!"

Seth slammed his door shut behind him with a loud bang, then toed off his shoes and gave them a kick toward his closet. One made it through the doorway, and the other knocked against it before falling on its side.

He still felt sick. His body was shaky, and a sense of nausea clung to him. Worse, though, was the embarrassment he felt over how he'd treated Gabriel. After the guy had come looking for him out of concern, no less.

Several minutes of pacing and a guilty conscience had him drunk texting an apology before crawling into bed.

# TWENTY-FOUR

Seth couldn't stop thinking about Gabriel. The happy memories he had were now soured and only made his stomach twist. Yet he couldn't stop turning each one over in his head as he wallowed in heartache and abandonment.

Seeing him at that party had only made it worse. So had the text he'd sent going unanswered.

Sometimes when Seth managed to find the energy to drag himself from his bed, he'd visit with Isaac rather than force himself to go to his classes.

On those days, Seth would pull a chair up beside Isaac's bed and talk to him. About anything and everything. Not that he replied much these days. Isaac's mind had faded with the rest of him, and the pain that came with that had Seth retreating back to bed as soon as he got home.

"Get up."

His father's voice broke into the monotony of his thoughts, and Seth grudgingly peeked at him from beneath the pile of blankets he'd sequestered himself under.

"Now."

Seth tugged the covers back over his head. "Go away."

"You moping around has gone on long enough," his father said as Seth turned his back on him and curled in on himself, only to have the warmth of the blankets that shielded him from the cold of reality yanked away. "No man is worth this kind of doom and gloom."

"How would you know? You've never dated Gabriel."

"Seth, seriously, get up." His father took hold of his arm and pulled him bodily from the rumpled bed before he could protest further. His rear hit the floor before his feet, which were still on the mattress. "Come on. Up."

"I like you better when you're drunk," Seth grumbled from where he lay sprawled out on the floor.

His father turned away to pull clothes from Seth's dresser. "Yesterday was your birthday, and you spent the whole day up here sulking like a lovesick sixteen-year-old."

Seth snorted. "If Lesley Gore were still alive we could do a duet."

His father dropped some clean clothes on him in response. "You're not funny. Get showered. Get dressed."

With a sigh, Seth pushed himself up to his feet and stooped to pick up the clothes that he'd let fall to the floor.

Seth obediently trudged his way to the bathroom, where he dropped the clean clothes on the counter and stared into the mirror. He seemed even paler than usual, as if his tears had washed the color from his skin. His puffy, red-rimmed eyes clearly betrayed the fact that he'd been crying off and on for days.

He took his time in the shower, letting the heat of the water bring life back into the numbness of his limbs. By the time he got out and had dried off, he felt a little more like himself.

He finished up his morning routine in the bathroom and dressed in the clothes his father had chosen for him before he headed downstairs.

Coffee and a bowl of fruit were waiting for him when he reached the kitchen. It made Seth smile a little, because it was the closest thing to a home-cooked breakfast his dad had ever made for him.

"Glad to see you amongst the living again," his father said by way of greeting from the other side of the kitchen island, his own mug of coffee in hand.

"Ha ha, hilarious," Seth said as he took a seat in front of the bowl of fruit.

His father said nothing for a time while Seth sat and ate between sips of coffee.

"You feeling any better?" his father asked hopefully, as though he thought coffee and a bowl of fruit could heal a wounded heart.

"I feel sad," Seth admitted. "Betrayed. Jilted." Jilted was the perfect word for it, Seth decided. "Yeah. Jilted."

"He's just trying to protect you."

"From what?" Seth spread his arms in exasperation. "We've already done everything. What could he possibly be protecting me from?"

"The guilt of getting him arrested, the ensuing media storm if the press found out, the legal proceedings. And that's just for starters."

Seth hid his frown behind his coffee mug. He hadn't considered that his relationship with Gabriel would shine a spotlight on him as well if they were found out.

"You're visiting mom today, right?" Seth asked, changing the subject.

His father looked over at him. "I was planning to."

Seth's heart clenched in his chest when he thought of seeing his mother again. An ache that was part longing, part fear. But he'd made up his mind the other day while he'd sat by Isaac's side.

Even if the decision made him feel fragile inside, like he'd fragment into a thousand pieces with the slightest misstep, he had to go see her.

"Do you think I could go with you?"

His father nearly dropped his mug. Hot coffee sloshed over the rim before he could steady his hold.

"I want to see her." It came out so quiet that Seth wasn't entirely sure his father had heard him, but then he nodded in agreement.

"We can go now if you want," his father said before Seth could second-guess his decision.

"Let me grab my coat," Seth replied.

He headed out of the kitchen and to the closet where they kept their jackets. The door was already open and Seth's hands shook as he took his coat down from its hanger. Once he had it on, he headed back in the direction he'd come but didn't make it entirely to the kitchen as his father stood in the hallway with his keys in hand.

"You ready, son?" he asked. A hesitant smile pulled at his mouth, as if he expected Seth to change his mind.

Seth nodded though, and his father's smile grew.

Together they made their way down the hall and out the front door to the car.

The drive wasn't long, but Seth spent the entirety of it staring out the car window but not seeing any of the scenery as it passed them by. His mind was filled with questions, with worry.

How would his mother react to seeing him after all these years? Would she turn out to be like the woman of his nightmares? Or had the years gentled her?

The two-story brick building came into view up ahead and Seth's stomach twisted. Nerves made the skin along the back of his neck prickle and his face go numb, a shiver running down into his gut.

How was he supposed to do this? How was he supposed to look the woman that had held his head underwater while he'd struggled for his life in the eye and call her "mom"? Fear sat like a cold ball of lead in his stomach and all he wanted to do now was run. Run, and never look back. Run and forget her. Forget everything. Forget his questions and his guilt and his pain.

The car came to a stop. The engine stuttered to a halt when his father turned the key, pulled it out of the ignition, and glanced at Seth as if to ask, "Are you ready? Are you sure?"

Seth gave a quick nod in reply to the silent question that resided in his father's blue eyes. A lie to push them forward. A lie that ached in Seth's chest as he stepped from the car and closed the door before he moved to follow his father.

In truth, Seth wasn't ready. He wasn't sure.

The lobby of the building was dimly lit and had scuffed linoleum floors. A picture of flowers hung crooked between two chairs that sat up against the wall. The space was otherwise empty save for the front desk.

His father didn't give any of it a glance. He headed straight for the woman who sat with a polite yet tired smile behind the screen of a computer.

"Seth." His father beckoned him over with a wave of his hand.

Seth stepped up beside him to turn over any items that could be potentially dangerous if his mother were to get a hold of them. He didn't have much. His car keys. A few coins. His cellphone.

Seth's eyes drifted to the heavy door with a black keycard reader next to it. The light on the scanner was red and solid, the door locked like a prison. Like the place his mother should have been.

When the light clicked over to green, the door opened and a man with graying hair that Seth assumed was one of the doctors stepped into the lobby. He wasn't wearing a lab coat, but the way he carried himself spoke to some form of authority.

The doctor introduced himself, but Seth forgot the name almost as soon as he heard it, distracted by his thoughts. It barely registered when he kept on talking.

Seth knew he should listen. That it was probably something important about procedure or safety. His safety, most likely, because he was the one she'd go after if something went wrong. The one in the most danger was him.

Before he knew it, they were being directed through the entrance, then down a hall to a pair of double doors. They opened with the swipe of a keycard and the press of a firm hand like the last one.

Another hallway lay before them, this one with rooms on either side. The doctor led them to a door on the right, three rooms down from the place they'd come in.

It was white with a number on it that Seth didn't even process before it was opened and they were led inside.

The room was small. With only a table, a few chairs, and the cause of so much grief—his mother.

She sat in a chair in front of the table. Her long brown hair falling down around her shoulders. She was dressed plainly and looked older than Seth remembered. There were lines around her mouth and crow's feet he had no memory of pulled at the corners of her eyes.

Her eyes widened when she saw him, surprise clear in the way her gaze swept over him and how she straightened in her chair, like she thought maybe this was some cruel joke of her mind.

Maybe this was a bad idea. Maybe he shouldn't have come. How could this help either of them?

His mother's chair scraped against the floor, and the sound was enough to make Seth flinch. This had definitely been a bad idea, but she was already moving toward him, her hand reaching out, like something from one of his nightmares. Seth wanted to hide behind his father. He wanted to back away from the cool press of her fingers against his cheek. He felt like that terrified six-year-old boy all over again.

This wasn't a nightmare, though. This was really her. His mother. His attempted murderer.

Seth's mind was torn between memories. Between contradictions. The mother who'd loved him and the woman who had tried to drown him. One and the same, and he wasn't sure which stood before him now.

Did she still think him evil? A monster? Did she still want to end his life? Or was she now more the mother that had dropped marshmallows in his hot chocolate and pushed him on the swing when he was little?

"You came?" Her voice was soft, questioning, as if she could hardly believe it herself. As if she thought it entirely possible Seth was a figment of her imagination, no more real than the spirit she had thought possessed him.

"Hi, Mom," Seth managed, even though he still half-expected her to wrap her hands around his throat.

Her gaze softened, as if hearing him call her "Mom" meant the world to her. "Baby, I'm so sorry. I never wanted to hurt you like that."

For years he'd wished to hear those words, but now that he had it did nothing to soothe him. It made rage swell in his chest, an angry flush spreading up his neck into his face.

"Then why did you?"

"Seth—" his father said from behind him.

"No, Dad, I need this. I need to know why."

His mother looked at him sadly as she smoothed a hand over his hair. "Because you're dangerous, sweetheart."

A chill ran down Seth's spine. A dogged sense of fear made him pull back and away sharply.

"Is that what the voices tell you?"

"It's what Myra tells me, and it's what I've seen for myself." His mother took a step toward him again and Seth took two back. "There's a spirit living inside you, Seth. The oldest raven familiar in existence. One of the first ever created."

It should have been nothing more than one of his mother's delusions. Only Seth knew exactly what she was talking about—and he could see the black in her eyes, the way he remembered the yellow in Gabriel's.

"You're a famirian. That's why you had the locket with the lavender," Seth realized in a broken whisper. A hand went to the silver chain around his neck. "And you think I'm one—"

"I know you are!"—His mother grabbed him around the throat, and Seth's hands caught at her wrists, trying to pull her hands away—"He's inside you! Don't you understand? Silas is inside you!"

His father made it to him before any of the staff. He only just managed to pull him free on his own. His arms around Seth as he dragged him back and toward the door that the doctor already held open. Seth dazed and not much help in the process.

"No. Wait. Seth!" his mother cried, an orderly holding her back when she tried to follow. "Seth! You can't let him out! You can't let him out!"

Seth sucked in mouthfuls of air once he was back in the hallway to calm the way his heart raced. He could hear his mother on the other side of the door, still screaming that he was dangerous. That they needed to kill him.

Seth turned and punched the wall in front of him. A dull thunk sounded under his fist when it bruised against the plaster, but the pain that radiated through his hand barely registered. He was too angry to care about the throb of his knuckles or his father yelling his name.

A hand caught his arm when he pulled back for a second swing and Seth tried to jerk away.

"Seth, stop. Stop."

Seth turned, defeated, to hide his face against his father's jacket. Each stuttered breath he took pulled in the smell of dry wall and whiskey. It was the smell of the construction sites his father worked and the after-hours bars he frequented to escape his own pain.

Seth wanted to yell, but instead he cried—great heaving sobs that tightened the knot in his chest and made his heart throb with the tug of despair.

# TWENTY-FIVE

Seth fought back a second wave of tears as they drove away, his head against the window and his arms wrapped tightly around himself.

It had taken his father nearly forty minutes to get him calmed down enough that he could walk himself to the car, another twenty once he was in the vehicle for the tears to stop completely, and he still barely felt like he could hold it in.

Seth hadn't told his father the truth behind what was said between him and his mother. If he was honest about the famirians he'd probably find himself locked up at Oak View just like her.

What Seth needed was some space to think and figure out what to do. A quiet place where people weren't likely to bother him.

"Could you drop me off at the train stop up ahead?"

His father looked over at him, those pale-blue eyes of his trying to get a read on Seth.

"I want to go see Isaac."

"I could drive you," his father offered.

"I think I'd rather take the train."

His father sighed, and idled the car to a stop along the side of the road.

Seth unbuckled his seat belt and hurried to get the door open to slip from the car. He didn't wait for his dad to pull away before he walked off.

The train pulled up a few minutes later and the sound of footsteps milled around him as he stepped on board with the other passengers before collapsing into a seat near a window. His gaze followed the scenery as the train moved along without really seeing any of it.

The revelations about his mother were a struggle to accept. All these years, he'd thought she was out of her mind. That the things she'd yelled that night had been part of an elaborate delusion. But she knew about the famirians, was apparently one herself, and she was certain Seth was as well. If that was true—what did that mean for him?

Seth wished he could talk to Gabriel. That he could ask him if it could be true. If there was some sign that he could look for. But Gabriel had blocked his number days ago.

He was on his own.

That simple fact had Seth squeezing his eyes closed. It shouldn't hurt so much. Being alone with his pain was a burden he was used to bearing. But it felt heavier now that he remembered what it was like to not carry it all on his own.

He got off at the closest stop to the hospital, glad he could finally step off the musty train and walk in the open air again. Even if the walk was a quick one from his stop.

Isaac's mother was dozing in a chair not far from the bed when Seth arrived at the room. Her head rested awkwardly against the back of it, her body slumped low and tilted to the side.

Seth touched a hand to her shoulder, and she startled from her doze. Then her gaze lifted. Her eyes were red-rimmed and bleary as she stared up at him.

"Have you been here all night?" Seth asked.

"It's hard to leave him. He doesn't have much time left and I..." She trailed off, and her eyes moved from Seth to her son, who lay still and quiet save for the labored sounds of his breaths. "I don't want him to die surrounded by strangers, because I left him for a few hours to sleep."

"You need to look after yourself too though."

Isaac's mother gave a tired sigh. "I don't feel right leaving him. Not when... They said it could be any time now. Noah went home to pick up Nell."

"You need to look after yourself too though."

Isaac's mother rose from her chair. Unsteady on her feet with exhaustion. "I might step out for a moment to get a coffee at least."

"I'll sit with him while you're gone."

"You're such a kind boy," she said softly as she hugged Seth to her. "I can see why he loved you so much."

Seth returned the hug and said, "I loved him too." A part of him still did. A part of him always would.

Finally, she relinquished her hold on Seth and headed for the still-open door, her shoes tapping quietly on her way out.

Once she'd gone Seth dragged a chair closer to the hospital bed with a scrape of metal against the tile floor before he dropped his backpack to the floor with a thud. Isaac didn't stir with either sound, and Seth pulled in an anxious breath as he looked him over.

He looked frail. Too thin in the white hospital gown that made his already sallow skin seem even sicklier. His eyes were sunken and ringed in deep shadow. They were closed like he was asleep, but Seth wasn't sure he'd wake up this time.

He didn't know how long he sat and stared at Isaac. Maybe a few minutes. Maybe over an hour. He'd meant to get the book he'd left from last time out to read to him, but hadn't been able to drag his eyes away from the rise and fall of Isaac's chest.

Seth lifted his head at the sound of a knock. A woman with brown hair that fell well past her shoulders stood in the doorway, the strap of a green handbag resting on her shoulder.

"Are you Seth?" she asked, and when Seth nodded, she added, "I'm Ruth. Gabriel sent for me."

Seth stared at her, nonplussed. After everything Seth had done. After every lie he'd told. Gabriel had still sent the healer he'd spoken of. He'd still kept this promise.

Ruth wasn't anything like what Seth had expected. He had thought she'd be older. Maybe dressed in clothes that were a little eccentric, or even dark, with talismans of gold around her neck or bracelets that clinked on her pale wrists.

But the woman that stood before him looked younger than his mother—somewhere in her twenties, maybe—with gray eyes and a rounded nose that softened the angles of her face, the point of her chin.

The clothes she wore were simple. Jeans and a green blouse. As if she were just an ordinary woman come to visit a sick friend.

"Thank you for coming," Seth finally said as he rose from where he sat.

He'd never told Isaac's parents about the healer. He'd never managed the courage, and then after Gabriel had left him, he'd thought it no longer mattered.

"Did you get his parent's permission?"

"I... um..."

Isaac's mother walked back into the room. A cup of coffee in her hand. Her timing was so perfect it was almost as if they had summoned her.

"Who's this?"

"This is Ruth." Seth moved to stand before Isaac's mother. "She might be able to save Isaac."

"How?"

"I'm a healer," Ruth explained. "My methods aren't conventional, but they work."

Isaac's mother looked more than skeptical. She looked downright wary.

"Please let her try," Seth pleaded. "Please. If there's even a chance this could work..."

Isaac's mother looked between them and then at her son. Her eyes brimming with tears as she watched the shallow rise and fall of his chest.

Seth took a relieved breath when she nodded her agreement.

"Please do what you can," Isaac's mother implored.

Ruth closed the door and turned the lock before she crossed the room to set her handbag down on the bed at Isaac's side. Something within shifted, alive, agitated. The green pleather seemed to breathe with it before it settled.

"What was that?" Seth asked, staring nervously.

"How much did Gabriel tell you about the process?" Ruth asked as she shut off the heart monitor.

"Nothing really," Seth admitted as he folded his arms over his chest and watched her warily. "He just said that you could help."

"Well, then, this may be a bit alarming for the two of you."

"Alarming how?" Isaac's mother questioned.

Ruth undid the metal clasp at the top of the bag with a soft click. A restless hiss rose from within when she opened it. Her hand went inside without hesitation.

Seth took an instinctive step back from her, from the snake she held carefully when she pulled her hand out, its wide body coiled around her arm.

A copperhead by the looks of it. Reddish markings shaped like hour-glasses ran along its length between crossbands of tan, except the end of it. That part was brown, like someone had dipped its tail in a bucket of paint.

The snake looked at Seth with dark orange eyes that made his skin crawl. Its black slitted pupils studied him as its pink tongue flicked out to smell the air, and it turned its V-shaped head away from Seth and toward Isaac when Ruth spoke to it.

Her words didn't seem like a mystic or foreign language. They sounded like English. But it was spoken so quietly Seth couldn't pick out exact words.

The sound of it was melodic. Soft, yet somehow lofty. Like a song or a prayer.

The overhead lights flickered in time with Ruth's voice, the hum and crackle of electricity an accompaniment to her aria, and the very air in the room seemed to simmer with its energy.

A warmth settled over Seth's skin and seeped into him. A tingle ran through his whole being with its presence, and something deep inside him stirred.

The swell of heat inside Seth built with the energy in the room. A twinge that pricked like needles climbed up his spine and pain spread out in his head, sharp enough that he closed his eyes briefly and drew in a harsh breath.

Another hiss reverberated from the snake as it slithered forward through light and shadow, lowering itself gradually from Ruth's arm to dangle over Isaac's chest.

Isaac's mother took a few hurried steps forward, no doubt thinking this couldn't be right. This couldn't be how they saved her son.

"Don't," Ruth said as she raised her other hand in warning and Isaac's mother stopped. "This part is delicate."

The snake swayed, letting out another hiss, and Isaac stretched beneath the sheets with a feeble breath. His head turned slowly to face the snake, his eyes blinking open with effort.

Even with how weak Isaac was, Seth had expected some kind of reaction from him. Some response of fear. It'd only be natural. But there was nothing other than the movement of his lips—a response to the snake's next hiss that Seth couldn't make out.

Ruth smiled, pleased. "It's done."

"What's done?" Isaac's mother asked.

She didn't answer. Instead she reached out with steady hands and snapped the snake's neck. The sharp crack of bone made Seth stumble back, but his eyes never left the snake that now hung limp from Ruth's hands.

She set its body on the bed next to Isaac. Who had started seizing in much the same way Gabriel had that day at the farm, and it was horrifying then, but it was terrifying now, because Isaac was so weak. So sick.

When Isaac went still and limp like the snake at his side, Seth was convinced that he'd died. But then Isaac jerked, his eyes going wide as his mouth panted open.

He turned in the space of a second, leaned forward over the bed railing, and heaved. A spray of grayish-pink gunk spattered over the floor while more leaked from his ears.

Seth grimaced at the sound of it, at the quake and shudder in Isaac's body as he retched.

"Oh god, what did you do?" Isaac's mother exclaimed.

"I saved him," Ruth said with a smile.

And sure enough, when Isaac stopped vomiting, he took a deeper breath.

A full breath. The first breath Seth had heard him take in a while that didn't sound like it was a heartbeat away from a death rattle.

"Isaac?"

Isaac raised his gaze to Seth with his name. That grayish pink goo was smeared around his lips and oozed from the corner of his mouth, but his eyes were clear. Focused. Cognizant.

"Seth."

It was the sound of his name that drew Seth in closer at last. It was the orange in Isaac's eyes that made him falter before he reached the bed.

A burst of brightness around the pupil bled into the rest of the iris, similar to what Gabriel had, but colored like the eyes of the copperhead that now lay lifeless beside him. The similarities were unmistakable, even if Isaac's eyes were ringed in orange, and Gabriel's in yellow. Isaac was a famirian now. Just like Gabriel.

There was an ache behind Seth's own eyes, a buzz of noise in his ears that made him blink and shake his head.

Ruth was saying something to Isaac and his mother, explaining things to them probably, but Seth couldn't seem to focus on the words. He stumbled out of the room, hoping a more open space might help. It didn't stop the pain, or the way spots danced in front of his eyes.

A wave of dizziness had him sitting on the floor so gravity couldn't bring him to rest across the tiles against his will. He told himself it was the adrenaline of the situation, the shock of witnessing what could only be defined as magic. But even as he thought it he knew it wasn't true.

Seth wept breathlessly as the pain in his skull spread like a hot knife through him and he tipped over onto his back, darkness hemming in along the edges of his vision. He opened his mouth to scream, but he couldn't get any sound out. He felt a rush of panic and heard a ringing in his ears before the world blinked out.

# TWENTY-SIX

It was the pain that woke Seth, a steady throb behind his eyes that made his brow furrow and his eyelids squeeze closed again.

His chin felt strangely damp, and when he licked his lips, they tasted like pennies. Like copper and grit.

He opened his eyes with some difficulty, not to see the ceiling of the hospital, but a cloudy night sky through the bare branches of trees.

He struggled to sit up. His body heavy. Numb. The forced movement made his head spin and sweat break out on his skin.

He pressed his palms to the dirt, thinking for a moment as he sat and shuddered that he'd be sick.

A sound came from somewhere behind him. Distant, but not so much so that he couldn't tell it was the rumble of an engine. If he headed in that direction, he'd eventually find a road, and maybe from there he could get his bearings.

Sticks and dry leaves pricked his socked feet as he stood. His legs shook like he hadn't used them in days, and with his first step he stumbled and fell back to the leaf strewn ground.

His hand shot out to catch himself, pain radiating up his arm as he took the impact on his wrist. With a groan he buckled under his own weight and his hands slipped through something wet as he landed on his stomach. Whatever it was felt slick and warm in a way mud wouldn't.

Seth raised his head with a grimace. The sleeves of his hoodie were soaked, and he could feel dirt and dead leaves sticking to the skin of his hands with the dampness he'd landed in.

A melodic ring cut through the air. Repetitive. Insistent.

His phone. He'd forgotten he'd put it in the pocket of his hoodie, but it wasn't there now. No. The ringing came from out in the darkness.

It sounded close. Somewhere ahead of him, maybe.

With a shaky breath Seth shifted forward on his stomach in the direction he thought the noise was coming from. He reached a hand out into the darkness as he went, trembling fingers patting along the ground blindly.

The ringing stopped just as abruptly as it had begun. The renewed silence was almost as unnerving as the darkness that pressed in on him, yet still he searched.

Where is it? Where is it? Where is it? he thought frantically as he pushed himself forward with legs that didn't want to cooperate, his mind just as repetitive in his desperation as the ringing of his phone had been.

His breath caught when his hand happened upon something else. His fingers sunk down into whatever it was with a wet squelch before he could snatch his hand away.

He recognized the smell of blood before he saw it, before the moon slipped from beneath the cloud cover to bathe the forest floor in subdued light that painted everything in shades of gray.

A body lay motionless only a short distance from him, the mouth slit from ear to ear and the chest and stomach cavity a gaping wound.

Splintered ribs poked up through flesh to reflect dully in the moonlight, and viscera stretched out over the ground. A few piles lay here and there in twisting spires, as if someone had been trying to make sandcastles out of the intestines.

One such pile sat only inches from where Seth lay, glistening in the moonlight and sending steam rising into the air. Still warm. Still dripping with the blackness of blood.

Seth opened his mouth to scream, but his voice seemed trapped. Only a squeak of sound escaped him.

Adam. It was Adam.

Even with the ghoulish grin carved into his face, Seth still recognized his ex-boyfriend.

An irregular lump lay on the ground just beside the pile of intestines closest to Seth, caked in the same oily black that covered Seth's hands and sleeves and spilled from Adam's body. It took him a moment to realize it was a heart, with large bloody chunks torn free of the muscle. Missing, Seth thought. Swallowed, he realized, as he remembered the dampness on his chin and the taste on his lips.

Seth's hand went to his mouth then dropped just as quickly to the ground as his stomach clenched and he heaved. His body rocked forward as a sour metallic taste coated his tongue and chunks of what he'd eaten pressed against the inside of his throat.

The smell of bile and chewed muscle made his stomach twist as it hit the dried leaves of the forest floor in clumps, made him press a hand to his belly as he retched again.

His body shook with the strain, and with the knowledge of what he was throwing up.

His hand trembled when he wiped it over his mouth to clear his lips and chin of saliva and bits of gore once his stomach had settled enough that he could raise his head. He only smeared blood over his skin.

*You wanted this,* a voice accused, the sound of it so close it made Seth's head snap around, thinking someone had spoken right up against his ear. He brought his hands up as the voice continued, pressed his palms flat to his ears. *You know you did.*

Dry leaves scraped Seth's skin. His hair and cheeks were sticky with blood and smudged with bits of the forest floor, but he didn't care. He didn't care because that voice was as clear and as real as the panicked thump of his heart in his chest. But it was inside his head. A hollow echo in his skull that he couldn't block out with the pressure of shaking hands over his ears.

*You hated him. You wanted him dead.*

Yes. Yes, he'd hated Adam. Had fantasized about horrible things happening to him. Had toyed with imaginings of his death. But he hadn't really wanted him to die. He'd only wanted to know he was safe from him.

Seth's breaths came quick and shallow as he choked back tears and stared transfixed at the wide, lifeless eyes and the too-long grin from Adam's mouth being sliced upward at the corners.

He remembered the first time he'd kissed that mouth. Sweet and slow, and full of all the promises of what could be between them. But things hadn't ended up that way. Things had gone so horribly, terribly wrong.

*It's what he deserved.*

Seth touched a hand to his face with the words, with the memory of pain blossoming hot and sudden across his cheek.

The voice in his head seemed all too happy to pluck forth those memories from Seth's mind and play them for him on a loop.

*We should have killed him sooner.*

"Who the hell are you?"

*You already know who I am.*

Seth's eyes widened as he recalled the name his mother had shouted that day at Oak View.

It was true. He knew exactly who it was.

"Silas..."

A ringing from the pile of intestines in front of Seth cut his thoughts short. His body went cold on realizing in the same instant where his cellphone was.

Seth grimaced, his eyes squinting with disgust as he slid his hand into the slick lopsided pillar in front of him. The intestines leaned toward him to slide down over his wrist while he worked to reach his phone. They seemed to follow him when he pulled his hand back, his phone clutched tight between his fingers.

The wet folds of tissue coiled around his wrist like a snake and moved to slither up his arm, warm and alive and wet with the black of a serpent that would have been a brilliant red in the light of the sun.

It shifted in the moonlight, winding tighter, and with a stuttered cry Seth jerked his arm free.

The intestines toppled over the forest floor. Not alive. Dead. Just as dead as the rest of Adam.

A low rumble reverberated in Seth's skull like thunder, and he realized the thing inside his head was laughing at him.

Seth's eyes darted away from the guts strewn over the ground. The thing in his head was toying with him—maybe for the simple pleasure of it, or maybe for some agenda Seth couldn't even fathom.

He turned his attention to his phone, not letting whispered words or the stink of death distract him.

The light from the screen made the blood smeared over it look red instead of black. Seth did his best to ignore the numb horror of his reality, to look past the film of red to the list of missed calls. The last two had been from Isaac. The one before that from Evelyn.

Seth's finger hovered over Evelyn's name. They hadn't spoken since the day they'd fought and he wanted to call her back more than anything, but the blood on his hands stopped him.

He looked at Adam, his guts spilling out of him and his mockery of a Cheshire Cat grin.

Seth couldn't call her. He couldn't call anyone. Not while he was covered in the blood of his ex-boyfriend.

With a shaky breath, he shoved the cellphone in the pocket of his hoodie and rose unsteadily to his feet. His first few steps almost sent him sprawling to the ground once more, but he caught himself against a tree. The rough bark dug into his palms as he leaned heavily against the trunk.

He heard water hit the leaves overhead. It was starting to rain.

He pushed carefully off the tree with a deep breath once he felt steady enough, resigning himself to slow, measured steps as he made his way in the direction he believed the road to be. He held the flashlight on his phone up in front of him to light his way when the moon slipped back behind the cover of clouds.

It was when he looked back the way he'd come, the light on his phone held up in front of him, that he saw them.

Ravens.

Dozens of them. Hunkered down over Adam's body like it was just any other animal carcass, curved beaks pulling strings of skin and meat free of the corpse to gobble down.

The large black birds were clearing up the evidence. One swallowed chunk at a time.

He wondered who would come for the bones, if wolves would claim them. Where there were ravens, there were often wolves, and the thought had Seth turning to check the darkness, light held aloft as he scanned for the reflection of eyes in the underbrush.

The fact he saw none did little to ease his fear. His heart still beat like a caged bird against his ribs, but he dared to turn his back on Adam's corpse to continue his trek through the woods.

The rumble of the engine was his only guidance through the trees. It grew louder, closer, and eventually light filtered in through the branches up ahead, an artificial glow that had Seth quickening his steps the best he could to reach the road. Only, when he stepped from the tree line, he found not a road but a parking lot for a campground.

It was dark here too, except for the streetlamps like the one he stood under that spilled yellow light out across the semicircle parking lot in front of him, illuminating the few cars that occupied the space and glancing off the brick rest station up ahead.

Seth knew this place. He'd been here once before, back when he and Adam had been dating. Adam had invited him on a camping trip with his family.

He recognized the van up ahead too. The motor still running, but the seats empty. One of the rear doors ajar. A bloody streak along the metal, as if someone had fought to hold on to the door while being dragged away.

Seth heard the echo of a scream in his memory. The sinking feeling in his gut told him it was Adam's blood from when he'd fought for his life.

He wondered how long it would take the rest of the Fuller family to come looking. Or were they dead as well? Had they been dragged off into the woods somewhere? Their bodies left bloody and broken out among the trees for the ravens to feast on?

It was raining harder now. The blood slipped down the car and off Seth in rivulets.

Seth's socks squelched against the pavement of the parking lot as he made his way to the still-running car. Each step left behind a red footprint that was washed clean almost as soon as it appeared.

There was a duffel lying in the back seat, half open and spilling its contents over the floor of the car. Seth pulled a pair of jeans loose from the tangle of clothes that poured out of it. Then a green shirt, simply because it was the closest one to his hand.

He moved on to the brick building. The door was locked, but the handle came off with some convincing from a rock, and the door swung open with a groan when Seth curled his fingers along the edge and pulled.

After a few moments of fumbling along the wall, he found the switch for the lights. They flickered to life overhead and cast the small space into a greater brightness than he had expected, and he blinked through the sting in his eyes until they adjusted.

Seth dropped the clean and now damp clothes to the floor once inside, then shucked off his hoodie. He barely heard it land when he dropped it, too consumed by the image he saw in the mirror.

He was covered in blood. Bits of leaves and dirt were practically glued to his skin. But it was his eyes that had him leaning forward.

His pupils looked dilated, but the black fanned out into the brown of his iris, the way the orange in Isaac's and the yellow in Gabriel's did.

Whatever had happened to them, it was happening to Seth too.

His phone rang. The name on the screen told him it was Evelyn calling again. This time Seth answered.

# TWENTY-SEVEN

Seth didn't know how long he waited out on the road, soaked by the rain and staring off into nothing, doing his best to keep his mind just as blank as the darkness that stretched out before him.

He didn't look at his phone again to check the time, but eventually headlights broke through the dark as a car drove up. Evelyn had arrived at last.

She stepped from the vehicle, though she left the motor running.

Her eyes flicked over him and he wondered if she could tell the clothes he wore weren't his own, that he'd stolen them from a dead man.

"Seth." She took a step closer to rest a hand against his arm. "Hey, are you okay?"

"Fine." Seth glanced back toward the woods.

"Is that blood?" Evelyn asked as she gestured to a spot on the sleeve of the shirt he wore.

"Can we just please get out of here?"

Evelyn looked wary, but nodded all the same, and Seth let her lead him to the car—her hand still on his arm, her steps slow to keep pace with his own.

At last he was inside the vehicle and watching the darkness swallow up the tree line in the rearview mirror. Only when it was no longer visible did Seth sag back in his seat.

"I'm sorry I hadn't gotten back to you until now," Evelyn said. "Nana has been having issues, and this whole thing with you and that guy—"

"Gabriel."

"Gabriel, yeah. I want to be happy for you. It's just—"

"You don't have to worry about him and me anymore," Seth said sullenly. "He found out I was lying, and we broke up."

"Oh," Evelyn said quietly. "I'm sorry."

Seth looked out the car window as they drove onto the overpass that led toward Twin Oaks, and his eyes drifted to the concrete barricade along its side. His mind was still filled with the image of Adam's eviscerated body. The way his eyes had been almost doll-like, vacant and glassy. His face forever carved into a ghoulish grin.

*You enjoyed it, though,* Silas whispered.

"No!" Seth protested aloud and Evelyn shot him a perturbed look, brow furrowed and mouth slightly open in concern.

*You don't have to lie. Not to me.*

Seth clapped his hands over his ears. He couldn't block Silas out though. He was inside him. He could feel him roil beneath his flesh. An itch like a rash in his bones, in his blood, making his fingers twitch and his teeth scrape together as he fought to keep control.

*What do you think Evelyn will taste like when we get our teeth in her?*

Seth squeezed his eyes shut. He still had blood under his nails from the last life it had taken. Moments in time came back to him in bits and pieces of memory that weren't quite his. Fragmented and incomplete, but enough for Seth to understand what it had used him to do.

Adam had been alive when they'd disemboweled him. He'd been conscious as his intestines were pulled from his belly and played with in the dirt. His heart was only ripped from his chest when they'd grown bored with the panicked sounds he'd made.

*I always found witches tasted sweet, but a little tart. Like blackberries with honey.*

"Stop the car!"

Evelyn looked at Seth like he was crazy. Maybe he was. Maybe he was just as sick in the head as he'd thought his mother to be all this time.

"Seth—"

"Just stop the car!"

Evelyn looked worried, but she did as he asked, idling to the side of the overpass near the thin strip of sidewalk to put the car in park.

Seth immediately stepped from the vehicle and staggered a short distance away before he stopped in front of the barricade. He clung to the wall as he took deep, shaking breaths.

He could feel it shift inside him. Its energy made his very marrow thrum. He was losing himself to it.

We can't let him out. No, no, no. We can't let him get out. His mother's words from that awful night rang in his ears so clearly she could have been right beside him.

Maybe the pond had been meant as a mercy. Because she'd been right. They couldn't let him out.

Seth's hands shook as he pushed them flat atop the concrete barricade. His arms ached as he raised himself.

"What are you doing?" Evelyn yelled, and he could hear her approach quickly as he pulled himself up on the wall.

He didn't look back at her when she spoke. He kept his gaze focused on the traffic below.

Suicidal ideation was nothing new to Seth. But anytime he'd gone beyond just the thought of it to staring at a handful of pills, or pressing a razor blade to his skin, something had stopped him.

He'd thought it'd been spite. The thought of giving his mother the satisfaction of his death rising inside him each time to leave a bitter taste in his mouth. Now he wondered if it had been the thing inside him influencing him in ways he hadn't even realized.

"Seth, this isn't funny."

He looked back at her then. At the tears on her cheeks and the red locks of hair that blew around her face in the wind. She looked like she was caught between grabbing him and the fear of causing him to fall.

Cars zipped past behind and below. If the people that drove by saw him, they made no effort to stop. He wondered if one of them would call the police, though.

"Please just come down," Evelyn begged. "Please. Whatever has happened, we can figure it out. We can fix it."

Seth looked away from her and laughed. A bitter, hollowed out sound that just made his body hurt. No one could fix it. He was the problem.

"She was right all along," Seth said. "She was right. We can't let him out."

"Seth—"

"Take care of my dad for me."

Seth let himself fall forward.

He let gravity take him, and he heard a gut-wrenching cry from Evelyn just for a moment before the sounds of the wind and the traffic below eclipsed it.

He was prepared for the hard impact of the asphalt, or even the sharp crack as his body broke against a windshield. He wasn't prepared for something to grab him. Thick and dark and swirling around him, it jerked him to a stop so his feet hovered above the ground.

Cars blared their horns in warning. But their headlights barely penetrated the inky blackness as they careened around him with a squeal of tires and crashed into one another.

Seth looked down at himself, at the oil-like substance that seemed to have come out of the night, only to realize it rose out of his skin.

It didn't hurt. It actually felt familiar, in a way. Like he'd always known it and it had always been with him. And then he realized why—it was the darkness from his dreams.

Seth stared at the stuff that poured out of him and now he could see it wasn't black after all. It shimmered with flecks of brightness. Flickering dots and swirls of color. Seth swore he saw galaxies taking shape inside it as it shifted and sparked, and he wondered how something so beautiful could be so terrifying.

Reality seemed to bend in on itself as the ever-shifting mass wrapped more tightly around him and tugged him forward with a sharp jerk. The suddenness of it made Seth's stomach drop, and as he kept moving, flying forward, he squeezed his eyes shut against the streaks of light and sound.

The sensation stopped without warning and Seth was dropped to his knees, disoriented by the wet grass he felt beneath his hands rather than the road he had plummeted toward only moments ago. The way reality had twisted around him along with the suddenness of the change in his environment made his already queasy stomach clench and he had to fight his body's urge to vomit.

When his stomach had settled and the ground no longer felt like it would spin away from beneath him, he looked around.

He was home. The familiar blue Foursquare was just in front of him, its porch light shining over the lawn.

Seth rose shakily to his feet and took slow steps to the porch in a daze. He stopped when he reached for the doorknob and the blood on his sleeve reminded him what he'd done. No. What it had done. The thing inside him. The thing his mother had tried to kill that night.

He wished she had. He wished his father had helped her rather than pulled him coughing from the water. It would have changed everything. It would have saved a life. A person was dead because he'd lived. If he didn't figure out a way to stop this thing, more would likely die.

The television inside the house was just loud enough to be heard through the wood of the door. Some kind of comedy by the sound of it. The muffled noise of his father's laughter hung in the air above the voices on the television.

Seth wondered what his father would do if he found out the blood wasn't Seth's own. That bloody chunks of what had once been Adam were now strewn through the woods. A human being that Seth had once loved more than anyone. Even if he shouldn't have.

*We should kill the rest.*

The rest.

Isaac. Seth's first love. His first everything. The boy with the beautiful blue eyes and wavy dark-blond hair that used to slip poetry into Seth's locker and reach back to hold Seth's hand beneath his desk in language arts class. Who kissed Seth with a smile on his lips every time.

And then there was Gabriel, who was only ever trying to do the right thing. Who broke Seth's heart out of integrity rather than cruelty. Who Seth ached for even now.

*You'd feel better if they were dead,* Silas promised in a voice that had grown weaker. Seth didn't feel him stir beneath his skin so viciously, though his words felt like oil inside the folds of his brain, slick and cloying all at once. *Hearts taste like closure.*

"No," Seth said back to him. "No. You don't touch them."

Silas seemed aggravated by his words, his choices, or maybe hiss inability to do anything about it. Whichever it was, whatever strength Silas had over him seemed to have faded. Maybe saving them had taken some power from him.

The door was unlocked when Seth turned the knob, a small blessing given he didn't have his keys on him.

If Seth was quiet, maybe he could make it up to his room without being noticed. The door closed behind him with a soft click as he eased it shut, and he held his breath, praying that his father hadn't heard.

When the TV didn't shut off and there were no footsteps that came down the hallway, Seth tiptoed to the staircase. He picked his way carefully up the steps, doing his best to avoid the ones that would creak and alert his father to his presence.

He'd made it about halfway up before his cellphone went off in the back pocket of the jeans he wore. The melodic noise sounded more like a death knell to his panicked ears than a ringtone as he fumbled to pull the phone from his pocket.

The volume on the TV lowered and after a beat of silence, his father called out, "Seth?"

"Yeah," Seth called back.

"I thought I told you to go to your room," his father said, and Seth heard the creak of the sofa with the broken spring as his father rose from where he'd been seated.

"I was just getting a glass of water," Seth lied as he hurried the rest of the way up the stairs with the approach of heavy footfalls. "Sorry. I'm going back up now."

The darkness of Seth's room felt like safety as he shut the door quickly behind him. He closed his eyes and leaned back against the cool wood with a deep breath.

"Where have you been?" a voice asked from the darkness, and Seth let out a terrified squeak as he dropped his phone to fumble his hand out along the wall for the light switch. His body moved sideways until he found it.

The light came on with a brightness that made Seth blink against it and he squinted at his bed, where Isaac sat staring back at him.

"Isaac? What the hell are you doing?"

"You didn't answer your phone."

"Okay. Well, there are better ways to deal with that than lurking in the dark of my bedroom like some crazed stalker."

"Would you have preferred I showed up under your window blasting 'In Your Eyes' on a boom box?"

"No," Seth replied with annoyance as his eyes drifted to his open bedroom window. "But I'd prefer it if you didn't climb in through it in the middle of the night."

Isaac's eyes roved over Seth from head to toe and back again as a slow smirk slipped across his face. "You used to like me climbing through your window in the middle of the night."

Seth grit his teeth against the memory of those nights. He could still remember all too clearly how Isaac's hands had felt on his skin. The warmth of his mouth. The press of his body.

"I never really wanted to break up with you, you know."

"But you did." Seth shook his head then bit at the inside of his cheek as anger swelled in his chest. "I still don't understand why, though. Did you think I wouldn't be there when you needed me? Were you scared I'd push you away?"

"No. You would have run yourself into the ground for me. I knew that," Isaac admitted solemnly. "I ended things because I didn't want my cancer to be the thing that broke you."

"I was already broken," Seth snapped. He took a step forward abruptly enough that Isaac actually leaned back, his eyes blinking up at Seth in bewilderment. "I didn't need to be abandoned and lied to on top of it!"

Isaac looked away. "Seth I—"

"What if you had died?" Seth demanded while doing his best to keep his voice steady. Hold firm in his convictions and push ahead, but his voice wavered when Isaac raised his eyes to meet his glare once more. "Did you think no one at school would ever mention it? Or that your mom wouldn't call me about your funeral?" His hands shook as he pressed them to his chest like he could physically hold the hurt and anger back. "Did you even think for a second what that would have felt like for me? To find out you'd died when I never even knew you were sick or had the chance to say goodbye."

Isaac nodded, accepting the truth of the position he'd put Seth in. "I'm sorry."

"Which changes nothing." Seth shook his head. "So if you came here to try to get back together with me, it's not going to happen. I care about you. I do. But not like that. Not anymore."

"You can't blame a guy for trying."

"Sure I can," Seth replied. "I'm petty that way."

Isaac fell silent. A few minutes passed in which he seemed to contemplate Seth.

"You seem off," Isaac said at last.

Seth blinked at him. Thrown off by the unexpected assertion. "What do you mean?"

Isaac rose from the bed, a fluidity to his movements that hadn't been there back when Seth had dated him. "Like you're nervous."

"I'm fine," Seth lied. "I've actually never been better."

Isaac crossed the room without another word. He reached for him when he got close enough, the touch of his hands heavy on Seth's waist, and Seth drew in a sharp breath as Isaac leaned in. Something about the movement, the way he smelled, gave Seth the horrifying sensation that this wasn't Isaac. This wasn't the boy he'd fallen in love with all those years ago. This wasn't the Isaac that lay dying in a hospital bed only a few hours ago.

What had happened to him? What had happened to the boy with the clumsy habits and the gentle touch. The boy that smelled more like a smoky vanilla than a cloying nutmeg.

The wet flick of a tongue against the skin of his throat made Seth jerk back to clamp a hand to his neck. It had been more of a tickle than a flat-out lick, but it still set Seth's nerves on edge.

"What the fuck, Isaac?"

"You smell like blood."

Seth narrowed his eyes at the lunacy of the statement. "And your tongue is supposed to tell you that how exactly?"

Strong hands pushed at Seth's shirt sleeves, causing them to rise as Isaac's hands slid up along his arms to examine his skin.

Seth sagged back against the wall when he realized what Isaac was doing. "I'm not cutting myself, if that's what you were thinking. I don't do that kind of thing."

"I still worry. When you left the hospital so suddenly I thought something might be wrong."

Isaac's hands slid down. His grip stopped at Seth's wrists and his thumbs moved in soothing circles against the skin there. An old habit of comfort that Seth was tempted to give into after the awful night he'd had.

"So you came to check on me?"

"Partly. The other part, well, you figured that out already."

Seth looked down at the hands on his wrists. He wanted to tell Isaac what had happened. Why he smelled the blood on him, but the thought of putting it out there terrified him.

"Are you sure you're okay?" Isaac's thumbs pressed more firmly to the skin of Seth's wrists. "Your pulse is racing." There was a teasing tone to Isaac's voice when he continued that made Seth bristle. "So either you're excited to see me, or—"

Seth tugged his wrists from Isaac's hold before he could finish.

"I guess it's safe to say it's not your blood?"

Seth shook his head, and he remembered another time Isaac would have been around this same blood. That day in the lunchroom when Isaac had attacked Adam. There'd been so much blood.

The same blood Isaac would smell now. The same blood that Seth could still taste in his mouth.

*The pretty boy will taste better.*

Seth drew in a shaky breath as he remembered Silas's earlier words, how he wanted to eat Isaac's heart, and Seth could feel the hunger he'd tried to ignore inside him like a gnawing void. Whatever little of Adam he'd kept down hadn't been enough to satiate them.

Isaac took a step to the side, then ran a hand over Seth's back. Somehow, that just made it worse. Made the hunger grow. Made the smell of nutmeg flood his nostrils and seem more tantalizing than off-putting.

"You need to leave," Seth said as a wave of nausea rolled through him in opposition to the way his mouth watered, forcing him to swallow back spit before he could speak again. "You need to leave, now."

"Do you really want me to go?"

"Yes." Seth nodded and gestured toward the window with each word. "Go. Get out. Now."

Isaac pulled back from Seth. He looked hurt, but he didn't argue. "Okay. I'll go then."

Seth watched him head for the open window—the one nearest his bed that had the trellis just outside it where ivy grew, the one Isaac had come through so many times before.

Silas wanted Seth to lunge forward to grab Isaac, but he forced himself flat against the wall. His nails tingled, and he arched his palms with a sudden flare of pain, digging the tips of his fingers up through paint and plaster that gave way like old chalk.

Not Isaac, Seth begged in his head. Please. Please. Not Isaac.

*Then who?* Silas hissed back. *You couldn't keep the last one down.*

The last one. Adam. It meant Adam. It meant his heart.

Isaac started to climb out the window, but paused with a hand on the sill. His long legs hung over the edge as he looked back at Seth.

"Isaac, go! Just go!"

Isaac finally disappeared out the window, and Seth squeezed his eyes shut as the thing in his head howled with rage and hunger. He wanted to scream with it, to lash out against what had happened to him. What it had stolen from him.

Seth carefully slid his fingers from the holes they'd made in the wall and stared down at his hands. Long, hooked talons flecked with drywall curved off each digit, the skin just beneath them rough and scaly and black as the foot of a raven.

Seth did scream then. A long, low wail that made his chest ache and his throat raw.

He curled in on himself on the floor as his screams dissolved into tears. He tried to hide his hands in the folds of his shirt as the door slammed open, terrified of how his father would react to him turning into a monster.

"Seth?" his dad called to him gently, like he was far away, and a hand came to rest on his shoulder as he knelt beside him. "Seth, what is it? What's wrong?"

Seth curled his fingers more tightly into the fabric of his shirt. "Go away."

His father didn't leave. Of course not.

"Was it a bad dream?"

"It's my hands." Seth got out a choked breath. "There's something wrong with my hands."

Seth didn't resist when his father tugged his hands away from his chest. Better he see the horror of what Seth truly was sooner rather than later. It wasn't as if he could keep it hidden for long.

"There's nothing wrong with your hands, Seth."

Seth opened his eyes slowly. His vision was blurred by tears, but he could manage to make out ten perfectly normal fingers, five of which currently clutched at his father's hand.

"No." Seth straightened, his damp eyes staring down at his perfectly human fingers. "No. There were talons."

His father squinted at him. Like Seth had lost his mind.

"I-I'm not crazy," Seth whispered to his father, and his voice cracked as he blinked up at him. "They were there. I'm not crazy."

"No one's saying you're crazy, son," his father replied. "You probably just had another one of your nightmares."

Seth shook his head. He'd been awake. He knew he'd been awake. None of it was a dream. It was real.

# TWENTY-EIGHT

The call earlier had been from Evelyn. And it was a call that Seth returned with no small amount of trepidation once his father had left the room.

Evelyn answered after only a single ring. "You're alive?"

A pang of guilt lodged itself in his chest at the sound of her tear-strained voice and the sudden recollection of her screaming his name when he'd jumped.

"Yeah," Seth said. Because what else could he say?

"Good. Because I'm going to kill you!" Evelyn snapped. "What the holy hell were you thinking jumping off like that? And that thing. That darkness that just swallowed you up—"

"Something's wrong with me, Eevee." Seth turned his back on his window and curled in on himself as he stared at the wall from where he lay in bed. "I don't know how to explain it. But something's really wrong with me."

Evelyn huffed brokenly. "That might be the biggest understatement I've ever heard."

"Eevee, I'm sorry," Seth said when he realized he hadn't even apologized for leaving her alone and scared next to her car.

"You know you say that a lot."

The line went quiet and for a moment Seth thought she'd hung up on him, but then she added, "Whatever is going on, though. Whatever this is, I'm here for you."

Seth blinked back tears.

"Come over tomorrow," she continued. "We'll try to figure out what's going on."

"I'm not sure that's a good idea. This thing is dangerous."

"I'm not going to take no for an answer. I'll hunt you down if I have to. You know that."

"I do," Seth agreed. He could hear traffic over the phone and wondered if Evelyn was still out on that overpass, shaken and alone.

"So, I'll see you tomorrow?"

"I'll be there."

"Good."

She hung up, and it left Seth to stare at his phone. There was a smudge of blood on the bottom corner.

He remembered how he'd scrubbed water across the screen with his fingers while in that small brick restroom. How he'd looked up to see several ravens strut in casually to carry his bloodied clothes away.

That was when he'd noticed a dark halo around the heads of the birds. It fluctuated like the shimmer of a heat mirage over a roadway. A sign of Silas's influence over them. One Seth hadn't been able to see when his eyes were ordinary.

He wondered how far such aberrations would go. How long it would take for him to change with them. If he'd be something completely different by morning, or if he were safe for the time being.

Seth set his phone down, shut his eyes against reality, and tried to force his mind to quiet. It was a hopeless endeavor. Silas whispered to him all through the night, the violent pictures he painted with his words more vivid than Seth's nightmares had ever been.

Morning came slowly. The sun gradually painted Seth's room in the colors of sunrise while he stared at his wall. When it was late enough that his dad wouldn't question him being up, he headed for the bathroom where he used the toilet and brushed away the taste of vomit that still lingered from his mouth.

Next he stripped out of the clothes he wore and took a quick shower to rinse the last of the blood and dirt from his body. A shiver ran through him at the thought that he'd laid in bed like that all night, but he'd been worried his dad would ask questions.

With a towel wrapped around his waist, Seth headed back to his bedroom and dressed quickly in jeans and a red T-shirt beneath a bluish-gray hoodie that was soft enough to comfort him. Layers had always made him feel more at ease in the world, like a socially acceptable armor he could wear without people looking twice.

His dad wasn't up yet. Seth knew this just from the sense and silence of the house as he made his way downstairs, stowing his cellphone in his pocket as he went.

He made sure to close the door softly behind him so he wouldn't wake his father, then walked the few blocks to Evelyn's house. It was safer than trusting himself at the wheel of a car with the ache that still lingered behind his eyes, and the way Silas's voice rattled in the space between his ears.

Evelyn was seated out on her front porch when he arrived, a cup of coffee clasped between her hands. Her eyes were red-rimmed and blinking slowly as she stared into her drink.

Seth sent her a hesitant, albeit strained, smile. He felt terrible over what he'd put her through, and didn't know what words could ever make it right.

Evelyn set her mug down on the porch, got to her feet, and pulled Seth into a fierce hug. One that squeezed the air from his lungs and made him gasp for breath.

"Don't ever do something like that again."

Seth nodded when she pulled back, and he could breathe normally again. "Promise."

Evelyn retrieved her coffee mug, then led Seth into the house. He followed her through the living room that was under repair to the staircase, his hand trailing along the banister as they headed up to her room. Evelyn closed the door behind them once they were inside and Seth sat himself on the end of Evelyn's bed. The pink vertical stripes on the bedspread stood out sharply from the white that matched the rest of the furniture in the room.

"So..." Evelyn began, as she leaned back against her desk.

"So..." Seth echoed. He fingered the matching pink blanket that lay folded and draped beside him over the foot of the bed.

A stretch of awkward silence, and then, "Has anything like that happened before? The smoke stuff, I mean."

Seth shook his head. "Not like that." His stomach clenched with what he was about to say. "But, I think the ravens, and what's happening with Mary might be because of me." When Evelyn's eyes widened, Seth added quickly, "I didn't mean to hurt her. I didn't mean to hurt anyone." He looked down at his feet. "It just kind of happened."

Evelyn blinked at him. "The blood on your shirt—"

"It was Adam's," Seth said dully. "I killed him, or the thing inside me did. I woke up in the woods. I don't even know how I got there... And he— he was..."

"Dead," Evelyn finished for him.

"Yeah."

"What did you do with the body?"

"I left it but, there were these ravens... They started eating it."

Evelyn blanched at the words. She took a step away from the mirror that hung above her desk and Seth's eyes caught on a photograph tucked into the corner of the frame. It was of the two of them on their first day of third grade together. Her with her pigtails, and Seth with his Pokémon lunchbox. Things had been simpler back then. Things had made sense. Well, mostly.

"You think the ravens are protecting you?"

"I do."

Evelyn glanced away. "Now that I think about it, I've noticed ravens around you before."

"My mom said there's a raven familiar inside me."

"A familiar? Like a witch's familiar?"

Seth nodded. "Yeah."

"You really think that's what's causing all this?"

Seth opened his mouth to tell her what happened after he'd gotten home. About the talons that had sprouted from the tips of his fingers, but stopped himself. Somehow, out of everything, that felt like the thing that would make him sound insane.

"What I think is that I need to see my mom again," Seth said instead. "She knew. Somehow she knew all along."

The thought of seeing his mother on his own made Seth feel sick. Especially after what she had said last time.

Evelyn seemed to realize because she asked, "Do you want me to come?"

"Would you?" The thought of seeing his mother alone made Seth feel sick. Especially after what she had said last time.

"Of course. Like I said, I'm here for you."

They headed out to Evelyn's car. Evelyn adjusted her rearview mirror once they were inside and buckled in before pulling out onto the road.

"What about you?" Seth asked as they drove along.

"What about me?"

Seth stared at her. "You cracked your living room floor open a few days ago."

"So now you believe me?"

"You being a witch wouldn't be the weirdest thing to happen."

Evelyn gave a shocked laugh. "A witch?" She glanced over at him with a shake of her head. "You're joking, right?"

"If there are familiars, then there must be witches. Besides, the familiar inside me said you were one."

"If I was a witch, wouldn't my parents know? Wouldn't they have said something?"

"What about your grandmother?" Seth asked. "She never said anything?"

"Just the stories she stitched into her quilts. She'd tell me them sometimes when I was little," Evelyn said. "But that's all they are. Just stories."

"I think it's safe to say that they're more than just stories." Seth looked back the way they'd come. "Maybe we should go back and talk to her instead?"

Evelyn shook her head. "She's been really sick lately, Seth. I mean, really, really sick. My mom is with her now anyway."

"Has anything else happened?"

Evelyn was quiet for several long moments. "The worse Nana gets, the clearer that voice I've been hearing becomes, but I don't know what it could mean."

"Did she ever tell you who Timmons was?"

Evelyn narrowed her eyes, confused, and shot a side-long glance at Seth. "Timmons?"

"Your grandmother is always mentioning him. I thought he was a cat she had once, but maybe he's a familiar."

Evelyn rolled her eyes. "Timmons is a stuffed pine marten Nana gave me when I was three. I haven't even had him in forever. I lost him on a family trip years ago."

"Okay, well, maybe there's another Timmons. A real one."

Evelyn sighed. "I don't know, Seth. Let's just hope your mother on the other hand does know something, because I'm starting to feel like I'm crazy."

Evelyn pulled into the small parking lot at Oak View another ten minutes later. Seth stepped from the car first and Evelyn trailed close behind him as he made his way into the building. The receptionist looked up at them as they entered. It was the same woman that had been on staff when Seth had last come for a visit, and she seemed surprised to see him.

"Hi." Seth greeted her with what he hoped was a pleasant smile. "I wanted to see my mom, Eliza Cunningham."

"I'd just need to clear it with Dr. Maddox. I believe your mother is in a morning session with him right now."

Seth stubbed the toe of his shoe against the floor and fidgeted with his hands while they waited for a decision. Evelyn was quiet and still beside him, composed in a way that Seth couldn't manage.

They were told after the woman hung up that the doctor would be by shortly.

Dr. Maddox joined them in the lobby as he had the first time to lead them back to the series of doors along the hallway that Seth had seen once before.

"I admit I'm surprised you came here after what happened the last time," Dr. Maddox said. "But maybe you can help. She's been rather closed off this morning. Hasn't spoken a word since last night before bed."

Dr. Maddox opened one of the doors, a different one from the last time Seth visited. But the room was just as softly lit from overhead lights as the other had been, brightened only slightly more by the subdued sunlight that filtered in through a reinforced window. The glow of it made his mother's silhouette seem almost surreal where she sat in a chair at the table, just like the last time.

"Mom?" Seth said as he crossed the room with an ease he didn't feel in the rest of his body.

*Crick.* The sound caught Seth off guard, making him jolt back a step and when he looked at his mother again, he realized a crack had appeared along her cheek.

Her gaze finally lifted to meet his, but there was something entirely empty in the way she stared at him. No light of cognition. No dawning awareness of who he was or the words he'd spoken.

"Mom?" Seth repeated, horror in his voice as he watched tiny cracks climb up his mother's neck from beneath the collar of her shirt. An eyelid collapsed inward with a sound like sand slipping from a shovel, and Seth stifled a scream behind his hand.

A rush of noise came from behind him. The shouts of the doctor. Someone opening the door. Evelyn's startled cries.

His mother just sat there, motionless, while bits and pieces of her continued to disintegrate. There was no blood, no gleam of bone or muscle. Just clumps of gray that gave way and rolled down her pale skin like ash from burnt wood.

The bridge of her nose buckled as if pressed down upon by some invisible weight, and Seth wanted to look away, wanted to turn from the sight of it, but he couldn't. He couldn't stop watching as she crumpled in on herself, still staring vacantly at him with the single eye she had left, just as silent as she had been when he'd first entered the room.

The shirt she wore dipped into a depression where her stomach should have been. A finger fell from her hand and broke into powdery flakes when it hit the floor. Then all at once she caved in on herself, sending a dust cloud billowing outward.

Seth sucked in a shocked breath, then coughed as the dry specks of what was once his mother's flesh tickled the back of his throat. He pressed a hand over his nose and mouth. His eyes watered. There was a real chance he was about to be sick.

Seth stumbled back out of the room before anyone could stop him, his shoes leaving a trail of dusty footprints across the floor, and his mind trying to comprehend what he'd just witnessed as his back hit the wall and he slid down it to the floor.

He barely registered Evelyn's presence beside him when she touched her hands to his shoulders. When he realized at last that she was speaking to him, he raised his eyes and stared at her, not comprehending a single word, but not able to pull away when she hugged him close.

Ash fell off him like snow with the way her arms tightened around him. It was then, as he watched the gray flakes gather on the floor, that he processed the fact he was covered in what had once been his mother. He could feel bits of grit on his skin beneath his clothes. In his shoes. Against his scalp. She was all over him.

He felt tears on his cheeks at the realization, and he brought a hand up to his face to wipe at them. His fingers were caked in what looked like soot when he pulled them back.

This couldn't be real. This couldn't be happening. People didn't just turn to dust like that.

"This is a dream. This is a dream. This has to be a dream."

"You're awake, Seth," Evelyn said gently. "You're awake. This isn't a dream."

It was a truth that Seth didn't want to hear. His mother was dead. It was something he'd silently wished for in his darkest moments, when the pain and the anger became too much.

Guilt twisted in his gut, a sense that he'd somehow caused this overtaking him. Silas only confirmed over and over again that it was his fault. All his fault.

He could see the ash through the door. Dr. Maddox and the orderlies were still shouting among themselves. What Seth wouldn't give to be anywhere but there at that moment.

He thought of when he was younger as that need to escape swelled inside him. How his family had visited that beach in California—the one where his mother had built a sandcastle with him, and kept him close when he'd swam in the ocean.

He could feel the waves almost, but inside himself, and he latched onto that sensation without thinking. His breath caught as warmth spread through him, chasing away the numb of shock.

Evelyn stumbled back from him, her eyes wide. "Seth, what are you doing?"

Seth looked down at himself. At the same smoking oil-like substance that had seeped from beneath his skin and closed in around him last night at the overpass.

"Stop! Seth, stop it!"

He looked up at her helplessly. "I don't know how."

It covered him like a sheet, the way it had at the overpass, the way it must have when he ended up in the backyard of that house and the woods of the campground. He'd wanted to be somewhere else and now he was going to be, whether he wanted to go this way, or not.

Seth fell the next instant. He had just enough time to register the water below him before he broke the surface in a cold rush that flooded his mouth and stung his eyes with salt. His body sank down, down, down into the dark below.

He kicked his legs and flailed his arms out toward the surface. His fingers stretched out to the light above. Still, he sank.

He didn't know how to swim. Isaac had tried to teach him once, but all Seth had learned was that being up to his neck in a swimming pool was enough to give him a panic attack.

Isaac. It was a Sunday. He'd be at church.

The flickering darkness was growing thicker around Seth. Almost cradling him. He was jerked upward then sideways abruptly, only to find himself dropped once more in a splash of water that echoed almost as loudly as the heavy thud his body made when it hit the ground. This time he landed on a carpeted floor and people in pews gasped as he coughed up water and struggled to pull in air.

One person he recognized tried to scramble out of a pew a few rows back. It was Isaac, and he looked terrified, like he was watching the devil himself take hold of Seth.

The glinting darkness still hovered around him in thick undulating tendrils that had to look like something demonic to the paled faces of the congregation that now stared Seth down with wide, shocked eyes.

"Isaac," Seth choked out, and he tried to get to his feet only to stumble and fall. He landed hard with a pained cry, and for an instant, he wanted his father.

An instant was all it took.

The darkness arced around him again, sparked with that strange life it had, and something in Seth broke. A litany of "No, no, no" falling from his lips.

He reached out a hand for Isaac, who had made it to the aisle and was sprinting toward him even as the dark twisted around him tighter and tighter. He screamed Isaac's name as he was hauled away again.

# TWENTY-NINE

Seth stared up at the ceiling from the glass-strewn floor of his father's bedroom. Pain radiated through his body from being tugged brutally from one place to another.

He used to have a yo-yo back when he was a kid, and he remembered how he'd flick the plastic part out, only to tug it back in toward him. Back and forth. Back and forth. Hours spent just watching it spin along the taut white string. Until he'd broken a vase with it and his father had thrown it out.

It had been a red one. The same color as the blood speckled across the carpet and pooling around a shard of glass lodged in his palm from when he'd crashed through the window.

Seth had a certain amount of sympathy for that yo-yo now as he lay on the floor, dreading the next jerk on his body that would yank him somewhere else entirely. He couldn't take much more this. Not just physically, but mentally as well.

Silas scolded him for his panic and his loss of control, the way he'd latched onto the power inside him without thought or understanding. He told Seth again and again what a pathetic, sniveling, worthless fool he was while Seth begged him to stop. His hands pressed over his ears and fingers trembling.

Seth turned on his side slowly and curled in on himself as Silas continued to berate him. Like prey in the sight of a predator, he tried to make himself small. As if he could ever hide from the thing living inside him.

The carpet was rough against his cheek and smelled musty. Which seemed strange given that he'd vacuumed in here not too long ago.

He realized he could smell other things as well. Things he probably shouldn't be able to from where he was. Like the lavender perfume in his bottom drawer of the dresser.

The scent of it had him blinking away tears. He could remember his mother smelled like it most days. His mother, who was now a pile of ash on the floor of a visiting room in a psychiatric hospital.

How did something like that happen? Had it really been him, somehow? Had Silas been telling the truth, or was it just another way to play games with Seth's head?

When nothing pulled at him after another twenty minutes or so, Seth dared to move. He got a grip on the glass in his hand. His face scrunched up, and tears rolled down his cheeks as he pulled on it. The shard moved at a stubborn pace, sliding out gradually bit by red-streaked bit, and Seth grunted with the effort, his teeth clenched.

A scream broke free when it came loose with a spurt of blood, and Seth pressed his other hand down over the cut to staunch the flow.

He rolled so he could get his knees under himself and staggered to his feet. A few smaller scrapes made themselves known with sharp stings as he moved, pieces of glass falling off him as he rose. His hand clasped tight over his trembling palm, his nerves on edge, still waiting for the next flight. The next jerk of motion that would send him careening somewhere else.

The closet door was already open when Seth stepped toward it and he pulled the cord to turn on the bulb overhead. It swayed slightly as it bathed the small space in yellow light.

Seth looked up to the shelf. It was easy enough to locate the first aid kit, half tucked beneath a hat box that had more likely belonged to his mother than his father, given it was decorated with a pattern of daisies. His mother had always liked daisies.

He got a hold of the red bag, but in the process of pulling it down, the hat box tumbled from the shelf.

It landed with a soft thud on the carpet, spilling photographs and papers over the floor.

Seth left them there and went into the bathroom with the first aid kit. He dripped blood from the cut on his hand across the floor and then the counter when he moved to set the bag down on it.

More blood speckled the white basin of the sink when he held his palm under the faucet once he turned it on. The shock of water against his skin made him wince as his blood circled the drain.

Seth dried the cut with a piece of gauze padding, but it was bleeding again by the time he bandaged it. He'd probably need stitches.

He wondered where his father was dazedly as he taped the end of the bandage down. He should find him. Tell him what had happened at Oak View. The smaller scratches on his skin he'd take care of later, after that was done.

His hand shook as he turned off the sink. He felt dizzy. Almost numb. But whether it was from the physical strain on his body, or the shock of his mother's death, he didn't know.

He almost walked through the mess of photos on the floor when he trudged his way out of the bathroom. Only stopping before he did because Silas drew his attention to an older photograph that was faded and creased, like it had been in someone's pocket for too long.

It showed his mother standing among a group of women with a man beside her. A man who was decidedly not his father, though he had an arm around her in a way that seemed more than friendly considering how close they were standing.

Seth would have shrugged it off as an old photo of a past boyfriend of hers before she met his father. Except that she held a baby swaddled in a blanket in her arms.

The photo was the kind that came from one of those instant cameras, with a white border along the edges and the colors slightly off, but he could still tell that the modest dresses his mother and the other women wore were white in a way his mother's wedding dress had never been. She'd hated white dresses, said it reminded her of a time she'd rather forget.

Seth kneeled and let his fingers comb through the pictures, shuffling them out across the floor to get a better look at them. He was desperate for an answer to the one he held in his hand, but all he found were family photos, smiling faces that looked up at him from scenes of outings and vacations.

One of the papers that lay partially beneath the photos caught his eye and he pulled it out to look it over. It was a birth certificate, but different from the one he'd used his entire life. It had all the same information except for one thing. On the line for birth father, the name read "Isaiah Morrison." The same name was on the back of the photograph with his mother's and several others when he turned it over.

A door opened and closed downstairs. The voice of the man he'd thought was his father for the past eighteen years called out to him from down below.

Seth stood slowly at the sound of steps on the staircase as the weight of the truth sank into him. The birth certificate and photograph clutched in his hand felt heavier than paper had a right to.

He left the rest of the photos and papers scattered over the floor around the hat box, his anger greater than his need to honor his mother.

"What happened?" his father asked when he caught sight of the bandage on Seth's hand as he stepped into the hall. "And why are you all wet?"

"Who the hell is Isaiah Morrison?" Seth demanded, rather than answer the questions, and his hand shook around the birth certificate.

His "father" stood still before him. He didn't speak right away, and it gave Seth a moment to look him over. Though he was going gray, he'd once been blond-haired, and his eyes were a light blue. The only similarity between them was his fair skin, which was looking fairer by the second as he paled.

Now that he really looked at the man that stood before him with panic written into his features, Seth wasn't sure how he could have ever thought they were related. They looked nothing alike.

"Seth—"

"You're not my dad."

It was an accusation, not a question. There was no doubt in Seth's mind. But it hurt to be so sure of it. It hurt to know that this man he'd spent all his life calling his dad wasn't his father.

"I am your dad. Maybe not by blood, but I raised you, and I love you. You're my son."

*He's a liar,* Silas whispered harshly in Seth's head. *A dirty, dirty liar. He only ever wanted your mother. You were just the baggage that came along with her.*

Seth took a step back when arms reached out toward him—to pull him into a hug, probably, but Seth didn't want a hug. He didn't want to be comforted. He didn't trust it.

"Were you ever going to tell me?" Seth asked as tears slipped down his cheeks. He felt lost. Broken.

"What good would it have done you? You were already hurting so much."

Seth shook his head but said nothing. Instead, he ran. Down the stairs and out the door. He let it slam closed behind him and kept running.

# THIRTY

Seth ran down the sidewalk, his steps carrying him further and further from his house. An ache in his side finally brought him to a halt, his breaths harsh puffs of air that he could see in the cold.

He took a stumbling step back. His hands pressed tight to his chest, where he felt like he was shattering in on himself.

Now that the anger had passed. Now that he was alone. The despair settled into his being with an ache that dug deep into the core of everything he thought he knew himself to be.

Seth pulled in one heaving breath after another. He did his best not to cry again. Only a few tears slipped free to be wiped away viciously before they could run the full length of his cheeks.

His hands shook as he ran them up through his hair and he tipped his head up toward the sky. A raven circled overhead just as he expected. A reminder of his mother's truth.

Seth ended up on the side of the road in front of someone's house. His rear on the curb and his head in his hands.

His thoughts were a mess. He couldn't think straight. Too consumed by everything that had happened and everything he'd lost. Silas's voice in his head an added distraction on top of it all.

He desperately needed Gabriel. He was the only one that could help Seth now. The only one that might have answers, or at least know where to look for them.

Seth's only way to contact him though was to show up at his door. Which was a terrible idea, but he had nothing better to fall back on.

It was then, while Seth was standing to head to the train stop, that a familiar voice called out his name. Not his father's voice. But he knew it and he raised his head to see his math teacher coming toward him from across the street.

Seth blinked at her, confused about why she would be here.

"Do you have a minute?" Mrs. Fields asked amicably enough, but there was something in the way her eyes watched him that made Seth uneasy.

Seth took a step back from her as he tucked the photograph and birth certificate into the back pocket of his jeans. His body was tense, ready to run again if needed.

"I'm actually supposed to head home," Seth lied.

"But you just came from there."

Seth's skin crawled. How long had she been watching him?

"Really, it'll only take a moment," Mrs. Fields insisted. Her hand closed over Seth's wrist to tug him forward when he tried to back further away. "I just want to show you something."

She reached into her coat pocket. Seth half expected her to pull out a weapon. A knife. Maybe even a gun. But she only pulled out her cellphone, and Seth relaxed, feeling foolish that he had suspected his teacher of being a killer. At least until she played the video she wanted him to see.

It showed Seth as he jumped from the overpass, that sparking darkness billowing around him like a shield before it encircled him and darted forward through the air, the headlights of crashed cars glinting off it.

"It was on the news last night, and more reports are flooding in today. Including some from a local church," Mrs. Fields informed. "That is you in the video, isn't it?"

Seth shook his head and tried to pull away. He turned in time to glimpse dark skin and black hair tipped with red. The next moment, a sharp pain spread up his side and he stumbled back, tripping over the curb to land in an undignified heap on the asphalt.

Other people came out of hiding from around the sides of houses and behind hedges. All of them carried a weapon. Most had guns, but a few held crossbows and even fewer carried a blade.

"I'm sorry, Seth," Aaliyah said with a tremor to her voice. "But you're dangerous. Maybe the most dangerous thing alive."

Seth got a knee under himself and pushed up to his feet unsteadily. Aaliyah took a step back, as he did. She was one of the few who gripped a knife in her hand. Some kind of dagger.

A smile crept over Seth's face that was not his own. "*You're all always so damn sorry.*"

A shudder of heat ran through Seth, familiar and frightening. Wisps of that oily smoke-stuff seeped from his back and flared like wings on either side of him before it raced toward Aaliyah.

"Aaliyah!" Mrs. Fields shouted. "Don't let the aether touch you!"

But it was too late. Aether licked across Aaliyah's cheek like flame, and like flame, it left her skin looking charred. Dark red lines ran like cracks through the rough patch of her face. She dropped to the ground with a strangled howl, her body contorting into inhuman and unnatural shapes.

"Shoot him!" Mrs. Fields yelled, seeming to regain her senses enough to give orders to the small group that followed her.

There were at least eight of them. Then seven as the aether shot forward from Seth to twist around one man's body as he raised his gun, pulling him into the air. Bones snapped as easily as kindling, and Seth felt each one as they broke. The man's head faced the wrong direction when he fell limp to the ground with a heavy thud.

Silas stop! Seth screamed inside his head. Please, stop!

Another gun raised. Another body snapped. Another person down.

"Shoot him!" Mrs. Fields screamed more urgently when another body hit the ground. It was a woman this time, her limbs bent at odd angles and blood seeping from her mouth to run down the pale skin of her cheek. The gun she'd held now lay on the bloody grass beside her.

Seth's side throbbed. Blood soaked his shirt and ran hot over his cold skin. Silas didn't seem to understand they were already in danger of dying.

We're bleeding, Seth tried to convince him as he watched the aether whisk toward another person. We need to get somewhere safe. We need help. A hospital.

Silas seemed resistant to the idea. He could feel the emotion even without him speaking a word. But there was blood spreading down Seth's shirt to his pant leg and Silas had to know they were weakening. He had to know they would die without help.

He dropped to one knee. Or maybe Silas did. He wasn't sure which of them was in control anymore.

Seth thought of Gabriel at that moment, of the kindness in his touch and the warmth in his smile.

The aether wavered, then drew back, pulling in close to Seth's body. It wound about him like a cloak, warm and strangely comforting. There was that sickening lurch that Seth had come to fear, and gravity shifted as the now familiar rushing sensation pulled at him and his body soared between one point and the next.

Seth landed hard on his back. The aether circled around him as if to check their surroundings before it slowly retreated inside him.

For half a minute, Seth didn't know where he was. Then recollection set in when he saw the two couches and an armchair. It was the living room of the farmhouse Gabriel's parents owned.

Seth's vision swam when he tried to sit up. He ended up falling back against the carpet with a sharp throb of pain in his side. His shirt was warm and wet when he pressed a hand there.

Hands cupped Seth's cheeks. They turned his head gently until he met dark-brown eyes set in a round face with a nose that widened at the tip. Diana.

Even with the way Seth's vision blurred, it was unmistakably her, her black hair tousled, T-shirt blue and rumpled. She looked as if she'd just rolled off the couch from a nap.

Diana's hands pressed to Seth's side, pushing the hand Seth had there already down more firmly into the wet heat.

She screamed for someone the next second. Seth had never seen her look so stricken, so panicked.

Seth's eyelids fluttered as his thoughts spun and sound filtered in like the sporadic buzzing of an insect up against his ear. He caught the tail end of what Diana yelled, only it was in Spanish and Seth wasn't clearheaded enough to even try to understand it.

There were hurried footsteps from down the hall, light and quick across the floor as if the person's feet barely touched the ground.

A woman appeared in Seth's field of vision. She looked like Gabriel. Her skin was darker than his but her hair and eye color were the same, as was the softness in her gaze when she looked at Seth.

It had to be Gabriel's mother—Daniela. Seth had never met her before, but she looked kind. Her touch was as gentle as it was sure when she had Diana move their hands aside so she could lift Seth's shirt to check his wound.

"Help him." Diana's face was wet with tears. Her voice strained. "Please, you have to help him."

"How did he get here?"

Diana shook her head. She looked as lost as Seth felt. "I don't know."

Her mother turned her attention back to Seth's wound, and Seth angled his head to see how bad it was for himself. He immediately wished he hadn't.

A jagged slash was cut into his flesh, a growing puddle of red spreading out beneath him.

"Sorry," Seth mumbled stupidly, because he had ruined the carpet. Because he kept ruining everything.

Diana hushed him as she held one of Seth's hands with blood-soaked fingers. A man Seth didn't know stepped up beside her, his features blurry, and Seth blinked his eyes as his vision swam.

"Diana, go get your brother from the barn," Daniela instructed.

Diana gave a nod and seemed to vanish from Seth's side. He could hear her running.

"Can you get him up, Carlos?" Daniela asked the man hurriedly, Gabriel's father most likely. "We need to get him to the clinic."

Carlos didn't reply, instead he got one arm beneath Seth's knees and the other under his back to lift him.

Seth whined in the back of his throat as the movement lanced pain through him. He knew he was would die without their help. By their hurried steps and fussing voices, so did Gabriel's father and mother.

Maybe it's better if I'm gone, Seth thought as he let his eyes close and his head loll. Maybe...

Something patted against Seth's face. A hand, he thought, and he opened his eyes reluctantly when it persisted. Then he tilted his head away from the too-warm touch with effort. Cold metal pressed against his cheek instead of the softness of a shirt and he blinked slowly, the counters and cabinets around him blurring in and out of focus.

Someone was cutting his shirt open. He could hear the snip of the scissors and feel the cool air of the room against his bare skin the next moment as the fabric fell away.

There were gloved hands at his side the next moment, pinching his torn flesh together. He choked on his own spit at this new agony, at the sharp pokes and the quick tugs at his flesh that started shortly after.

Seth didn't look. He didn't want to see.

His fingernails scraped against the metal table and cold sweat broke out across his skin on a wave of nausea. Gabriel's name came out on a gasped breath when he shuddered with a fresh wave of pain. His hand twitched against the table, but he found he didn't have the power to reach out.

A strong hand wrapped around Seth's and squeezed gently. Seth's gaze slid over in the direction of the touch.

"I'm here." Gabriel's free hand smoothed back Seth's hair as he spoke. "I'm right here. It's going to be okay."

Seth clenched his teeth with the next pull of the thread. This wasn't right. There was no way it should hurt this much. Something was wrong. It had to be.

Seth begged, or at least tried to. The words didn't feel right in his mouth. His tongue felt sluggish, and his voice cracked.

But Gabriel seemed to understand because he squinted at the wound in confusion at Seth's words. It drove him to lean forward the next moment. The hand he'd been petting through Seth's hair now touched the skin just on the outside of the gash, pulling slightly like he was trying to get a better look at something at the edge.

Daniela had stopped stitching the wound with Gabriel in the way, but this was almost worse. Seth felt like he was on fire there. Like his insides were scorched, raw and blistered just beneath the skin. The pressure of

Gabriel's touch was too much to bear, despite how gentle Seth was sure he was trying to be.

"I'm sorry. I'm sorry," Gabriel murmured when Seth whimpered and tried to move away, but he didn't pull his hand back.

"Gabriel, what are you doing?" his mother demanded.

"Do you see that?"

Daniela leaned forward to have a better look.

"The blade he was stabbed with must have been coated in witchbane." She shook her head in disbelief. "But he'd have to be a famirian for it to react that way. I thought he was human."

"He is, or at least he should be."

"Then when—"

"Look, we don't have time to sort this out now. He's going to start seizing soon and I'd rather he not go through that." Gabriel pulled on the chain Seth wore around his neck to raise it from beneath his shirt. He let go of Seth's hand to get a palm under his head so he could lift it and slip the necklace free. "Get me some water."

Daniela must have done as she was told, because there was a glass of water being handed to Gabriel in the next instant. By then, Gabriel had already opened the locket and removed the sachet.

Seth lost track of what Gabriel did after that. Though he could hear him talking in that soothing tone he had. The one he used when an animal he was caring for was hurt and frightened. The one he'd used that night in his apartment when Seth had woken screaming in his arms.

The words barely made any sense to Seth through the haze of pain and the dizziness of blood loss.

A hand pressed to Seth's side. Damp bits of what he knew must be lavender being worked into his wound, and at first it was torture, but then came the heat. A warmth that somehow soothed the fire in his skin. It was followed by a gradual cooling sensation. One that left him numb where he needed it most. He couldn't even feel the needle and thread when Daniela started lacing his skin closed again.

Seth curled his fingers over Gabriel's hand when it slipped into his again and he let himself close his eyes. His mind and body were exhausted. He just wanted to sleep now that the pain had gone.

# Thirty-One

It was too quiet, and as Seth sat up, his hands and feet slid through the dry brown leaves that littered the forest floor.

There was movement off to Seth's left. Some sort of animal darted through the trees. Not a raven—it was too large and quick to be a bird.

Seth scrambled to his feet and looked around. He saw it again, this time more clearly as it moved in closer. Its yellow eyes fixed on him. He didn't feel afraid, though. Not even when it halted less than a foot from him, its tail sweeping the ground and its eyes looking up at him.

A wolf. Its black fur flecked with gray. The moonlight made it almost look a silvery blue. No, not the moonlight, but a light that seemed to emanate from within it. Soft and ethereal, like he imagined a ghost light might look.

There was something strangely familiar about it, a pattern of gray around its eyes and mouth that sparked a sense of recognition.

"Kit?"

The wolf's ears twitched at the name and it stepped closer when Seth held a hand out toward it, his fingers bent slightly and his palm facing down. "It is you, isn't it?"

The wolf sniffed Seth's hand, then licked and nuzzled his fingers before it pushed its head up into his palm, its dense fur coarse against his skin.

"Hey, boy." Seth smiled and scratched his fingers through the wolf's fur just behind its ears. His smile dropped as he remembered where he'd been moments before. The cold metal of the table. The warmth of blood that spilled from his body. So much blood.

The wolf leaned into his touch and whimpered softly, almost as if it could read Seth's thoughts.

"This has to be a dream."

Seth glanced around as he patted Kit. He could see a light just outside the circle of trees—a yellow house with white shutters and a flower garden along the sides of the porch. Seth recognized it instantly as the Caballero Ortiz farmhouse. He wondered if he'd find Gabriel inside, or at least some memory of him.

Seth stiffened when he heard a familiar *kra-kra-kra* in the distance and the wolf growled, shifting uneasily.

"It's okay," Seth said, even though it was more for his own benefit. "It's just a bird."

He was about to stand when water rose out of the grass beneath him. The blades shriveled and turned brown as Seth scrambled back and away. Small white stones poked through the dirt, piling one on top of the other with dry clicks. Others soon followed. Some larger, some longer, some curved like the crescent moon overhead and almost delicate looking. It was only when Seth noticed the eye sockets in one of the rounded ones that he realized the stones weren't stones. They were bones. Thousands of them. Spread over the ground so completely that there was no chance he could walk anywhere without stepping on them.

He stared at them, mostly at the skulls, some of which were barely bigger than his fist. Distinctly human and so small that they couldn't have belonged to anything older than an infant.

Seth felt sick all over again. He rose shakily to his feet, the crack of bone beneath his shoes unavoidable.

Kit was gone from his side, though Seth thought he heard a raspy howl in the distance, a searching cry in the still air.

Even more forest lay ahead of him now, where before the farmhouse had shone like a beacon in the darkness.

The trees looked like oaks. Old and bark knotted. Their naked branches reached toward the sky, obscuring the moon and what little light it provided.

Water had appeared behind Seth. A lake rather than a pond, but just as dark and calm as the waters his mother had held his head under.

His mother. Was she here?

Seth looked around, almost desperate to see her. Even if it meant she would drown him. He just wanted to see his mother once more.

A figure rose from the ground in the distance, a dark shadow that stepped closer to him through the fog.

"Mom?" Seth called out shakily.

Tears slipped down his cheeks when she came into view, and his chest constricted painfully. Even after all she'd done, he still loved her. She was still his mother.

Seth didn't wait for her to come any closer. He took a few steps of his own until he was running, toward her rather than away for once.

He could hear the brittle snap of bones beneath his shoes as he ran, but he didn't care. It was his mother. It was her.

He threw his arms around her when she was within reach. She'd been the monster in his dreams for so long. But now he held onto her like she meant everything.

"Mom," Seth choked out when she wrapped her arms around him in return. She was just as silent as before, but something seemed different, more real, or maybe that was just his mind drawing off his own wishes. But she was dressed differently than usual, in blue jeans and a white blouse rather than the faded nightgown from that night all those years ago.

His mother stroked his hair gently and Seth closed his eyes as he wept with the gentleness of her touch. He remembered this now. From when he was younger. The way she used to stroke his hair when he was upset. It was like something right out of his memories.

"Poor Seth. Always looking for a love that doesn't exist."

Seth looked up, then stumbled back. He tripped over a skull and landed hard among the brittle bones that littered the ground. The splinters of the ones that snapped with his fall pricked his skin, drawing droplets of blood.

A young man wearing his face now stood where his mother once had.

"You know she did all this." He looked at Seth with eyes as brown as Seth's own, and he spread his arms as if to indicate all that surrounded them. "So many have died because of her and her ilk."

"What?"

"Your mother helped drown all these children," the other him clarified. "I've lost count of how many have died. How many they killed hoping it was us." He strode forward with sure steps that snapped the bones that covered the ground like snow. "I'm sure somewhere it's happening even to this day, because they don't know about us."

Seth stared at the other him. He'd never had a dream like this one before. Never seen himself stand before him on a hill of bones with downcast eyes and a heavy frown.

"You're lying," he said.

Seth leaned away when the other crouched in front of him.

"I promise I'm not."

"Why would she...?" Seth trailed off as he glanced around with watery eyes at the white and uneven landscape, at the skulls that stared back at him from dark and vacant holes.

"Because she hated us that much."

A tear slipped down Seth's cheek. "Stop saying 'us.'"

"Why? She hated you too." He touched a hand to Seth's cheek. Wiped at the tears on his skin with his thumb. "She tried to drown you just as she did me, and then she left you." More tears slipped down Seth's cheeks as he continued, "But me, Seth? I'll never leave you. I've always been with you."

"Go to hell."

The other him smiled, something wrong in the crook of his mouth and the way it pulled at his features.

Seth blinked as the world around him started to falter, and Silas gave an annoyed frown as the surrounding trees faded like smoke caught in the wind.

The weight of sheets and covers became more recognizable as the haze of a medicated sleep faded, and a dull throb echoed up Seth's side with his movements.

Light stung his eyes when he blinked them open, and he turned his head in the other direction, away from the lamp and toward the door that stood ajar. A chair had been pulled close to the bed. Its occupant was leaning forward, dark head of hair pillowed on his arms, which rested atop the bed just beside where Seth lay. He seemed to be fast asleep.

Seth reached out, noticing as he did that the hand he'd cut was wrapped in a fresh bandage. The skin beneath pulled like it had been stitched.

"Gabriel." The name came out in a croaked whisper and Seth let his fingers brush against Gabriel's arm, the touch rousing him into lifting his head. He had always been a light sleeper, which made the fact he'd been able to put up with Seth's more restless nights some kind of miracle.

"You're awake," Gabriel said, his voice dry with sleep and a weariness to his tone that made the dark circles beneath his eyes even more pronounced.

*Weak. The both of you.*

Seth clenched his teeth at the voice in his head, at the way he had to push back against the consciousness that tried to strangle out his own.

"Can you tell me what happened?" Gabriel asked.

Seth remembered in a rush the events of the past few days. He'd wanted so badly to have Gabriel with him then. To find comfort in him. But now that he was here, Seth couldn't get the truth out.

Tears slid down Seth's cheeks to soak into the pillow beneath his head, a lump in his throat and an ache in his gut that wouldn't go away.

"What happened?" Gabriel asked again.

But Seth couldn't tell him. How could he tell him he'd killed people? That he'd eaten someone's heart. That a girl he'd considered a friend had tried to kill him. That he, and Silas, they were hungry, *ravenous,* and craved to rip bloody strings from muscle with their teeth. That the steady *ba-dump, ba-dump, ba-dump* of Gabriel's heart was making the hunger worse. That it was a temptation that they wanted to gorge themselves on.

*Ba-dump. Ba-dump.* The thumping grew closer as Gabriel leaned over him to press a hand to his shoulder, and Seth squeezed his eyes shut.

His fingertips prickled, the beginnings of talons taking shape, and he curled his hands into fists beneath the blankets.

Wisps of aether rose from him. A glimmer of what they'd been before, but there, and the sight made Seth's heart race. His breaths came in stops and starts.

"Don't panic," Gabriel said, and Seth turned his head to look at him. "You're stronger than you think. You can do this. You can control this."

Gabriel was right that he needed to control it. Seth had to control these powers. These impulses that weren't his own, but twisted around his mind like a fever that tried to burn his humanity out of him.

He couldn't lose himself to Silas. He couldn't let him have control. He couldn't let him out.

This was his body. His. Not Silas's. Not theirs. *His.*

But Seth could feel Silas more acutely than ever. He was right there at the surface of his thoughts, trying to claw his way free to make a nest out of Seth's brain.

"Seth, breathe. Just breathe."

Gabriel was so close now that all they'd have to do was reach up to sink talons through the skin of his chest. His body would open for them in a rain of blood like it was nothing. Because it *was* nothing. Just tissue and muscle and bone that could be snapped easily enough. It'd be simple. So, so simple to get to such a vital thing.

"No..." Seth tried to pull away when Gabriel reached out. "I—I don't want to hurt you."

"Trust me. I can help."

Seth pushed back against the urge to feed when Gabriel leaned in again. His body arched and his eyes rolled back in his head when Silas dug into his mind harder.

Gabriel's hand came to rest against Seth's forehead, warm and steady, and Seth felt his body relax under the familiar touch.

He found himself back in that space again, recognizing it for what it was even though the lake and the bones had gone. But Silas was there, as was Kit, who stood at Seth's side to stare the other him down with yellow eyes and bared teeth.

"You think you can protect him, Kit?" Silas sneered. "You think you can stop me?"

The wolf simply bared its teeth, a vicious display that almost made Seth step away.

"All this time, you've been keeping an eye on me, and holding me back as best you could, haven't you? It was never a coincidence that you showed up on that road." Silas shook his head. "You know, you used to believe in me, and what I was trying to achieve. We were like brothers, you and I. What changed you?"

Kit snapped his jaws. His fangs were a warning that Silas didn't heed as he stepped forward.

Seth didn't know what Silas's goals had been in the past, or what history he had with the wolf at Seth's side. He only knew Silas was dangerous.

Debra had told Seth to imagine a box or room that Seth could shut his problems away in. He'd thought it childish, but he couldn't think of anything else he could try as Silas stalked toward them with talons growing from his fingertips and aether that fanned out from behind him like wings.

Seth pictured a room with concrete walls as he took a step back. He didn't imagine a door because he wanted to keep this monster locked away forever. No exit. No escape.

He willed his concrete box to appear, and the earth rumbled in answer as four thick walls rose out of the ground. Kit shone more brightly beside Seth, and he knew the spirit was lending him its strength. He could feel it flowing through him like a current.

Silas disappeared from view as the walls ascended. He wasn't quick enough to outrun them, and it hurt when he fought to break out, when he raged and beat his fists and scraped his talons against the walls that were a part of Seth's mind. But it was a pain Seth could manage.

The wolf raised its head to look at Seth, its yellow eyes appraising him. And Seth didn't hear him speak, but he felt a sense of meaning all the same. An urging more than anything else, telling Seth he should open his eyes now. He should talk to Gabriel. Silas was trapped, but this was far from over.

Gabriel's hand was still a comforting weight against Seth's forehead when he blinked his eyes open. He could remember other times like this, when he'd woken to find Gabriel's hand on his forehead. He hadn't thought much of it then, but now he suspected there was something more to it than a simple act of affection.

"They knew each other," Seth mumbled. His mind fuzzy. Tired.

"What?"

"Silas and Kit. They knew each other."

Gabriel leaned forward again. "Who's Silas?"

"The familiar inside me."

"What? How long has he been with you?"

"Since I was a baby." Seth fought against the urge to cry again, but the tears came anyway. "He's—he's why my mom tried to kill me."

Gabriel wiped away the tears on Seth's cheeks and smoothed back his hair. The touch soothed something inside Seth. That hunger inside him calming somewhat.

Silas had said Kit had been trying to hold him back, and Seth wondered if that could have something to do with it.

"Gabriel." Naomi was leaning in through the doorway, worry etched in her eyes and the tight line of her mouth as she held a phone out to her brother. "It's Josh. Haley's gotten worse."

Gabriel's heartbeat quickened and Seth's stomach twisted painfully around the hollow of emptiness inside it as he watched Naomi pass Gabriel the phone.

Seth couldn't make out what Josh was saying on the other end of the phone, but from what he could catch of Gabriel's part of the conversation and his deepening frown, it wasn't good.

When the call ended, Gabriel looked at him, an unspoken apology in his eyes. "I have to go. Something's wrong with Haley."

"What is it?" Seth asked, doing his best to sit up. The burn in his side made him grit his teeth.

Silas was laughing, an echo of a sound in the prison of Seth's skull, and it made dread pool in the emptiness of his stomach.

Seth remembered that day at the marina. The way electricity had sparked between his and Haley's hands when their skin had touched. The same way it had with Mary when Seth had grabbed her, and now

Mary's skin was turning red and pebbled, like ink left to curdle in the sun.

He couldn't help but wonder what effect his touch had on Haley. If she was so far gone that Gabriel was leaving in a panic, it had to have been just as bad, if not worse.

Naomi stepped aside to let Gabriel pass her on his way out of the room. She stood there silently after he'd gone, her eyes on Seth with something like disdain in the downward curve of her mouth, and Seth forced himself up despite her staring.

Silas was still talking in his head, but his voice was muffled now. Barely loud enough to be heard.

With a wince, Seth threw aside the blanket to find he was still wearing his pants from earlier, but the shirt he wore was a blue Henley he recognized as belonging to Gabriel. On him it was just long enough to hide the blood stains on his jeans.

It felt like his body was against him as he stumbled from the bed. Not like it had in the woods with the numbness that had made him fall. No. This was a different weakness. The kind that sent jolts of pain lancing up his side with each step.

Naomi made an exasperated sound. "Are you stupid? Get back in bed."

Seth shook his head and continued on out of the bedroom, then down the hall toward the front door, Naomi glowering after him the whole time.

"Gabriel, wait." Seth picked up his shoes from where they sat by the door and pushed the screen open. "I'm coming too."

"Go back inside, Seth," Gabriel said as he opened the Jeep door.

Seth stalked stubbornly to the vehicle and yanked the passenger side door open, sliding inside before Gabriel could object. Only then did he tug his shoes on and tie up the laces. "We need to finish talking."

"No. What we need is for you to get back to bed before you pop your stitches," Gabriel retorted. "You're lucky to even be alive. If you'd been bleeding internally, I'm not sure we'd be having this conversation right now."

Gabriel stood tensely in the open space between Jeep and door, waiting for Seth to get out. But Seth had made his decision, and he had no intention of leaving.

With a sigh Gabriel got in the car and sank into the driver's seat before he closed the door. He started the vehicle with a sidelong glance in Seth's direction before backing out of the driveway.

The drive was short. Shorter than Seth needed to get his nerves together to say the things he wanted to say and ask for the answers he was dying to know.

A library rolled into view before Seth could even figure out where to start. The building was red bricked and one story high. Old, but well cared for, with a few bushes that probably flowered in warmer months along its sides.

Two figures stood outside the building. One of them was yelling, long hair falling across her face as she stumbled back from the other when he reached for her.

It was Josh, the angles of his face recognizable even in the fading light of the sun. Which meant the woman had to be Haley.

She looked sick, her hair matted to her face in strings with sweat, skin paler than Seth had ever seen it, except for the spidery red lines that twisted up her arm. The infection visibly spread even as she stood there.

Gabriel parked the Jeep just as Haley took off running, and Josh followed her with a desperate shout at Gabriel.

"Gabriel, wait—"

But Gabriel was already out of the Jeep, and slamming the door behind him.

"Stay in the car."

Seth kept his eyes on Gabriel as he fumbled with his own seat belt. He saw him duck around the brick building just as he got free.

"Wait!" He flung the door open and half jumped from the Jeep. "Gabriel! Come back!"

There was no answer, and Seth took off after him, ignoring the throb in his side with each hurried step forward.

He skidded around the corner of the building, almost missing the door that stood open a crack in his haste. It looked as if the deadbolt had been snapped clean off.

He wondered briefly what could cause metal to break like that. But the thought didn't stop him from pulling the door open and stepping inside.

# THIRTY-TWO

It was darker than it had been outside and Seth stood just inside the
doorway as he waited for his eyes to adjust. Gray shapes slowly took
form in the darkness. Rows upon rows of bookshelves came into focus,
desks off to one side of a wall by a section of windows, computers off
to another. A collection of various more comfortable chairs than the
wooden ones at desks were scattered here and there. But no Gabriel. No
Josh. Not even Haley.

Seth was about to turn back when he heard a sound. A kind of shuffling, like feet being dragged across the floor.

"Gabriel?" Seth called out, letting the door drop closed behind him to
move further into the library. "Gabriel? Is that you?"

A figure stumbled out of the dark and toward him. The moonlight
from an overhead window reflected off blond hair and the soft curves of
a round face. Seth's eyes widened with recognition. It was Haley.

Haley clutched at the bookcase closest to her, and when she looked at
Seth with her teeth bared in a grimace, her eyes shone yellow.

"Run," she rasped. "Go!"

Seth didn't move. He wanted to move. He wanted to run. But it was
as if his feet were tethered to the floor as he watched Haley dig claws into
the side of the bookcase. The sharp tips left deep gouges in the wood as
she sank to the ground with a groan.

Her head dropped forward. Long blond hair obscured her face as her
bones seemed to shift and protrude at odd angles beneath her skin with
brutal cracks of sound.

Seth took a step, but in the wrong direction. Toward Haley instead of away from her.

Haley raised her head with a jerk at the sound of Seth's approach. Wisps of aether clung to her when she looked at him, the same aether that he and Silas had used before.

"Run!" Haley repeated, this time through sharp teeth that glinted even in the low light of the library. "Run! Ru—" Her words cut off as her face elongated.

Seth moved back out of shock, the quick step off balance, and he fell to land hard on his rear. His eyes widened as he stared at the shift of bone beneath reddening skin, the build changing, growing.

He tripped to his feet with a particularly sharp crack of bone, and ran toward the door, but a flashlight beam shining in his face stopped him.

"What are you doing in here?" a policeman asked as Seth raised a hand to shield his eyes from the light.

He didn't have time to respond. A guttural howl rang through the air and the beam of the flashlight moved to light the area behind him.

"What the hell?" the cop cried.

Something inhuman leapt forward with a snarl and Seth threw himself out of its path to the floor, just barely missing the teeth that had snapped at him.

The cop shrieked in panic and the flashlight clattered from his hand to the ground. The light glanced off the surrounding area as it spun across the floor.

Seth scrabbled forward behind a bookcase on hands and knees to press back against the shelf. The thump of the policeman's body being slammed to the ground made him clamp a hand over his mouth to keep from screaming.

The flashlight finally stopped with a *thunk* against a table leg, the beam of light pointing at the bookcase Seth was hiding behind.

A mangled hand clutched at the edge of the wood, smearing blood across the smooth surface. The pinkie finger stuck out at an odd angle and the index finger was nothing more than a stub, as if it had been chewed off.

Seth's stomach twisted. His own hand groped off to the side of him to grip the bookshelf as he leveraged himself to his feet.

A second later, the cop's eyes peered around the bottom of the bookcase and up at him as he dragged himself painfully forward.

"Help— Help me..." he pleaded in a desperate voice as he fumbled a hand out toward Seth. Blood ran over his lips and streaked his face from deep scratches, his hair stuck to his skin in wet, red clumps. "*Please.*"

Before Seth could even move there was a sharp, wet crunch. The cop's body jerked, then lay still in a growing pool of his own blood. His eyes stared vacantly at Seth and his body moved roughly every so often as whatever Haley had become fed on him.

Seth shook his head. Terror made him inch further away and guilt sent tears rolling down his cheeks.

The movement halted abruptly. As did the sloppy wet sounds of viscera and flesh being ripped apart.

There was a different sound now. One that filled Seth with dread. A loud breathy sniffing as if the thing was smelling the air.

Slow steps crept along the other side of the bookcase that Seth cowered behind, almost as if it had caught his scent and was stalking him like prey.

Seth stayed still. He held his breath, pressing his lips together tightly as he willed his heart to stop beating so loudly.

There was a huffing sound just behind him. The bookcase rocked, and a heavy book toppled to the floor as a snout wreathed in aether pushed its way through the shelf right next to Seth's head with a snarl.

Seth ducked and ran. The shelf came down above him as the creature slammed into it from the other side with a growl of frustration. It knocked into the one next to it and that toppled as well, the bookshelves grinding against each other as they fell.

Seth sprinted for the rapidly closing gap at the other end of the shelves.

But the side of the bookcase knocked him down when he'd almost made it out. Pain blossomed sharply across his side and he landed on the ground with the heavy pine and metal bookcase slamming down on top of him.

Seth groaned. His body throbbed, and he blinked his eyes against the sting of pain. He could hear the heavy footfalls of the creature drawing closer.

He turned his head toward its panting breaths. Tears blurred his vision, but he could still make out the mass beneath the aether that billowed around what had been Haley.

Its body was a raw, blistering red as if it had been skinned alive. The shape of it looked almost like an enormous wolf, but with longer legs and arms. Its extremities more closely resembled hands and feet than paws, with curved claws that clicked against the floor when it walked.

Werewolf. It was the first word Seth's overwhelmed brain landed upon, and he wondered if creating one was Silas's sick attempt at humor.

Numb panic gripped Seth as the thing prowled toward him with a *click, click, click* of claws against the floor. He could barely breathe through his tears as he tried to shift out from beneath the bookcase, tried to drag himself forward with his hands and elbows. But he couldn't move.

He screamed when the werewolf stepped onto the wood over his back. He felt like his spine was going to snap, that his body would break under the pressure.

The shelf creaked as the thing leaned forward to sniff him, the shift in weight making the shelf dig even deeper into his skin.

Seth squeezed his eyes closed with the hot breath against his face and the smell of bloody flesh. He was going to die. He was actually going to die. This thing was going to kill him.

When Seth opened his eyes again, fangs coated with blood glistened inches from his face. There was a cracking sound and the beast's jaw seemed to unhinge, its mouth gaping open as it moved in closer to his head. As if it planned to crack his skull open like an egg.

"Haley, please," Seth pleaded between panicked sobs, even though he was sure the girl he'd known could no longer hear him. "No— Please, don't—"

Something slammed into the werewolf just as it started lowering its mouth. The impact sent it tumbling over the floor in a snarling fit of aether and long limbs.

Seth looked up at the figure that stood next to him. He knew that build. Intimately.

"Gabriel."

The beast howled in rage and rose up on its hind legs. It towered over Gabriel now, but he didn't back away. Instead, he almost seemed to challenge it with a low growl from between bared teeth.

It bristled visibly at being kept from its prey, and dropped back down to all fours, hackles of aether rising along its neck and back. A clawed hand pawed at the ground in agitation, before the creature slunk to the side. Its yellow eyes narrowed and darted from Gabriel to Seth as if looking for a point of attack.

With a growl it stepped closer to Seth, and Gabriel did the same, his fangs snapping in a vicious retort to the werewolf's continued snarls.

Wisps of aether trailed behind the beast as it lunged at Gabriel, who caught the larger clawed hands in his own. Even with his body braced for the attack, it still sent Gabriel skidding back before he held his ground.

Seth tensed in fear as the creature let out an enraged roar that shook the library.

Gabriel gave one of his own, but as terrifying as it was to hear that sound come out of him and see the length of his fangs on full display, it wasn't anywhere as loud or frightening as the rage of the beast he struggled to hold at bay.

It yanked Gabriel forward with the very grip he had on it, a clawed hand breaking free to slash at him. The blow swiped from side to stomach and Gabriel stumbled back, his shirt torn and blood dripping from deep cuts.

"Gabriel!" Seth yelled as Gabriel was grabbed by the throat and slammed against a table near the windows.

The wood cracked with the impact and a whimper fell from Gabriel's lips as long claws sank into the sides of his throat.

No. He can't die like this. It can't end like this, Seth thought frantically, watching blood stream from the wounds on Gabriel's neck.

Seth tried to twist out from beneath the bookcase. He started slapping back against wood to try to shove it off.

His palms smacked down against the floor once more with a cry of frustration, and in the next moment, Seth felt Silas stir—a thin crack opening in one of the walls he'd trapped him behind. Not enough to break free, but enough for some of his power to slip out.

Seth felt it flow through him as he scraped his nails over the floor again, trying to drag himself forward. This time, talons grew from his fingertips and he was able to dig them into the vinyl flooring for leverage. The skin of his hands turned black and scaled as he pulled himself along the floor.

Seth let the power build beneath his skin, sharp and hot like lightning before a storm. His eyes never left Gabriel as he focused the energy between his shoulder blades, doing his best to obey the muffled voice in his head.

The thing that had been Haley leaned in over Gabriel, its mouth opening wider than was natural, and Gabriel tried to kick out at it. Push it back. Stay alive. He twisted at the last second so its fangs sank into his shoulder rather than his face.

With a strangled cry, Seth forced a wave of aether from his back, letting the power flare out like wings to shove the bookcase up off him.

He was certain from the warmth along his side that some of his stitches had torn, but he made it out before the aether gave way and the shelf toppled back to the floor.

The beast had turned yellow eyes on him now, a snarl rattling from its blood-soaked maw while Gabriel struggled against its hold. His thrashing only made its claws sink deeper into his neck.

Seth stepped forward, his talons flexed, their tips gleaming like hooked knives.

The werewolf snarled and squeezed down on Gabriel's throat. The added pressure making Gabriel cry out and twist, his body bucking against the pain. It hurt to see him like that.

Helpless. Wounded. Gabriel's blood everywhere. On his skin. The desk. The floor. On claws that loosened then withdrew as the beast turned its full attention on Seth. Gabriel slumping from the desk to the floor, body bloody and shaking.

Seth wasn't sure what to do now that the beast faced him down. He only had talons and an inkling of power he barely understood how to control. This thing had claws and teeth and a body that slammed into Seth like a truck.

The impact sent him sprawling through a pile of books. his head knocking hard against one of the shelves that had fallen.

Dazed and in pain, Seth wasn't quick enough to react when it grabbed his leg and pulled him forward to fling him into the side of a desk like a rag doll. He could feel blood dripping from his side when he landed, the last of his stitches having torn.

It grabbed at him again, and Seth swiped at it. A few deep stripes of red marred its face where his talons met flesh.

The beast flinched back, but only for a moment. Not long enough for Seth to get to his feet. Not long enough to save himself.

Lips curled back from fangs with anger. Claws sank down into Seth's chest, and he let out a choked sob as blood seeped up to soak his shirt.

A different set of claws wrapped around the beast's throat. Strong enough to pull its head back, leaving its neck exposed, and Seth slashed out, his talons rending flesh easily.

Blood sprayed out over him and the surrounding area as the werewolf stumbled from Gabriel's hold with a wet gurgle and fell to the ground. It heaved a shuddering breath once, twice, and fell still.

Gabriel took several steps toward the corpse that lay on the ground. Seth watched the heave of his shoulders as he breathed, the sound of it rough and unsteady, as if he were fighting back tears.

Seth flinched back when Gabriel turned his gaze toward him. His eyes were dry, but still yellow, and his clawed hands dripped blood.

Gabriel moved at a measured pace toward him. His claws and teeth retracted with each careful step he took, and by the time he knelt next to Seth, he was deceptively human in appearance. Right down to the green of his eyes.

Seth's talons hadn't retracted the way Gabriel's claws had. They stayed just as they were, hooked and sharp and glistening with Haley's blood.

Gabriel reached a hand out toward him and Seth jerked back. Not because he was afraid of him. But because Seth knew now what his touch could do, how it could rot the very spirit of a person.

Gabriel's hand dropped back to his side, his mouth a thin line but his eyes narrowed with concern as Seth sat staring at his hands.

"I— I don't know how to make it stop." Seth hated the way his voice broke. The way his hands shook. "I don't know what to do. What do I do?"

"Okay. Just calm down."

"Calm down?" Tears welled in Seth's eyes, and he struggled to blink them back, to hold on to some semblance of his sanity. He felt like he had lost his mind. "Are you crazy? I have talons growing out of my fingers!"

"Adrenaline can trigger it," Gabriel said, "so if you want them to go away, you need to *calm down.*"

Seth drew in a breath and let it out slowly, doing his best to calm the pace of his heart and the rush of blood that set his nerves on edge.

The talons retracted gradually, until even the pointed ends had slipped away. Seth looked past his fingers when they'd gone. To the hideous corpse only a few feet away.

"I did that to her." Seth realized.

"She would have killed you."

Seth shook his head. Gabriel didn't get it. He wasn't understanding.

"She turned into that thing because of me. I saw it happen with Aaliyah," Seth said. "Something came out of me. It did something to her, to Haley, and Mary." He raised his eyes to Gabriel, terrified of what Gabriel would think of him.

"I'm sorry," Seth said, more of a plea than an apology now. Tears streamed down his cheeks as the panic took over. "I'm so sorry."

The blood on Seth's chest drew Gabriel's attention. "You're not healing like I do though."

Seth stared at him. "What does that have to do with any of it?"

"It means you're not a famirian. It's a dominant trait across all types."

"Then what the hell am I?"

"I don't know. I thought you were a raven famirian since they control aether and I saw it come out of you at the farmhouse but"—Gabriel shook his head, and Seth followed his gaze to where the thing that had been Haley lay—"I've never seen anything like this before."

"Never?"

"I mean... There are stories about how the first familiars had immense powers, but I thought they were just that—stories. Tall tales about things that no longer exist."

Seth drew in a sharp breath and dropped his gaze. His hands curling into fists in his lap. "My mom told me the thing inside me was one of the first raven familiars ever created."

"Are you serious?"

"You think I would joke about that?" Seth asked as he looked at Gabriel with narrowed eyes.

"No. No of course not," Gabriel replied with a shake of his head.

"What should we do?"

"You should go back to the Jeep. There's a first aid kit in the glove compartment."

"What are we going to do about Haley, though? We can't just leave her here like this." Seth looked to Haley's body, or rather, what should have been Haley's body. Blood splashed over the muzzled face and broad chest, an ugly slash where its throat should have been. "We have to do something. We have to tell someone."

"Josh and I will take care of it. He went to check the woods, but he'll be back soon."

Seth looked back at Gabriel with his toneless reply, not knowing what to say or how to help him. He knew pain when he saw it. Even when people didn't want it seen. But Gabriel was trying to be strong for him, even though he shouldn't have to be. Not when it was his best friend's mutated body that lay dead only a short distance away.

"Just go to the Jeep, Seth."

Seth got shakily to his feet, using the desk he'd backed into as a brace. He took a step toward the door, his eyes still on Gabriel, who hadn't moved.

When Gabriel swallowed back a choked sound, Seth's eyes were drawn to the reddened skin of his throat. There was blood on the side of his neck, where claws had dug in deep, but the wounds already looked less serious than they should have. Gabriel's skin a mottled bruise where bloody gouges of torn flesh should have been.

There was light enough here from the streetlamps just outside the windows that Seth could make out the tears that slid down Gabriel's cheeks. The sight pushed Seth to his knees in front of him, and Seth's hand shook as he reached out toward Gabriel only to pull back at the last moment, his arm recoiling with memories of Mary's reddening skin and Haley's broken sounds as her body contorted—the sound of bones inside her cracking and pressing up beneath her skin like her very insides would split her open.

A wounded sound escaped Gabriel, animalistic and wretched. He hunched in on himself with his head bowed into his blood-stained hands. His forehead pressed to the floor as he shook, and for a moment, Seth feared he'd turn too. His breath caught in his throat, thinking of all the times he'd touched him. All the times the infection that had ripped Haley asunder from the inside out could have wormed its way beneath Gabriel's skin.

Seth held his breath, waiting, while tears stung his eyes and fear churned inside him like a sickness. Like something that would take on mass and crawl up his throat if given half a chance. But Gabriel only cried, wet and shuddering and awful in a way that broke Seth's heart, but his bones didn't break into new shapes, and his flesh didn't pucker or darken to a sickly red. And for that, Seth was grateful.

"I'm sorry," Seth whispered, because it was the only comfort he could give without touching him. "I'm so, so sorry."

Gabriel raised his gaze to Seth. His eyes seemed to shine when a door opened and the light from outside fell across them, bright and reflective, the way Kit's had been in the headlights of Gabriel's Jeep.

"What happened?"

Josh's voice sent a chill of dread down Seth's spine and he closed his eyes. It should come from him. He should be the one to tell Josh, but like a coward, he kept his mouth shut and let it fall to Gabriel. He let him explain to a wide-eyed and pale Josh what had happened.

That the thing lying in a puddle of its own blood with its tongue lolling out of its mouth used to be the woman he loved. That it had been her or them, and Seth had chosen them.

# THIRTY-THREE

They made Seth go back to the Jeep while they figured out what to do with the body. Seth didn't argue with the decision. He just stumbled his way silently back to the car and sat inside it while his head throbbed and his wounds bled.

He was pretty sure his head was bleeding too, and when he touched the source of the pain there, his fingers came back red and sticky, just like he expected.

There was a clang of metal and Seth looked up in time to see the library door bang against the brick of the building a second time as Gabriel and Josh carried the bloodied corpse outside. His gut clenched at the sight of it as they passed beneath a streetlamp. It was even more gruesome-looking in the light, the wound along the neck a ragged mess of torn meat, the beast's eyes gaping wide and its tongue dangling from its fanged mouth, the length of it swaying as they carried the body.

Seth wanted to look away, but something made him watch them carry it to the trunk of Josh's car, where they deposited it carefully.

*If you'd let me out, I could have controlled her,* Silas whispered to him. *She'd be alive right now.*

Seth ignored the urge to respond and hugged his arms around himself, his eyes fixed on Gabriel and Josh and the body in the trunk until he couldn't stand to see their pain anymore.

He told himself that Silas was lying as he looked away. That even if it were true, he wouldn't have had the strength to manage such a thing.

When Gabriel got back inside the Jeep after Josh had driven off, he took one look at Seth and leaned over him to get to the glove compartment. It clicked open and Seth watched as Gabriel took out the first aid kit.

"I can do it myself," Seth said.

"Don't argue with me, Seth. I'm really not in the mood."

"Fine. Okay."

Seth shrugged halfway out of his shirt to let Gabriel patch him up. His breath caught with even the slightest pressure from Gabriel's hand as he tended to Seth's wounds.

"I think you are healing," Gabriel said while he worked. "Just not as quickly as expected. Probably because of the witchbane. You shouldn't need stitches again, though."

"Thank god. That was torture. They couldn't have at least used an anesthetic?"

"Not safely. We don't typically treat human patients."

Seth sat and considered things for a moment before he asked, "So, if I am healing, were you wrong before? Am I a famirian?"

"Maybe. The bond I have with Kit though is a kind of mutualistic symbiosis, and it's consensual. What's happening with you and Silas, I think it's more—"

"Parasitic?"

"Yeah, or at least something close to it."

Seth slid his shirt back on with slow movements when Gabriel had finished. His entire body felt like one long bruise.

"What's going to happen—with Haley?"

"Josh is taking her to the rest of the pack. He's already called them."

"Do they know about me, then?"

Gabriel didn't reply right away, and Seth's heart gave a panicked flutter.

"Gabriel?"

"I told him to say that I did it."

Seth blinked at him. Taken aback. "They won't come after you for it, will they?"

"I don't know," Gabriel replied, and the vacancy in his voice tore at Seth. "Hopefully they'll understand it was self-defense."

Self-defense. Seth tried to accept it as the truth—but it didn't feel right—what he'd done felt like murder.

"Were you hurt anywhere else?" Gabriel asked.

Seth didn't reply. Too busy remembering the warmth of Haley's blood as it had sprayed over him. He couldn't get the sight of her monstrous and bloodied corpse out of his head.

"Seth—"

A laugh bubbled up out of Seth, the sound of it brittle and on the edge of hysteria. A completely inappropriate response given the situation.

Then something gave out inside him, and his laughter snapped off into a ragged sob, his body bowing forward.

"I've killed other people. Silas... He made me kill so many people," Seth blurted, and he couldn't meet Gabriel's eyes. He could only wrap his arms about himself as he cried. "He killed Adam. He killed— These people came after me with knives and guns, and he killed them."

Gabriel stared at him. He was silent, but Seth could see that the pieces of the puzzle were clicking together behind his eyes.

"Take a breath."

Seth breathed in deep. Let it out slowly.

"Now, tell me what happened," Gabriel instructed. "From the beginning."

Seth took another breath and let the words he'd been holding back fall out of him. He felt sicker the longer he talked. He lost his nerve partway through telling Gabriel about waking up to find Adam in the woods, about the heart he'd found more than half-eaten lying next to him with the taste of blood in his mouth. The Jeep door thunked open as he leaned out to puke up thin strings of bile from an empty stomach.

Gabriel didn't force Seth to keep talking when he closed the door and leaned back in his seat. He just started the Jeep and drove to his apartment, because Seth begged him not to take him home to his father.

Seth wouldn't let Gabriel touch him to help him out of the car when they got to the building, even though he stumbled on his way to the door. Still convinced that the less physical contact they had, the better the chance Gabriel would go uninfected. But when he tripped into the wall of the hallway, Gabriel slung one of Seth's arms over his shoulders, despite his protests, and steadied him as he got them inside the elevator.

"Did Kit ever mention a Silas ?" Seth asked quietly when the metal doors slid closed and he had a moment to think.

"No."

"How could you not know about him? I thought the two of you were supposed to be bonded on a some kind of soul level. How could you *not* know?"

"I'm not sure," Gabriel replied. "Kit's been hiding things from me somehow. I don't understand it either."

A nod and a frown were the most Seth could manage in response, not having the energy to argue further. His head turned back to the elevator doors as they opened on Gabriel's floor.

Seth staggered his way into the bathroom once they were inside the apartment, unsteady on his feet from the blood loss, and the memories plaguing his conscience as he turned on the sink to wet a washcloth.

He wanted to lie down. He didn't much care if it was a bed or a couch he collapsed on. He just wanted to escape into unconsciousness for as long as his nightmares would allow.

When Gabriel knocked on the doorframe a few minutes later, it was to find Seth leaning over the sink taking steadying breaths. The washcloth was now soaked in blood and wadded up in his hand against the edge of the sink.

"Are you okay?"

Seth nodded, then after another moment, he shook his head, his hand reaching out to turn off the still running faucet. "No. I'm not okay." Seth took another deep breath. "What am I going to do, Gabriel?"

"We'll figure it out."

Seth took the clothes Gabriel held but didn't meet his eyes. He thought of Haley every time he looked at him, and couldn't understand how Gabriel could want to be anywhere near him. If Seth had watched Gabriel kill Evelyn, he'd never be so forgiving.

He closed the bathroom door when Gabriel stepped away so he could change. The clothes were similar to the ones he wore now, though the shirt was black rather than blue.

When he stepped out of the bathroom, he wandered to the bedroom on hearing noise in that direction. He found Gabriel sitting on the edge of the bed, just staring straight ahead like everything had caught up with him.

Seth moved over to the bed to sit beside him, silence filling the space between them. At any other time, Seth would have reached out to comfort him, but he thought better of it now.

"It's my fault."

Seth looked up at Gabriel's words and his eyes searched his face before they dropped to the cellphone in his hand. He'd obviously just gotten off a call with someone.

"In what world is this your fault?"

"In the one where I asked Ruth for her help."

"What do you mean?"

"The spell she did." Gabriel looked away. "It's meant to make the body a more receptive host."

"More receptive?"

Gabriel looked back to Seth as he said, "Isaac doesn't come from a bloodline that is capable of bonding with a familiar. So Ruth did a spell to open his spirit up to the attachment process. The thing is—she didn't think to set up a barrier to contain the magic."

"So, the spell—"

"It didn't just help the snake familiar bond with Isaac, it helped Silas get some control too," Gabriel explained. "Before that, he would have been more of a passenger. A hitchhiker almost. Able to influence your actions with suggestion, and use a modicum of his powers, but not much else. Now though—"

"He can take the wheel?"

"For lack of a better term, yeah."

"What are we going to do?" Seth asked. "Can Ruth help? Is there a spell or something she could do?"

"No. Once this magic takes hold, it can't be reversed."

"Gabriel—"

"Get down!"

Seth was pulled to the floor in the next instant just before the sound of glass shattering erupted through the room and padding flew from the mattress where Seth had been sitting only a second ago.

A second bullet pinged into the wall. A wide shot, probably meant to startle them out into the open, and it almost worked. Almost had Seth running before Gabriel could drag him back down to protect him from the next bullet that whizzed past and left a splintered hole in the wall.

Seth could feel tears on his face and Gabriel tugged at his sleeve to get him to look at him as hands checked over his body.

"Are you hurt?"

"I don't think so. No."

Another gunshot and Seth shielded his head at the sound of something else shattering. A picture fell from the dresser to the floor just in front of them, a hole punched through the center of the image.

"Move for the door and stay down. Watch out for the glass."

Seth nodded. He crawled on his belly to the door, doing his best as he went to not cut himself on the shards from the picture frame.

They made it out into the hallway, both of them pressing their backs against the wall.

Gabriel's hand was on his shoulder, a pained sound escaping him as he hunched in on himself. Seth had his hands on him before he could think not to, his fingers pulling back the collar of Gabriel's shirt.

Seth had expected to find a messy hole from a bullet, blood dripping down olive brown skin. What he found instead was a cluster of vein-like webbing crawling up from where Gabriel had been bitten by the beast. The mottled bruise now looked like a festering wound. Thinner, more delicate lines of gray and purple ran through the deep, almost rotted shade of red.

Whatever this was, whatever Silas had done to Haley... It was contagious.

# THIRTY-FOUR

The longer Seth stared, the more he noticed the way it pulsed and squirmed along Gabriel's skin. Alive. Malignant. Like some kind of tumorous leech.

It didn't seem to be spreading the way Haley's had, but that might have just been a matter of time.

"Gabriel—"

"I'm fine. I'll be fine."

Seth shook his head. His tears came faster now, because he knew Gabriel's words couldn't be true. Not after Haley. Not after what she'd become or how she'd died. Not trapped as they were.

Gabriel raised his head, his eyes on the front door and head cocked as if he were listening.

Seth held his breath, pushed his panic down for when they were safe. It took some focus, but eventually he picked up on the sound of four heartbeats in the hallway outside Gabriel's apartment. The steady *thump-thump-thump* deafening the sound of their footsteps.

He wondered if that was what Gabriel heard. The heartbeats. Or if that was something more in Silas's range of sensory perception.

Gabriel pulled Seth forward. Both of them crouched low, and tried to avoid being seen from the windows by the hunters who were no doubt on the roofs of the buildings opposite them.

There were apparently more gunmen aiming for this room because the next instant, it practically exploded. Bullets ripped through couch cushions, lamps, the television.

Gabriel shielded Seth with his body, his chest pressed to Seth's back and Seth's head cradled beneath his arms, protecting him from the shower of glass and sparks that rained down on them.

Seth shifted beneath Gabriel and raised his head enough to see the door that splintered a short distance from them. More hunters on the other side of it. Bullets punching through and creating holes in the wall opposite it.

*Let me out.*

Seth squeezed his eyes shut. Shook his head at the sound of Silas's voice.

*Now!*

The word boomed in Seth's skull, the force of it slamming through him like a physical blow, and the echoes sent tremors through his body that made him twist beneath Gabriel.

A ringing in Seth's ears drowned out the sound of gunshots and shouting. He couldn't move, but he could feel movement inside himself. Silas's essence seeped like a poison out through a hole in the walls he'd made to ooze through the folds of his brain.

"No..." Seth whimpered.

"Seth?"

Seth's back arched as Silas spread like fire through every muscle and bone, taking everything Seth was and shoving him down into the recesses of his own mind. His consciousness faltered as he was smothered beneath a wave of smokeless heat.

Gabriel's voice came again, calling Seth's name, a distant echo of urgency that Seth couldn't answer. But Silas did.

*"Not even close."*

Gabriel let go of them, moved back enough that Silas could rise.

Aether swirled around him like a barrier and bullets dropped to the ground with metallic clinks before they could even reach him.

Gabriel turned as one fell behind him. Silas's eyes were on him, a smirk pulling at the corner of his mouth, a wave of aether still curled around Gabriel like a crooked wing.

Darkness fluttered across the window. A flock of ravens blocked the glass panes. A few flashes of light from the streetlamp outside appeared now and then when one would take a bullet, only for the light to flicker out when another took its place.

The aether retracted as Silas stepped toward the front door. His hand rose, and the door blew outward. The hunter just on the other side of it was blasted back, thick slabs of wood pinning him to the wall. Blood gushed from the wounds and dribbled from his mouth as his head lolled forward, his body slumping lifelessly.

Silas took in the wood lodged in the man's chest, and Seth felt a spark of disappointment from him. *"Such a waste."*

The other three hunters had frozen. A man stood to the left of Silas and the other two stared at him from the ground. One woman. One man.

The hunter on the left was the first to react, his gun leveling with Silas's head.

The gunshot was a sharp crack. One that didn't faze Silas.

The bullet was stopped by the aether. It clinked to the ground harmlessly and Silas's hand shot out, his fingers digging into the man's throat.

The man's legs kicked uselessly in the air as he was lifted up. blood spurting from his neck as Seth felt the prick of Silas's talons extending.

The woman stood, then ran forward, a hunting knife readied in her hand as if she thought she could gut them like a deer.

Silas flicked a hand in her direction. The motion stopped her in her tracks as tendrils of aether curled around her arms. It turned the knife in toward her. Her arms struggled as she stared down at the gleaming point of the blade.

Her eyes went wide as it pierced her flesh, sank into her stomach and pulled upward swiftly with a jerk of Silas's hand.

Seth wanted to close his eyes and couldn't. He was forced to watch as her organs flooded out of her with a splat. She dropped to her knees in the same instant, then fell forward into her own guts.

"Please," the last hunter begged as Silas turned eyes on him. "Please, no…"

*"You can die…"* Silas smiled. *"Or you can serve."*

The man crawled forward, a placating gesture, yet another plea on his lips.

Aether lashed across the man's cheek, almost seeming to spark with the contact. Inky red lines curved over his skin when it withdrew. His face almost seemed to melt, and Seth watched helplessly as the man screamed, his fingers clawing at his own flesh as if he could peel the affliction off.

Silas turned his attention back to the man still thrashing in his grip. The man's eyes were wild with panic—the look of someone who knew they were about to die.

"*I think you'll be okay with me killing this one.*" Silas glanced at the man's boots then back at his face. "*I can smell Gabriel's blood on his shoes. He's the one that shot him.*"

A jolt of anger ran through Seth as he remembered how Gabriel had suffered. How he had almost died.

Silas looked over as Gabriel stepped out into the hall. His eyes widened when he saw the face of the man they held pinned to the wall. The recognition clear in his stare and the half step he took back. There was fear there.

"*I know you want him dead. I can feel your rage.*" Silas sneered. "*I'm happy to kill him for you.*"

Silas pressed the man to the floor and Seth could feel a smile on his lips, the fabric of the shirt as it was ripped open, the heat of blood as Silas dug into the hunter's chest, his talons working to split muscle and break bone.

Seth wanted to scream when his hand closed around the beating heart. He wanted to claw free of his mind, go blind and deaf and numb so he wouldn't have to see, hear, or feel any of it.

Silas was going to eat this man's heart. He was going to use Seth's lips and teeth to feed on the beating muscle, and there was nothing Seth could do to stop it.

Hands hauled him back abruptly, and the heart slipped from their grasp.

Silas scrabbled forward against the hold, practically rabid for the heart now visible in the man's chest.

"Seth! Seth, snap out of it!"

Seth screamed out in his own head at the sound of Gabriel's voice and he felt another presence alongside his own, Kit trying to help him push Silas back into that box of a room.

Seth blinked his eyes once the wall was sealed back up, then blinked again just to be certain he was the one blinking.

He flexed his blood-soaked fingers and turned his head to see Gabriel behind him looking stricken. His arms were wrapped around Seth still, but to steady him now, rather than hold him back.

Seth took in the broken bodies around him. The blood splashed over the walls and the floor. The man on the ground writhing in agony as he clutched his face. "I'm sorry. I didn't mean to—"

"It wasn't you." Gabriel shook his head as he pulled Seth to his feet.

Seth leaned into him, his body unsteady and trembling.

"You wouldn't do this."

They moved down the hall as voices sounded from below. Seth stumbled and Gabriel had to half carry him.

People shouted from the other side of the doors as they passed, more than one person mentioning the police.

They took the stairs up since down wasn't an option, Gabriel helping Seth along the best he could.

The doorway to the roof was locked, but the doorknob snapped off easily enough beneath Gabriel's hand. The sight of the crumpled metal made Seth realize how easily Gabriel could have hurt him if he'd wanted to.

The door that led out onto the roof swung open and Gabriel pulled Seth along after him. Seth skidded to a halt that dragged Gabriel to a stop before he could reach the edge of the rooftop.

There was nowhere left to run. No safe space to hide.

"Shit!" Seth swore. "What now?"

Gabriel nodded to the gap between where they stood and the next building over. "We're going to have to jump."

"Are you joking? No. Gabriel, I can't!" Seth's eyes widened, taking in the distance between the rooftops. "There's no way in hell I can make that!"

"We don't have a choice."

Seth looked back over his shoulder at the sound of footsteps pounding up the stairwell. "You're going to have to go without me."

"No! I'm not leaving you!"

"You have to!" Seth shouted back. "There's no way I can make that jump!"

"Seth—"

"Just go! Please!"

The footsteps were getting closer. Seth could make out voices now.

Gabriel pulled Seth toward him, got an arm under his legs.

"Don't be stupid! You'll fall!" Seth protested as Gabriel lifted him into his arms.

Gabriel didn't answer. He was already taking a half step back, as if preparing to run.

"Gabriel—"

"Hold on to me."

Seth wrapped his arms around Gabriel's neck, pressed his tear-stained face to his chest, and murmured blasphemies into the fabric of Gabriel's shirt that would have sent Isaac's head rolling when Gabriel sprinted across the rooftop. The wind ruffled through Seth's hair as he charged forward.

Seth felt when Gabriel pushed off the roof and he squeezed his eyes shut, held his breath while they sailed through open air, waited for the fall.

Seth's breath hitched at the jolt that raced up Gabriel's frame with the impact of his landing. His feet slid a short distance across concrete with the momentum.

Gabriel didn't put Seth down. He kept his hold on him as he jumped off the edge of the roof onto a fire escape, then moved lower along its side, one arm still around Seth and the hand of the other gripping the metal. He finally jumped to the ground, skipping the last level entirely.

Seth was shaking when Gabriel set him on his feet, still shocked that they hadn't died.

"We need to get to the Jeep. Can you run?"

Seth looked at Gabriel with wide, frightened eyes. "You want to go back there?"

"They're coming around this way after us. If we double back now, we may have a chance."

"This is insane." Seth wept. "This is insane. This can't be my life."

"Hey." Gabriel shook Seth as if it could shake him free of the trauma of being shot at like an animal and jumping across rooftops. "Don't lose it on me now. We need to move."

Seth let Gabriel drag him forward, back in the direction of the building they'd just escaped. His feet tripped forward until he matched step with Gabriel's pace.

He was fast. So much faster than Seth had known, and he knew now that he was probably slowing Gabriel down. That he could no doubt run faster than this if he just let go of Seth's hand and left him behind to die.

They crouched low when they reached the edge of the building, Gabriel peering around the side to the parking lot where the Jeep was.

Seth was gasping for air, a hand pressed to his side where it ached.

"There's two of them standing watch out front. I think we can make it, but we need to move quick and quiet."

Seth nodded and let Gabriel lead the way as he crept forward with his keys gripped tightly in his hand so they wouldn't jangle together.

Gabriel unlocked the passenger side door when they reached it, grimacing at the click of the lock, and Seth pressed a hand to his mouth as if his breathing might give them away instead of the creak the door made as Gabriel inched it open.

The hunters didn't seem to notice the noise. Gabriel took the chance to crawl inside and to the driver's seat, his head ducked and the key waiting to turn in the ignition.

He motioned for Seth to wait to close the door when he got in. Counted silently to three. Seth read his lips and slammed the door shut as Gabriel set the engine running.

Gabriel shifted the Jeep into reverse and backed out of the parking space as the two hunters started shouting. Seth only narrowly got his seatbelt buckled before they were peeling forward, the Jeep careening around the corner and out of the parking lot, its front wheel bouncing off the curb with the sharp turn but still managing to avoid the gunfire that followed them.

Seth looked back over his shoulder at the hunters as they scrambled to get to their vehicles to follow.

They sped down the city streets, ignoring traffic signals and taking turns at speeds that had Seth clutching at his seatbelt and bracing a hand against the window to keep from smacking into it.

A barricade blocked their path on the next turn and Gabriel didn't even slow down. The Jeep crashed through it, sending splinters of orange and white plastic flying.

Seth wondered if the hunters had set road blocks like this one up to deter people from the area around the apartment building. It would explain why the streets had been deserted until now.

Gabriel pulled out onto a busy street and weaved his way through cars where he could. Still trying to put distance between them and the hunters.

When they lost sight of the hunters behind them, Gabriel pulled off the road into a parking garage. He stopped the Jeep in one of the parking spots and shoved Seth's head down to hide him.

Seth held his breath as if it would somehow help. Gabriel's hand was a heavy weight along the back of his head, warm and protective despite everything.

They waited for the sound of approaching car engines to slow, for people armed with guns to crowd around the Jeep and put them down like dogs. But the cars passed them by. The sounds of shouting and engines eventually died out.

Minutes passed in silence before Gabriel raised his head to check over the dashboard. His hand slipped from Seth's hair a second later.

"Are you okay?"

Seth glanced at Gabriel. "I feel like I should be the one asking you that."

Gabriel pressed a hand to his shoulder, flinching slightly. "I don't think it's spreading yet. It didn't with Haley right away..." He said the last part more quietly. Like it hurt to say her name.

"God, Gabriel, I'm so sorry. This is all my fault."

Gabriel winced and dropped his hand from his shoulder. "It's my fault too."

Seth shook his head and looked away from Gabriel to stare out into the darkness of the parking garage. His eyes flicked over to the entrance where the hunters had passed recently.

"My dad," Seth gasped. "I need to call my dad. The hunters know where I live. They may try to—"

Seth could feel Gabriel's eyes on him as he searched his pockets, only to find nothing.

"My cellphone," Seth said in a near panic. "I can't find my cellphone. I must have dropped it."

"When? You didn't have it on you back at the farmhouse."

"It's probably at the bottom of the ocean."

"What? How the hell did you end up in the ocean?" Gabriel thought for a moment. "Is that why you smell like salt?"

"I don't know how it happened, okay? I've been getting jerked around from one place to another," Seth replied. "It's like I teleported or something."

"You mean you flew."

Seth stared at Gabriel with the absurd statement. "Excuse me? Flew?"

"Some raven famirians can fly, but it's a rare ability."

Seth felt like his brain was short-circuiting. There was only so much he could process.

"Okay, I can't with this right now." Seth gave a flustered wave of his hands. "Do you have your phone? I need to get ahold of my dad."

"They won't go after him. He's human," Gabriel said. "Too many bodies would draw attention."

"Right, because subtle is definitely what just went down at the apartment."

Seth patted himself down one last time to be sure it was gone. It was. The photograph was there, though, crumpled but untorn when Seth pulled it from his jeans pocket.

The faces stared back up at him. All solemn, but for the hint of a smile on the man's face.

Seth's eyes caught on the woman just behind Isaiah. Her hair was longer, and her face younger, but he still recognized her.

"I know her."

"Who?"

"The woman behind my dad. My real dad."

"Your real dad?"

"Apparently the guy I thought was my dad adopted me when he married my mom," Seth said bitterly. "Anyway, the woman behind him is Debra Thompson, I went to her for a therapy session."

"Really?"

Seth nodded.

"Do you think she realized who you were?"

"Maybe? She acted weird when she first saw me. She would have known my mom. My real dad too." Seth smoothed his thumb over the photograph. "Maybe she can tell us about Silas."

"Or maybe she's in with the hunters." Gabriel shook his head. "We should lie low. It's not safe."

Seth gestured toward Gabriel's shoulder. "I don't think we have the time to wait."

"Kit is holding it back."

"But how long can he manage that for?" Seth frowned. "I mean, I assume it was the same with Haley, that her familiar helped her, but she succumbed to it eventually anyway."

"I don't want you in danger."

"I'm already in danger. We might as well try to figure out why."

Gabriel looked frustrated, but he pulled his cellphone out all the same. He seemed to think for a moment before sending off a text himself, probably to his family, and then handed the phone to Seth.

"Call your dad and then look up Debra's address."

The first person Seth actually called was Evelyn. Who was out of her mind with worry and Seth felt terrible for not thinking to contact her sooner. But she understood why he hadn't after he explained things.

It was when he got to the part about the hunters that she seemed skeptical.

"Hunters? Really?" she mused.

"Just... stay away from Mrs. Fields. She's one of them."

"What? Our math teacher is one?"

"Just trust me. I should go."

Seth hung up without a goodbye and called his dad next. Even as he explained things, he knew his father wouldn't believe him. Hunters. Familiars. Witches. It sounded insane.

The response was what Seth had expected, his dad asking him to stop playing games and come home so they could talk.

Seth went back and forth a few times with him before he hung up, a lump of worry in his throat as he looked up Debra's address rather than keep arguing. He couldn't make his father believe him. The best he could do was try to find a way to end all this.

# THIRTY-FIVE

Dr. Debra Thompson's house was in a small suburb just a few miles outside of Portland. It was a quaint, unassuming house, white-sided with a few potted plants sitting on the front porch. The windows were dark and curtained, unsurprising for the hour of their visit.

"Are you sure about this?" Gabriel asked warily as he pulled the keys from the ignition.

"No, but I need answers." Seth gave Gabriel an imploring look. "I need to know about my dad. My real dad. And I need to know where Silas came from."

Gabriel finally gave a nod and pocketed his keys. Then he followed Seth's lead in exiting the car.

They stepped onto the darkened porch. Seth reached out a hand to rap on the front door. No response. So he knocked again, harder, louder.

A light went on inside the house, shining out through the narrow windows alongside the door. Then came the quiet padding of footsteps.

The front door opened a moment later to reveal Debra in a pink bathrobe, the legs of her floral pajama bottoms sticking out from beneath her robe a few inches above her bare feet.

She'd clearly just risen from bed, her eyes bleary and her hair in disarray.

Seth didn't apologize for waking her. He just held the photograph out between thumb and forefinger. His hand shook as he stood there waiting, with the light from the hallway glinting off the image.

"You knew my mom." It came out like an accusation, his voice rising on a swell of anger.

She'd known. Known all along who he was, and said nothing.

Debra took the photo from Seth. Her eyes distant, somber, as if remembering something from long ago. Something unpleasant.

"You knew my mom," Seth said again. More softly this time.

"Eliza. Yes. I knew her." Debra raised her eyes from the photo. "We'd kept in touch over the years, and I saw photos of you when I visited her at Oak View. I'm sure your father found my practice because of your mother. She probably mentioned me."

Debra gestured them inside with a sigh and a wave of her hand. They obliged, stepping into the entryway, Seth first and Gabriel following in after.

"Take a seat. I'll make tea. We'll need it," she said as she closed the door, then swept past the living room and toward what must have been the kitchen.

Her exit left Gabriel and Seth standing awkwardly side by side until Seth ventured to take up her instructions, going into the living room to sit on the mauve sofa.

There was so much green in the room. Not from the walls, which were a soft blue, but from the many plants that decorated the space.

Seth took a seat on the couch and did his best to ignore the fact Gabriel had sat on the opposite end. The space between them was substantial enough that if Seth reached out, he wouldn't have even been able to touch him.

They were back to this then. The avoidance. The distance.

Debra returned, a wooden tray with a tea set on it in her hands.

They watched silently as she set the tray down on the coffee table with a soft clack of wood and a rattle of china. The kettle looked like an antique, white-bodied with a spray of delicate pink flowers on green leaves along its sides. The teacups had been painted to match and rimmed in gold.

Debra's hands were steady when she lifted the kettle, one hand on the lid and the other on the handle as she tipped it forward carefully. An aromatic yellow-brown liquid filled the first cup.

"Now then," she said as she passed the cup to Seth before moving on to fill the next, "I suppose you have questions for me."

Debra held the second cup out to Gabriel, who declined the offer with a shake of his head and she took it as her own as she settled into one of the high-backed chairs across from the couch. There was an air of patience about her that reminded Seth of his time in her office sitting on a different couch opposite her.

There were so many things Seth wanted to ask. Things he should ask. Important things. Things about the spirit inside him.

"My father," Seth asked instead. "My real father, what's he like?"

"Isaiah. He's charming. Well spoken. I guess you could call him a preacher of sorts," Debra explained. She puckered her lips as if tasting something far more bitter than the tea she'd sipped. "But that'd be putting it kindly. More kindly than he'd deserve, I'm afraid."

"And if you put it unkindly?" Gabriel asked.

"Then I'd call him a cult leader. Not of a very well-known cult. But a cult all the same."

Seth recoiled at the words, his full teacup clutched tightly in his hands, his fingers numb around the still-hot china.

He was the son of a cult leader. That was where he'd come from. That was who he was.

"We all believed in Isaiah," Debra continued. "In his teachings. His promises."

"And what teachings were those?" Gabriel prompted when Seth remained silent.

Debra took a drink from her own cup of tea before answering, as if to steady her nerves. "About spirits mostly. About the doorways between our world and others. And when he found a pocket dimension—we believed him even more."

"A pocket dimension?"

"A small world connected to our own. It was a beautiful place, and we made it our home."

"Is the cult still active?" Gabriel asked.

Seth glanced at Gabriel. He didn't seem surprised by Debra's words, and Seth wondered if he'd already known that such places existed.

"Yes. Though I don't believe its numbers have ever been the same since the incident."

Seth blinked at her, finally looking up. "The incident?"

"Isaiah had been searching for a specific door. One that the witches had locked a powerful spirit behind."

"You mean Silas." Seth realized.

Debra nodded with a grim frown, "Isaiah found the door, and he opened it. We thought it our salvation. But instead..." She trailed off, her hands trembling so badly around her teacup, she had to put it down. The fine china clinked against the wood of the coffee table.

"What happened?" Seth asked.

"The children were offered as vessels." Debra sniffed. "It took Peter," She paused as if to take a steadying breath and tears welled in her eyes. "My son." Another pause, then, "Your half brother."

The teacup slipped from Seth's fingers to shatter against the floor. The sound of it breaking barely registered.

Gabriel's voice came to him closer than before. A hand brushed Seth's shoulder briefly before he pulled away, not up to being touched in that moment.

He blinked back tears. Because he'd had a brother. A brother he'd never known. Would never know.

"Including you and Peter, there were six of you."

"S-six?"

"All from different mothers, but yes. Six. Five boys, and one girl."

He thought of the bones in his dream. The skulls staring at him with empty eye sockets. Some would have been his family. All that would be left of his brothers. His sister.

"Seth..." Gabriel started, but trailed off.

Seth rose unsteadily from the couch, picking his way around the broken glass with all the care of someone treading on a grave.

"I need some air."

Seth said nothing about the teacup, and Debra didn't seem fazed as she knelt on the floor to clear up the mess. Gabriel helped her as Seth slipped out of the room then through the front door.

It was cold outside, Seth's breath fogging in front of him as he sucked in deep breaths that he exhaled shakily.

He'd had a family. Brothers. A sister. And from what Silas had told him, his mother had helped drown them all.

But why had Seth been spared then? It made no sense why he would have been allowed to live longer than the others.

There was a noise out in the darkness, a soft rustling that made the hairs on the back of Seth's neck stand on end.

He stepped hurriedly back toward the safety of the house, where he locked the door behind him once he was back inside. His eyes remained on the dark wood just in front of him, waiting for whatever was out there to get in. Had the hunters found them? Or the ravens maybe?

Seth spun around when someone touched his shoulder to find Gabriel standing just behind him.

"I just wanted to see if you were okay."

"I'm fine," Seth lied, shaking off his uneasiness. "It's just a lot. You know?"

Gabriel nodded, understanding. "Do you want to go?" he asked in a whisper.

Seth shook his head. "No." He took in a breath and then wet his lips nervously. "No. I need to know the rest."

Gabriel didn't object, though he didn't look like he agreed with Seth's decision either. He followed him back into the living room all the same, where he sat back down on the couch, nearer Seth this time than before.

"What happened next?" Seth asked quietly. "What happened to Peter?"

Debra took a thin breath, and Seth felt guilty for making her relive it all. But he had to know.

"Isaiah tried to convince me it was an honor for my boy to have been chosen, but it made him into something else. Something monstrous. He wasn't my son anymore. That thing killed him. Burned him right out of his own body as it took him over."

A few tears slipped down Debra's cheeks and Gabriel handed her a tissue from a box on the table next to a potted lily.

Debra took the Kleenex with a nod of thanks before drying her eyes.

"How did you get away from him?" Seth asked quietly. "How did my mother?"

"Hunters came," Debra replied. "They killed Peter, but the spirit escaped by jumping into another boy. So the hunters started drowning the potential vessels. All of them. Even the infants. They thought if the spirit had no where to go they could manage to trap and kill it."

"Hunters killed them?" Seth said, and a sick sense of relief washed over him. "Silas told me my mother had done it."

"No." Debra shook her head. "Your mother, she took you, and she ran. You were only a baby back then, not even four months old yet. How either of you survived out in the woods in the dead of winter, I can't even imagine. You so young and her without even her shoes."

"My dad found us," Seth realized out loud. "He saved us."

Seth could almost see it. His mother in that modest white frock he'd seen her wearing in that photo, running through the woods with Seth clutched to her tightly. Her feet red and blistered with the cold as she moved through the snow as quickly as she could manage, the wind whipping around her and an infant heavy in her arms.

She would have been barely visible with the snow swirling around her when she'd found a road. But his dad would have seen her in the headlights of his car. Would have stopped in time, the car swerving a bit on the snowy road when he'd hit the brake.

His dad would have done his best to help her. He'd have given her his coat bundle Seth up in and helped her into the back of the car, then taken them away from that place.

"He saved us..." Seth said again, and he thought of the words he'd screamed at his father the last time he'd seen him. The memory of how hurt his father had looked coming back to him. The sadness in his eyes. He wished he could take the things he'd said back now.

"As far as I know, your mother and I were the only two of Isaiah's wives to survive the hunters' attack," Debra said. "I saw a few drowned before I managed to escape myself."

A hush fell over the room, somber in its stillness. A moment of silence for the dead.

"You said the cult was still active," Seth said after several minutes had passed. "Can you tell us where it is?"

Gabriel's eyes widened at Seth, clearly not liking where this was going, but he didn't stop Debra when she reluctantly wrote an address on a small pad of paper after Seth insisted, nor when she tore the sheet free to hand it to him.

"This is in Nevada," Seth noted as he stared down at the words.

"Isaiah relocated after the incident," Debra explained. "I heard what followers remained went with him."

Seth supposed that explained why his mother had agreed to settle down in Oregon. They'd moved from state to state until Seth turned five.

"I'd think twice before you go though, Seth," Debra advised. "It's really not safe. If he gets ahold of—"

A shadow flitted by on the opposite wall, catching Seth's attention. A moment more, and it barreled forward.

The world seemed to explode with a breaking of glass from behind them. Seth thought it had to have been a gunshot. Hunters that had tracked them down. But then he heard a wounded *kra* and the flap of wings—the enraged call of many ravens.

Seth had ducked and dropped to his knees on the floor, hands over his head, more for the shower of glass than the birds that flew past him. If this were anything like what happened at the café, they wouldn't touch him.

The bird that had paved the way for the rest had somersaulted over the couch to lie motionless on the carpet beside Seth, its neck bent at an odd angle and its eyes unfocused. Blood seeped from between its feathers where the glass had pierced its flesh.

There was a scream, and Seth raised his head. Bits of glass slipped off him to clink to the floor with his movements. His eyes fixed on Debra, who was trying and failing to keep a dozen ravens at bay.

Gabriel was getting to his feet, his focus on Debra, no doubt thinking he could somehow save her, and Seth flung himself forward to hold him back.

"Seth! What are you doing? We have to help her!"

Seth didn't listen. He dragged Gabriel back, his grip tightening around him as Debra flailed and fought, her fists beating back at the birds that dove at her.

The hooked tip of a beak stabbed through one of her eyes with a soft pop, and a gush of fluid ran down Debra's cheek as the beak dug in deeper.

Debra's struggles ceased, and she dropped to the ground. The bird in her eye pulled back. A bit of something bloody and grayish, like a worm, clutched in its beak that it quickly devoured.

The ravens continued to pick at her body, pulling bloody chunks from it where they could and swallowing them with very little chewing involved.

Seth kept his eyes on the ravens, two of which were fighting over a strip of flesh torn from Debra's cheek, tugging it between them until it snapped in two.

None of the birds seemed interested in either of them, but that could change, and Seth wasn't willing to risk Gabriel.

"Come on. We need to go. We need to go now."

Seth pushed Gabriel toward the front door when he hesitated, those wide green eyes taking in the sight of Debra lying lifeless and the ravens plucking bits of flesh from her body.

"Go," Seth hissed, and gave him an urgent shove. "*Go.*"

He pushed Gabriel forward. Made him run. The entire time, he kept his body between Gabriel and the ravens.

They stumbled from the house and hurried down the porch steps, Gabriel fumbling with his keys on the way to the Jeep. The lights clicked on when he hit the unlock button.

The rustle of feathers was not far behind. A dozen angry squawks filled the air with the slam of the Jeep doors after they'd piled inside the car.

"Drive!" Seth shouted as ravens flew from the broken window of the house.

Gabriel hit the gas, and the Jeep lurched forward. When Seth chanced a look behind them, he found the ravens hadn't followed. He didn't ask Gabriel to slow down though.

"I should leave town."

Gabriel looked over at him. "What about your dad? Or Evelyn?"

"They'll be safer away from me. So would you. You should go back to your family."

Gabriel shook his head. "Josh already convinced them to clear out. Besides, I don't feel right leaving you on your own."

Seth let his gaze settle on Gabriel. His eyes mapping out the features he knew so well.

Gabriel cleared his throat when he caught Seth staring and Seth snapped his gaze back to the road ahead of them. He leaned back in his seat and took a breath, the sheet of paper Debra had given him still clutched tightly in his hand.

# THIRTY-SIX

They drove for hours, only stopping at an outlet mall to use the restroom and pick up a few things, including clothes and jackets for the days ahead of them.

That first night they slept in the Jeep when they were too exhausted to go any further. Well, Seth slept, he had a feeling Gabriel spent most of the night on watch to keep them safe. At least that's what Seth figured from the dark circles under his eyes.

It worried Seth. Especially since he couldn't get Gabriel to let him have a turn driving.

They came across a motel when it was nearing two o'clock in the morning. A dingy place, on a bleak road, surrounded by woods. The red neon sign like a beacon in the still dark early hour of the morning.

Gabriel reluctantly pulled into the parking lot when Seth insisted they both needed some real sleep.

"Wait here," Gabriel said as he opened the door and Seth's mouth pulled tight at the command, his hand already shoving his own door open out of spite.

Seth wasn't a kid. He'd never really known what it was to have a childhood, and yet here his ex-boyfriend was thinking he could boss him around because he was younger. Well, he wasn't having it.

Gabriel rolled his eyes at the glower Seth sent his way. He didn't protest to Seth's company though as they walked together to the doors of the motel lobby, but he clearly didn't welcome it either. His discomfort clear in the way he held himself, the stiff hunch of his shoulders and the hurried gait of his walk clear signs he wanted space from Seth.

A plump woman with blond hair sat behind the desk, thumbing through a magazine, a cigarette between the index and middle finger of her other hand that she set in an already cluttered ashtray when they entered the lobby.

Seth looked up at the flicker of a shadow to find a moth beating its wings against one of the dust-covered bulbs in the light fixtures overhead. The walls the shadows played over might have once been white but had yellowed with the stain of cigarette smoke and age.

The woman stood from her chair with a sweet smile to greet them, her hands pressed flat to the wooden counter she was behind to help her stand. The name Lucy was spelled out in black letters against the white of the name tag she wore pinned to the front of a pink blouse.

"We need a room with two beds for the night," Gabriel said before the woman could speak.

"I'm afraid we don't have any double bedrooms left," Lucy informed him without even bothering to check the computer in front of her. "But we have a queen." Her eyes darted between them. "If the two of you don't mind sharing."

Gabriel looked like he'd swallowed his tongue and found the taste of it vile. Seth tried not to feel insulted.

"A queen is fine," Seth said, since Gabriel had gone quiet.

Lucy shuffled round. Her steps carried her over to the wall behind the counter where brass hooks held the few keys that hung there.

She took one set off the wall and handed them to Seth since Gabriel remained as still as a statue.

"I'll just need a credit card to put on file."

At that, Gabriel did move, his hand going to the back pocket of his jeans to pull out his wallet.

Lucy took the credit card Gabriel held out to her. She then turned to the computer, her eyes glancing from the card in her hand to the screen, then back again as she typed in the required information.

"The room's out the door and to the left." Lucy handed Gabriel back his card. "Checkout's eleven in the morning."

Seth didn't wait for her to say anything else. He turned back the way they'd come to escape the staleness of the lobby and gulp in mouthfuls of clean air.

He tried to not think about sharing a bed with Gabriel. It hurt to think about it. The thoughts inevitably led to ones that had once brought him such happiness to remember. Those times together. Wrapped up in each other. Knowing he was safe. Knowing he was loved. Really and truly loved, for once. Until he'd lost it. Until Gabriel had found out he'd lied. And, just like that, it was gone.

Seth shook his head free of the melancholy and blinked too fast as he forced himself to put one foot in front of the other. His steps were hurried while Gabriel trailed after him, slower than before, weighted down with the same thoughts as Seth, maybe, but that would have to mean Gabriel still cared for him in a way that could only ever be wishful thinking.

Gabriel looked defeated when he dropped the duffel bag at the foot of the bed. This Gabriel didn't love him.

Seth watched as Gabriel went to the small closet and took down the two extra blankets and four extra pillows from the shelf up top. The sight of it confused him until Gabriel went back to the bed and began arranging the pillows in the middle of it.

"You're joking," Seth groused as he crawled onto the opposite side of the bed.

"Just stay on your side."

"So are you mad at me, or trying to avoid temptation?" Seth asked as Gabriel stacked one pillow on top of the other like bricks. The comment earned him a glare that he stared down with a clenched jaw and furrowed brow.

Gabriel looked away first, but Seth didn't feel any sense of victory over it. He felt nothing but broken as he watched Gabriel straighten a pillow.

Once satisfied with his makeshift barricade, Gabriel turned on his side, away from Seth. His arms crossed over his chest and his shoulders hunched, tense and angry.

Seth lay down himself so he couldn't see Gabriel anymore. But the anger was still there, as was the hurt beneath it.

"You know I'm not a little kid," Seth snapped as he smacked the topmost pillow off Gabriel's wall.

"Then stop acting like a child."

"You're the one building pillow barricades, but *I'm* the child?"

"Yes. You are."

"If I was a child, you'd be a pedophile. So it's probably a good thing I'm not."

"Yeah, because the statutory rape you tricked me into is *so* much better."

A hollowness settled in Seth's chest with those words, and his mouth closed without a rebuttal. The truth felt like a punch to the gut, and he stared at the ceiling from where he lay on his back, feeling winded. He didn't have any witty comeback for that. No scathing retort. It was a truth he couldn't talk or think his way out of.

Gabriel was quiet now, and Seth turned his head toward the other side of the bed but couldn't see past the pillows to know whether it was regret, anger, or kindness that lived in Gabriel's silence.

"Do you hate me?" Seth dared.

"I hate what you did," Gabriel answered quietly after an agonizing moment when Seth thought he'd chosen to ignore him. "I hate that you lied. I hate that you made me fall in love with you."

That last one hurt. That last one had Seth blinking back tears.

Gabriel regretted them. He resented the love they'd had. He hated that he'd felt anything for Seth at all.

Seth sat up. He couldn't be here anymore. He couldn't lie here next to Gabriel with the pillows stacked between them like some metaphor for the rift that ran between their hearts. Not when Gabriel regretted everything they'd been to each other.

He needed to get out of this room. Out of his head. His heart.

"Where are you going?" Gabriel asked when Seth rose from the bed, found his shoes, and started putting them on with numb fingers.

"I need some space," Seth said flatly. With that, he stepped to the door and headed outside. The sound of the door as it closed behind him felt like an ending in more ways than their actual breakup had.

A chill wind brushed across Seth's skin as he stood on the sidewalk, reminding him he'd left his jacket inside. He refused to go back in for it though, so he ignored the way the cold bit into his skin and headed toward the back of the motel where he'd spotted the woods earlier.

He wondered if it was possible to get lost in there. He wondered if Gabriel would bother to look for him if he didn't come back out.

Something moved in the grass not too far from where Seth was walking. A rabbit. He could just make out the brown of its fur in the dim light from a streetlamp.

The soft yet rapid pitter-patter of its heartbeat made Seth's stomach ache. It hadn't seen him yet, preoccupied with its own meal of wilted grass.

*We're hungry. You want it too. I know you do,* Silas hissed through the cracks in the walls Seth had boxed him behind. *It's alright to want it.*

Seth took a step, spurred on by the hunger in his gut and that voice in his head. It was only a rabbit, after all. It wasn't like he'd be killing a person.

The rabbit froze. Its body tensed in preparation to bolt and Seth flung himself forward with a speed he hadn't known he possessed, a hand closing around a hind leg as it leapt forward toward a safety it would never know again.

He dragged it back across the lawn, its body twisting against his grip. Its paws scrabbled at the ground in desperation. In fear. As if it knew what he was planning. As if it could already feel his talons rending it apart.

The rabbit broke open easily beneath Seth's hands, his talons barely out before he was in.

Blood sprayed over his shirt, spilled over the grass and his hands as they snapped bone to get to the heart. It beat red and warm in the still-heaving rabbit.

He plucked the heart from the rabbit's fractured chest and popped it into his mouth with only the slightest hesitation.

The thump of the heart felt disconcerting behind his lips, against his tongue. The edges of his teeth thrummed briefly when he bit down on it, a taste both familiar and strange coating his tongue as it went still with his chewing. A part of him wanted to spit it out, but it was good. It was so good, and he needed it. His body needed it. It needed more.

There was an iron-like sweetness to it. An almost buttery richness to the flesh he didn't have a word for. The bits of muscle slid over Seth's tongue and down his throat easily. Hardly satisfying with the way it barely made a dent in the hunger lodged in his stomach like some unwanted houseguest, but at least it was something.

*See. There's nothing to be afraid of. There's no reason to resist.*

He couldn't help silently agreeing. The reassurance was a welcome balm to the ache in Seth's own heart.

Seth looked up as a pickup truck rumbled into the parking lot—blue and the type of old that had rust eating at the chipped paint. It came to a halt in an empty parking spot, one of the back tires over a faded white line.

The engine shut off. Then the creak of a door filled the air, and a man stepped from the cab, frame lanky and blond hair pulled into a ponytail through the back of a red baseball cap.

Seth's stomach growled at the sight of him. It was harder to force his cravings back with blood still on his lips and the flavor of muscle in his mouth. He had a taste for it now, and he was *so* hungry.

# THIRTY-SEVEN

The driver glanced in Seth's direction as his feet hit the pavement, and the light that shone from the open door of the cab glinted off his glasses when he turned to get a better look at him. Seth tried to step back from the streetlamp into the shadows, hoping that the darkness would obscure the blood smeared over his skin and staining his clothes.

"Aren't you a little old to be trick-or-treating?" the man joked, but there was a wariness in his tone, a dread in his chest that Seth could hear.

The man took a step back when Seth didn't reply. The smell of his fear and the skip of his heartbeat fanned the flame of hunger that burned in Seth's gut.

Silas was whispering to him again. Warm and encouraging. Like Gabriel had been once, only Silas didn't shy away from Seth's darkness. He didn't hate him for his lies. No. He accepted him. Wholly and completely.

Seth stepped forward, letting the streetlamp bathe him in yellow light. His talons were still drawn and wet with blood.

The man's eyes went wide as he turned to run, but Seth was faster.

The man barely had time to scream before Seth was upon him. One hand went around the man's throat as he dragged him to the ground to silence him, while the other sliced through cloth, then skin to the fat and muscle beneath. Blood rose in a spray, then a gush from the wound as Seth pressed his hand inside the body beneath him, knees digging into the man's belly to pin him down.

The man thrashed and coughed blood. Lips red. Eyes wide. Seth's hand pressed down harder on the man's throat to keep him quiet as his talons scraped across his insides to find a handhold on the bone that blocked him.

Seth's talons hooked beneath the edge of the breastbone. An audible crack rang through the air when it snapped with the pull of his hand.

He yanked the obstruction out, flung it aside, greedy fingers reaching in past shards of bone to wrap around the still-beating heart.

Seth licked his lips when he felt the heft. Thick and meaty and so much larger than the rabbit heart he'd been able to hold between his fingers.

He brought the heart to his lips, tore strips off with his teeth and slurped them down. His control lost to the hedonistic satisfaction of finally getting what both he and Silas wanted.

When there was no more to be consumed, Seth sucked the blood and bits of gore from his fingers before he rose to his feet. It was only after there was nothing left to consume that Seth came back to himself enough to process what he'd done. The body he'd left ripped open on the pavement and the blood that now drenched his clothes.

An icy wave of panic washed over him, threatening to drown him in its wake. What had he done? What was he going to do? He couldn't leave the body here, and it was too heavy to be dragged into the woods to hide without Silas lending him his strength, and he had gone quiet after getting what he wanted.

Seth dropped to his knees again, this time to shove at the body—shove it hard until it moved and rolled under the truck. In a strange way it reminded him of that time when he was eight and had rolled a sausage of dry salami under his bed because he didn't want his dad to know he'd snuck out of his room in the middle of the night to get food. The body was also about as well hidden.

His dad had found the salami three days later when his room had begun to stink. Seth was pretty sure a dead body would be found in less time than that.

He staggered to his feet after it was done, choking back the urge to vomit. As sick as the whole thing made him feel, he needed to keep what he'd swallowed down or Silas would push him to find another person to feed on.

Seth walked back to the lawn after a quick look around to be sure no one would see him. Once there, he wiped his shoes on the damp grass.

His footprints didn't come up red when he stepped back on the pavement and he spared a glance at the body he knew was tucked beneath the pickup truck.

A lump rose in his throat as he crept back to the room he shared with Gabriel, avoiding patches of light and sticking to the shadows. His steps were cautious, slow, so as not to drip too obvious a trail with hurried steps.

The knob of the door to their room felt like both his salvation and his end. He'd be safe from prying eyes once inside, but Gabriel would know. Somehow that felt worse, and yet somehow Seth still opened the door.

Gabriel was sitting up in bed, his back stiff and his eyes pinched with worry, like he knew what Seth had done before he'd even walked into their room covered in blood and closed the door hastily behind him.

"I found a rabbit," Seth said after too long a beat of silence as he stood there caked in blood. Not a lie. But not the truth, either.

Gabriel swallowed and looked away, but Seth didn't need to see Gabriel's face to know he knew what he'd done. There was too much blood for it not to be a lie.

Seth crossed to the bathroom in silence and once inside, leaned back against the door until it clicked shut.

Slowly, Seth stepped away from the door and peeled off his clothes. The fabric clung to him with blood. Sickeningly wet, his shirt and pants landed on the floor with a sloppy sound, flecks of red spattering out to tarnish the pristine white of the tiled floor.

He put his shoes in the sink to wash later, blood running down the porcelain to circle the drain.

Seth stood in his boxers for several long minutes just watching the blood from his clothes seep out across the floor. Blood that used to be inside a person. Blood that had pumped through the beating heart that now sat heavy in his stomach.

He was only half-aware that he'd turned the shower on. The water against his skin barely registered when he stuck his hand under the spray to check the temperature, and he turned up the heat until it stung his fingers.

When it was hot enough that his skin pinked beneath the spray of water, Seth pulled off his boxers and got in the shower.

The steady stream sluiced over his body, the water running red then yellow around his feet as he washed the blood away, scrubbing it desperately from his skin, his hair. He even took the time to clean his fingernails of the bits of bloody flesh embedded beneath them.

Tears welled in his eyes as he worked. He didn't bother to wipe them away.

He cried quietly, but he was certain Gabriel could hear him. Certain that even through the doorway and the sound of running water, he could pick out the sound of each tear as it slid down Seth's cheeks. He had bonded with a wolf familiar after all, and wolves, from what Seth could remember, had an acute sense of hearing.

The taste of the man's blood was still in his mouth, a sharp metallic tang against his tongue that had him tipping his mouth up into the hot spray of water. It scalded his lips and tongue, but he didn't care. Pain was as welcome a distraction as any other.

He could still hear the man screaming. The sound of his flesh as it tore and the crack of his bones echoed in his ears, the memory playing over and over on a loop in his head.

In the steam of the shower, beneath the too-hot spray of water, Seth shivered.

His hand itched, and he peeled back the bandage on his palm to find the sutures dissolving as his skin knit itself back together, though Seth wasn't entirely sure how. There was so little of this he understood.

The wounds that had been along his chest and side were the same when he checked, the flesh warm and oversensitive to the touch with how new it was, but completely healed.

Yet another sign that his body was becoming less and less his own. How it tapped into Silas's power like a reflex more and more. The occurrence had become as automatic as breathing with things like healing and hearing. Less so with abilities like strength, speed, and the appearance of their talons.

Seth forced himself to turn off the water and step out of the shower. He stood there for a time, tired in a way that ached into his bones. His eyes roved over the white-tiled room with the truck driver's blood smeared over the floor and sink and tub like something out of a slasher film.

He sank to the floor, where he pulled his knees up against himself, his arms wrapped tight around his bent legs. He sat there in the middle of the mess he'd made, tears streaming down his face as he shook. With cold. With fear. With the hunger that had already started to gnaw at his gut.

"Seth?"

Gabriel was outside the bathroom door. Seth could hear his heartbeat as surely as Gabriel could hear his tears. But Seth didn't want to move. It felt like too much work to push himself to his feet and cross the room to open the door. His body felt so heavy. As if the weight of everything that had happened was holding him in place.

Seth dropped his head against his knees when the doorknob rattled. "Just— just *go away*."

Leave, Seth thought bitterly. Leave like you want. Like you did before.

Metal creaked, wood splintered, and Seth didn't have to raise his head to know Gabriel had broken his way inside.

He didn't look up at the hesitant footsteps that crossed the floor to him. He didn't look up when something soft settled around his shoulders. Or when Gabriel spoke his name.

He'd killed someone. Seth had killed someone, again. To make matters worse, a part of him had liked it. Some part of him he couldn't blame on Silas had wanted to hurt and maim and feed until the ache inside him went silent. Until someone else was the one in pain for once, bleeding on the outside the way Seth always felt like he was bleeding on the inside.

Seth finally looked up at Gabriel with wet eyes. "Kill me."

Gabriel shook his head, eyes going wide with horror and lips moving soundlessly like he couldn't find the words.

"Please, I can't do this anymore," Seth implored as he brought Gabriel's hands up to his neck, his own fingers forcing Gabriel's to curl around his throat. "I can't live like this. I don't want to."

Gabriel's expression had gone hard. His jaw clenched and brow fur-rowed, but his hands didn't tighten in the way Seth wanted. His fingers weren't pressing in the way he needed.

He needed claws and the pressure of suffocation pushing him down and under. He needed Gabriel to drown him in his own spit and blood the way his mother had failed to drown him in the pond.

"I can't do it on my own. It won't let me. When I jumped—" Seth took a deep breath with the way Gabriel's eyes had gone wide. There was a sadness there that made Seth look away.

Gabriel said nothing as he pulled Seth to his feet and made him walk into the main room, where he shoved clean clothes into his hands before collecting the plastic bags they hadn't even unpacked yet.

"Get dressed," Gabriel instructed, already halfway out the door when he spoke.

Seth stood in the blanket Gabriel had wrapped him in and stared at the now closed door. Gabriel was outside packing the bags into the Jeep because, of course, they would have to leave now. Because of him. Because of what he'd done, they'd have to run from the consequences of Seth's actions the way they'd been running from the hunters.

Seth swore under his breath and started pulling the clothes on. He only stopped when he had everything on except his shoes, which were still in the sink. His socked feet curled against the ratty old carpet as he stared into the blood-spattered bathroom with its desecrated tiled floor and white walls. He didn't want to go back in there.

Gabriel took one look at Seth when he got back and walked past him into the bathroom. He pulled a hand towel from the rack to wet and began scrubbing the blood from Seth's shoes in a way that was almost clinical.

Gabriel was still trying to help him after everything, and Seth had to push down the urge to cry again. Because there shouldn't have been any part of him worth saving left.

# THIRTY-EIGHT

Seth opened his eyes to daylight and snow, a rare occurrence for this early in November. If he'd been home, he probably would have gone outside to watch it fall, or maybe headed over to Evelyn's to hang out and drink hot cocoa on her front porch. The thought had him wondering after his best friend. Was she safe? What about his dad? Or Isaac and Micah? He hoped they were okay. He hoped leaving had kept them alive.

The life he'd known seemed so long ago, so foreign with the hint of blood lying heavy across his palate.

He'd fallen asleep sometime after Gabriel had hustled him into the Jeep and driven from the motel. Exhaustion set in quickly after the panic of adrenaline had left him.

A part of him still felt sick and tired. Shaky. Like his body was rebelling against its own chemical responses.

He looked at Gabriel, who hadn't said a word since Seth had woken. He looked upset again. His face was set in a stony expression, eyes tight and mouth even tighter.

"Do you want me to drive for a while so you can get some sleep?" Seth offered.

Silence. The uncomfortable kind that made anxiety curdle in Seth's gut.

"I'm sorry about what happened back at the hotel," Seth tried instead. "I didn't mean to lose control of Silas. I thought I had him contained. I didn't know he'd be able to influence me like that."

Gabriel took a heated breath in and out through his nose, but still didn't look at Seth or speak to him.

"Pull over," Seth said when the silence became too thick to swallow. "Now."

Surprisingly enough, Gabriel responded to that, pulling the Jeep off to the side of the road and putting the gear in park.

"Are we seriously back to this again?" Seth demanded.

"Back to what?"

"Oh, look, he speaks."

Gabriel glared, and Seth stared him down. He was angry, and terrified, and he couldn't take this silent hostility from Gabriel anymore on top of everything else. He just couldn't.

"You keep going back and forth between concern and anger," Seth said, and Gabriel narrowed his eyes in confusion when he added, "I'm starting to feel like I'm trapped in that one Katy Perry song."

"What?"

"Don't make me sing it. We both know I can't carry a tune."

Gabriel rolled his eyes, then sighed as he glanced away, then looked back. "It's hard for me, okay? There's a lot going on in my head right now."

Seth's brow rose at that. "A lot on your mind?" He gestured at his head. "I have a literal evil spirit banging around in here."

"You're not the only one affected here, Seth."

"Yeah, well, I can't take your mood swings on top of everything else. It's giving me emotional whiplash. So could you please, for the love of God, just tell me what I can do to fix this?"

"You can't fix it."

"Look, I know that you're mad at me—"

"You have no damn idea how I feel."

"Well, I mean you're obviously upset so—"

"Yes! I'm upset!" Gabriel shouted. "You just killed someone, and I know you couldn't help it, but it's still terrible! Not to mention you asked me to kill you, Seth! As if I would ever, *ever*, hurt you like that! And then there's all the stuff from before I'm still furious about!"

"You mean that I lied—"

"No! I mean yes, I'm mad at you for lying, but I'm... I'm angrier with myself."

"Why?"

"Because I should have known better! Naomi realized right when she met you! I should have listened to her! I should have realized too, and it's rape! You were seventeen! I raped you! Don't you get that? I'm like that woman now, and I can't..." The retort came out shaky, Gabriel's calm fraying at the edges, but the silence that came afterward was worse.

Seth stared at Gabriel's panicked face while his brain turned the words over and over in his head. It didn't surprise him that Gabriel was caught up in the legality of what they'd done. It was the "I'm like that woman now" that had Seth going cold.

He kept trying to twist the words into a different order. Make them fit a different meaning than the one that made his stomach clench with nausea and his eyes burn with unshed tears.

"What are you saying?" Seth asked, even though he already knew the answer.

Some things made a little more sense now, like Gabriel's seemingly unending patience with Seth's nightmares. It made a sick kind of sense if he'd had to contend with his own demons. His own restless nights where he'd woken crying and more exhausted than when he'd closed his eyes. Experience could be a cruel teacher of empathy.

Someone had hurt Gabriel. No. Not just hurt him, raped him. And what Seth had done had brought that all back up for him. Had made Gabriel feel like a perpetrator rather than a survivor.

"You di—"

"I can't do this. I can't—" Gabriel broke off with a pained sound as he clutched at his shoulder and doubled over, his other hand clenched on the steering wheel.

"Gabriel—"

"Don't touch me," Gabriel snapped when Seth reached out to him, and the flash of yellow eyes and a sudden streak of red crawling up his neck had Seth coming up short.

"Gabriel..."

Gabriel was out of the Jeep before Seth could stop him, off and away at a clipped pace like he was planning to flee into the woods. Maybe it was the wolf in him longing for the familiar safety of the trees.

Seth flung open his own door to follow, cold air hitting him in the face and wind blowing snow into the Jeep.

His seatbelt jerked him back in his hurry before he remembered to unbuckle it so he could step from the vehicle. His shoes skidded on black ice when his feet hit the ground, and he had to grab the door as he slid forward to keep from falling.

Gabriel was ahead of him. His shoulders hunched, his head bowed, and whether it was because of the wind or his shame, Seth wasn't sure. He only knew Gabriel was still moving away from him, but along the side of the road rather than off into the trees, like Seth had expected.

"Gabriel, stop!"

Not a pause in Gabriel's steps, and Seth was running now. His shoes leaving footprints in the thin layer of snow that had gathered. His eyes stung with more than just the cold as he ran.

"Where— Where the hell are you even going?" Seth demanded when he'd almost reached him. "We're in the middle of nowhere."

Gabriel didn't respond, and Seth closed the last few feet between them, his hand catching at Gabriel's sleeve only to have Gabriel turn on his heel and shake him off.

The look Gabriel gave him hurt his heart, his face flushed and eyes wet.

The infection was even worse now. Red spidery lines arched up the skin of Gabriel's throat to his face and wove together like a second skin, the shadowy tips reaching for his eyes, the corners of his mouth.

It was spreading. Right in front of Seth's eyes.

He was going to lose him. Gabriel was going to end up like Haley, and there was no way for Seth to save him.

There was so much pain in Gabriel's stare. So much guilt and shame, and Seth couldn't let him go like this. He couldn't let Gabriel end thinking he was a monster.

"Just..." Seth rested his hand on Gabriel's arm again, more slowly than the last time. "Listen to me."

Gabriel shook under Seth's hand, but he didn't move to pull away this time. His gaze was wary and his breaths came out shallow as he fought back his tears.

"You did *nothing* wrong. I'm the one that crossed the line. *Me.*" Seth took a steadying breath and gave Gabriel's arm a gentle squeeze. "Whatever happened to you, whatever you're trying to tell me happened, it's nothing like what was between us. You didn't force me, and you didn't hurt me."

Gabriel's shoulders hitched as tears slipped down his cheeks, leaving damp trails across red patches of skin that pulsed with the infection.

"I'm so sorry, Gabriel. I'm so sorry for what I did to you, and for what happened to you. None of it was your fault."

It was like watching a dam break. Gabriel's face screwed up before he pressed his hands to his eyes. Fresh tears for old wounds. And Seth hadn't even needed to use talons to get to the heart this time. He'd torn it out of Gabriel just by being in his life.

Seth pulled Gabriel into a hug when he reached for him. After everything he'd done, the least he could do was offer some form of comfort.

Seth had to swallow against his own urge to cry as Gabriel wept in his arms. Because Gabriel was hurting, and he loved him. He didn't know how to stop loving him.

"Shh. It's okay. It's okay," Seth soothed, one hand cupping the back of Gabriel's head while the other rubbed circles into his back. "Ella ya no puede hacerte daño. Estás seguro ahora."

*She can't hurt you anymore. You're safe now.* It was something Gabriel had said to Seth sometimes when he'd woken from a nightmare.

Gabriel had always seemed to have the right words to ground Seth. Maybe because he'd been saying all the things he'd needed to hear once, and maybe he needed to hear those things now.

A car honked at them as it sped past and Seth guided Gabriel further off from the side of the road.

They ended up at the edge of the woods, where it was safer, less visible with the trees and the shadows they cast.

Seth leaned back against the trunk of a tree with Gabriel pressed close. It smelled like pine there beneath the branches. Like Christmas mixed with damp earth and grief.

Seth bit back a cry as something inside Gabriel cracked then shifted beneath his skin.

*This is it. This is when you lose him forever,* Silas hissed.

"You need to get away from me," Gabriel said. His voice almost lost beneath another sickening snap of sound.

"No. I'm not going anywhere."

Seth held Gabriel more tightly when he made to pull away. He didn't care if it cost him his life. He wouldn't leave him. Not now. Not like this. Not with Gabriel making sounds like he was trying to swallow his pain back down inside him and was choking on it.

If the end was coming, Gabriel would go with Seth's voice being the last thing he heard. He'd go knowing he was loved, and accepted, and good.

Seth talked to Gabriel softly, and waited. Waited for the body in his arms to contort and twist into something he didn't recognize.

The change didn't come, though. Just the snow, and the wind through the branches of the trees, and the passing of cars with the sound of tires rolling over the wet road.

With a deep breath, Seth chanced a look at Gabriel's neck and found the marks receding. Like a shadow being chased away by the sunrise, the tendrils unwinding as they slipped back to hide beneath the collar of his shirt.

Softer pops of sound came as Gabriel's body shifted back to normal. The noises drawn out like it took effort.

Seth wasn't sure how much time passed before Gabriel's tears started to taper off. He only knew that his body ached with the cold by then. Neither of them were wearing coats and both were damp with the snowfall.

There was an even damper spot on Seth's shirt that he only noticed when Gabriel pulled away, the sudden loss of his warmth against Seth's shoulder leaving the area cold and more noticeably wet.

"Are you okay?" It was a stupid question. One Seth already had sense enough to know the answer to. He couldn't help but ask it anyway.

Gabriel looked away as he swallowed hard and wiped a hand over his face. "I don't know how much longer Kit can hold the infection back. He's weakening to it, and I'm no help to him like this."

"Was it like this with Haley before she changed? I mean… was she able to stop it once the shift began?"

"Yeah," Gabriel answered softly. "But Essie wasn't able to hold it back for long."

It took Seth only a moment to realize Essie must have been the spirit Haley had bonded with. He felt ashamed he hadn't ever thought to ask her name when she had died as well.

"For how long after it started was Essie able to hold it back?" Seth asked.

"About two, maybe three days. Josh had taken Haley out by the library looking for the alpha, because she sometimes frequents the woods and trails out that way." Gabriel sighed. His eyes downcast. "They thought she might be able to help somehow, but they hadn't been able to find her at home or reach her by phone for the past several days. So they went looking. But it was too late."

"Hey." Seth touched a hand to Gabriel's elbow. "We'll find a way to help you, okay?"

Gabriel didn't answer, either too worn down or too unconvinced.

"Let's go back to the Jeep. It's freezing out here, and you should rest. I can drive for a while."

Gabriel didn't argue. In fact, he said nothing at all as he let Seth lead him to where they'd left the Jeep running with a hand to his back.

"Just be careful. It's slippery on the road there," Seth said when Gabriel broke away from him to get in the passenger side.

It was cold in the Jeep since they'd left both the doors open, and Seth turned the heat up once they were inside and had the doors closed. Then fished around in the back until he found the bag with the last bottle of water in it.

"Here," Seth said as he passed the bottle to Gabriel, who took it without a word. "You should drink something."

Gabriel stared at the bottle of water in his hands with more consideration than it probably deserved.

"Look, if you're feeling embarrassed or anything, get it out of your head, okay?" Seth said with a wave of his hand. "I'm the last person who's going to judge you."

Silence. But for once Seth didn't feel slighted by it. Gabriel was probably just trying to wrap his head around everything that had happened. Everything that had come out.

"I never told anyone before."

Seth couldn't even imagine what it must have been like for Gabriel to deal with it all on his own. As alone as Seth had sometimes felt, he'd never really been alone. He'd always at least had someone who knew what had happened.

"Did you think your family wouldn't believe you?"

"There was that, but"—Gabriel wet his lips and drew in a shaky breath—"I was more worried they'd see me differently."

Seth nodded. "Yeah, I can understand that."

He'd had similar worries around his own trauma. Worries that had turned out to be well founded with some people. People who weren't in his life anymore, but whose memories still haunted him. Like Adam.

"You know I don't though, right?" Seth asked, and Gabriel looked over at last. "See you differently, I mean. You're still just Gabriel to me."

"Am I?"

"Yeah. Of course."

Gabriel fell into silence as he rested his head against the window and Seth put the Jeep into drive, then pulled back out onto the road.

They still had no destination in mind, only the road ahead of them and the hunters somewhere behind. The police now probably as well with what Seth had done.

A plan would be a good idea. Something to put into motion to get them out of this mess. But all Seth had was a voice in his head and Gabriel next to him, looking like the light had gone out in his eyes.

"My parents wanted me to keep going," Gabriel said suddenly.

"To what?"

"To piano lessons."

"Oh, so, *oh*..." Seth trailed off, a sinking feeling in his chest. "That's why you wanted to quit? Because your piano teacher was—"

"Yeah," Gabriel interjected before Seth could get the last words out. "My dad was so mad though." His voice deepened to what Seth could only imagine was supposed to be an imitation of his father. "'We're not quitters, Gabriel. We see things through to the end.'"

"Yeah. I think Naomi mentioned they made you keep going."

Gabriel looked back out the window, the inside of the Jeep quiet for a time before he said softly, "I didn't know what to do. I was a kid, and I was confused and embarrassed and I didn't want to cause a problem. I mean, I did get out of going eventually, but I just... I feel like such an idiot for going back again and again."

"You're not an idiot." Seth shook his head. "And it wasn't your fault. I know that, and I don't think your family would blame you either if you told them."

"No, they'd just blame themselves," Gabriel said, and Seth's heart ached at the words. "I'd only hurt them if I said anything."

Quiet again except for the soft snick of sound from the cap on the bottle of water being opened. Gabriel took a long drink before putting the bottle in one of the cup holders.

With a heavy sigh, he leaned his head against the window and closed his eyes.

"That cannot be comfortable."

"It's not."

Seth reached back behind him and snagged the first coat he felt beneath his hand. When he pulled it up front, he found it was his, but it didn't matter.

"Hey, here," Seth said as he held the coat out and Gabriel turned his head enough to look over. "You can use it as a pillow."

Gabriel took it without comment. He folded the coat up a few times, then stuck it between his head and the window. His eyes fell closed again and his arms wrapped around himself almost protectively.

There wasn't any talking after that, Gabriel's body relaxing a short time later. He'd fallen asleep if his breathing were anything to go by, and Seth hoped his sleep was peaceful. He needed the rest.

It was strange to be driving this way, aimless and picking exits at random. But there was one for Nevada coming up, and if Seth took it, then maybe they could have a destination after all, or at least the beginnings of a purpose. Finding his father. His real father.

Seth changed lanes, slowing the Jeep as he made the turn and headed out of Oregon.

# THIRTY-NINE

Seth stopped at a diner hours later, figuring Gabriel should eat something with it being well past noon, and wanting to stretch his legs.

"Hey, Gabriel." Seth pressed a hand to Gabriel's shoulder, and he stirred at the touch, his head rising from where it was nestled against Seth's jacket. "I thought maybe you might want some food."

Gabriel shifted up and blinked out the window at the diner.

It wasn't much to look at—a red, wooden building, with a sun faded sign on the front and white doors—but it would suit their needs.

They headed inside from the Jeep, Seth shrugging on his coat as he went. The fabric was warm from Gabriel lying on it.

They claimed one of the empty booths with padded seats and brown tabletops when they got inside. Gabriel avoided eye contact as he slid into his side and Seth watched him turn to look out the window in that far off way he got sometimes.

Only a few other people sat at the booths around them or up at the counter. Some talked, while others sat quietly and watched the news on the TV, the volume muted, but the screen closed-captioned.

A waitress brought them menus and took their orders a few minutes later. Her smile reminded Seth of the one he used to give customers at the café when he was tired and had to pretend he cared.

"Be honest with me, Gabriel," Seth said when she'd gone and they had the space to themselves again. "Are you okay?"

Gabriel shrugged. "It happened a long time ago, Seth. It's been ten years now."

"But it still hurts you."

Gabriel looked at him and sighed. "Sometimes a memory will hit me out of nowhere, but it wasn't happening that often anymore."

"Except now, because of me," Seth said as he slouched back in his seat.

Gabriel scrubbed a hand over his face. "It's all been a lot, Seth."

"I know."

"Where are we anyway?" Gabriel asked, changing the subject as he glanced around.

Seth grimaced when Gabriel caught sight of a display rack stocked with Nevada souvenirs and maps. "Yeah, about that—"

"Are you out of your mind?" Gabriel demanded.

Seth's brow rose. "Wow, don't hold back Gabriel, tell me what you really think."

"This isn't funny," Gabriel said sharply. "There is a *reason* your mother kept you hidden from them, and Debra didn't want you going either."

"We need answers Gabriel. We need a way to stop what's happening with me, and with you," Seth said, and Gabriel pressed a hand to the spot just beneath the collar of his shirt where the infection still lingered. "You said yourself you're not sure how much longer Kit can hold it back."

"What if they try to hurt you?"

"They won't. They need me, right? I'm what they want."

Gabriel shook his head and Seth watched the way he leaned back in the booth, his arms crossed and brow furrowed in thought.

"It's my father, Gabriel. My actual father." Seth held his gaze, imploring him silently to understand. "Would you do any different if you were me?"

"Probably not," Gabriel relented. "I still think it's a bad idea."

"I can go alone—"

Gabriel shook his head and his eyes fell closed on an exasperated breath. "You're not going alone."

Their food came, and they broke off the conversation. The waitress set their meals and waters down in front of them with a quick question if they needed anything else. They both shook their heads, thanked her, then turned back to each other when she had gone.

"You'll go with me?" Seth asked.

"Someone has to make sure you're safe."

Seth smiled, relieved that Gabriel cared enough to stand by him.

"You should try to eat something," Gabriel said, already having taken a few bites from his burger and starting in on his fries.

Seth stared down at his own uneaten plate of food. It was nothing close to what he craved, the greasy burger and fries entirely unappetizing when he could still remember the rich taste of fresh muscle.

The diner was a cacophony of noises—people talking, utensils clinking against dishes, meat sizzling in the kitchen—and still, underneath it all, was the steady thump of a little over a dozen heartbeats. The sound of them made Seth's mouth water.

The plate scraped softly against the table when Seth pushed it away from him, sick with himself.

"You really should eat," Gabriel pressed as he picked up the squeeze bottle of ketchup and squirted a small pile onto his plate.

Seth leaned back in the booth, his arms crossed, and a frown planted firmly on his face. "I know. It's just... It's not what I want to eat."

"That doesn't mean you shouldn't."

Seth glanced away. "Don't tempt me."

Gabriel stared him down. "Look, there's what the familiar spirit needs, and there's what your human body needs."

"So I'm like, what? Eating for two?" Seth joked with a grin that didn't reach his eyes. His smile faltered the next moment, and he asked in a softer voice, "Do they all eat hearts?"

"Different spirits feed on different things."

"What does yours feed on?" Seth asked hesitantly, not entirely sure he wanted to know.

"Dreams."

Seth blinked at Gabriel, shocked by the answer. "Are you serious?"

"Yeah. I am."

"I thought it was going to be something bloody, or something to do with the moon at least." Seth waved a hand. "Because of the whole wolf famirian thing, you know?"

"The energy from dreams is strongest during a full moon, but I can feed on any dream or nightmare at any time."

A slow smile crept over Seth's face when he remembered Gabriel's hand on his head when he woke some mornings beside him, and he realized, "You took my nightmares."

"I ate them, technically."

Seth leaned forward, his arms coming to rest atop the table. "Can you enter dreams too? Is that how I could see Kit in my mind?"

"Kit can. I still haven't figured out how to follow him into a person's mind. I only know how to siphon dreams."

"What about snakes?" Seth asked with a thought for Isaac.

"Depends on the serpent," Gabriel replied as he swiped a fry through the puddle of ketchup on his plate. "Some feed off sexual energy, and some off pain."

Seth paused in thought as Gabriel chewed and swallowed, then reached for another fry. "Wait. So why do all the rest of you get the clean energy menu, and I get the bloody lump of muscle?"

"Adaptation. It was advantageous for familiars to find other food sources so they wouldn't be discovered so easily. Yours just didn't evolve with the rest of them for some reason."

They fell into silence, Gabriel eating his food and Seth waiting for him to finish. He wanted to get back out on the road. To find his father. To find some place he could belong, and someone who could help them.

Seth dragged his plate back toward him at Gabriel's steady insistence that he eat something. He managed to eat half the burger and a few fries even though it tasted oily and bland.

He was sure it would stave off the hunger only briefly, but it was enough to satisfy Gabriel, who left a few bills on the table to pay for their meal and tip their waitress, then followed Seth from the booth.

Seth stopped at the sound of several startled gasps, then turned when someone clicked the volume on the television up, a newsman's voice permeating the hush that had fallen over the diner.

A warning of disturbing and graphic content scrolled across the bottom of the screen. The video footage looked shaky, as if it had been shot on someone's cellphone. It showed people running and screaming as one of Silas's creations chased after them, her hands grasping out with fingers that were caked in blood.

It was the eyes that had Seth shaking though, or rather the stubs of bone that curved up out of where the eyes should have been. But even with the horn-like protuberances, Seth still recognized the face, and the sight made his stomach roll.

It was Aaliyah.

Thorns had ruptured up through her charred skin, white like bone and sharp like knives. A simmer of something fiery and not quite fluid moved through the cracks in her flesh that spread out from where the thorns had sprouted.

*Not my finest work,* Silas said, almost sounding disappointed. *But I was short on time and resources. You can understand, I'm sure.*

Seth turned to hide his face against Gabriel's chest. Gabriel brought an arm up around him as he pressed in close.

*You know, the humans are always so much more fun to reshape than the famirians,* Silas continued. *You can only push the corruption of a famirian so far, but oh, you can do so much more with a normal person. They're just so malleable.*

Someone in the diner screamed and Seth forced himself to look at the television again. Aaliyah had caught someone. A man Seth recognized, his eyes brown, but his hair as red as his daughter's.

Seth's stomach twisted as he watched thorns pop through his cheeks in a spray of blood and Seth could see where they'd lodge in his mouth when he opened his lips to scream. Blood ran down his face and purplish red lines crawled up his skin from wounds that seemed to boil.

Evelyn was yelling a short distance behind her father, tears streaming down her face.

A gun went off. The shot only grazed Aaliyah, but it was enough to make her release her hold on Evelyn's father. His body hit the sidewalk as Aaliyah ran away.

Gabriel led Seth from the diner and Seth dropped to the ground heavily once they were outside. The pavement was unforgiving against his knees, and his guilt choked him with each strangled breath he tried to drag in through his sobs.

Gabriel pulled him from the ground and Seth let himself be guided to the Jeep. He didn't argue when the door opened and Gabriel gave him a nudge to get him inside.

Seth curled in on himself once he was tucked into the passenger seat, the reality of what he'd just seen crowding in on him.

"We'll fix this," Gabriel said as he climbed into the driver's side. "We'll find a way."

"Fix it?" Seth started, and if his voice reached the level of hysterics, he really couldn't be blamed. "Fix it? How the hell do we fix it? People are dead, Gabriel! And the others... the others aren't even human anymore!" He shook his head frantically, then banged it back against the headrest in frustration. "God dammit! I don't know what to do! I'm all alone with this thing inside me and I don't know how to stop it!"

"Seth—"

"Don't tell me it's not my fault," Seth snapped as he stared straight ahead and tears ran down his face. "I don't want to hear it!"

Seth looked over and down at the touch of Gabriel's hand, his fingers intertwining with Seth's own.

"I was going to tell you that you're not alone."

Seth sucked in a breath as he looked over at Gabriel, taking in the sympathetic downward pull of his mouth and the sincerity in his gaze. He blinked to clear his eyes when Gabriel squeezed his hand.

"I'm not leaving, okay? This time I mean it."

Seth gave a small, reluctant nod as he sniffled and rubbed the sleeve of his jacket across his face. Gabriel's hand was a warm reassurance in his own as he tried to pull himself together, his head falling back against the headrest once more as he sucked in one shuddering breath after another.

"My best friend's dad was attacked, and what if Evelyn is hurt too?" Seth wondered aloud. "What if she's dead?"

"That was Evelyn and her dad?"

Seth nodded.

"Do you want to call her? Make sure she's okay?"

Seth looked to Gabriel. "Can I?"

Gabriel handed Seth his phone, and Seth took it with trembling fingers to punch in Evelyn's number before holding it up to his ear.

Each rhythmic ring had Seth's chest tightening, his hand gripping the phone tight enough for it to hurt as he waited for an answer. It finally came on the third ring.

"H-hello?" Evelyn's voice cracked as it came over the line.

"Eevee, it's Seth."

"Seth, my dad— He—"

"I saw on the news," Seth said, wiping at his face when fresh tears ran down his cheeks. "I'm so sorry. Is he..."

"He's hurt really bad, but he's alive. I'm at the hospital now."

"Are you okay?" Seth asked.

"I'm not hurt. I'm scared for my dad though, and Aaliyah. I could tell it was her. I feel so helpless," Evelyn replied, and Seth nodded even though Evelyn couldn't see him. "What about you? Where even are you?"

"It's a long story. But I'm safe. I'm with Gabriel, and we're going to try to find a way to fix all this."

"Please be careful. I have a feeling all of this won't be stopped so easily."

"I'll try," Seth promised. He paused for a moment then said, "Stay safe, Eevee. I hope your dad will be okay."

"Wait. Let me talk to Gabriel real quick."

Seth hesitantly handed the phone over. "She wants to talk to you."

Gabriel took the phone and pressed it to his ear, his gaze drifting over to Seth as he listened.

"Yeah, I will," Gabriel agreed in return to whatever Evelyn had said. "I promise I'll keep him safe."

Gabriel handed the phone back to Seth to say his goodbyes, Evelyn making him promise once again to be careful before hanging up.

Seth tried to call his father next. But it went straight to voice mail and Seth's gut twisted with what that could mean.

"Did you want to call your family?" Seth asked Gabriel in a heavy voice after trying two more times to reach his own father.

"I called them after we left the hotel while you were sleeping," Gabriel replied. "They're safe. They're with family."

"Good."

"You have the address for the GPS?"

Seth nodded and dug the address Debra had given him out of his pocket, hoping as he unfolded the paper that whoever it led them to would have the answers they desperately needed.

# FORTY

The drive was slow. The route took them off paved roads, and along a dirt one that meandered through the desert. A set of houses and several low-lying buildings came into view hours after turning onto a dirt road. It was greener here than Seth had expected, with rolling hills and rows of crops. Like some kind of oasis. It even had a decent-sized pond and an area of woods.

Gabriel parked a short distance from the commune and they both left the Jeep behind to walk the rest of the way.

A woman had spotted their approach, having looked over from where she'd been hurrying down a path, a girl's hand clasped in her own. She paused as they made their way over to her, pulling the girl Seth assumed to be her daughter in closer to her.

"Hi," Gabriel said stiffly when they reached her. "We're looking for Isaiah."

"He's holding evening service."

Seth was only half listening, too busy looking her over. The white frock she wore reminded him of the dress his mother had worn in the photograph he'd found, and he looked at the girl dressed in beige at her side when she raised her head to stare at him. She looked about ten, if Seth had to guess, with lighter skin than her mother, but the same dark hair and eyes.

"Have you come to hear the word?" the woman added when Seth didn't respond.

"Not exactly," Seth replied. "I'm his son."

"Seth? Is it really you?" The woman in white cupped her hands to Seth's face, her eyes bright as she looked him over. "Oh, child, look how you've grown."

Seth blinked at her, startled by her words, but then he realized she must have been there all those years ago when he was only a baby. Another survivor of the day the hunters attacked.

"Isaiah will be overjoyed," the woman said. "Come. I'll take you to him."

She took Seth's hand in her own, like his hand belonged in hers as much as her daughter's did.

"You too," the woman said to Gabriel with a glance over her shoulder when he hesitated. "Isaiah will want to meet you."

The four of them headed toward the largest building, a white rectangular structure with wooden double doors that the woman released Seth's hand to push open.

She ushered them inside. The space beyond the doors was packed with people seated on the floor, smiles on their faces as they listened to a man who stood on a stage preaching about spiritual transformation, and Seth couldn't help the way he stared. His eyes swept over Isaiah to take in his tall, lean stature. His bearded face. The part of his dark hair.

This was him. His father. His real father.

Isaiah trailed off and his eyes widened as if in realization when his gaze settled on Seth. The others in the room murmured as they followed Isaiah's gaze, taking in the newcomers with curious stares.

"Hi, Dad." The words tumbled out of Seth before he could think on them, his heart beating shallowly in his chest with a nervous ache.

"It can't be." Isaiah stepped down from the stage and the crowd seemed to part for him like the Red Sea when he moved forward. "Ena, where did you find him?"

"He found us," the woman at Seth's side answered with a smile.

Seth's eyes squeezed shut as Isaiah pulled him into a fierce hug when he reached him. He tried not to think of the man who had raised him in that moment, the one no doubt out of his mind with worry and searching for him.

"The spirits brought you back to us."

"Actually, I brought him back to you," Gabriel said, and Isaiah pulled back from the embrace to look at him.

"And you are?"

"Gabriel."

Isaiah smiled. "Like the angel."

A few curious onlookers had gathered, five of the women dressed in the same white frock as Ena.

"My son has returned!" Isaiah announced, and a cheer of joy rose into the air as more people stood and moved forward to greet them.

Most of them dressed in simple red clothing that looked homemade. All except for the five women Seth was certain now were Isaiah's wives, who wore white, and their children, who wore beige.

One such woman in white stepped forward, a smile on her face and words of rejoicement falling from her lips as if Seth were Jesus come to walk the Earth again.

One after another, they came to Seth. Some clasped his hands in welcome. Others were bold enough to press a hand to his cheek.

The prodigal son, they called him. The lost one has returned, they said.

Some of the praise they espoused sounded familiar from Seth's time around Isaac. Some Abrahamic ideology but mixed with foreign ideas and talk of spirits. Spirits that Seth actually believed in, with Silas living inside him. Banging on the door of Seth's mind. Demanding to be let out more than ever since they'd returned him to his worshipers. Silas's fury was a dull ache that started at Seth's temple.

Isaiah ended the evening service early in favor of speaking with Seth. His followers were sent off to their tasks for the evening, leaving Gabriel and Seth alone with Isaiah.

The three of them walked about the commune while Isaiah pointed things out and explained how their community worked.

From the look and sound of the place, Seth couldn't see what Debra had found so frightening. The people here seemed happy. They laughed and talked as they went about their chores. A few even danced while a man sat beneath a tree strumming a guitar.

Gabriel fell behind when a little girl approached him with a crown of yellow flowers in her hand, and Seth couldn't help smiling at the way Gabriel knelt to speak with her. The girl placed the flower crown on Gabriel when he bowed his head.

"So who is he to you exactly? Someone special?" Isaiah asked quietly as he watched Gabriel. "I mean, he did come all this way with you."

"We're together," Seth lied, wanting to see how his father would react.

Isaiah nodded, not noticing the way Gabriel tensed or frowned. "I thought as much."

"Am I going to get a lecture?" Seth asked. "Because I mean, you have, like, six wives. So I'm not sure you're really in a position to judge."

Isaiah laughed. The sound surprised Seth, who had expected a sermon on the sins of lying with a man, or at least a disapproving comment on the age gap. Though given the ages of two of the women in white, the latter probably wasn't seen as an issue.

"You get that sense of humor from your mother."

Seth ducked his head with a bitter smile.

"It looks like I've struck a nerve. Is she not well?"

"No." Seth pulled in a breath to steady his nerves. "She passed away recently."

"I'm sorry to hear that. She was very dear to me." Isaiah cupped a hand to Seth's head. "As are you."

Seth looked away at the words, his gaze straying to Gabriel.

A few more children had gathered around him—two boys and two girls—the girl he'd seen with Ena among them. All of them seemed curious about the newcomer in their midst. And all of them were dressed in beige.

"Are they..." Seth trailed off, searching for the words as he looked at Isaiah. "Are they my family?"

"We're all family here, Seth," Isaiah said, then smiled when Seth looked at him pointedly. "But if you mean in the old way, by blood, then yes."

The children looked up when Isaiah called to them, their attention drawn from Gabriel to Seth and their eyes grew even wider than before.

They ran to Seth in the next instant, almost knocking each other over in their haste. Excited to meet him. The missing brother they'd probably been told stories about.

Seth crouched when they circled around him. One boy reached out to touch his face, as if to check that Seth was real. He looked about three, round-faced and his hair lighter than the others, but that would no doubt change.

"That's Caleb," Isaiah said of the boy with his hand on Seth's cheek. "You know Lilian, of course." He gestured toward the girl Seth had seen with Ena when he'd first arrived. "The other girl is Abigail, and the boy hiding behind her is Elijah. He's always been shy."

All of them had similar features. Brown eyes. Dark hair. Lilian's being the darkest. An undeniable resemblance to their father. But Seth could still pick out things that must have come from their mothers.

Caleb's brown skin, Abigail's freckles, the hint of green in Elijah's eyes, and the epicanthic fold of Lilian's.

Seth caught sight of Gabriel hanging back to watch him as he was introduced to his siblings. To the family he'd never known he'd had, but on some level, had always longed for.

Isaiah allowed them to sit and talk, Abigail coming forward to hug Seth at one point. Apparently she was the most affectionate of the children, and the second youngest at five years of age.

Isaiah sent the children to help their mothers bring dinner out about an hour later, and Seth stood to watch them go, happy in a way he hadn't thought possible any longer.

Strands of lights clicked on as the sun set. Round bulbs illuminated the area, and with them a line of women carrying bowls of food walked along paths worn in the dirt to a grouping of long wooden tables.

The children tagged along after their mothers with silverware or plates in their hands. The dresses the girls wore were almost long enough to sweep the ground.

When the tables were set, they all took seats, Seth being seated at the center of the main table between Gabriel and Isaiah.

They passed the serving dishes around and food was ladled generously onto plates.

One wife told Seth to wait before he could take a serving for himself, that they had something special for him.

A few moments later, another woman came down the path leading to the table where Seth sat. She held a single plate in her hands. Something red rested in the center of the chalk white dish that was placed in front of him.

Seth's eyes widened. A heart sat on the plate, droplets of blood slipping down its glossy sides into a gathering pool.

"It's lamb," supplied the woman who had brought the plate. "From one of the finest in our stock."

Seth slid a glance in Gabriel's direction, more concerned with what his reaction would be than anyone else at the table. He knew what Seth fed on, but he'd never seen him feed firsthand. Had never witnessed the ecstasy he ultimately gave into as he pulled bloody chunks loose with his teeth.

"There's no need to be ashamed, son," Isaiah said with a hand clasped to Seth's shoulder. "Eat."

Seth looked back down at the heart on the plate in front of him while the cult stared. Waiting. Expectant. Placid smiles on their faces, as if they were about to witness a miracle.

Silas was whispering reassurances to Seth that in his current state of hunger were all the nudging he needed. His hands reached out, disregarding the knife and fork by his plate in favor of his fingers. Blood coated his palms as he lifted the decently sized hunk of bleeding muscle from the plate, his lips slipping over the slick surface before his teeth caught and ripped a chunk free. His eyes fell closed again as he savored the richness of flavors against his tongue.

He knew Gabriel was watching, but didn't look his way to see if it was disgust or pity that colored his expression. He focused on chewing. Swallowing. Tearing another strip of raw muscle free and shuddering with satisfaction as he swallowed it down into the void that howled inside him.

They watched him eat with reverence, quietly bearing witness to his sacrilege and the way blood smeared over his mouth, like they were witnessing the birth of a god and not the desecration of a once beating heart.

All except Gabriel, who, when Seth finally looked at him, stared at him with sadness, his brow knit and eyes wet. It was enough to make Seth drop the more than half-eaten heart back to the plate despite the hunger that still gnawed at his insides. The plate rattled against the table, upsetting flecks of blood that splattered over the wood.

"Sorry," Seth apologized, more for what Gabriel had seen him do than for the mess the blood had made. He pushed away from the table in the next instant. "I'm sorry."

"Seth!" Isaiah called after him.

Seth kept moving. He needed to put space between himself and the heart that lay abandoned on his plate. He needed to get as far from those smiling faces as he could. From the way Gabriel had looked at him.

A hand caught at Seth's wrist, stopping him. Isaiah stood behind him when he turned and he tried to jerk free.

"Let go of me," Seth hissed.

"Seth—"

"He said let go," Gabriel said from behind Isaiah, who reluctantly dropped his hold with a look at Gabriel's stern frown.

"How'd you know?" Seth demanded as he backed up toward Gabriel. "How did you know it was in me?"

"I didn't." His father took a step closer. "Not for certain, anyway. But we've suspected for a while that it hid itself away inside someone who had left us."

"I want it gone."

"Son—"

"It's ruining my life! It's hurting the people I care about!"

"It's a blessing in disguise."

Seth shook his head. "It's a curse."

"I know it must feel that way now. With all that's happened and all that you've no doubt lost," Isaiah reasoned, and his hands moved to clasp Seth's shoulders, "but there is so much good that can come from the spirit you carry. We'd have an end to war, famine, even death. All of that is possible through you."

Seth stared at him, his eyes wet and his chest aching. "It's not a savior. It's a sickness. People I care about are hurting because of it."

"Isn't the promise of salvation for the many greater than the sacrifice of a few?"

Seth looked away. Isaiah wanted him to see promise where all Seth could see was death and suffering. He didn't know how to convince him of how wrong he was, how naive.

"Sleep on it tonight," Isaiah advised. "We'll discuss it more in the morning." He looked beyond Seth and gave a nod. "Ena will show you two to your rooms. I'm sure you're tired after your travels."

"But—"

"Tomorrow, Seth," Isaiah insisted sternly.

Seth gave a defeated huff as Isaiah strode off and he glanced at Gabriel who shook his head with a helpless gesture, not knowing what to do any more than Seth did, and not liking it just as much.

They were at the mercy of Isaiah's choices. With his followers ever present, there was no way either of them could threaten or force answers from him even if they were so inclined. They had no choice but to wait.

Ena's voice drew their focus to her.

"The two of you will stay in the main house," Ena explained. "It's typically only for Isaiah, us wives, and his children. But then none of the children have ever had a partner before you. You'll be staying in separate rooms, of course."

"I'd rather stay with Gabriel."

"I'm sure you would. But it's not our way." Ena gave Seth an imploring look. "Please, Seth. Don't cause a fuss. We're being as accommodating as we can with this."

Seth nodded reluctantly and let Ena lead them up to the large wooden house that sat at the center of the commune on top of a hill.

# FORTY-ONE

Seth followed Ena to the front of the house with the stucco exterior and large square windows. The double doors before them opened into a spacious foyer with white walls, and arched entrances on either side that led off into dim hallways.

Ena led them up a staircase straight ahead that diverged left and right into separate sections of the house. When she reached the top of the landing she turned right, explaining as she did that this was the wing where the boys had their rooms.

She stopped at one of the first doors with a look to Gabriel as she opened it. "You can sleep here for the night."

Seth caught at Gabriel's hand before he could move away. "I don't like the idea of being away from you."

"I know, but we'll be just down the hall from each other." Gabriel glanced at Ena. "Right?"

Ena nodded and pointed to a door toward the end of the hall. "Seth will be just in there."

"I still don't like it."

"Neither do I," Gabriel admitted. "But what else can we do?"

Seth gave Gabriel's hand a squeeze. He would have liked to hug him at the very least, but he wasn't sure how Gabriel would feel about it, and was even less sure how Ena would respond.

Gabriel gave Seth a reassuring smile as he stepped back. "I'll see you in the morning."

Seth watched Gabriel disappear into the room before he followed Ena to the door she'd pointed to earlier. She stopped in front of it with a smile at Seth then turned the brass knob to open it. Seth stepped inside ahead of her when she moved aside.

It was bigger than his room back in Twin Oaks, with white walls like the rest of the house and a large window across from the bed and opposite the door. The furniture looked handmade and Seth slid his fingers across the smooth surface of a desk that sat with one edge near the door.

There were pencils and pens in a holder and notebooks tucked to one side. A drawing of five children lay on one of them, and Seth picked it up.

"Abigail drew that."

Seth couldn't help but smile as he looked down at the squiggles of color on the page. He assumed the tallest boy was meant to be him.

"She always wanted to meet you. They all did. Not just your brothers and sisters, but your mothers too."

"Mothers?"

"We raise the children together here. All the children are my children, and all the mothers are their mothers. Though I'll admit, back when you were still with us, I helped your mother with you the most." Ena smiled. "We're not supposed to play favorites between the children, but I did always have a soft spot for you over my other sons."

"You don't find it weird raising children that way? Not having them just be yours?"

"It may seem strange to you. The way we do things," Ena said in a patient voice as Seth set the picture down on the desk, "but there's a certain sense of belonging that comes with it."

Seth nodded. He could understand what she meant on some level. How there was comfort to be found in knowing there would always be someone there for you and your child.

Ena was silent as Seth continued to explore the room and the items it held. The stacks of books on the bedside table that were classics. The paintings on the walls that he was told Navaeh, one of the wives, had done. It was when he reached the photos on the dresser and picked up one of them to get a closer look that Ena spoke again.

"That's Peter."

Seth looked up from the picture of the boy he held. "This is Peter?"

"You know about him? I didn't think your mother would have mentioned any of us to you."

Seth stared back down at the photograph. At the boy who could have been his twin. "Debra mentioned him before she died."

Ena's eyes had widened when Seth looked at her again, a mix of shock and sadness in her gaze.

"Sorry." Seth shook his head and set the photograph back down. "I didn't think—"

"It's alright, Seth. Death is a natural part of life."

Seth didn't respond to the statement. There was nothing particularly natural about any of the deaths happening around him.

He looked at the rest of the photos on the dresser. Some of the other faces were familiar. The siblings he'd met today. The women from the photograph he'd found in the hatbox. Though he couldn't put names to all of them.

"What were they like?" Seth asked quietly. "My sister and other brothers and... mothers?"

Ena joined him at the dresser where she put names to the faces Seth hadn't recognized. Told him stories about the siblings he'd never known, but had loved him, and the mothers that had helped care for him.

All Seth could think about was how they died. How their heads had been forced beneath the water while they struggled. The way their lungs would have burned with the need for air, an agony Seth was far too familiar with himself. It was a horrible way to go.

"Oh, and Josephine. She was always wanting to hold you, and sing to you." Ena plucked a frame from the dresser to give to Seth who took it in both hands. "She was so excited to be a big sister again."

Seth brushed his fingertips across the glass covering the image. The girl in the photo stared back at him with deep amber eyes. Her skin was a medium brown, and her dark hair fell in tight curls past her shoulders.

"How old was she... when she died?"

Ena's voice turned somber. "She'd turned eighteen just a few days before she passed."

Seth blinked back tears, his hands shaking around the picture he held.

"It's getting late. There are clothes in the dresser if you'd like to change for bed," Ena said in a gentle voice as she took the frame from Seth's hands to place back on the dresser. "The third drawer has pajamas. We traded out the old clothes for new ones when appropriate, since you would have grown. We always kept several sizes, though. I'm sure something will fit."

Seth crouched as she spoke to open the drawer, sorting through the clothes he found there. All beige and hand-sewn, though neither of those things was a surprise.

He rose when he found a set he thought would work, the top long-sleeved and the bottoms just the right length.

Seth used the bathroom to change. A blue toothbrush still in its packaging and a new tube of toothpaste caught his attention when he'd finished putting the clothes on. Yet another sign that they'd been waiting for him to return.

The plastic crinkled beneath his fingers as he opened it. He ran the head of the toothbrush under the water, then squeezed a dollop of toothpaste out onto the bristles, and brushed his teeth. An act so incredibly ordinary that it felt out of place.

The used toothpaste came out red and flecked with bits of muscle that had been caught in his teeth when he spit in the sink. That, somehow, seemed more normal. More like the life he was growing used to, and it was a strange relief to watch the splotches of bloody toothpaste circle the drain.

Seth found that Ena had turned down the bed when he'd finished up in the bathroom and came back out, closing the door behind him as he did.

"I don't really want to sleep."

Ena looked at him with a tilt of her head. "You're not tired?"

"I have nightmares," Seth admitted reluctantly.

"About your mother?"

Seth nodded after a moment of hesitation. "Most times, yeah."

"I heard you tell Isaiah she passed recently. Is that what you dream about?"

Seth shrugged. He didn't want her to know the whole truth. He didn't trust her enough for that.

Ena sat, patting the spot on the bed next to her, and Seth padded across the room to sit beside her.

"You know, in some places, a white butterfly is sometimes said to be the spirit of someone who has passed." Ena held out her hand, palm facing up, and Seth watched a swirl of aether manifest. It shifted size and shape, finally solidifying as a butterfly that sat on the tips of Ena's fingers, its white wings giving a gentle flutter. "Maybe now that you're home. You'll be able to see their spirits and find peace."

Seth sat up, his eyes transfixed on the butterfly. "How in the world did you do that?"

"It takes some practice, but most chosen by ravens have the ability to manipulate the world around them, and all of us wives were chosen by some kind of familiar spirit. Most of them ravens." Ena smiled. "It's how the old one can live in you. A child of the chosen is a child of both man and spirit. It makes you strong enough to be a vessel. An ordinary person would have been torn apart by the power an old one contains."

Seth shuddered at her words, sickened by the thought of being ripped apart from the inside out.

The butterfly had gone still. The tips of its wings taking on a grayish tone that spread swiftly over the rest of it. Bits and pieces of it fell away in small clumps.

Seth frowned as he watched the ash accumulate on the floor. "What happened?"

"I can create a shell, but I can't grant life. Only the illusion of it," Ena explained, and Seth met her eyes. "I don't have that kind of power."

Seth remembered the way his mother had crumbled apart in very much the same way as the butterfly, bits and pieces falling off her to pile on the floor or drift in the air.

He thought of the voice in his mother's head. The one she'd called Myra.

"What about my mother? Could she do what you can?"

"Oh, she was so much better at it." Ena smiled. "You should have seen the things she could create, and she could get them to last for hours."

Seth's eyes widened and his gaze fell to the ash on the floor, the possibility that his mother was alive taking root in his heart. The ache it brought was both haunting and hope-filled.

He watched Ena rise and dust her hands off. A few more flakes of ash drifted from her fingers to the floor.

"So, I'm like the two of you then? I can do the same things?"

"You can alter things at your whim, Seth, but you could also create life itself if you wanted."

Seth thought of those the aether had touched. The way they'd changed. Their bones rearranging and flesh contorting. He'd made monsters out of people, and it occurred to him then that somewhere out there a fawn was running about, horribly disfigured.

"Or take it away entirely," Ena added in a softer, more reverent voice.

Seth lowered his gaze. "By eating their hearts."

"You can't give life without taking one. So you feed on life itself, and store it within you."

"It makes me a monster."

"No, sweet boy." Ena tilted his head up to look at her. "It makes you a God."

# FORTY-TWO

It took a while for Seth to fall asleep after Ena had gone. She'd pulled the covers up over him and kissed him on the cheek before leaving, something that felt odd given his age and how he barely knew her, but he hadn't complained. In a weird way, it felt nice to have someone play mother to him.

Seth knew he'd fallen into dreams when water lapped at his bare feet and he looked up to find he stood before a lake. Clear and dark and almost as still as the sky above it.

He could feel Silas there with him, both of them united in their desires for once. Seth wanting his family back, and Silas eager for more potential vessels.

*Don't be afraid,* Silas said when Seth hesitated at the water's edge out of fear. *You can't drown here. This is our world.*

With a deep breath, Seth entered the lake. His anxiety spiked with the touch of the water against his skin, but he waded deeper at Silas's urging. His insistence pushed Seth forward.

"Peter."

A butterfly broke the surface of the lake, and the water rippled red from where it rose. Its body was somehow dry as it fluttered in the air, the moonlight catching on its white wings.

He could hear the other names come out of his mouth with each step he took forward into the lake. "Aaron. Levi. Noah. Josephine."

One after the other, they surfaced with their name, the water turning redder with each one, until there were five white butterflies hovering over a brownish-red lake.

Seth strode deeper. With each step, he felt their bones beneath his feet. But it was the butterflies he was after. Not their bones. He could make new bones. What he needed were their spirits. Those were irreplaceable.

It was the closest he reached for first, and his hands cupped its delicate body to draw it toward him, being careful as he did to keep it from the water that was stained with old blood.

Seth could feel the thrum of energy against his hands with every flutter of those tiny wings, his skin prickling where its legs pressed to his palms.

He concentrated on the vastness inside himself, the way Silas instructed, until he found a heartbeat that didn't belong to him—the one that had belonged to the lamb that he'd swallowed down only a few hours ago—and now gave it as an offering to the spirit in his cupped palms.

A flutter of acceptance and the butterfly shone with a bluish-white light that warmed Seth's hands. It was gone a moment later, disappearing to the place in the physical world it had been tied to in its final moments.

Seth raised his eyes to the other butterflies. All of them were waiting patiently for him, but he only had the life energy from one heart left. The smaller one from the rabbit. Enough for the youngest among them, maybe.

He reached his hand toward the one he knew to be Noah, the brother Ena had told him was only a few months old when he'd died. But a hand rose from the lake to grip his arm before he could capture it.

Yellow eyes shone up at Seth from the water when he looked down, eyes he recognized, and he plunged both hands beneath the surface to drag the body up.

"Gabriel," Seth choked as he pulled the body closer. New blood mixed with the old blood, the surrounding water deepening to a brighter, fresher crimson.

Seth didn't understand where all the blood could be coming from. Gabriel usually healed so quickly.

That's when he saw the ends of the tubes that stuck out of Gabriel's arms, blood flowing steadily from both of them.

"This isn't real," Seth breathed, and his fingers shook as he traced up along the hard line of tube he could feel beneath the skin, a faded bruise resting over it like someone had sliced open Gabriel's arms and forced the tubes in before his flesh had knitted itself back together. "It's a dream. It's just a dream."

It was a horrible, impossible dream. It had to be.

"*It's not just a dream*," insisted a voice that wasn't Gabriel's own but came from his mouth, and Seth knew it was Kit speaking to him. "*We're dying*."

Seth bolted upright with a ragged cry that would have certainly woken the other sleeping boys in the hall. Daylight was already filling the room through the white curtains that offered little resistance against the light of the morning.

He stumbled from the bed, his feet catching in the sheets and his hands smacking the ground as he tripped.

The sheets piled by the bed when he kicked free, and he pushed himself to his feet. He was out the door and running in the next instant, calling for Gabriel as he went. His younger brothers poked their heads out of their rooms as he passed them.

Gabriel's room was empty when Seth flung the door open, the bed made and the rest of the room spotless, as if he'd never been there at all.

Seth stumbled back. His body hitting up against the wall as he stared through the open door at the immaculately clean room. The horror of his nightmare, the possibility it was real after all, made him push off the wall and break into a run once more.

The mothers were in the foyer by the time he'd reached the stairs, no doubt drawn by his shouting. All of them. Navaeh, Courtney, Helen, Avis, Mandy, and Ena, who broke away from the rest to go to him when he stumbled down the last step and landed hard on his hands and knees.

"Where's Gabriel?" Seth demanded of Ena when her hands clasped his shoulders. "Where'd you take him?"

"Seth—"

"I need to see him," Seth begged, his eyes wet and his hands grasping at her arms. "I need to know he's okay."

"Sweetie, you were having a nightmare."

"No." Seth shook his head and pulled away from her, pushing up to his feet as he did. "No. Something's wrong."

"What's all this now?" Isaiah demanded as he strode past those of his wives that were clustered near one of the arched doorways leading to a hall on the main floor.

"Gabriel—"

"Left early this morning."

Seth stared at him, his eyes searching Isaiah's face for anything that would tell Seth he was lying. He found nothing but a patient frown and a sympathetic gaze. But the dream was still clinging to the edge of Seth's consciousness, Kit's words repeating in his head. "*We're dying.*"

"What have you done?" Seth demanded, staring at his father with wide, horrified eyes. "Where is he? What have you done?"

"I've done nothing," Isaiah assured him in a placid voice. "Gabriel simply left."

"No. No, you're lying." Seth shook his head. "He wouldn't leave like that. He promised he wouldn't do that again."

"If he left you once, what made you think he wouldn't again?"

"I don't believe you," Seth hissed. "You're a *liar*."

"Sweetheart, please calm down. It's okay." Ena pulled him into a hug, and Seth pushed away, only to hear her whisper, "Listen *carefully* for him."

Seth moved backward to the center of the foyer when she let him go. He needed space to concentrate, to calm his own heartbeat as he closed his eyes.

He listened the best he could, letting that sense of hearing he could draw on from Silas take in his surroundings and doing his best to listen over the pulsing noises from the people that stood around him.

Seth found it eventually, that familiar sound he'd fallen asleep to some nights with his head pillowed on Gabriel's chest, and instinct made him hold his breath to hear it better.

The sound was faint. Muffled, and off in the distance, but Seth could just make it out. It came from the direction of the woods, and it was to the woods Seth ran, the doors of the house banging open as he burst through them.

He ran for the tree line, not caring that his feet were bare, or that rocks and sharper branches stabbed at them. He ran until that heartbeat was right beneath him.

For a horrifying moment, Seth considered the possibility that they'd buried Gabriel alive. That he was suffocating in the cold, dark earth right beneath Seth's feet. But then he saw the metal door set into the ground. A bunker they'd hidden away in the woods.

Seth could hear people moving through the forest behind him, twigs snapping and leaves rustling beneath steady footfalls as he worked to heave the door open on his own. He managed it finally, with a little help from Silas and his strength.

A staircase of stone led downward, and Seth didn't hesitate. Didn't think. He took the steps down two at a time until his feet hit the ground.

# FORTY-THREE

The room Seth found himself in was hollowed out from the dirt and rock of the earth. No windows. No other doors. Only rough walls and a circle carved into the floor, spiraling outward and marked with rune-like symbols.

Seth spotted Gabriel by the light of a lantern that sat in a corner. He was restrained near the center of the stone carving, on his knees and strung up by his wrists. His eyes were closed and his body motionless as blood dripped steadily from him.

It was real. The tubes. The blood. It was all real. Seth hadn't just dreamed it.

Seth hurried across the space and dropped to his knees in front of Gabriel, his hands going to the tubes in his arms to stem the flow of blood, but the warm red only seeped out from between his fingers and slicked his palms, making it difficult to keep his grip.

A series of rivulets had already tracked their way along the grooves of the stone floor as if drawn by some unseen force to snake their way through the carvings, and Seth thought he saw older trails staining the ground.

"Gabriel?" Seth said, taking his hands from the tubes as he leaned in to clasp the face before him between his bloodied hands. "Come on. Open your eyes."

Gabriel didn't respond and Seth stroked his hands over his cheeks, trying to rub some semblance of warmth and consciousness back into him.

"God dammit, open your eyes!" Seth shouted. "You promised you wouldn't leave me! You promised!"

Gabriel's eyes blinked open slowly and with effort, but he didn't move aside from that. He stayed limp in the rope's grip and Seth moved in closer to let Gabriel rest against his shoulder, taking some of the unbearable weight from him while he worked to untie the knots that bound his wrists.

It would have gone faster with talons or if he had the strength to snap the ropes, but Seth couldn't reach the power himself, and Silas had gone silent inside him, refusing to answer Seth when he called to him. It sent a chill through him. He couldn't shake the feeling that this was all exactly what Silas wanted.

"I'm going to get you out of here," Seth promised, his voice thick and catching on his fear. "You're going to be okay."

Seth looked up at the sound of footsteps against stone as Isaiah and his wives descended the stairs. They moved to block them in once they'd reached the bottom, a half circle of women in white, daggers glinting with promise in their hands.

"Aren't you curious what it is?" Isaiah asked, and Seth looked over his shoulder to catch Isaiah's nod toward the intricate design engraved in the floor. "I had it brought with us when we left Oregon."

Seth glanced at it, and now that he knew what to look for, he could see where the edges were set into the floor.

"It's a doorway," Isaiah continued, undeterred by Seth's silence and how he turned his focus back to the rope. "To another world."

"I don't care," Seth bit out, finally getting one knot undone and unwinding the rope from Gabriel's left wrist. "I don't care about you, or your plans, or— or any of it."

Gabriel made a soft sound between pain and relief when Seth lowered the arm he'd gotten free.

"The hunters interrupted the ritual all those years ago, so a part of you is still trapped on the other side."

Seth reached for the next knot while Isaiah spoke, a chill running through him when he realized this was what Debra had tried to warn him about before she'd been killed. The other half of Silas that still lay trapped beyond that door.

He tried to stay focused on the rope in front of him as his father droned on. His fingers searched along the thick coil for a place he could more easily loosen, Gabriel's blood smearing over the rough fibers.

"You must have noticed how unreliable your powers are. Once that part of you is freed, no one will be able to stop you."

"No. Not me. Silas." The knot budged slightly when Seth worked the tips of his fingers into a groove and tugged. "He's the one you've wanted all along, and I won't let him out."

"You'd rather your lover die?"

Seth ignored Isaiah and the women in white, but he could feel the weight of their stares as he worked stubbornly at the rope. A choked sound of relief escaped him when it finally gave beneath his persistent pulling, allowing him to unwind it from chafed skin.

Gabriel's breath hit Seth's neck in shallow, strained pants. His head hung heavy on Seth's shoulder as he took his full weight before he moved him down to the floor, his hand cupped to the back of Gabriel's head as he lowered him so he wouldn't knock it against the ground.

"Well done," Isaiah said. "Now, how are you going to get the tubes out and stop the bleeding? You have to know only a miracle could save him now."

Seth pressed his fingers to the tubes again, this time examining the way the skin gripped them tight, how it had healed around the rubber.

He couldn't get them out. Not without ripping Gabriel open, and Seth wasn't sure he would have the strength left to heal from the damage that would cause.

Gabriel blinked up at Seth like he was fighting to keep his eyes open, like all he wanted was to drift off to sleep. And Seth squeezed his shoulder, trying to get him to focus.

"Why do this to him?" Seth demanded, his voice cracking, and he looked at Isaiah. "He doesn't deserve this."

"Because you love him," Isaiah said, "and you would never stay without him. And he was never going to stay. Besides, the gateway becomes dormant if it's not fed properly."

"Fed?" Seth stared at the blood-soaked symbols, the way the fluid grew lower inside them, a soft sucking sound coming from the space beneath. A living door with the same hunger that ached inside Seth.

"Yes. Fed. Now, call on Silas and set him free."

Seth looked at the women that stood around him, the mothers that he'd been told were supposed to love him.

"You're just going to let this happen?" Seth demanded. "You're going to let us die?"

"You're not dying, Seth," Isaiah assured him. "You're being remade into something better."

Seth shook his head and tears ran down his cheeks.

"There's no need to cry. This is a joyous moment. We're going to change the world together."

Seth lifted his head, his wet eyes finding Ena at the end of the line of women, the only one of them that didn't seem elated. Maybe he could at least get through to her.

"Ena, please. You can't let this happen to us," he cried. "Silas isn't what you think. You don't know what he'll do to me. To everyone."

But she did know. Seth could see it in her face when she stole a glance at him. The fear there was enough to make Seth shake.

Isaiah moved behind Ena, his hands gripping her shoulders, and she turned her gaze from Seth.

"She's not going to help you, Seth." Isaiah said, and Seth let his gaze search among the faces desperately. "None of them are."

Seth bowed his head as Isaiah stepped closer. He couldn't bring himself to look at the man who called himself his father, the man he'd come looking for hoping he'd find not only answers but some place he could belong.

"You're killing him, Seth."

Seth stared down at Gabriel with the words. At the blood that still ran from his body. At how ashen his skin had gone.

"You have the power to save him, and instead you're letting him die."

*We still have the rabbit's life energy,* Silas reminded him, speaking for the first time since they'd reached this hole in the earth, and his voice was cold, calculating. *I'll give it to him so he can heal. But only if you surrender your body to me.*

Seth bowed his head. "I'll do it."

Gabriel moved his head slightly, as if he were trying to shake it. His eyes pleaded with him silently, the yellow in them dimmer than Seth had ever seen it.

"You can have me. Just save him."

*Deal,* Silas replied, and Seth could almost hear the smirk in his voice.

Seth pressed a kiss to Gabriel's forehead and smoothed his hands down over his face. "I love you." He nodded and wiped at the tears that spilled from Gabriel's eyes. "I'll always love you."

*There is no always,* Silas said. *Not for you. But I promise Gabriel will live.*

The words didn't leave Seth reassured. They felt dark and twisted like the aether that curled its way down his arms when he tore down the walls in his mind.

His hands shifted with Silas's release, the skin turning dark and rough as his nails lengthened to familiar points.

Seth could feel his consciousness being pushed under with the change, his panic rising with the jarring, claustrophobic sensation of being disconnected from his own body and shoved into a corner inside his head. Back in that space where he and Silas had first stood face to face. Only now it was just a vast emptiness. No bones. No lake. Just Seth seated alone in the darkness, unable to touch or feel the world outside him.

He couldn't move his body. He couldn't even twitch a finger or draw his own breaths. It was maddening, the sudden and utter loss of control.

His body was Silas's now. Every action. Every word. All Silas.

Silas smirked as he flexed his fingers and slid his gaze to Gabriel, who stared up at them with panicked eyes.

"Scared?"

Gabriel flinched when Silas pressed the sharp point of a talon to the start of the bruise that marred his left arm. The rubber hidden beneath the skin shifted only slightly at the touch, but Gabriel groaned all the same.

"I'd say something soothing, but you're right. This is going to hurt."

Seth wished he could reach for Gabriel with the way he screamed when the talon dug in, that he could offer comfort where Silas wouldn't as the blood welled from the long gash Silas had made in Gabriel's arm. His talons reached into the open wound to catch and pull out the tube, blood gushing with the press of fingers beneath skin.

Gabriel made less noise when Silas sliced into the other arm, but the sounds that came out of him were worse. Broken, weak whimpers of agony and stuttered breaths for air that made Seth feel so helpless, because all he could do was beg Silas to give Gabriel the life energy he'd promised.

"Your ex-boyfriend is *very* annoying," Silas said with a roll of his eyes like he was confiding in Gabriel, even though Seth could hear every word. "After I'm whole again, the first thing I'm going to do is kill him."

Gabriel squeezed his eyes closed as tears rolled down his cheeks.

"Oh, don't cry." Silas tilted his head with a mock frown. "You're getting what you decided you wanted days ago. A life without him."

"Get... out of him."

"Careful, Gabriel." Silas placed a hand on Gabriel's chest, his talons pressing down hard enough for him to feel the danger he was in. "You don't want to make me angry when I'm holding your life in my hands."

*Please,* Seth begged. *We had a deal.*

"A deal which I'll break if you don't shut up."

Silas splayed his hand out on Gabriel's chest more carefully when Seth went quiet. It didn't take him long to find that smaller heartbeat and push the steady rhythm of energy into Gabriel. The yellow in his eyes stood out bright against the green as his skin knit itself back together, thin strings of tissue and veins to start, then thicker ribbons. The different parts fused and pulled until the wounds were closed.

Gabriel's chest rose and fell shallowly, his body struggling to normalize after the trauma. He wouldn't be strong enough to keep Silas from his purpose, from the door that he stepped toward with a relaxed gait.

Something on the other side of the doorway called to Silas in a way that made Seth shrink in on himself. It was awake. Alive. Primed for this moment. Ready to be opened. And Silas moved to kneel at its edge.

A set of small circular grooves were hollowed out in the center, an irregularity in the stone to anyone who didn't understand their purpose. Silas, though, understood exactly what they were for, and his talons slotted into the openings. A smile curled the edges of his new mouth as he turned the inner circle first one way, then the other.

The outer rings moved in opposing directions as he twisted the keystone this way and that, a grinding sound echoing off the walls as they turned. The individual sections crumbled one after the other, leaving behind a gaping maw.

Aether spilled out around the edges and rose into the air to twist around itself and Silas opened his mouth wide when it came toward him to let it worm its way inside.

Seth felt his body choke around it, and he wished he could go numb again, but Silas wanted him to feel this. His throat spasmed and limbs he had no control over tensed.

It pushed in deeper, leaving the taste of ozone in his mouth and making his eyes water. He could feel every inch of it slowly cramming itself inside before fanning out through him.

It scorched every nerve in Seth's body and invaded every cell of his being until it rose out of his pores like smoke, the power too great and his body too small.

A howl reverberated through the air, and Seth wasn't sure if it was Gabriel or Kit that had cried out in despair. It sounded like pleading, like he was calling for help.

Seth's consciousness faltered, flickering in and out of awareness beneath the surge of aether, and he couldn't fight it. He couldn't move. He couldn't think.

A speck of blue rose from the gateway, hovering momentarily before it shot forward. Too quick for Seth to process what it actually was. He only knew it cut straight through the aether like a knife, and Silas shuddered when it darted in through his mouth. A sense of rage emanated from him as that tiny ball of light made its way into their mind.

It shone through the darkness that Seth was suffocating beneath. The aether retreated as it flitted toward his consciousness, still unrecognizable as little more than a streak of light until it perched itself on Seth's shoulder protectively, and Seth stared at the small, winged thing. The heat and pain receded with its energy.

The tiny light was actually a hummingbird spirit, its ruby throat almost purple with the blue glow that emanated from inside it. The curve of its long beak looked as fragile as a needle and just as sharp as it licked up the wisps of aether that ventured within reach, feeding on the darkness, and only shining brighter in return.

Seth could feel Silas's anger at being kept at bay. His impotent rage made the darkness pulsate and twist around them as the last of his essence settled inside Seth's body.

Silas rose from his crouch by the gate, his eyes flicking over the people that stood in the room. All of them had bright smiles upon their faces, except for Ena, who cowered from her place in line, and Gabriel, who had gone rigid on the other side of the gaping hole in the floor.

*Who should we eat first?* Silas taunted Seth in a voiceless drawl, and Seth would have caught his breath if he had breath to hold when Silas licked his lips.

Silas's gaze slipped from Gabriel, and Seth could feel a flutter of sentiment from Silas that left a bitter twinge in their gut, some memory of Kit no doubt stirring in him. He'd said Kit had believed in him once, and such things weren't always easy to shake.

"You." Silas pointed to the woman standing beside Ena—Elijah's mother, Avis—and she stepped forward obediently with her head bowed in respect, her long blond hair sweeping forward across her shoulders as she moved. "It's time for you to fulfill your purpose."

Silas pressed his talons into Avis's chest without further preamble and Seth shuddered inwardly at the spray of her blood, then the snap of her bone, and the small gasps she gave even as a smile lit her face. As if she were truly happy to give her life for Silas's wishes.

Avis collapsed to the floor when Silas drew his hand back with the sickening snap of her heart being pulled free. That wide, adoring smile was still on her face even as she landed in a bloody and crumpled heap.

Silas brought the heart to his mouth to feed, his teeth peeling away bloody strips while his aether sparked brighter.

Silas raised his head from the heart he'd been feasting upon when Gabriel stood and stared at him with a grimace.

"Does it disgust you, Gabriel?" Silas asked before he took another bite from the bleeding heart like an apple, chewing and swallowing it before he continued. "Kit always found it unseemly. He thought I should evolve. Grow past my taste for such things. The way he did."

Gabriel watched while Silas licked a line of blood up from the morsel he still held before popping it into his mouth like candy and swallowing it down.

"Seth—"

"You can't save him." Silas tilted his head, and a crooked smile lifted the corners of his mouth. "Seth is gone." He shrugged a shoulder casually. "I burned his consciousness right out of this body."

Seth bristled at the lie, and the hummingbird took measured steps along his shoulder until it could press its tiny head to Seth's cheek, a small gesture of comfort that Seth clung to emotionally, and he quietly named the spirit Colibrí after the constellation Gabriel had traced on his skin.

"I don't believe that." Gabriel rounded the gateway, closing the space between them. "I think he's still in there."

Silas's hand shot out when Gabriel was within reach, and his talons drew lines of blood where they pricked his skin. "You think because I made a deal with Seth to assume control that I won't hesitate to gut you where you stand? You may have mattered to him, but you mean *nothing* to me."

"But Kit does," Gabriel managed, and Silas's eyes widened marginally, his nostrils flaring. "That's why you saved me back at the apartment, isn't it? You were protecting *him*."

Silas sneered and dropped his hold from Gabriel's throat, letting him fall to his knees with a gasp for air and his fingers pressing to the already healing scratches on his neck.

"You've always been the clever one, haven't you, Gabriel?"

Gabriel didn't reply. He kept his head down, and Silas knelt before him, a hand coming up to Gabriel's jaw with a gentler touch that tipped Gabriel's head up until he met Silas's gaze. His eyes narrowed and his teeth clenched, a slither of red working its way up his neck with Silas's touch.

Silas leaned in closer as a smile curled his mouth. "Do you know why the First Witch made me?"

Gabriel stared at him. "The stories say she carved the first familiars from wood and brought them to life so she wouldn't have to work alone."

"That was only part of it." Silas rocked on the balls of his feet before leaning forward, perching precariously on his toes and putting himself nose to nose with Gabriel. "She dreamed of creating this world anew. Kit and I, we are meant to fulfill that dream, *together*."

Silas moved swiftly to grip Gabriel's head between both hands, his talons a sharp warning against Gabriel's scalp not to move.

"And I will have him back," Silas continued. "Even if that means I have to change him."

*You promised,* Seth wept from his corner in his mind when Gabriel lurched forward with a ragged scream, the crack and shift of bone beneath his skin eventually drowning out his cries. *You promised you'd let him go.*

"No," Silas corrected. "I said he'd live."

*Please,* Seth whispered to Colibrí, desperate, and having nowhere else to turn. *Please, help him. Please.*

Colibrí raised his head, his body shining brighter. The blue light built to a blinding flash of energy that Seth could feel thrum through every inch of him, pushing him toward the surface of his mind. Silas was a screaming whirlwind of rage that threatened to swallow Seth back down, but he could feel Gabriel's skin beneath his hands now, clammy and trembling, but there. The light surrounding them was bright enough to force the others in the room to shield their eyes.

The glow from Colibrí spread from the tips of Seth's fingers as the talons retracted, and he gentled the touch. His fingers grazed lightly through Gabriel's hair as the blue invaded the red of the infection. Gabriel's body shifted back to normal as the mutation receded until all that was left was the olive brown of his skin.

"Run!" Seth forced out as his hands slipped from Gabriel's head and their eyes met. He could see Gabriel's anguish at the words, his hesitation at leaving Seth behind. "I can't hold him back much longer." He glanced at Ena, hoping he could trust her. "Take Ena with you. She may be able to help you save the children. You can't leave them behind. I can see into Silas as much as he can see into me now. He's going to use the children to make more like him."

"I'll get them out of here," Gabriel promised, "and I'll find you again. I'll bring you back."

Seth wanted to believe him. He wanted to hold tight to the spark of hope Gabriel's words kindled inside him.

Gabriel ran for the stairs and Seth watched him catch hold of Ena's wrist to pull her along after him. She stumbled at first, before she found her stride in the time between one step and the next. Both of them made it past the line of startled and blinking women.

"What's wrong with you?" Isaiah demanded of his wives, some of whom still rubbed at their eyes. "Go after them!"

Seth sank back into the darkness as the women rushed from the room, trapped once again in the prison of his mind while Silas circled around him. Colibrí's light was dimmer now from where he still perched atop Seth's shoulder.

*He can't protect you forever. At some point, he'll make a mistake,* Silas said to Seth and Seth alone. *When that happens, I'll kill the both of you.*

Seth looked at the hummingbird spirit on his shoulder and watched the way its light flickered like a candle. The energy it had used to save Gabriel had taken a toll, but the aether that circled it would only strengthen it in the end.

*I don't think you can kill him,* Seth said. *I think it would take more power than you have.*

Seth brushed a knuckle gently over Colibrí's back. He was warm and soft, the feel of him a relief, a small bit of tactile sensation that eased Seth's sensory deprivation. He could feel this at least, even if the outside world was barred from him once again.

He only hoped it was enough to keep him sane.

# A Humble Request

Thank you for reading The Raven Key. If you loved the characters, found the plot engaging, or appreciated the underlying themes, I have a humble request for you. Please consider leaving a review.

Leaving a review is a great way to support indie authors and it helps other potential readers find books they will enjoy. Did the characters make you laugh or leave you wiping away a stray tear? Did the plot twist you up inside over what would happen next or sweep you off your feet with the romance? Let others know!

If you would like to know more about me, you can visit my website at HarperLCarnes.com or find me on most social media under the username HarperLCarnes.

# A Thank You

I would like to start off by thanking the friends that stood by me not only on my writing journey, but through the trials of my life as well. Julie, Tabby, Amanda, and Rue, thank you for all the help you've given me. A special thank you to Gina as well, who would often check in on me during some of the hardest years of my life, and who has sadly passed away. You are missed dearly.

To all the new friends in the writing community who have come into my life on this storytelling adventure I've embarked on, and especially those who have offered much needed wisdom and advice. Erica, Alura, Nicole, Jean, everyone in the campfire group, my proofreader Kate, and many others. Thank you for all the help you've given to get me to this point.

For my family, who has been there for me through all of it, and endured my obsessive writing habits. Especially my mother, who in many ways supported my journey to becoming an author. Thank you for your love and support.

# Trigger Warnings

Explicit sexual content
Graphic violence and gore
Discussions and depictions of the drowning of children
Non-descriptive discussion of childhood sexual assault
Animal injury and death
Shapeshifting and forced mutations
Cannibalism
Past abusive relationship and further abuse by perpetrator
Homophobic bullying
Depictions of cancer
Depictions of seizures
Depictions of mental illness
Depictions of therapy and visit to a psychiatric hospital
Depictions of trauma and PTSD
Attempted suicide and brief mention of suspected self-harm
Loss of autonomy
Underage drinking and alcoholic parent
Swearing and ableist language